New Arrivals

SURPRISE BABY
FOR HIM

BARBARA HANNAY
DONNA ALWARD
MELISSA McCLONE

MILLS & BOON

Published in Great Britain 2015
by Mills & Boon, an imprint of Harlequin (UK) Limited,
Eton House, 18-24 Paradise Road, Richmond, Surrey, TW9 1SR

NEW ARRIVALS: SURPRISE BABY FOR HIM
© 2015 Harlequin Books S.A.

The Cattleman's Adopted Family © 2010 Barbara Hannay
The Soldier's Homecoming © 2008 Donna Alward
Marriage for Baby © 2007 Melissa Martinez McClone

ISBN: 978-0-263-25366-5

010-0315

THE CATTLEMAN'S ADOPTED FAMILY

BARBARA HANNAY

Barbara Hannay was born in Sydney, educated in Brisbane, and has spent most of her adult life living in tropical North Queensland, where she and her husband have raised four children. While she has enjoyed many happy times camping and canoeing in the bush, she also delights in an urban lifestyle—chamber music, contemporary dance, movies and dining out. An English teacher, she has always loved writing and now, by having her stories published, she is living her most cherished fantasy. Visit www.barbarahannay.com.

PROLOGUE

AT FIRST, when Amy saw two policemen at the ballroom's grand entrance, she felt no more than mild curiosity. She didn't dream they were about to turn her life upside down.

She was way too excited to entertain such dark thoughts. For weeks, she'd been on tenterhooks planning tonight's high-gloss corporate launch. Its success or failure rested almost entirely on her shoulders, and she was relieved that everything was turning out well.

'Love it, love it, love it!' her ecstatic clients cheered.

As far as they were concerned, Amy hadn't put a foot wrong. They were thrilled with the venue she'd found on Melbourne's Southbank. They were especially thrilled with the video walls that showed off their brilliant new range of environmentally friendly lighting systems.

Amy was equally pleased with the way she looked tonight. She'd dieted for three weeks to squeeze into her divinely chic, but frighteningly expensive little black dress. She'd paid another outrageous sum at a trendy salon in Chapel Street to have glamorous blonde highlights added to her rather ordinary, pale brown hair.

Now, with the addition of killer high heels and her

grandmother's diamond earrings, she'd received oodles of compliments about both the launch party and her appearance. Tonight it was clear—in Melbourne's competitive, pressure-cooker world of marketing and corporate events, Amy Ross had *arrived*!

But before she could take her first celebratory sip of her champagne cocktail, she saw the deepening sombreness on the policemen's faces.

Why on earth were they here?

Surely they must have come to the wrong function. At any moment they would move on.

But no, the older of the two men approached the doorman and Amy saw the look of concern on his face. She felt a cold ripple of anxiety. Hastily, she scanned the crowded ballroom, searching the sea of guests. Could a criminal be lurking in their midst?

Her stomach tightened as she glanced to the doorway again. The doorman was turning.

He pointed directly at Amy.

Oh, God.

The glass in her hand shook, spilling wine onto her gorgeous new dress. Dismayed, she set it down. Any second now, the policemen would come marching into the very centre of this ballroom, and she had visions of the guests falling silent, eyes agog as they stepped aside to make a wide path for the blue uniformed men.

Amy knew she mustn't let that happen.

Sending her clients a brave thumbs-up gesture, she started off across the vast expanse of highly polished floor, knees knocking, thoughts racing and skidding through distressing possibilities.

Had she accidentally invited one of Melbourne's infamous gangland criminals to this party?

Or was this personal? Was *she* the policemen's target? Had her car been towed away?

Had something happened to her parents? *Please, no!*

Her stomach gave another sickening lurch as she drew closer to the grim-faced men, but she forced a smile. 'Good evening, gentlemen. How can I help you?'

The older policeman nodded to her gravely. 'Are you Miss Amy Ross?'

'Yes.'

'You live at Unit 42, 67 Grange Street, Kew?'

'Y-yes.' *Oh, cringe.* Had she forgotten to turn off the iron? Had her flat burned down?

'We've been informed that you organised this event and sent out the invitations. Is that correct?'

Amy gulped. 'That's right.'

'Could we speak with you privately, please?'

She couldn't hide her alarm any longer. 'W-what's the matter?'

'We're making enquiries, Miss Ross. We don't want to cause any unnecessary fuss, so, if you could just come this way, please?'

Enquiries. Surely this was a euphemism to cover all kinds of awfulness?

Stomach churning, Amy followed the men out into the marbled splendour of the hotel's lobby. She felt too ill to ask questions, so she stood very still while the younger policeman drew a piece of paper from his pocket.

She recognised it as one of the invitations she'd sent out

for the launch party. Was she about to be quizzed about her guest list?

Amy's mind whirled. Her clients had vetted her guest list and her only addition had been her best friend, Rachel. It was all above board. She'd been allocated one private guest and although her initial choice had been Dominic, her boyfriend, she'd changed her mind at the last moment and invited Rachel instead.

Rachel had been her best friend since they were fifteen, and she really understood how BIG this night was.

Besides, Rachel was a single mum and a writer, and since her daughter's birth she hardly ever got out. This party was a terrific chance for her to exercise her social skills before her first book was published and she became famous.

Amy had no doubt that her brilliant friend would become famous. Of course, she wasn't surprised that Rachel was running late tonight—she'd probably had trouble leaving Bella with a babysitter.

The policeman tapped the invitation with a long finger. 'Are you the same Amy Ross who's listed as Rachel Tyler's next of kin?'

A strangled cry broke from Amy. She tried not to think the worst, but she was gripped by numb terror.

'I—I suppose Rachel might have named me as her n-next of kin,' she stammered. 'She has no family and I'm her b-best friend.'

'Your name came up when we checked her driver's licence,' the policeman said gently. Too gently.

Shaking, Amy wished with all her heart that she didn't have to hear what these men had come to tell her.

'We found this invitation and realised you'd be here,' he said.

Amy almost screamed. She wanted these men to go. Away. Right now.

Instead they were beating around the bush, driving her insane with terror. 'Please,' she sobbed. 'Just—tell me.'

'There's been an accident,' the older man said. 'A fatal accident. Only a block away.'

CHAPTER ONE

AMY stood at the open window of the shabby hotel room in Far North Queensland, and watched a utility truck emerge out of the heat haze to the north. She felt an anxious flutter tremble from her stomach to her chest. The driver was almost certainly Seth Reardon.

Her hair was damp against the back of her neck and her cotton clothing stuck to her skin, but as the ute rattled down the street and came to a halt directly opposite the pub she wasn't sure if her discomfort was caused by the tropical heat or her nervousness.

The driver's door opened and, with an excessive lack of haste, a man unfurled from the cabin.

His build was tall and lean, a perfect match for his faded jeans and well-worn riding boots. He wore a milk-blue cotton shirt, with long sleeves rolled to his elbows to reveal sun-darkened skin on his forearms. His hair was very black.

From this angle, Amy couldn't see his face, but he crossed the empty street with a slow and easy stride that commanded attention.

Without warning, he looked up.

And saw her.

Gulp.

She swung away from the window, her heart thumping strangely. She'd gained a fleeting impression of masculine strength, of a grim mouth and a proud and resolute jaw, and eyes that were a breathtaking vivid blue.

'Oh, Bella,' Amy whispered, sending a glance back to the two-year-old playing with a toy pig on the bed. 'This man is your daddy.'

It was too late to change her mind, but suddenly, for the first time since she'd left Melbourne, Amy wondered if she'd done the right thing to come all this way.

Rachel had been so cagey about Bella's father. She'd always confided in Amy—*always*—and yet she hadn't breathed a word about Seth Reardon until Bella's second birthday.

Rachel had finally made the big confession after the birthday party, a very casual gathering in her backyard— a few playgroup mums and toddlers, with colourful cupcakes, jelly oranges and chocolate frogs.

Afterwards, Amy had helped to wash coffee cups and once Bella had been tucked into bed she and Rachel had opened a bottle of wine and made spaghetti. They'd eaten on the back patio and talked long into the night.

When Amy brought up the subject of Bella's father, Rachel groaned. 'Do you always have to act like my conscience?'

'But Bella's two years old now,' Amy protested. 'And she's such a gorgeous little thing. I can't help thinking there's a guy out there who's missing out on so much by not knowing her.'

To Amy's surprise, Rachel actually agreed.

'You're right,' she said, and, after almost three years of silence, the confession tumbled out.

Rachel had met this absolutely amazing guy when she'd been working on a cattle property on Cape York, in Far North Queensland.

'I suppose I was totally overawed by him,' she admitted. 'He was the most attractive man I've ever met.'

'You mean,' Amy whispered, 'he was *The One*?'

Rachel's face was white, her voice edgy. 'Yes, I'm afraid he was—but that's what scared me, Ames. That's why I never kept in touch with him. If I'd told him about Bella, he would have wanted me to live up there with him.'

'But if you love each other you'd live happily ever after,' Amy declared. It seemed incredibly simple and romantic to her.

But Rachel's mask slipped to reveal raw fear. 'I couldn't live there,' she said. 'He's the boss of a massive cattle station. It occupies his whole life, and it's so hot and wild and remote. I'd be mad with loneliness and I'd drive the poor man insane.'

A glass of wine later Rachel said more calmly, 'You're right, Amy. God help me, you're always right. I really must make contact with Seth again. I do want to take Bella to meet him. I just need to find the right time.'

But she'd never found the right time…

Which was why Amy was here now, in the Tamundra pub, almost three thousand kilometres north of Melbourne.

When Seth Reardon heard footsteps on the bare timber stairs, he stood in the empty hotel dining room, facing the doorway, shoulders squared, hands lightly fisted at his sides.

He wasn't looking forward to meeting this friend of

Rachel Tyler's, and he frowned, sensing something odd as he listened to Amy Ross's approach.

He was here for a business meeting and he'd expected to meet her alone, but he could hear another set of footsteps—eager, small footsteps.

Without warning, a tiny girl burst, like a small torpedo, through the doorway.

'Hello, man!'

Arms outstretched, the child greeted Seth with a huge grin, as if a reclusive cattleman, whom she'd never met, was the one person in the world she most wanted to see.

Seth's stomach dropped as she headed straight for his knees, blue eyes dancing, dark curls bouncing. He knew next to nothing about children, would rather face an angry scrub bull than a small, toddling female.

To his relief, an anxious young woman, the same woman he'd glimpsed in the window upstairs—Amy Ross, he presumed—came hurrying behind the child.

'Bella!' She reached for the little girl's hand and halted her headlong dash to embrace Seth's legs.

'I'm sorry,' she huffed, slightly out of breath and blushing brightly. 'I'm afraid Bella's very friendly.'

'So I see.'

Seth's dryly drawled response was the result of habit rather than displeasure. Now that the child was safely perched on her mother's hip, he could see that the two of them formed a charming picture.

The child's dark, curly hair, dimples, and blue eyes were in startling contrast to her mother's brown eyes and straight honey-brown hair. Amy Ross's complexion was warmer than her daughter's, with the slightest hint of a golden tan.

But in spite of the differences in their appearances, the close bond between the two of them was clear, and Seth was suddenly lassoed by unexpected emotion. He'd been stoically resigned to his life as a loner, but now he felt strangely left out, excluded from a very special unit.

He'd thought he'd thrown off his urges to be a family man.

'Perhaps we should start again,' Amy Ross said, and she held out her hand with a smile as appealing as her daughter's. 'I'm Amy and you must be Seth. How do you do?'

He accepted her greeting with a stiff nod, and as they shook hands he was super-conscious of the soft warmth of her skin.

'You didn't mention that you were bringing your daughter,' he said with an asperity he immediately regretted.

Amy's eyes widened. 'I hope you don't mind. I'm afraid I couldn't leave Bella behind. She's usually well behaved.'

Seth made no comment and the little girl continued to regard him with enormous delight, which he found quite extraordinary.

He swallowed to clear the tightening in his throat. He was mad with himself for allowing a total stranger—a woman, no less—to convince him to drop everything and race into town.

Admittedly, Amy Ross's phone call had delivered alarming news that Seth couldn't afford to ignore. He'd been shocked to hear about Rachel Tyler's death. He hadn't heard from Rachel since she'd worked on Serenity, and he'd tried to put her clear out of his mind.

Her death was a tragedy.

And already, there'd been too much tragedy.

Amy hooked the straps of her shoulder bag more

securely and held Bella's hand. But the child immediately began to squirm.

'Man, up!' she demanded, running to Seth's side and tugging at his denim jeans with determined little hands.

'Bella, no.' Grimacing with embarrassment, Amy pulled picture books from her shoulder bag. 'Come and sit here quietly and look at these books while I talk to Mr Reardon. Come on now, be a good girl.'

Seth tried to be patient while Bella was persuaded to sit cross-legged on the carpeted floor with books and a handful of toys. He and Amy sat at one of the dining tables.

'Hey, diddle, diddle,' the child announced gleefully.

He stifled a sigh of irritation. 'Does your daughter usually accompany you to business meetings, Mrs Ross?'

'Cat an' fiddle,' chanted Bella.

Flushing, Amy nervously lifted her hair from the back of her neck. Clearly, the heat and the tropical humidity were bothering her. Her hair was damp against her skin, and her neck was flushed and shiny with perspiration.

'I'm not married,' she said.

It was only then, as Seth watched her elegant hands securing a twist in her honey hair, that he noticed she wasn't wearing rings.

So she was a single mother. He supposed he should be more tolerant. He'd heard all the news reports about the excessive costs of day care.

'I don't usually have Bella with me while I'm working,' she said. 'But I had to travel such a long way this time, and I didn't want to leave her.'

He bit back a question about the child's father, but he

couldn't help wondering where the guy was and why he hadn't been able or willing to help out.

'You've come quite a distance,' he said.

'Don't I know it? It's so hot and muggy here.' She lifted the limp collar of her cotton shirt away from her skin. 'The tourist agency told me it's as far from Melbourne to Tamundra as it is from London to Moscow.'

Seth nodded. 'And you've chosen the very worst time of the year to make such a long journey.'

Her lower lip pouted. 'I had no choice. There's so little time to get publicity organised. Rachel's book is coming out in April.'

'Ah, yes, Rachel Tyler's book,' Seth said quietly and he narrowed his eyes.

'Aren't you pleased about it?'

'Why should I be pleased? When Rachel was on Serenity three years ago, she never once mentioned to anyone that she planned to write a book. I was very sorry to hear about her accident, but I can't say I'm happy that there's a book coming out now, after such a long silence.'

'Rachel's—Rachel was—a brilliant writer. She had a wonderful gift for description.'

That was all very well, but what had she described? As a reclusive bachelor, who prized his privacy, Seth was distinctly unhappy that a former employee had written a book about the six weeks she'd spent on his cattle property.

On the phone last week, Amy Ross had gone to great lengths to assure him that the book was a work of fiction and people's names had been changed to protect the innocent. But Seth wasn't at all confident he could assume that Rachel Tyler had been discreet.

Rachel had claimed to have been on a backpacking holiday, but she'd never hinted that she planned to race off and write a book about it.

To Seth, Rachel's behaviour had been sneaky. People in the bush were upfront and open and the whole business of this book made his gut churn with apprehension. Even so, he was determined to find out what he could. It was why he'd agreed to this meeting.

He frowned at Amy. 'You were Rachel's best friend, so I assume you can shed some light on this book.'

Amy smiled awkwardly. 'I'm afraid I don't know much at all. I'm here because the publishers have a limited budget for the promotion, and I wanted to do as much as I could for—for—'

Her eyes rested on the child. 'I wanted to do this for Rachel.'

The little girl looked up suddenly. 'Mummy?'

To Seth's surprise, Amy paled and closed her eyes, as if the child had upset her.

When she opened her eyes again, a moment later, Seth was struck by their dark, liquid beauty.

There was something very graceful and feminine about Amy Ross that he found eminently watchable. On the other hand, there was something about her story that didn't quite add up.

The child's presence...Amy's nervousness... Her insistence on coming now at such an inappropriate time when the wet season was about to break over their heads.

He knew Amy hoped to return to Serenity with him to take publicity shots, but already he was convinced that even agreeing to this meeting had been a huge mistake.

* * *

Amy could feel her heart beating in her throat. It had been such a shock to see Seth and Bella together. She'd never dreamed there could be such a strong likeness between a grown man and a baby girl, and she found it hard to believe that he hadn't seen the resemblance for himself.

How much time did she have before he began to notice and to ask difficult, searching questions?

She was pretty sure he could see huge holes in her claim that she'd come here solely to gather promotional material for Rachel's book. She was terrified Seth Reardon might change his mind about allowing her to spend a couple of days on his cattle property, and if that happened she would have no choice but to reveal her real reason for coming north.

But she couldn't tell him yet.

It was too soon.

To surprise this cold and forbidding cattleman with the news that he'd fathered a daughter was a delicate and difficult exercise. The timing was crucial, and there was no way she wanted to tell him such distressing news now in this strange hotel, miles from anywhere.

This exercise couldn't be rushed. She needed a chance to get to know Seth Reardon first. She wanted to win his confidence and trust—if that were possible, which right now she seriously doubted. She had hoped that together she and Seth could work out the best way to care for her precious Bella.

Amy forced a shaky smile, uncomfortably conscious that Seth Reardon was an exceptionally good-looking man. Rachel had always had good taste in men, and Seth's lean, rugged physique and arresting blue eyes were enough to make any young woman forget her mother's warnings.

Last night, when Amy had arrived here, she'd mentioned his name to the publican's wife, Marie, and the woman's reaction had puzzled her.

'Seth Reardon?' Her eyes had widened with sudden surprise. 'Oooh… He's a quiet one. Doesn't hang around the pub much. He's…cold. But there's something about him though. Eyes that make you wonder.'

'Wonder what?' Amy had prompted, hoping to hear a positive comment.

The woman had actually blushed, and then she'd shot a quick glance at Bella, who'd been sitting at the dining table, absorbed in drinking a glass of iced milk with a straw.

'What?' Amy had asked again.

'Oh, I've always had a soft spot for a man with blue eyes,' Marie had said lamely and she'd become very busy clearing dishes while she muttered about needing to get back to the kitchen.

Amy had been left with the impression that Seth Reardon was dangerous.

Even Rachel had admitted that Seth had been cool and distant at first, until she'd got to know him. Not that Amy would allow her mind to dwell on thoughts of Rachel and Seth becoming familiar…

Or intimate.

The very idea…of Seth Reardon making love…was like a close encounter with a lightning bolt.

He sent a frowning glance to the window and Amy saw that it had started to rain rather heavily. 'When you phoned last week you said you planned to take photographs, but this weather's going to rule that out. I did try to warn you that this is the wet season.'

'I suppose I could take photos of the rain. Rachel might have written about the wet season.'

'I doubt it. She was here in the dry season, in the winter.'

'Oh, yes, of course.'

Seth frowned at her. 'Haven't you read her book?'

'Actually…no.'

Her friend had been uncharacteristically protective about this story and she'd never offered Amy so much as a peek at the manuscript.

After the accident, Amy hadn't liked to search through the files on Rachel's computer. It had felt too much like snooping. She had sat down once to read a section of Rachel's poetry, but she'd been overcome by grief. It was like hearing Rachel's voice—and the thoughts expressed had been too intensely personal.

Amy had been in tears as she'd shut down the computer.

She hadn't opened it again.

Seth's eyes widened. 'How do you plan to promote this book, then?'

'These are early days, and I'm just starting my research. I have the publisher's back-cover copy, and a picture of the front cover. It's rather beautiful. Would you like to see it?'

She dug a folder out of her bag, and handed it to him. The book's cover depicted a balmy tropical beach at sunset with palm trees and white sand. Distant islands floated in the background, and the sun melted into a smooth golden sea.

'I know it's not very accurate,' she admitted, sending another glance out of the window. She'd been dismayed by Tamundra's rather desolate main street and the drab gum trees beyond it, and red earth that stretched for miles. She was pretty sure the whole of Cape York looked just as bad, so the cover was deceptive to say the least.

Seth Reardon shrugged. 'There are sections on the eastern edge of Serenity that look exactly like that.'

'Oh.' Amy looked again at the idyllic palm trees and golden sand and felt her jaw drop with surprise.

Seth's blue eyes froze her. 'You haven't done your homework, Amy Ross.'

'I—I've done my best,' she spluttered. 'I—I told you I've only just started. It's only two months since Rachel died and I—I've been busy. With Bella.'

They both looked down at Bella, who was sprawled on the carpet, busy with a scrapbook and fat crayons.

'My drawing Amy,' the little girl announced proudly as she made a lopsided circle with a purple crayon. 'An' here's Amy's eyes.'

Happily, Bella drew small purple squiggles inside the circle.

Amy gave her an encouraging smile. 'That's lovely, Bella. Now draw my mouth.'

A small sigh escaped Seth and he lifted his gaze from the child and studied Amy.

She resisted an urge to squirm beneath his scrutiny. It was important to appear calm and in control.

'I'd like to know more about Rachel's stay up here,' she said, hoping to convince Seth that she wasn't wasting his time. 'What kind of work was she doing? How did she fit into life on a cattle station?'

To her dismay, his frown deepened. With a long brown finger he tapped the book's back cover blurb. 'But the answers to your questions are right here.'

'They're generalities,' she countered, desperately trying to ignore the niggling of her conscience that told her he was right. 'I'm looking for details.'

His expression was immediately guarded. 'What kind of details?'

Amy gulped. 'Nothing too personal.'

His frown deepened and she felt her face redden.

'I'm looking for anything quirky or interesting,' she said. 'Rachel was a city girl. I doubt she'd ever touched a cow before she came here, or cooked on an open fire, or slept in a swag on the ground.'

Abruptly, Seth stood, making his chair scrape on the wooden floor. He strode to the window, where he leaned a shoulder against the wall, looking out into the rain as he thrust his hands into his jeans pockets.

'I'm afraid you've wasted your time.'

'What do you mean?' She knew she sounded too scared, but was he going to refuse to take her to Serenity?

Seth's eyes narrowed. 'If you've come all this way in search of scandal to spice up the promotion, you should leave now,' he said.

'Scandal?' Amy was dumbfounded. 'Why would I want to tarnish my best friend's name?'

'For money? To sell more books? You're in marketing, aren't you?'

'How dare you?'

Seth shrugged again. 'Whatever. But you haven't been straight with me.'

Oh, help. Already he was pushing her towards making her confession. But if she told him about his daughter now, he might be so immediately shocked and angry that he stormed back to his cattle station alone, without giving her a chance to really discuss what was best for Bella.

'Rachel was my best friend,' Amy told him, softly. 'And—and I've lost her.'

She tried to go on, but suddenly the difficult, grief-filled weeks since Rachel's death seemed to overwhelm her. It had been a nightmare trying to deal with the horror of her best friend's death while taking on the responsibility of her little daughter.

She'd been trying so hard to do everything right, including coming all this way.

Now, on the brink of failure, Amy couldn't look at Seth, didn't want him to see her tears.

'Look,' he said suddenly, clearly uncomfortable with her evident emotion, 'I'm prepared to take your word.'

Her head snapped up.

Grimly, he said, 'But if you're coming to Serenity with me, we'd better get cracking, before this weather really sets in.'

Her jaw dropped, she was so surprised by his sudden hasty about-face.

'Did you drive here from Cairns?' he asked brusquely.

Amy blinked. 'Yes. I hired a car.'

'A small sedan?'

'Yes.'

'With four-wheel-drive capability?'

She shook her head.

'You'd better travel in my vehicle, then,' he said quietly and with grim resignation.

Seth was actually offering her a lift. Was it wise to accept? Would he also be willing to drive her back here in two days' time?

'Wouldn't it be simpler if I followed you in my car?' she said.

'The road's too rough and in this rain it'll be slippery. I don't want you or your little daughter's safety on my conscience. But let's not waste time. It's a long drive.'

CHAPTER TWO

SETH wasn't exaggerating his desire for a hasty departure.

Fortunately, Bella didn't kick up a fuss when she was suddenly strapped into a booster seat in the back of his dual-cabin ute. The little girl was mildly puzzled, but she'd lunched on Vegemite and cheese sandwiches, a banana and milk, so she obligingly fell asleep soon after they left Tamundra.

Rain streamed down the windows, making the sky and the trees a grey blur. Amy could see nothing but a small view, cleared by the wipers, of the muddy red track in front of the vehicle.

Apparently it would be dark by the time they got to Seth's property, but despite the prospect of a long journey he didn't seem inclined to talk. Whenever Amy stole a glance his way, he looked utterly relaxed and competent, his sun-browned hands resting lightly on the steering wheel as he skilfully negotiated the rough and slippery surface.

Amy supposed he would look equally relaxed and competent on the back of a horse, or driving a tractor.

She was surprised that she wasn't more worried about heading into the wilderness with a man she hardly knew. Seth Reardon was different from almost any man she'd ever met, and she could totally understand how Rachel had been both attracted to him, and cautious about sharing her life with him.

He was clearly at ease in his own skin, but he had the wary intelligence of a loner—the Outback equivalent of street smarts, she supposed. More than likely, he never allowed anyone to get too close, which meant it wasn't going to be easy to find the right moment to tell him that Bella was his daughter.

And yet, the weight of her secret loomed large. She would be relieved to finally get it off her chest.

Needing to make conversation, she asked tentatively, 'Have you lived here on Cape York all your life?'

Seth shook his head. 'I moved up here when I was twelve.'

Amy waited for him to expand on this and when he didn't, she dived in with more questions. It was ridiculous to waste this golden opportunity for a getting-to-know-you chat.

'Where did you live before that?'

'In Sydney.'

'Really?'

'Does that surprise you?' he asked, sliding a quick glance her way.

'I was expecting you to say that you moved here from another cattle property in Queensland.' Bustling, metropolitan Sydney was as alien to this environment as her own home in Melbourne. 'Coming here must have been a big change for you.'

Seth nodded. 'I came after my father died, to live with my uncle.'

'So it was a very big change,' Amy said quietly, and she was unexpectedly moved by the thought of him as a grieving, lonely boy, on the cusp of adolescence, leaving his friends in the city to live so far away.

She wanted to ask him about his mother. Why hadn't she been able to look after him when his father died? Why had he been moved into an uncle's care?

A glance at the set lines in Seth's face, however, silenced further questions.

The rain continued as they drove on.

The relentless downpour and Seth's rather grim silence were enough to make Amy feel sorry for herself. It wasn't her habit to be self-pitying, but the weeks since Rachel's accident had been rough and she wasn't quite sure how she'd managed, actually.

She'd made the decision to care for Bella swiftly. On the night of the accident she'd gone to Rachel's house, numb with shock, and paid the sitter, then tiptoed into the little room where Bella lay innocently asleep.

She'd looked down at the little girl's soft, chubby-cheeked face, at her closed eyes and her soft, dark eyelashes and her heart had almost broken.

There'd been no question. She had to devote herself to caring for Rachel's daughter. A succession of babysitters could never provide the round-the-clock security and stability a two-year-old needed.

But the transition from marketing to motherhood hadn't been easy, especially when in the midst of it all, Amy's boyfriend, Dominic, had suggested that they both needed time out…to give each other some space.

Amy had known it was the thin edge of the wedge that would crack their relationship irreparably apart. Dominic was jealous of the closeness she'd quickly developed with

Bella. He'd started to snap at the little girl when she'd innocently interrupted his computer games. Being upfront as usual, Amy had told him that things had to change now that Bella had arrived.

In the end they'd had the most appallingly ugly and bitter row over Bella. Dominic couldn't see why Amy should automatically assume responsibility.

The fact that she'd been named as Bella's guardian was a mere technicality, he said. It didn't mean she had to care for the child day in, day out—which proved that, after almost twelve months together, he didn't really know Amy at all.

She'd reminded him that he was living in her house, that she always had to jog his memory to get him to pay for his share of the food, the phone and the electricity, and she'd also let him know how annoying it was when he disappeared into the spare room and spent hours on computer games, racking up a huge Internet bill as well.

Whether Dominic had left her or whether she'd finally shown him the door was academic now. The whole catastrophe had been draining, and Amy might have collapsed in a complete heap if Bella hadn't been so resilient and such an utter darling.

It was amazing how quickly the little girl had transferred her trust to Amy, and the nights when she'd cried for her mummy had gradually lessened, but it still cut Amy to the core that she was now the focus of the little girl's love, the love that rightly belonged to Rachel.

She'd get weepy, though, if she thought too much about that.

For much of the journey the vehicle rattled down a long straight track, which every so often climbed a low hill, then dipped down again to cross a rising creek. Yesterday, on her journey north to Tamundra, the creeks had been mere trickles, but already these gullies had begun to swell with fast-flowing muddy water.

Seth drove in silence and Amy felt the beginnings of a tension headache. She let her head fall back and tried again to relax as she watched the rain slide down her window. Every so often she caught the blurred outlines of cattle hunched together in mobs, looking desolate. A stalwart few continued to graze, apparently untroubled by the driving rain.

Bella woke up and was immediately chirpy and eager.

'Moo cow!' she announced importantly. And then 'Moo! Moo!' over and over.

Amy stole glances in Seth's direction and she was quietly pleased to catch him smiling at Bella's enthusiasm.

He looked incredibly gorgeous when he smiled.

Amy wondered if he'd been infatuated by Rachel. Most guys had been. Had there been other girlfriends since? She supposed there wouldn't be too many available women here in the wilderness, but perhaps there was a beautiful girl who waited impatiently in Cairns for Seth's visits.

'How long were you and Rachel friends?' Seth asked suddenly, much to Amy's surprise.

At first she was nervous that he'd guessed the direction of her thoughts, and almost as quickly she worried that he'd somehow made the link between Bella and Rachel. But he looked too relaxed, and Amy let out a huff of relief.

Actually, she was really pleased that he wanted to talk, especially to talk about Rachel. It would pave the way for the news she had to share.

'Rachel and I were both fifteen when we met,' she told him, 'and we were in hospital, having our appendixes out.'

'Ouch. I suppose you cheered each other up,' he suggested with a smile.

Heavens. A smile *and* conversation. Things were looking up.

Amy returned his smile. 'We had a great time. We were in a small hospital run by nuns and we had beds side by side in a room to ourselves. We soon discovered we were in the same year at school, so we had tons to talk about.'

'And you stayed in touch afterwards?'

She nodded. 'Rachel went to a very snobby, private girls' college and I went to an ordinary co-ed state school, so we didn't see much of each other, but we kept in email contact. And we got together on weekends sometimes. Rachel even came away with my family to the beach for the summer holidays.'

'You really clicked,' Seth said quietly.

'We did, and then we ended up at Melbourne University, and that's when we truly became best friends.'

She took a packet of butterscotch from her bag. 'Would you like one of these?'

'Thanks.'

'I'll unwrap it for you.' Carefully, she untwisted the ends of the paper and as she offered him the sweet his hand bumped hers. She felt a zap of electricity that made her gasp. *Good grief.* She shouldn't be getting the hots for this guy.

To cover the reaction she said quickly, 'I suppose you went to a boarding school.'

Seth nodded, and finished chewing before he said, 'I used to fly down to school in Townsville.'

'I've always thought boarding school would be great fun.'

'Yeah. We had plenty of fun.' He looked genuinely happy as he said this.

'And what about after school?' Amy prompted, more tentatively. 'Did you go straight back to your uncle's property?'

An almost imperceptible sigh escaped Seth. 'I spent a year in England, playing rugby.'

She was so surprised she almost cried out. She struggled to picture Seth Reardon in a rugby jersey on a soft green English playing field, surrounded by his teammates. He was athletic, certainly, but was he a team player?

She'd had him pegged as a natural-born loner. 'Was it hard to come back to Cape York?'

'Not at all.'

He said this quickly, almost too quickly, and his eyes became very bright and hard, as if he was warding off any further discussion.

After that, they continued their journey in silence once more, while Amy's mind seethed with unasked questions. There were so many gaps in Seth's story, things he plainly had no intention of sharing with her. Where was his mother? Was she dead too? Did he miss Sydney? Or rugby? Or England?

Most of all, she wondered if he really liked living on Cape York. If he didn't, why had he stayed up here in the north? If he'd been willing to move south, he and Rachel and Bella might have been a family.

One thing was becoming very clear to her, however. She'd underestimated Seth Reardon.

She'd come north with the vague idea that she'd meet a guy wearing an Akubra hat, a suntan and a smile. She'd imagined an attractive, but uncomplicated, country fellow, who'd had an affair with her best friend and who now deserved to know that the affair had resulted in…consequences.

She'd been a fool to think that it would be easy and straightforward to share the news about Bella with him.

Twisting around in her seat, she looked back at Bella, who'd dozed off again, but then woken up to gaze around the interior of the vehicle with a slightly dazed frown. Amy felt her heart swell with love for the dear, innocent little scrap.

It was hard to believe that she'd grown so close to her in two short months, but the truth was her emotional connection to Rachel's daughter was so strong at times it shocked her.

They'd been on quite a journey together, she and this little girl, as they'd slowly learned to cope with unbearable loss, and to live with each other.

To love each other.

These days, more often than not, Amy woke when Bella bounced into her bed, eager to greet her with hugs and kisses and laughter.

With Bella, Amy had discovered the joy of simply being alive. She'd relearned the pleasure of simple things like trips to the park to feed the ducks, riding slippery slides, and splashing in wading pools. She'd forgotten that it could be so much fun to blow bubbles at bath time, or to share bedtime picture books.

Already, it was hard to remember a time when corporate launches with champagne cocktails and gourmet canapés had been vitally, crucially important.

More often than not, meal preparation these days

involved oatmeal or boiled eggs and toast soldiers, and bunny-shaped mugs of milk. Amy had learned to always carry an extra bag, to accommodate Bella's sunhat and a change of clothes, as well as a drink and a banana, or tiny packets of sultanas for snacks.

Her life in marketing had been put on hold.

Being self-employed had made the transition possible—not easy, but possible—but there was a limit to how long she could continue this lifestyle without earning. She'd already gobbled up a major chunk of her savings. Luckily, she had no big debts hanging over her, but she knew she would have to return to work soon.

Just the same, she certainly hadn't come looking for Bella's father because she needed his financial help. Caring for Bella might require a few sacrifices, but Amy knew she would manage.

Eventually, they stopped at a gate and Seth got out to open it.

'Are we almost there?' Amy asked hopefully when he got back into the car. Bella was grizzling more loudly now. 'Is this Serenity?'

'This is one of the boundary gates,' he said as he steered the vehicle between timber fence posts. 'I'm afraid it'll be another half-hour before we reach the homestead.'

Another half-hour… It was already dusk, and growing dark quickly because of the rain. Amy found it hard to imagine owning so much land that you could drive across it for such a long time.

Seth got out again to shut the gate, and when he came back he said, 'Would you like to let Bella out for a bit, to stretch her legs?'

'I'm sure she'd love that, but it's raining.'

'You have raincoats, don't you?'

'Well, yes.'

Seth shrugged. 'This is the tropics, after all. The rain's not cold.'

'You're right.' In a matter of moments, Amy found their raincoats, which she'd packed in an outside pocket of her suitcase, and she was buttoning Bella into hers. She glanced at Seth, who was standing alone…looking…not lonely, surely?

A sudden instinct prompted her to ask, 'Are you coming to walk with us?'

For the first time, Seth lost his air of cool certainty. His bright eyes rested on Bella's eager face peering up at him from beneath the yellow hood of her raincoat. The lines of his face softened, then broke into a smile.

Wow! Amy felt the impact of his smile deep in the pit of her stomach.

'Why not?' he said and he snagged a dark oilskin coat from the back of the vehicle.

Amy's chest felt weirdly tight, but moments later they set off together along the red dirt track between straggling gumtrees and pandanus palms.

Bella was thrilled to be allowed out in the rain, skipping between the two adults. She insisted on holding their hands, but every so often she would let go and dash off to splash in a puddle, then she would turn and grin at them ecstatically and Amy's heart would leap into her throat.

Surely Seth must see how closely the little girl's smile resembled his?

But apart from that anxiety, Amy enjoyed the little

outing much more than she should have. There was something about being out in the rain in the middle of a journey through nowhere, just for fun, that felt impossibly rash and carefree. Seth was smiling almost the whole time and their gazes kept meeting. Every time his blue eyes met hers she felt a knife-edgy thrill zap through her.

It was inappropriate and foolish, but she couldn't help it. A strange, shiver-sweet happiness seemed to have gripped her and she felt as if she could have walked along the darkening, rain swept track for ever.

But at last she had to be sensible and to suggest that it was time to head back to the ute.

As they went on Seth had to get out to open and close gates at least another six times. Each time he got back into the car, he brought the smell of damp earth and a fine spray of rain.

'I should be looking after the gates,' Amy protested after the third stop.

'Outback gates are notoriously tricky.' He frowned as he looked at her more closely. 'Are you OK? You're looking pale.'

'Bit tired. That's all. I'm fine, thanks.' Truth was, she was feeling ill and scared, scared of the shivers of awareness this man caused. It was ridiculous to feel so hung up about him. He was Rachel's ex, and Bella's father, and once she revealed her real reason for coming here he might hate her.

'We're almost there,' he said, sounding surprisingly gentle.

Ahead of them, Amy saw lights winking through the rain, and then at last they pulled up at the bottom of a short flight of wooden steps.

She was familiar with pictures in magazines of homesteads on Outback cattle stations—ageing timber houses with corrugated iron roofs and wrap-around verandas, sitting in the middle of grassy paddocks.

It was too dark to see much tonight, but if she guessed correctly they'd arrived at the back of this house. Rain drummed loudly on the iron roof, and the veranda was in darkness but a light came on as they got out of the vehicle.

They hung their damp coats on pegs near the back door and Seth turned to Amy. 'I'll show you straight to your room,' he said, watching her with a thoughtful frown.

'Thanks.'

He walked ahead of them, carrying their bags, and Amy followed, hugging Bella close, reassured by the familiar warmth and softness of her baby skin. She wondered where Seth's uncle was. Wondered if she should tell Seth tonight, while they were alone, that this little girl was his daughter.

Surely it was better to get the truth out in the open sooner rather than later?

Fear rippled through her as she pictured the moment of revelation. She had no idea how Seth would react, whether he would be angry, or shocked, or disbelieving. Or suspicious of her motives.

Or all of the above.

Perhaps it would be prudent to wait till the morning. It had been a long, unsettling day. Her tiredness made her fragile and susceptible to tears and she wanted to be strong like a mother lion when she broached Bella's future with this man.

'I thought this room should suit you,' Seth said, pushing open a door.

'Oh.' Amy couldn't hold back an exclamation of surprise as she entered the room and he set their bags down. 'This is lovely.'

It was the prettiest room possible, with soft, pale green carpet and matching green and cream wallpaper. Romantic mosquito nets hung over twin beds and French doors opened onto the veranda.

'There's an en-suite bathroom through there.' He pointed to a door.

'Thank you, Seth. That's wonderful.'

Setting Bella down, Amy peeped around the doorway. The bathroom was sparkling clean and as lovely as the bedroom. Thick, soft towels hung on the rails and there was even a purple orchid in a cut-glass vase on the wash-basin. It was amazing, really, to find such comfort all the way out here, like coming across a mirage in the middle of a desert.

Perhaps Seth and his uncle were used to having guests. Amy wondered if he wasn't nearly as antisocial as she'd believed. This wonder was compounded when she turned back into the bedroom, and found Bella and the antisocial man in question trying to touch the ends of their noses with their tongues.

As she watched them Amy's throat tightened and her mouth wobbled dangerously. They looked so alike, giggling together and having such incredible fun being silly. Without warning, her guilty conscience got the better of her and she very nearly blurted out the truth. Right there and then, accompanied by tears.

I mustn't. Not now. It would be too cruel to walk into Seth's house and immediately dump the news on him like an emotional thunderstorm.

She pretended to be terribly busy, opening Bella's suitcase, struggling to feel calmer.

As if he hadn't noticed anything amiss, Seth said, 'I told Ming we'd be happy with something light for supper. How do scrambled eggs with tea and toast sound?'

'That sounds fine.' She was dazed with surprise. 'Who's Ming?'

Seth smiled. 'My cook.'

His cook?

Amy blinked. This was another surprise. From the way Rachel had spoken, she'd always imagined that life on this cattle station was pretty rough.

'So are scrambled eggs OK?' Seth asked.

'Yes,' she said. 'They'd be perfect. Bella would love some, too.'

'No problem. I'll let Ming know. Come along to the kitchen when you're ready. It's just down the hall.'

'One, two, five, six!' Bella chanted proudly as she counted the buttered fingers of toast on her plate, then beamed happy smiles at both Amy and Seth.

They were eating alone in the kitchen, the mysterious Ming having prepared their food and then disappeared before Amy could meet him.

Fortunately, Bella was quite adept at filling any awkward silences that lapsed during their dinnertime conversation. In between Bella's choruses, Amy answered Seth's questions about her work in marketing and he elaborated on the export beef market.

She wished she could follow up on their earlier conversation with more personal questions like how he'd felt about giving up rugby, or whether he planned to live on Cape York for ever. Or whether he looked forward to having a family one day. Most importantly, she wanted to know how he'd felt about Rachel.

Instead, she told him about her Melbourne flat and Bella's playgroup and the day care centre where she planned to leave Bella when she returned to work.

Seth's gaze met Amy's when she told him this, and wariness crept into his eyes, as if he sensed her underlying tension.

All of a sudden she was desperately, achingly tired and she realised she'd been tense for hours. The closer she got to telling Seth about his relationship to Bella, the more frightened she was.

The fact was, telling Seth was one thing. Handing her precious little girl over was another matter entirely. Amy had no intention of giving her away. As Bella's guardian, she planned to take the child back to Melbourne with her. Seth could stay in touch, certainly, but he couldn't expect to have Bella permanently.

Could he?

All through the meal, there was a question in his eyes, which Amy tried to avoid. She focused on his hands as he cut a piece of toast into the shape of a sailing boat for Bella. They were very workmanlike hands—sinewy and strong and suntanned. To Amy's intense dismay, she found herself imagining his hands on her skin and the thought caused crazy explosions deep inside.

By the end of the meal, Bella was growing sleepy again and Amy grabbed the excuse to escape, to put her to bed.

'Good idea,' Seth agreed easily, but as Amy was about to leave he said, 'Would you have time for a chat after Bella's settled?'

Time for a chat?

Her heart jumped with sudden fright. Why did his simple question sound ominous? His blue gaze was quiet and steady, in complete contrast to her hectic pulse.

'Yes, of course,' she managed to reply. 'It shouldn't take too long to settle Bella.'

'Half an hour?'

'That's plenty of time.'

For once Amy was pleased that Bella knew every word of her bedtime story by heart. She only had to turn the pages while the little girl happily pointed to the pictures and recited snippets of dialogue.

Meanwhile, Amy's mind raced, trying to guess why Seth wanted to chat.

Ever since Rachel's accident, her mind had developed the alarming habit of leaping to worst-case scenarios. She wondered if Seth wanted to talk about Rachel and Bella. Could he have guessed?

She wasn't ready to tell Seth the truth. She'd mentally prepared herself for a confession in the morning.

But would there ever be a right time?

Amy watched Bella's innocent little face as she snuggled down beneath the crisp white sheets with her favourite toy, a fat stuffed pig.

'Night, night,' she murmured, touching her fingers to a silky curl of jet-black hair.

Bella eyed her sternly. 'Say bed bugs.'

'Bossy boots,' Amy chided, but she obliged. 'Night, night, sweetheart. Don't let the bed bugs bite.'

Bella grinned with satisfaction and they hugged tightly. Amy kissed her warm, baby-soft skin, and tried not to think about distressing possibilities that involved handing Bella over, or nights in the future without this ritual.

An awful panic gripped her, and suddenly she knew with blinding clarity how vitally and deeply important Bella had become to her. She simply couldn't bear to give her up.

Sitting on the edge of the bed, she fought tears as she stroked the child's soft curls and watched her eyelids grow heavy. And she tried, frantically, to sort out a strategy in her mind for dealing with Seth Reardon.

CHAPTER THREE

SETH stood on the back veranda, staring out into the rain without really seeing it. Instead, he kept seeing a lovely young woman and her cute little daughter, so happy together, and the image gnawed at a private pain he'd tried very hard to keep buried.

With an angry groan he strode to the far end of the veranda, and stared out into the black, rain-lashed night, willing his reckless thoughts to the four winds.

He'd invited this woman and her child into his home, and already today, during a simple walk down a bush track, he'd let down his guard. But he knew that he mustn't allow a single mother's warm brown eyes and her daughter's appealing ways to slip under his defences.

It seemed there was no other man in the picture for Amy and Bella, but so what? Seth had given up all thoughts of domestic happiness, and he'd done so with the fierce determination of a smoker, or a gambler giving up an addiction.

Women, he'd learned after too many mistakes, were a health hazard. Families looked cosy and attractive when viewed from the outside, but he knew from bitter first-hand experience that the inside story could be something else entirely.

Closing his eyes, Seth saw his own mother—slim, elegant and beautiful, her sleek, dark hair framing her face like a satin cap. He remembered her tinkling laugh and the way she'd smelled of delicate flowers. Remembered her infrequent hugs.

He remembered, too, the many evenings he'd stood, nose pressed against the glass, watching her from his bedroom window as she stepped into a limousine. She'd always looked remote, like a goddess, in a glamorous red evening gown, in sequins, or gold lamé—a glittering evening bag in one hand, cigarette in the other.

Mostly, he remembered the day she'd left him for good.

The departure of females had become a pattern in Seth's life.

He was done with relationships.

This evening, he had to remember to be very careful when he talked to Amy Ross. There were important things about Rachel Tyler that he needed to know—an awkward mystery that he needed to clarify—but he couldn't allow himself to be sidetracked by any further discussion of Amy's life as a single mother. If she'd been abandoned by a gold-plated jerk and left to struggle with a baby on her own, Seth didn't want to know about it.

He didn't want to feel pity for her and her daughter. And he didn't want to feel concern. Or longing.

He simply needed to get to the truth.

When Amy heard the soft tap on her door she felt a hot rush of adrenaline. Anxiously, she snatched a glance at her reflection and hoped she'd achieved a small improvement by changing into a fresh T-shirt and jeans.

Her hand was pleasingly steady as she reached for the door knob, but as soon as she saw Seth, tall and dark and filling her doorway, her steadiness deserted her.

She stepped outside quickly, and through the open doorway he sent a silent glance to the bed where Bella slept.

'Yes, she's out to it,' Amy said quietly and she let out a huff of breath, hoping it would settle her nerves.

'Would you like coffee?' he asked. 'Or something stronger?'

'Not especially,' she said, wanting a clear head, although she suspected she would benefit from a stiff drink right now.

He gave a curt nod towards the back veranda. 'Perhaps we should go out there, if it's not too wet. We shouldn't disturb Bella, but you'll still be able to hear her if she cries.'

'All right.'

Leaving a single bed lamp on, she closed the door softly and followed him, and she felt nervous, as if she were going to a job interview she hadn't prepared for.

On the veranda, a wall light cast a soft glow over a trio of potted plants and two deeply cushioned cane chairs beside a wicker table.

Amy took a seat and she peered out at the curtain of rain, which was falling more softly now. She wondered what Seth wanted to 'chat' about. Avoiding that thought, she asked, 'How long will this rain last?'

'Hard to say.' He shrugged. 'In some wet seasons it rains non-stop for weeks.'

'That sounds depressing.'

'It can be. Most of us try to get away for at least part of the wet.'

'I've read about roads being cut off by floods.'

'That's why I have a plane,' Seth said in a dry, matter-of-fact tone.

A plane? Before Amy could register her astonishment, he said, 'So you've never been in the tropics before?'

'No, never.'

'You're not seeing it at its best. You should have come in winter.'

'But that would have been too late to help Rachel's book launch.'

'Ah, yes.' Seth looked out to the black and silent night, with only his profile showing to Amy. 'I was hoping we could talk about Rachel's book.'

Goosebumps broke out on Amy's arms. At least Seth hadn't guessed about Bella, but she wasn't sure if she was relieved or alarmed. What else could she tell him about the book?

If he realised that she'd come all this way, and imposed on his hospitality, on the pretext of promoting a book she knew next to nothing about, he would be justified in thinking she was crazy, *and* bad mannered.

She studied the dark lines of his brow and his nose and the angular jut of his jaw, but they gave her no clue to his thoughts.

He spoke without looking at her. 'You said you were Rachel Tyler's best friend.'

'Yes, I did, because it's true.'

'You've known her since you were fifteen.'

'Yes.'

'You've gossiped together.'

'I wouldn't call it gossip.' Amy sounded more prudish than she'd meant to. 'But sure, we talked a lot.'

'And yet she never talked to you about her book?'

'Not in any kind of detail.' Amy watched a moth dance into the pool of light. 'I—I think Rachel was superstitious. The book was terribly important to her, and I think she might have been afraid that it wouldn't be a success if she talked too much about it.'

'Did she tell you about her time at Serenity?'

'Very little,' Amy admitted with a sigh. Rachel had been totally absorbed by the aftermath of her trip north—her pregnancy and the birth of her baby.

'But she told you about me,' Seth said coldly. 'You knew how to find me.'

'Yes.'

Feeling hopelessly cornered, Amy closed her eyes. She hadn't wanted to tell Seth the whole story tonight. She'd wanted to wait till she'd been refreshed by a good night's sleep. She'd wanted to feel calm and composed, able to take her time and to choose her words carefully.

More importantly, she'd wanted to retain the upper hand in this, but Seth was pushing her, giving her no choice. She had to speak now. If he dragged the truth out of her, she would lose every ounce of credibility in his eyes.

And that mattered perhaps more than it should.

As she sat there, eyes closed, gathering courage, she heard the flutter of the moth's wings against the light globe and the sound of Seth's chair scraping on the wooden veranda boards. Her eyes flew open.

Seth was standing directly in front of her, towering over her. 'There's something you're not telling me, Amy.'

His voice was hard and as cutting as a sabre. He was trying to intimidate her, which was one thing Amy wouldn't tolerate. She'd learned in her own backyard to stand up to her brothers.

Bravely, she glared up at him. 'I don't like your tone.'

For a moment, he looked taken aback. 'I'm being very civil.'

He ran tense fingers through his hair, and time crawled as he stood there staring at her, while she stared back at him.

Eventually, his expression relaxed, and the next time he spoke his voice held no menace. 'Give me a break, Amy. I'm not used to playing these games. All I want is the truth. Why did you come here?'

'Because I need to talk to you.' Her eyes dropped to the moth, which now lay burned and dying on the bare floorboards. 'I have something very important to tell you.'

Even though Seth hadn't moved, she sensed the tension run through him, like a fault line in a wall of rock. She knew his mind was working at a million miles a minute and any second now he would put two and two together.

'If we're going to have this conversation, Seth, could you please sit down?'

He looked surprised, but to her relief he relented and resumed his seat, one long, jeans-clad leg crossed over the other, hands plunged deep in his pockets.

'I'm sorry,' he said. 'I didn't mean to upset you.'

'I'm sorry, too,' Amy admitted. 'I came here to do the right thing, but I've made rather a mess of it.'

Seth shot her a sharp glance, and she knew he was waiting for her to explain.

So this was it. The moment she'd feared.

'I'm not Bella's mother,' she said.

It was ages before he spoke, and in the stillness the rain continued to fall, needle-fine and shiny and silent.

'Is she Rachel's child?' he asked at last.

'Yes.'

Yes...

The word hung in the air, quivering like the vibrations of a tuning fork.

Amy wished she could feel relieved now that it was out, but she was too shocked by Seth's reaction.

Even in the subdued light, she could see the colour drain from his face. Then, silently, he slumped forward, elbows propped on his knees as he covered his face with his hands.

Shocked, she sat completely still, two fingers pressed against her lips, wishing she could recall the single word that had revealed so much.

Too much?

Yes. One little syllable had told him everything. There was no need to add that Bella was his daughter.

The fact that Amy had brought Bella all this way pointed to it, and a few simple calculations confirmed the facts. Seth only had to count back to know that Bella's conception had occurred during the time Rachel had spent at Serenity.

With him.

And, clearly, it was the worst possible news.

A cool breeze whipped onto the veranda, spraying fine rain over them.

Amy shivered and rubbed at her arms. 'Seth,' she said gently. 'I'm sorry. I know this is a shock.'

He didn't respond at first, then slowly he lowered his hands and let them hang loosely between his knees. He didn't look at her and he didn't speak, but Amy saw the movement of his throat as he swallowed.

'I came here, because I—I thought you should know,' she said. 'I thought it was important. Not because I want money from you, but because—well, because Bella's such a sweetheart.'

The thin, cold pricks of rain continued as she waited for a response from him. When it didn't come, she went on, desperate now to make her point. 'I think Bella's the cutest thing on two legs, you see. And, to me, it seemed unfair that you didn't know about her.'

At last Seth turned to her and she was shocked by the banked despair she saw in his eyes and in the deep lines that bracketed his mouth.

His eyes were bleak, but to her surprise he almost smiled. 'Don't feel bad. You've done the right thing.'

It was reassuring to hear this, but she wished he looked happier.

'I'm not planning to offload Bella,' she felt compelled to explain. 'You don't have to worry about that, Seth. I'm totally prepared to keep her with me and to take care of her.'

'I'm sure that's best,' he said quietly.

She let out her breath on a sigh. This was awful, so different from how she'd imagined everything before she'd set out on this journey. She'd anticipated the possibility of fierce anger, or disdainful disbelief. She'd been worried that Seth might try to take Bella away from her, but the last thing she'd expected was this shocked and horrified acceptance.

When his gaze met hers again, his eyes warmed just a little. 'So what's your relationship to Bella? Are you her guardian?'

Amy nodded. 'Rachel had no other family.'

'Really? No one at all?'

Amy was surprised he knew so little. 'She was an only child,' she told him. 'Her father has passed away, and her mother's in an aged care facility, and she's not at all well. Her parents were in their fifties when she was born. Apparently, they'd never expected to have a child, and Rachel was a huge surprise.'

After a bit, he said quietly, 'That might explain why Rachel was…*different*.'

'She *was* different, wasn't she?' Amy's mouth twisted in a wistful smile as she remembered her friend. 'She was brilliant, a ton of fun, but—yes—different.'

Seth nodded and looked away quickly, and she wondered if he'd been deeply in love with Rachel. The thought caused an unhappy pang.

'You're doing a great job with Bella,' he said.

'It's no hardship. I love her.'

His piercing blue gaze swung back to study her for a heart-stopping stretch of time, and then he rose abruptly.

'Thank you,' he said simply, and she knew their conversation was over.

They went back inside the house and Amy shivered as breeze from a ceiling fan chilled her damp skin. She felt miserable as she stood outside her bedroom door.

'Goodnight,' Seth said. 'I hope you'll be comfortable.'

'I'm sure I will.' Then she remembered. 'Just a minute, Seth. I have something you might like to see.' She went into the room and fetched a photo album that she'd brought with her, especially for him. As she gave it to him his hands brushed hers and her breath caught as she felt the heat of his skin.

'Thanks,' he murmured, gripping the album tightly.

The house was silent, listening.

He seemed to remember his manners as a host. 'Are you sure you wouldn't like something to drink before you turn in?'

'Could I make myself a cup of tea?'

'I can get it for you.'

'No, it's OK, honestly. I can find my way around the kitchen.'

'Be my guest,' he said, gesturing down the hallway to the kitchen, and with a curt nod he left her.

Amy's sense of anticlimax was overwhelming, and a warm shower and a brisk rub down with a luxuriously thick bath towel didn't help her to feel any better. Standing in her nightgown between the twin beds, she looked down at Bella, sound asleep and blameless, hugging her plush pink pig, her mouth slightly ajar as she slept.

She felt an urge to climb into the bed and to cuddle the little girl close, seeking comfort and reassurance from her small, warm weight in her arms.

Have I done the right thing, baby?

She padded on bare feet down the darkened hall to the kitchen and found an electric jug and the makings for tea. On her way back, mug in hand, she saw light coming from beneath a door just across the hallway.

Was it Seth's room?

The possibility made her skin flush hot.

Fool.

In her room, she piled up her pillows and sat in bed in a small pool of lamplight, nursing a mug of hot, sweet tea.

She thought about Rachel, and was swamped by a tidal

wave of grief. If only she hadn't invited Rachel to the launch party. For the trillionth time, she wished that she could go back into the past and change that night. Rachel had always been so full of life, so brimming with can-do confidence and charisma. She shouldn't be dead.

Their friendship had been so strong, an attraction of opposites. Rachel was brilliant and wild and she'd always claimed that Amy was calming and steadying.

'Amy's my anchor,' she used to tell people.

Guys were forever falling in love with Rachel—so much so that she should have had a warning light, like a lighthouse. Amy's brother, Ryan, had been smitten, but he'd come to his senses eventually and married his sensible, sweet Jane instead.

For her part, Rachel had loved the attention of men, always had a boyfriend on tap, but somehow she'd managed to stay immune, never really falling in love.

Until her trip north.

'You should have been there, Ames,' she'd said, on that night she'd finally opened up. 'I needed you there, to keep me on the ground. I lost my head completely.'

Swiping at tears, Amy thought about Seth. She wondered if he was looking at the photo album now. Would he sleep tonight? Or was he totally calm again?

Was he thinking about Rachel? About Bella?

He'd looked so terrible tonight when she'd told him her news, and the memory of the deep lines of pain etched in his face sent a throbbing ache to the middle of her chest.

It was so silly to care so much about a man she'd only just met, but she couldn't help it. There was something about Seth Reardon that *got* to her—something elemental and deep. Whether he was happy or sad, whenever she was near him, she felt in danger of drowning.

She'd known, from the moment she first saw him—gosh, had it only been this morning?—that he wasn't a man who would take fatherhood lightly. Chances were, Seth wouldn't take any relationship lightly—which meant there was a distinct possibility that he'd really, *really* loved Rachel.

Without warning, Amy's tears began to fall in earnest, and she buried her face in the pillow so she wouldn't wake Bella.

The photo album lay abandoned on the nightstand.

Seth had taken a look at it, leafing quickly through the pages, catching glimpses of Bella as a tiny newborn, and later, as a gummy, smiling infant…later still, as a sturdy toddler, learning to walk…

He'd seen pictures of Rachel looking surprisingly maternal, and healthy and happy. There'd even been a shot of Amy, hovering somewhere in the background behind a cake with pink icing and two striped candles. But he'd had to set the book aside. It was too hard to look at these happy snaps.

Amy had offered them to him in all innocence, but she had no idea of the size and force of the bombshell she'd dropped this evening.

She thought he'd fathered Rachel Tyler's baby.

He'd never dreamed that Rachel was pregnant when she left Serenity, but, hell, in many ways everything would be a whole lot easier if he were the little girl's father. He would face up to the responsibility, and he could have worked something out with Amy—a way to share custody of Bella, perhaps. Truth be told, the thought of spending more time with Amy was enticing.

But it was a fantasy.

He wasn't Bella's father. He hadn't slept with Rachel.

Not once.

Never.

The real story was something else entirely, and it smothered him with a mountain of guilt and heartache.

While Rachel had flirted openly with him almost as soon as she'd arrived at Serenity, Seth had sensed she could spell trouble and he'd given her the brush-off, so she'd set her sights…elsewhere…

With tragic consequences.

Those consequences were the cross Seth had to bear, but they were too painful to share this evening with a warm-hearted, soft-eyed girl like Amy.

With a harsh groan, he launched to his feet and began to prowl.

This whole business was more complicated than Amy could possibly have imagined and he needed time—days, weeks, *years*—to work out the best way to explain it to her.

Damn it, he didn't want to burden her with the truth. Not so soon. She'd been such a loyal friend to Rachel. She'd put her career on hold and she'd devoted herself to Bella, and she'd come all this way, to do something Rachel should have done three years ago.

Reaching for the album, Seth looked again at the photo of Amy, smiling in the background. Her dark eyes were so warm and pretty, and just looking at her made him want to smile.

She was as generous and open-hearted as his uncle had been when he'd taken Seth in after his father died, giving him a home, an education, a sense of belonging. Family.

Seth owed so much to his father's younger and much admired brother, after whom he'd been named.

But now…damn it…what was the right thing to do?

He couldn't turn his back on this little girl. How had Amy described her? *Cutest thing on two legs.*

Too true.

Thing was, it would be easy to wash his hands of this, to tell Amy she was mistaken, that he wasn't the father. Send her packing.

Except—he felt such a weight of responsibility…and it was all so painful…and even though Amy was warm and compassionate, he didn't feel ready to talk to a woman he'd just met about what had happened…

He needed time.

'Wake up, Amy! Wake up!'

Amy felt small fingers trying to prise her eyelids apart.

'It's too early,' she moaned, refusing to open her eyes.

She'd had a dreadful night, endlessly tossing and turning, and she felt as if she'd fallen into a deep sleep only five minutes ago. But a sudden knock at the door brought her smartly awake.

'Man!' Bella squealed, gleefully slipping from the bed. 'Man at the door!'

With a groan, Amy pushed her bedclothes aside and swung her feet to the floor. She had no idea of the time, but daylight was streaming through the shutters.

Bella was banging on the door. 'Hello, man!'

'His name's Seth,' Amy grumbled. She couldn't remember where she'd left her dressing gown and she grabbed up a silk wrap to throw around her shoulders to cover her nightgown. 'Bella, you can't keep calling him man. Say Seth.'

'Sef.'

'That's better.' Amy grimaced at her reflection. She looked a fright—hair everywhere, dark circles under her eyes.

There was another knock.

'Hello, Sef man,' Bella called through the door.

With one hand clasping the wrap modestly over her front, Amy ran frantic fingers through her hair, but she knew it wouldn't improve her appearance. She opened the door.

Seth, freshly showered and shaved, was rather too much at such an early hour, but she didn't have time to go weak at the knees. She was distracted by Bella's shriek of joy.

'Hello, Sef!' the little girl shouted, and she beamed a gorgeous smile up at him, holding her arms up to be lifted.

For a moment, Amy thought he might resist the appeal of those little outstretched hands, but after only the briefest hesitation he bent down and scooped Bella high.

'How are you this morning, possum?'

Giggling, Bella planted a wet kiss on his cheek and hugged him hard. Amy choked back her surprise. When had this pair become such firm friends?

She watched Seth's ears redden, but with the typical fickleness of a two-year-old the little girl was soon wriggling to be set down again.

Seth's smile was shy as he took in Amy's dishevelled appearance. 'I see I'm too early for you.'

'I forgot you cattlemen get up at the crack of dawn.'

His eyes shimmered with mild amusement as he took in her nightgown and her efforts at modesty. He glanced at his wristwatch.

'What's the time?' she asked.

'Seven-forty.'

'Oh…well…not exactly dawn, then.'

'Breakfast's at eight. Is that too early?'

'No, that's fine, thank you.'

She dropped her gaze, unsure what to say now. She wondered if Seth had adjusted to the news that he was Bella's father. Even though he looked calm enough, he could be angry that she'd come to Serenity under false pretences. Last night she'd lain awake worrying and imagining that he'd send her packing this morning, straight after breakfast.

'It's stopped raining,' Seth said. 'So you might have an opportunity to take some photos after all.'

'Really? That's great.' She felt her heart skip in relief. So, not straight after breakfast, at least.

Behind her, Bella began bouncing on her bed, treating it like a trampoline.

Amy whirled around. 'Bella, stop that, or you'll fall.' She reached out to catch the little girl's hand.

'I was thinking it would be good if you could stay on for a bit longer than we'd planned,' Seth said, ignoring the distraction.

Amy blinked at him from beneath tumbled hair.

'You came here because you wanted me to get to know Bella,' he said. 'So it doesn't really make sense that you should rush away too soon.'

'I—I—' Catching giggling Bella in mid-jump, Amy held her close to keep her still. 'I'd have to change my flights.'

'I'm sure we could arrange that.'

She rubbed at her forehead, trying to clear her sleepfuzzed brain. 'You were so upset last night. Are you sure you want us to stay?'

'I've had time to think, to get used to everything. I'd like the chance to get to know Bella. I'd like her—both of you—to enjoy Serenity.'

'Will your uncle mind?'

Seth's face seemed to cave in. Shadows darkened his eyes and his throat worked. 'My uncle's not here. He died a couple of years ago.'

'Oh, I'm sorry,' she said, but it was hard to feel the appropriate depth of sympathy when she hadn't known his uncle, especially when her stomach was fluttering madly at the possibility of staying on, alone with Seth.

Amy couldn't think why she was hesitating. This invitation was exactly what she'd come north to achieve. Twenty-four hours ago, time on Serenity so that Bella could get to know her father had been her primary goal. Her dream.

Twenty-four hours ago, she hadn't met Seth Reardon. She hadn't developed a silly, useless and problematic crush that would only get worse if she spent more time with him. But there were other problems, too. There was every chance that Seth would fall for sweet Bella as swiftly and certainly as she had fallen. How would she cope if Seth wanted to keep Bella?

Part of Amy wanted very much to whisk the little girl safely back to Melbourne and to resume her life. She couldn't give her little girl up.

She would have to make it clear that Bella couldn't stay at Serenity permanently. That had never been her plan.

Amy knew how Rachel had felt about remote Cape York, and yesterday she'd seen for herself how far Seth's home was from anywhere else. It was no place for a single dad to try to raise a sociable toddler.

'Look, I'll give you time to think about it,' Seth said, backing down the hall. 'We can talk about it at breakfast.'

'No, it's OK.' Amy sent him an apologetic smile. 'It's a good idea and we'd love to stay. Thank you.'

'Terrific.' Seth smiled in a way that put creases in the suntanned skin around his bright blue eyes. 'We'll have breakfast on the front veranda at a little after eight. You just have to turn left at the end of the hallway.'

'OK. Thanks.'

It was only after Seth had gone that Amy realised her wrap had fallen during their conversation—while she was trying to catch the bouncing Bella, no doubt. She'd been standing here, talking to Seth in her fine cotton nightgown, exposed in all its transparent glory.

A glance in the mirror showed her just how much of her Seth had seen, and a blushing river of heat flooded her.

At least he'd been too polite to stare at her breasts.

She wished she could take more comfort from that.

CHAPTER FOUR

HOLDING Bella's hand, Amy went down the hallway, turned left, as Seth had directed, and walked into a stream of sunshine.

And an idyllic tropical paradise.

'Goodness, Bella, where are we?'

Last night, entering by the back steps in the rainy dark, Amy had realised that Seth's home was comfortable—but now she saw that not one thing about it came even close to her idea of a cattleman's residence.

The veranda at the front of the house was so deep it formed large, outdoor rooms. She paused in the doorway to take it all in.

From here she could see a dining area and, beyond that, bamboo cane lounge chairs grouped around a coffee table, and, beyond that again, a desk with a telephone and a high-backed chair. Gently circling ceiling fans and huge potted palms gave the whole area an elegant, Oriental air.

She saw the garden beyond the veranda and gasped... Instead of hectares of dry, grassy paddocks, the Serenity homestead was fronted by terraces of smooth lawns and lush tropical gardens where delicate orchids grew side by side with bright bougainvillea and graceful palms. Heavens, there was even a swimming pool on one of the terraces.

The entire grounds were set in a haven of green on a densely wooded hillside, with views to white sandy beaches, a bright, glittering sea, and the dark emerald silhouettes of offshore islands.

It was gorgeous. Unreal. Amy felt as if she'd woken up at a resort and, at any minute, a waiter would appear to offer her a long, colourful drink with clinking ice cubes and a tiny paper umbrella.

Seth rose from the dining table and came towards them, smiling at the stunned expression on Amy's face.

'This is amazing,' she said.

'Glad you like it.'

'But—' She made a sweeping gesture that took in the gardens edged by rainforest and the view. 'Where are your cattle?'

Seth laughed. 'We passed through the grazing country yesterday. Over to the west. Not far away at all. There's only a narrow fringe of this rainforest along the coastal mountains.'

'But it's beautiful.' She could so easily imagine Rachel living here, soaking up the exotic atmosphere.

That thought brought Amy straight back to earth.

Which was just as well. She knew she couldn't allow herself to be carried away by the beauty of Seth's home.

It would be prudent to keep Rachel at the forefront of her thoughts. She had to remember that it was right here, in this setting, that Rachel and Seth had been swept away by a passionate liaison.

Bella was tugging at her hand. 'Look, look! A swimming

pool!' She tried to pull Amy towards the sparkling blue water. 'My go swimming.'

'Not now,' Amy told her. 'We're going to have breakfast.'

Bending quickly, she picked the little girl up and hugged her, and as they took their places at the dining table she wished she didn't feel so unaccountably afraid.

Her desire for Bella to know her father had been driven purely by emotion. Families were important to Amy. Her own family was big and noisy and loving and she hated that Bella knew no one who was related to her by blood. Now, suddenly, Amy was looking at this gorgeous property, and was forced to accept practical realities that outweighed emotion.

Seth Reardon was seriously wealthy. He didn't merely own vast tracts of land and mobs of valuable cattle. His home was beautiful and comfortable and he had domestic help, and an aeroplane, for heaven's sake.

Bella was his daughter, his potential heiress, and if Seth wanted to he could hire a nanny for her and she could live here with him quite happily and safely.

Last night, when he'd been stunned and shocked, Seth had agreed that Amy could take Bella back to Melbourne. Naively, she'd had no doubt that she was the very best person to raise the little girl. She'd even broken up with Dominic because she believed that so vehemently.

But already, less than a day after arriving at Serenity, she was having deep misgivings about her right to make such demands.

Had Rachel felt similar doubts? Was that why she'd kept her pregnancy secret?

'Let's eat,' Seth said, watching her with a puzzled smile, and she turned her attention to the food.

Clearly Ming was a genius, and their breakfast was a meal of stunning simplicity. A beautiful fruit platter of passionfruit, vividly hued pawpaw and mango, and a star-shaped fruit Amy had never seen before, was followed by perfectly delicious, lightly spiced mushrooms and tomatoes on toasted home-made bread.

Bella ate a banana cut up in a bowl of yoghurt with golden circles of honey drizzled on top.

'That's one of her favourite breakfasts,' Amy told Seth as she watched the little girl eagerly wielding her spoon.

'I took a guess when I suggested fruit and yoghurt to Ming. He's not used to cooking for a two-year-old.'

'Are you?' she couldn't help asking. 'Have you had much experience with children?'

'Only what I've observed with other people's kids.'

Which meant he was more observant than most bachelors, she decided unhappily. Again, she felt an anxious swoop in her chest at the possibility of giving up Bella.

'I'm guessing that Bella might enjoy a play in the pool before it gets too hot,' Seth said when they'd finished their meal.

'I'm sure she would. She loves the water.' Amy was grateful that she'd included their bathers when she'd packed, but she'd expected to be swimming in an Outback creek or a river, not a beautifully tiled, sparkling, manmade pool.

'Go swimming,' Bella announced, pulling at Amy's hand.

Amy gave her a wistful smile. 'When your breakfast's gone down.'

But it wasn't very long before she gave in and Bella was racing ahead of her down the smooth stone steps to greet Seth at the edge of the pool.

'Look, Sef!' the little girl announced with great excitement. 'I'm a ballerdina!' She spun around, so he could admire her red and white spotted swimsuit edged with cute frills.

'You're a beautiful ballerina,' he assured her. 'Bella the water-baby ballerina.'

His smiling gaze flickered to Amy and she was glad she'd splurged on a new swimsuit for herself. She knew she was no real beauty, but she'd always been told she had decent legs, and the swimsuit was dark green and perfectly cut to flatter her figure. Even though she wasn't trying to impress this man, she was quietly pleased that she looked OK.

Seth looked more than OK, of course, in black swimming trunks and with a towel slung around his magnificent shoulders.

It was hard to stop stealing glances at his bare chest and his deeply bronzed, fabulous physique.

'Well, let's have a splash, shall we, Bella?'

The little girl loved the water, but she couldn't swim, so she needed constant help and supervision and Amy was grateful that she was kept busy. It helped to ignore Seth while he swam up and down the pool with smooth, powerful strokes.

After a bit, he joined them. 'Your turn,' he told Amy, sending her a grin that made his teeth flash white against his tan. 'I'll look after Bella, while you have a swim.'

It was unsettling to hand Bella over, almost as if it was a foretaste of the future. Amy struggled with her reluctance. 'You need to watch her like a hawk,' she told Seth. 'She thinks she can swim.'

'I'll be careful.'

She had no choice but to trust him. 'She's not scared of the water, and she doesn't mind putting her face under.'

Bella was so excited and wet and wriggly that the handover was precarious. Amy almost dropped the little girl when she felt Seth's bare leg brush against hers and she fumbled again when their hands touched and they bumped elbows.

It was bittersweet relief to leave them at last and to swim away in a careful breaststroke to the deep end of the pool. As she swam she could hear Bella's delighted squeals and laughter.

When she reached the other end, she turned and looked back and saw them together—father and daughter, looking so alike with their dark wet hair, sleek against their skulls— and she felt another tremor of fear deep inside.

Was she being silly, or was she really in danger of losing Bella? Would Seth demand that his daughter live with him?

The thought brought a hot swirl of panic. She'd been so sure she was doing the right thing, that bringing Bella here was in line with Rachel's intentions.

But now she'd met Seth and seen his beautiful home she couldn't help wondering why Rachel had objected to living here. She wondered if there was a deeper reason behind Rachel's avoidance of this meeting with Seth. And was there also an equally good reason why she'd named Amy, and not Seth, as Bella's guardian?

Amy was sure she was entitled to the role. She adored Bella, had been involved in her life since her birth, had actually been present at her birth.

She would never forget that incredible, joyous morning. Now, the possibility that she might lose Bella made her want to weep.

She dived under the water to wash away the possibility of tears. She had to be strong, to remember that she'd come here for this—to allow Bella and her father to meet—and she was pleased they were getting on so well. He'd accepted that Amy was Bella's guardian and she had to have faith in her decisions and in her instincts that told her Seth Reardon could be trusted.

Even so, the few days that she would spend here suddenly felt like a dangerously long stretch of time.

'Everything's so different and exotic here,' Amy said later, waving her hand to the view of the terraced hillside and the bright blue sea framed by a tangle of rainforest jungle. 'I find it hard to believe that I'm still in Australia. I feel as if I've crossed hemispheres.'

'In a way you have.' Seth sent her a slow smile, aware that it was becoming a habit, this smiling at Amy. It was highly likely that, between them, she and Bella had made him smile more times in the past twenty-four hours than he had in the past twelve months.

He said, 'Weren't you telling me yesterday that Serenity is as far from Melbourne as London is from Moscow?'

She turned to him, giving him the full benefit of her warm chocolate eyes, and he was very glad he'd suggested that they take this time to sit on the veranda, drinking coffee after lunch, while Bella napped.

'It must have been quite a culture shock for you to move all the way from Sydney to here,' she said earnestly. 'You were only twelve. That's smack on the edge of adolescence, when everything looms larger than life.'

'Actually, I think the fact that everything was so different here helped me,' he said. 'I was overawed by this place, but I thought it was incredibly exciting, and my uncle kept me busy from first thing in the morning till I fell into bed at night. He turned my life into an adventure. I'm sure I'd have found it much harder to get over my father's death if I'd stayed in Sydney.'

Surprised that he'd told Amy so much, he reached for his coffee cup and drank deeply.

Her face was soft with sympathy, as if she was picturing how it had been for him. 'It can't have been easy though, when you didn't have a mother.'

From force of habit, Seth brushed her comment aside. He had no intention of explaining about his mother. She was a subject he never talked about. There was no reason to discuss her.

But Amy had hooked her elbow over the arm of her chair and she was leaning towards him, watching him with her complete attention. Two small lines of worry drew her brows low and her brown eyes were rounded with concern, her pink lips parted. Seth found himself wanting to lean closer, too, to kiss those soft, inviting lips, to kiss away that frown.

It would be so easy.

So incredibly satisfying.

And…totally inappropriate. She hadn't come here for a fling.

All day he'd been struggling to blank out the picture of Amy this morning in her flimsy cotton nightdress. He tried not to think about the soft round outline of her breasts, the smooth skin of her shoulders, the tapering curve of her waist.

But Amy was different from Rachel. Seth knew she hadn't been planning seduction, and he could have sworn that she hadn't even noticed when her wrap slipped from her shoulders.

There'd been no flirting in the pool today either. But, heaven help him, he could still see the back view of her as she climbed the pool ladder. World-class legs. Lovely behind. Movements so graceful and feminine he couldn't help but stare.

Damn it, the very fact that Amy's sexiness was unintentional, and the knowledge that she wasn't trying to seduce him, made his desire for her all the stronger.

But he shouldn't have been checking her out. Just as he shouldn't be thinking about kissing her now.

He couldn't afford to start an affair with little Bella's guardian when he knew that it could never go anywhere. The child needed stability in her life, and he'd learned the hard way that women and his lifestyle didn't mix. For the past few years, he'd worked hard at keeping his distance from women like Amy—intelligent, warm-hearted, home-and-hearth-loving women.

The marrying kind.

Even so, he knew it would only take the first taste of her tender mouth, the first touch of his lips to her soft, warm skin and he'd be craving more.

He drew in a sharp breath.

Don't even think about it.

Why was it so hard to remember his past mistakes?

For pity's sake, man, just answer the woman's question.

He said, 'My mother left after my father died.'

'Left?' Shock made Amy's voice tremble. 'Are you saying she left *you*?'

Seth shrugged and forced a smile. 'Ever since I can

remember, she'd had her sights set on Hollywood, and without my father to hold her back she was free to go.'

'But she wasn't free, Seth. She had you.' Amy stared at him, with a hand pressed to her throat. Her dark eyes were clouded, as if he'd told her something completely beyond her comprehension. 'You'd just lost your father. You were only twelve. Why couldn't she keep you with her?'

It was a question that had eaten at Seth for years. Even now, he could feel the agonising slug of loss that had flattened him, when he'd finally understood what his mother's choice had meant.

Her longing for fame and glamour had outweighed her sense of responsibility.

Bottom line, she hadn't loved him enough.

Regretting that he'd started this line of talk, he sent Amy another shrugging smile. 'I was better off up here with my uncle.'

'I can't believe that.'

'I didn't believe it at first, but with the benefit of hindsight I know it was best.'

Amy looked as if she couldn't possibly agree.

'Think about it,' Seth told her. 'What twelve-year-old boy would choose to live in a low-rent flat in a huge metropolis like Los Angeles, when he could be here, learning to ride horses, to raise cattle, to fish and to skin-dive, to explore deserted islands, and to paddle a kayak?'

'I guess,' she said uncertainly.

'I owe my uncle a great deal.'

As if she needed time to think about this, she picked up the coffee pot. 'Would you like a refill?'

'Thanks.' He held out his cup and he admired the unconscious elegance of her slim wrists and hands as she lifted the teapot and poured.

She was dressed for the tropical heat in a soft blue cotton dress, with loose sleeves that left her smooth, lightly tanned arms free. Her hair, which had dried in natural waves after their swim, was twisted into a loose knot from which wispy curls strayed.

Her citified neatness was beginning to unravel and Seth found the process utterly fascinating. He wasn't sure which version of Amy he preferred, but one thing was certain— he was finding it close to impossible to remain detached, an aloof observer.

But he had to keep his distance. In a matter of days she was returning to Melbourne. She was a city girl. End of story.

Amy filled her cup and added milk, then settled down to resume their conversation. 'So did your mother make it big in Hollywood?'

'She's had walk-on parts in daytime soap operas, but that's about it.'

'Has she made enough money to live on?'

'I have no idea, but it doesn't really matter. She remarried,' Seth said coldly. 'Found herself a cashed-up Californian.'

'Has she ever been here?'

'Once, when she dropped me off,' he said, unhappily aware that he'd revealed much more than he'd intended. It was time to put a stop to these personal questions. Years ago, he'd learned to live without his mother and he wasn't going to admit to a tender-hearted woman like Amy Ross that his only contact with her had been letters on his eighteenth and twenty-first birthdays with generous cheques attached.

He drained his coffee cup and stood. 'I'm afraid I have business to attend to and I'm sure you'd appreciate time to yourself while Bella's asleep.'

'I'd like to take photographs of your grounds, if that's all right.'

'Be my guest. But keep to the open areas. Don't go wandering off into the rainforest, or down the track to the beach.'

Amy frowned. 'Do you think I'll get lost?'

'I'm assuming you'd rather not come face to face with an amethystine python, or a salt-water crocodile.'

The colour drained from her face and he winced. In one breath he'd completely ruined her stay.

'I'm exaggerating the danger,' he said more gently. 'People have been living here for decades quite safely. But I'd rather you didn't go exploring without me.'

'Yes,' she acceded, still looking pale. 'That might be best.'

'So promise me for now that you won't go beyond the garden.'

Amy gave him her word.

CHAPTER FIVE

As SHE watched Seth stride away, Amy almost changed her mind about setting foot outside the house. The spectre of snakes and crocodiles scared her to death and in a panicky rush she ran back to the bedroom to make sure that Bella was still sleeping safely.

The windows and doors to their room were screened, however, and no creepy-crawlies could find their way in, thank God. Bella was fine.

She knew Seth's claim was true—plenty of people had lived here and avoided being eaten. Rachel had stayed here for six weeks and she'd never mentioned any special dangers. Then again, Rachel had kept quiet about a lot of things in the north.

Including Seth.

But Amy had already tortured herself enough over that man. All morning, she'd driven herself crazy fretting over his relationship with Rachel, his plans for Bella, and her own giddy pulse rate whenever he was near.

Taking several deep breaths, she swore to put him out of her mind, and she set off, camera in hand, to explore his garden.

Which was lovely. Really lovely.

Again she wondered why Rachel had never mentioned how gorgeous this place was. She'd made so few comments, hadn't shown any pictures. Nothing. Had she saved it all for her book?

Amy didn't know the names of many of the tropical plants, but as she walked she recognised hibiscus, orchids and bougainvilleas growing lushly amidst ferns and palms. She loved the showiness and variety of the lavishly hued tropical flowers and leaves.

The butterflies and birds were extra bright and beautiful, too. All living things here were wonderfully vivid. Nature at double strength. As she walked down twisting paths, she felt as if her senses were zapped onto high alert.

She was surrounded by fragrances—the scents of frangipani, of ginger and cardamom, mixed with a pervading smell of damp earth and vegetation. There was a constant peep-peep-peeping sound, which, Seth had already explained, came from tiny tree frogs in the nearby forest.

Here in the tropics there was a sense of life teeming and lush, pushing to the max, and she was aware of an indefinable something that stirred her, a constant pulse-raising excitement and restlessness.

Perhaps that was why her thoughts zeroed straight back to Seth.

She couldn't help it. He was such a fascinating puzzle.

He'd said he was fine about his mother's defection, but Amy had been watching him closely, and despite his brave words she'd seen dark pain in his eyes and in the tightening set of his mouth.

Her heart ached for him, but his brave stoicism also

frightened her. How could they come to an agreement about Bella's future when his attitude to mothers and motherhood was almost the polar opposite of hers?

Amy adored her mum and she adored caring for Bella, but if Seth had managed so famously in this remote place without any contact with his mother, he might easily assume that Bella would be fine here, too.

And where, Amy wondered, did that leave her?

It was a relief, on rounding a tall clump of pink ginger, to be distracted by an elderly man wearing a wide-brimmed hat of woven cane and happily hacking at palm fronds with a long-handled machete.

'Hi,' Amy called, waving to catch his attention.

In no time, she'd introduced herself and learned that he was Hans, who'd grown up in Indonesia, and had worked as a gardener on Serenity for more than twenty years.

'Can I show you my garden?' he asked in response to her eager compliments, and when she assured him she'd love that he grinned so widely his face disappeared into a mass of brown wrinkles.

For the next half-hour, Amy was highly entertained *and* educated, and she tried, once again, to put Seth Reardon and his potential threats to her happiness firmly out of her mind.

Seth didn't return to the homestead until it was close to dusk. By then, the sky had turned smoky aqua and pink and the garden was filled with purple shadows. Amy was about to take Bella inside for her bath when she saw Seth coming across the lawn to the house.

There was something tired about his shoulders that she

hadn't noticed before, but his smile was bright when Bella ran to greet him with her usual bouncing enthusiasm.

He scooped her up in his arms and swung her so high that the little girl squealed, then begged for more.

Seth laughed. 'That's enough for now.' He shot Amy a bright-eyed glance. 'Come with me and I'll show you magic fireflies.'

'Fireflies?' Amy and Bella chorused together.

He nodded towards the darkening forest. 'Over here. Come on, I'll show you.'

They went down a flight of stone steps to a lower terrace, crossed the lawn to a dark line of trees, and Amy saw a narrow track leading away into the shadowy depths of the forest. Seth, who was holding Bella with one arm, suddenly reached for Amy's hand.

Heat raced over her skin like a fire out of control.

'Stay with me,' he said quietly and for a giddy, heart-stumbling moment, she fancied he was asking her to…stay here…

To live with him at Serenity.

And then, crazily, even though she'd only known him for two days, she felt an astonishing impulse to say yes.

'We'll take this track slowly,' he said.

Oh, good grief.

Embarrassment flooded Amy as she realised her mistake. Seth wanted her to stay close to him on the darkened track. Of course he wasn't talking about a romantic future.

Of course, of course.

Silently, she cursed her ridiculous reaction. For heaven's sake. Her job was to protect Bella's future happiness, and she had to remember that Seth might yet make unreasonable demands and become their enemy.

'W-what about the s-n-a-k-e-s?' she whispered, spelling out the word so she didn't frighten Bella.

'You'll be OK with me. I know what to look for.'

'Are you sure?'

She saw the flash of his teeth as he grinned at her. 'Tree snakes aren't really dangerous, unless you're a bird or a little possum.'

Her heart was thundering like a Mack truck, but the problem wasn't so much her fear of snakes as the intimate warmth of Seth's hand enclosing hers. She registered every detail—the slightly rough texture of his palm, the individual pressure of each of his fingers.

Seth took them deeper into the forest, dodging hanging vines and buttressed tree roots. The frogs were silent now and the trees crowded close, but just when Amy wondered if they were mad to continue into the gathering gloom they reached a clearing—and Seth released her hand.

The sudden feeling of loss was alarming, but Amy was soon gasping with amazement as tiny pinpricks of light flitted and danced in the dusky glade. The fireflies flashed in front of them, behind them, and above them, and they looked exactly like tiny glowing fairies.

Seth was right—they were magic. Truly magic and utterly entrancing.

'They're so beautiful,' Amy said softly. 'Look Bella, see the fireflies. They're like fairies.'

'Fairies,' Bella repeated in hushed awe.

'Aren't they pretty?'

The little girl nodded, and for once she was too entranced to speak. She simply wound her arms around Seth's neck and hugged him more tightly, and he smiled and kissed her cheek.

'Is that firefly all right? It doesn't seem able to fly,' Amy said, pointing to a blinking light that had stayed on the ground the whole time.

Seth laughed softly. 'That's a female. She stays down there quietly, waiting till a flashing male appeals to her, and then she flashes back, signalling her interest.'

'Oh.' Amy wished she hadn't asked and she was sure she was still blushing when it was time to head back.

'I didn't bring a torch,' Seth told her. 'So you need to stay close.'

He took her hand again and she vowed to remain calm and sensible as they made their way back.

Conversation would be a helpful distraction, she decided, so she told Seth that she'd made friends with Hans, the gardener, and that she'd visited the kitchen to talk to Ming. Bella chattered about fairies, then promptly begged for another swim.

'Not till tomorrow,' Seth told her gently but firmly, as if he was already completely comfortable with his new role as her father.

Amy half expected Bella to ask again for a swim, pleading and putting on her whiny voice, but the little girl accepted Seth's ruling without a murmur.

They reached the edge of the trees where they could see the lights from the house spilling across the terraced lawns, and just when Amy expected Seth to release her she felt his thumb stroke the back of her hand. Slowly. Deliberately.

Just once.

A trembling thrill raced from her breastbone to her toes. She knew it hadn't been an accident.

She couldn't breathe, but then Seth released her hand and he set Bella down to run ahead of them over the smooth lawn.

Still trembling from his touch, Amy sent a quick glance in his direction, but his attention was focused entirely on Bella, and he was smiling as he watched her skipping and flapping her arms in the warm night air.

'She's trying to be a firefly,' he said.

'She's having a great time here,' Amy admitted softly.

'She is, isn't she?' He was still smiling.

She wanted to remind him of his intention to let Bella return to Melbourne at the end of their stay, but she was silenced by the shining light in his eyes. For the first time since she'd met him, he looked genuinely happy.

After Seth showered and changed into fresh clothes, he went through to the kitchen, where he found Bella at the kitchen table, glowing pink and clean after her bath, smelling of baby talcum powder and wolfing down a bowl of Ming's special chicken congee.

'Hi, Sef,' Bella called, waving her spoon at him. 'My eating dinner.'

'Lucky you.' He found himself smiling back at her. He'd been smiling so much lately it was a wonder his face hadn't cracked. 'Is Amy about?' he asked Ming.

'She's taking a shower.' Ming turned from the stove, shot a shrewd glance Seth's way, and grinned. 'I reckon she's doing the same as you.'

'What's that?'

'Getting spruced up for your dinner date.'

'It isn't a date.'

Ming's keen gaze took in Seth's clean moleskin trousers

and neatly pressed shirt and Seth felt the back of his neck grow hot.

'I thought I explained,' he said tightly. 'Amy's a friend of Rachel's. You remember Rachel? Rachel Tyler?'

'Of course.' The cook frowned and turned back to the stove. 'But Amy Ross is nothing like Rachel.'

'No,' Seth agreed as he helped Bella to scrape the last of the chicken and rice porridge from the bottom of her bowl. 'Amy's not remotely like Rachel. They're chalk and cheese.'

He heard a sound behind him and turned to find Amy in the doorway. Her hair was loose to her shoulders, brushed and shining, and she was wearing a white summery dress with no sleeves and a soft, floaty skirt. She carried an apricot silk wrap, and her skin looked natural and free from make-up. She was…in a word…

Lovely…

Breathtakingly so.

And she looked as if she might, at any moment, burst into tears.

Seth cursed beneath his breath as he realised she'd overheard his conversation with Ming, and the comparison with Rachel. *Damn.* He'd meant it as a compliment, but it could just as easily have sounded like a put-down to her. Problem was, he couldn't explain exactly what he'd meant by his 'chalk and cheese' statement without embarrassing her in front of Ming, and without casting her best friend in a bad light.

Despite the abrupt and awkward silence, Amy came into the room and flashed a bright smile, clearly determined to carry on as if she'd heard nothing. 'Has Bella finished her dinner?'

'She's eaten every drop,' Seth told her.

'Ming, you must be a genius.' Amy admired the empty bowl elaborately. 'Bella doesn't normally eat much in the evenings.'

Ming grinned. 'Everyone likes my cooking.'

'You should thank Ming, Bella.'

'Thank you, Ming,' the little girl parroted obediently, but her smile was genuine enough to melt the shy cook's heart.

'Now drink up your milk because it's time for bed.'

As soon as the milk was down Amy whisked the child away.

Not once did she look at Seth.

Amy took a deep breath as she walked across the subtly lit veranda, past a table set prettily for two, with a candle under a glass dome and a pink ceramic bowl filled with floating flowers. She found Seth sitting on the top veranda step, staring out into the vast, moony black night.

'Seth?'

His head whipped around and his gaze was fierce.

She swallowed. 'Would you mind saying goodnight to Bella?' Smiling awkwardly, she explained, 'I'm afraid she won't settle without a kiss from you.'

'Sure.' He stood quickly and looked as uncomfortable as Amy felt.

'I'll wait here,' she said steadily, but she was fighting tears as she watched him go. It was so silly. She was upset on all sorts of levels tonight.

Bella's demand that Seth be the one to tuck her in had hurt. Amy hated to think she was jealous, but the little girl was falling for Seth fast and hard. She seemed to be totally fascinated by him—utterly trusting, excited and enthralled.

Amy told herself it was because Bella had very little experience of men. Rachel had stopped going out with guys once she'd known she was pregnant, and, of course, Dominic had stayed well out of any scene that had involved Bella.

But now, it was almost as if Bella sensed that Seth was special, and connected to her. It was fanciful to think that the child knew he was her father. But very soon he would want her to know the truth, and, although she was too little to really understand, it would be an important step in cementing their emotional bond.

Leaving her wrap on the veranda railing, Amy leaned against a post and looked out at the inky sky where a silvery half-moon was glowing softly through a gap in the trees. She thought again about the conversation she'd overheard in the kitchen.

It was *really* silly to be upset about that. She knew very well she was different from Rachel. It was very true they were chalk and cheese. Their differences had kept their friendship in balance. But it was only logical that, if Seth had been madly attracted to cheese, he was unlikely to fall for chalk.

Of course she knew that.

She had never, in her wildest dreams, expected Rachel's ex to be interested in her. She just wished he hadn't held her hand this evening, hadn't made that one slow, deliberate stroke on her skin. She was quite, quite sure she would remember that slide of his thumb for the rest of her life.

But how idiotic was that?

Anyone would think she was a trembling virgin who'd

been locked away in a tower for a hundred years and knew absolutely nothing about men. Truth be told, she'd had experience, but she had a terrible habit of picking the wrong kind of guy. Each relationship had ended unhappily.

If she had any brains she'd avoid men completely. How on earth had she allowed this man, this *highly unsuitable* man, to reduce her to such a pathetic state in such a short space of time?

She was a *fool*!

At the sound of Seth's footsteps, she spun around.

'All quiet on the nursery front,' he said, smiling.

'Is Bella asleep?'

'Just about.' He came and stood close beside Amy. 'And judging by the aromas coming from the kitchen, I'd say our dinner's almost ready.'

'Something smells amazing. Is it curry?'

'Seafood curry. One of Ming's specialties.'

'Wow. So we're in for a treat.'

On cue, Ming appeared with a bamboo tray holding a bowl of steaming jasmine rice and a large blue and white covered pot, which he placed in the centre of the table.

'Thanks, Ming,' Seth said with the very slightest hint of an amused smile and a courteous dip of his head.

'Enjoy.' Ming bestowed them both with an eloquent grin before disappearing discreetly.

Seth pulled out a chair for Amy and, to her dismay, the old-fashioned gesture set her heart speeding again.

She kept her gaze lowered as he sat opposite her and she told herself again to remember that she was the guardian of Bella's future. That was her role here.

It was time to forget the handholding, the suntan, and

the heavenly blue eyes. Seth was her host and she was his guest. No more, no less.

She took a deep breath and smelled their fragrant meal and the scent of frangipani. In the glow of the candlelight, Seth's shirt gleamed whitely and his throat was a dark shadow above the V of his open collar. She concentrated on safer things—the smooth gleam of silver cutlery, the crisp white napkins and the fine matchstick placemats dyed a deep watermelon pink.

Helping herself to fluffy spoonfuls of the aromatic rice and curry, she made a stab at polite conversation. 'I have to keep reminding myself that this is a cattle station,' she said. 'I feel as if I'm on holidays at a beautiful resort.'

'Well, this should be a holiday for you. I'm sure you deserve a break,' Seth said with a smile. 'But tomorrow I'll take you and Bella to see the rest of Serenity. You'll soon see there are plenty of cattle.'

'How many?'

'At the moment we have around seven thousand.'

Amy's eyebrows lifted. 'More than a few, then.' Between mouthfuls, she added, 'This food is sensational.'

'Ming's outdone himself tonight.'

Seth looked and sounded amused, which confused her.

'Do you dine out here alone, when you don't have guests?'

He shook his head. 'Hans and Ming often join me here. Sometimes I eat in the kitchen, or over with the stockmen. It varies.'

'I wish I'd known that. I would have been more than happy for Hans and Ming to have joined us tonight.'

'What? And spoil their fun?'

Amy frowned.

'Those guys see so few women,' Seth explained, gesturing to the candle and the bowl of flowers. 'Hans adores his garden, and Ming loves his cooking, and they live for the chance to do this kind of thing.'

'But they probably think—'

'Relax. I've explained our situation to them.'

'What did you tell them?'

'That you're a friend of Rachel's. That you and Bella are in the north on business. Just passing through.'

Amy nodded, reassured. She wondered if Seth would tell the others about Bella's relationship to him once she was gone.

As she thought about their departure in a few days' time, she realised, with a start, how very far away Melbourne felt. Already, it was almost as if she'd lived there in another lifetime.

She looked out into the moonlit garden, to the dark wall of trees beyond, and the twinkling stars peeping above the forest canopy. This alternative reality had already wrapped itself around her senses. Her heart.

'I love these open verandas,' she said. 'They're such a good idea. Like living in the garden.'

'The best way to live in the tropics.'

'But what happens in bad weather? Don't you have cyclones here?'

'We have built-in storm shutters that roll down. This whole area can be made completely secure.'

'That's clever. Who designed that? Your uncle?'

Seth nodded.

'Was there a woman involved? It's all so—so lovely.'

'No woman. My uncle had a flair for design. He liked to be surrounded by beautiful things.'

A shadow crossed Seth's face like a cloud over the moon.

Ever so casually, Amy asked, 'Did Rachel stay here in this house when she was working here?'

Seth blinked and the cloud vanished. His eyes were suddenly bright and alert with more than a hint of wariness. 'No, Rachel stayed over in the barracks with the other staff.'

'I see.' Amy wasn't sure what to make of that information and she paid careful attention to her food.

'She also spent some time on one of the islands,' Seth said.

'With you?' Oh, good grief. Amy couldn't believe she'd asked such a pointed question, but now that it was out she couldn't take it back.

Seth, however, dodged her question with the practised skill of a politician. 'She liked to take the dinghy across to Turtle Island on her days off,' he said. 'She liked the view to the west, looking back to the mainland, especially at sunset.'

'I suppose that's why she called her book *Northern Sunsets*.'

He lowered his gaze. 'I dare say.'

She could all too easily imagine Rachel with this highly desirable man, alone on a tropical island, watching the sunset, but the thought made her ridiculously miserable and her throat prickled painfully as she tried to swallow.

'Let's not talk about Rachel.' Seth was watching her carefully. 'I'm sure the memories must be upsetting for you.'

She nodded.

'I'd like to hear all about you.'

'Me?' Her head shot up and she stared at him. 'Why?'

As if the answer was obvious, he shrugged. 'You're Bella's guardian.'

'Oh, right. Yes, of course.' Why else would Seth be interested in her? He had every right to check out his daughter's protector.

Tamping down the tiniest spurt of disappointment, Amy wondered where she should start.

'I know you work in marketing,' Seth prompted. 'Does that create difficulties for you with childcare?'

'I do some of my work from home,' she said defensively. 'But not all. Do you have a problem with day care?'

His eyes widened. 'I know very little about it. If you're single, I guess you don't have an option.'

'That's right. I don't have an option, but it's not a problem. There's a wonderful day-care centre quite near me, and I have a big, extended family so I have a great back-up team.'

'Is your family in Melbourne?'

She nodded. 'I have two older brothers, both married with kids. And my parents, of course. Aunts, uncles. We have tons of family gatherings—Christmas, birthdays, Easter, Mother's Day. You name it, we celebrate. Any excuse for a Ross family get-together.'

'Sounds like fun,' Seth said, but a tight note had crept into his voice.

Sensitive to his distinct lack of family, Amy took her enthusiasm down a notch. 'Most of our gatherings are fun. But big families can be claustrophobic at times.'

'How does your family feel about Bella?'

Was this a trick question? 'They adore her, of course.'

'Of course.' Seth's face was grim as he speared a piece of fish with his fork. 'And what about your boyfriend?'

Amy tried to keep her tone casual. 'What boyfriend?'

Seth's gaze locked with hers. 'There's got to be a boy-friend. A girl like you must have a host of admirers.'

She almost choked. 'I don't have anyone at the moment. There was someone, but it—it didn't work out.'

It was weird how quickly Dominic had faded from her thoughts. Did it mean she was shallow that, after two months of living with Bella, she rarely thought about him? Now, in Seth's company, she didn't want to think about Dominic at all.

In the glow of the flickering candle, Seth's eyes had turned such a deep blue she feared she might drown in them.

'If there's no boyfriend,' he said softly, 'why are you blushing?'

Because of the way you're looking at me.

'Amy?'

She chewed nervously at her lower lip, unwilling to admit to Bella's father the exact reason that had prompted Dominic's departure. If he knew Bella was involved he might try to persuade her to leave his daughter here.

'Did this man break your heart?'

'Is that any of your business?'

'I thought we were having an adult conversation.'

'Yes, we are.' She let out an impatient huff.

'Did he?'

'Break my heart? No. I—I don't think so.'

'You don't *think* so?' Seth skewered her with a search-ing, no-holds-barred gaze. 'That isn't possible. If your heart was broken you'd know about it.'

'You sound as if you're speaking from experience.'

He shrugged, but didn't answer, and she realised with

a sharp pang that it was true. Seth had been hurt badly and he still carried the scars.

With her eyes on the bowl of floating flowers, she forced herself to ask, 'Was it Rachel? Did she break your heart?'

'No, not Rachel. It was years ago—long before she came here.'

Puzzled, Amy looked up, but he smiled at her with a surprisingly gentle look that sent her pulse spiralling helplessly. At the same moment she caught a movement out of the corner of her eye and she turned to see Bella in her green and white pyjamas, coming towards them across the veranda.

'Baby.' Amy jumped to her feet. 'What are you doing out here?'

'I waked up.'

Hurrying to the little girl, Amy scooped her up quickly and hugged her close. She smelled warm and sleepy, and she was rubbing at her eyes with one fist while she clutched her pink pig with the other.

'You didn't kiss me goodnight,' Bella said with a hint of bossiness.

Aware that Seth was watching them, Amy tried to be stern. 'But you sent me to find Seth. You wanted him to kiss you.'

'Want you, too,' Bella said, sticking out her bottom lip stubbornly.

'If I take you back to bed now and give you a kiss, you must promise to go straight back to sleep.'

'Sef, too.'

'But you've already had a goodnight kiss from Seth.'

Bella looked mutinous 'Sef, too.'

Amy sent a helpless glance back to Seth, and saw that he was already on his feet.

'It's OK,' he said, coming towards them with a slow, easy smile. 'I can give Bella two kisses in one night.'

'Well, yes. Of course.' Amy hoped she didn't sound flustered.

He followed her to the bedroom, and she was far too aware of his presence as she turned on the lamp, and rearranged Bella's toys around her pillow, then helped the little girl into bed and retucked the sheets.

Sitting on the edge of the bed, she gave Bella's soft cheek a kiss. 'Night, night.' Gave her another hug. 'Don't let the bed bugs bite.'

She stood and shuffled in the narrow space between the twin beds to make room for Seth, who suddenly seemed enormously tall and broad shouldered. And excessively male.

Bella's eyes shone as he perched on the bed beside her and she grinned with delight as he kissed her.

'Goodnight, possum.' Gently, he tucked a strand of hair from her face. 'Now close your eyes.'

Bella obeyed.

'Sleep tight.'

As Seth stood up in the confined space his shoulder bumped Amy's arm and heat flashed through her like a sky-rocket taking off.

She struggled to sound calm as she spoke to Bella. 'I'm going to leave the lamp on for ten minutes, and you must go to sleep.'

Before the little girl could think up another reason to delay her, she turned and left the room, and Seth followed.

Outside, beyond the bedroom's closed door, she sent him a nervous smile. 'I do hope she actually nods off this time.'

'She's not used to this house yet,' he said smoothly.

Amy knew this was true, but his indulgent attitude surprised her.

'She's used to sleeping in strange beds,' she said, and then, to her annoyance, she blushed again.

Seth's eyes sparkled with poorly concealed amusement.

'What's so funny?' she snapped.

'I was thinking—' He paused, looking at her, and the light in his eyes made her chest squeeze tight. 'I was thinking that it wouldn't be fair if Bella gets all the kisses.'

Amy stopped breathing, and Seth took a step closer.

CHAPTER SIX

SETH told himself it was a simple thing.

He was merely being playful, giving Amy a friendly and innocent kiss on the cheek just like the one he'd given Bella.

So it made no sense that, from the moment he touched her—merely brushed a wisp of her hair from her cheek—he felt fine, electric tremors all over his body.

Amy was standing still. Very still… *Too* still…standing with her eyes closed…

Seth could see the delicate blue veins on her eyelids, and he could smell faint traces of the jasmine soap she'd used in the shower. He focused on her smooth, soft cheek and tried to ignore the softer-than-soft bow of her lips, but, for some reason that made no sense at all, he didn't find his way to her cheek…

He dipped lower…

Until his mouth brushed against hers…and they shared a beat of trembling hesitation…and then a gentle, lingering touch…the most tender of hellos.

And Amy didn't pull away.

Seth felt a subtle increase in the pressure of her mouth against his, and then her lips parted, yielding and warm. She tasted of the summer night and his blood began to roar.

His heart pounded, his skin burned…the homestead veranda faded and the entire universe became Amy.

Sweetly erotic Amy.

Her mouth was so soft and warm, just how he knew it would be. Oh, God. He'd been fighting this attraction from the moment he saw her in the Tamundra pub, and now she was offering heaven…

He wanted nothing but this…. Amy, breathless and needy, her skin silky and hot under his hand.

Her kiss…was such a perfect thing…

But she went suddenly still and pulled away.

Seth realised that Ming was there.

'I—I've left your desserts ready in the kitchen,' Ming said, eyes wide with poorly suppressed delight, then he scuttled sideways like a crab down the hallway, as if he couldn't hurry away from them fast enough.

As Seth struggled to breathe he heard Amy's voice calling, 'Thanks for dinner, Ming. The seafood curry was sensational.'

She sounded astonishingly calm, not at all like a woman who'd been drowning in a whirlpool of passion.

With her back very straight, her chin high, she turned and sailed ahead of Seth onto the veranda, leaving him reeling in her wake.

He took a swift, steadying breath. If there was one thing he'd learned to do well, it was to hide his feelings. No way did he want Amy to guess how seriously he'd been rocked by that kiss.

Once they were out of Ming's earshot he asked, almost calmly, 'Do you think Bella will settle now?'

Amy stared at him blankly, as if she hadn't a clue what he was talking about. Hastily, she looked the other way. 'Sorry, what did you say? I—I w-was distracted.'

This was better. Perhaps they were on the same wavelength after all.

She lifted her hands in a nervous gesture of helplessness. 'I—I was hoping Ming hasn't got the wrong idea.'

'He's discreet, like all my staff.'

'Well, yes, I'm sure he is,' she said unhappily.

Seth opened his mouth to apologise, but swiftly changed his mind. He wasn't about to apologise for kissing a lovely girl in the moonlight.

And he wasn't prepared to admit that the kiss might have been a mistake, even though it was almost certainly a huge error of judgement. He'd let his desire for Amy complicate a situation that was already thorny enough. He would have to tell her the truth sooner rather than later, but he couldn't face it now. The painful story was still raw inside him. *I'll do it soon,* he thought. *When I've had more time to prepare.*

For now, he decided, it was better to simply change the subject.

'Are you ready for dessert?' Before Amy could object, Seth added, quickly, 'You have to try Ming's watermelon balls in green ginger wine.'

The ghost of a smile flickered. 'That does sound tempting.'

'Take a seat. I'll be back in a sec—as soon as I collect the desserts from the kitchen.'

* * *

As Seth headed off Amy let out her breath on a shuddering sigh. She felt as if she'd been holding her breath ever since he'd kissed her, and now she was grateful for this moment alone, for this chance to close her eyes while she relived that astonishing experience.

It was too bad that Ming had seen them, but she wasn't nearly as worried as she'd made out.

What she wondered now was how she'd lived so long, and dated so many guys, without discovering that one kiss could be a phenomenal, life-changing moment.

Gently, with a sense of wonderment, she traced the soft skin on her lips as she remembered the hot, out-of-this-world thrill that had jolted through her body as Seth's mouth settled against hers.

She'd give anything to experience that sensation again—*everything*: her job, her life in Melbourne, the close contact with her family.

She'd never felt anything remotely as exciting when Dominic had kissed her. Small wonder their relationship hadn't survived. There'd been no real chemistry.

Chemistry. That was the secret ingredient in tonight's kiss, wasn't it? Mysterious, magical, astonishing chemistry.

But chemical reactions could also be dangerous and she had to remember that now as she heard Seth's footsteps returning.

She had to remember that Seth was potentially dangerous. Chances were, every woman reacted that way when he kissed them. Especially that one woman who'd broken his heart.

And Rachel.

A thud of disappointment brought Amy back to earth. What on earth had she been thinking? She couldn't afford to forget, even for a moment, why she was here. Clearly, this man was indeed dangerous. He had seduced her best friend and made her pregnant and here she was getting into a flap over a tiny kiss that probably meant nothing more to him than yet another woman falling at his feet.

'I think you'll find this dessert is the perfect second course after curry,' Seth said as he reached her.

'Thank you,' she said primly.

He set a green glass bowl in front of her and she caught the sweet scent of watermelon mingled with the deeper spiciness of the green ginger wine.

'That smell reminds me of Christmas,' she said, determined to steer her thoughts onto a safer track.

'It certainly reminds me of summer. Tuck in.'

She watched as Seth slipped a marble-sized ball of lush pink fruit from his spoon to his mouth.

Oh, for heaven's sake! Already she was thinking about his mouth, about his kiss—so perfect.

'What's Christmas like here?' she asked, trying again for a distraction. 'Do you usually have a big party?'

'Not any more. We used to throw parties, but they're not really my scene.'

'That's a pity.' She looked around her at the open-plan living spaces on the veranda, and she pictured paper lanterns in the garden. 'This is a perfect house for a party, and with Ming to help with catering it would be a breeze, and so much fun.'

'So you like parties, do you?'

'Most parties,' she said. 'I sometimes have to organise them as part of my job—to help clients with networking, or to launch new products.'

As she said this Amy was hit by memories of the launch party on the night Rachel died and she felt another sickening thud, deep inside, as if her heart had crashed from a great height.

'Amy, are you all right?'

She reached for her water glass and took a deep sip. 'I'm OK,' she said. 'It just catches me every so often—the pain, you know—when I think about Rachel.'

'Yeah,' he said softly. 'I do know what you mean. And it lasts a long time, I'm afraid. I still miss my dad after all these years, and it's been worse since my uncle died.'

She was surprised that Seth hadn't mentioned mourning for Rachel, too. Surely he must feel some degree of grief for Bella's mother?

For Amy the smallest memory of Rachel could trigger pain—Rachel's habit of flicking her long, pale hair over her shoulders. Her deep, throaty laugh. A punchline from the zany jokes she loved to tell.

But she wasn't prepared to share these memories with Seth. It was far safer to leave the intimate details of his history with Rachel where they belonged—firmly in the past.

Unhappily, she scooped up a spoonful of wine-drenched fruit. 'Can you tell me more about your uncle? Did he always live here?'

Seth shook his head. 'He started off in Sydney like the rest of my family. Moved to Cape York in his late twenties.'

'To be a cattleman?'

'Yeah.' Seth smiled. 'Left a thriving family business to become a struggling grazier.'

'That's intriguing.' She dipped her spoon into the bowl.

These watermelon balls were amazing. 'What was the family business?'

'Have you ever heard of Reardon and Grace?'

She shook her head.

'It's a very old importing and exporting business. My great-great-grandfather started it way back, and he owned one of the first warehouses in Sydney.'

'Wow.'

'All the men in my family have played a role in the firm, including my father. Seth was the first to leave.'

'Seth? Was that your uncle's name, too?'

'Yes. He was my father's younger brother.'

Amy frowned. Somehow, this information seemed significant, but she was too caught up in this story to stop and puzzle it out. 'Why did he leave Sydney?'

Seth's mouth twisted into a wry smile and she winced. 'Am I being too nosy?'

'Not really.' His steady gaze met hers. 'But it's rather a sad tale.'

Unwilling to push him, she took another spoonful of her dessert.

'You see, my uncle was madly in love,' Seth said quietly. 'And everything was fine until he brought his girlfriend home and introduced her to his older brother.'

'To your father?'

He nodded. 'He wasn't my father then, of course. This was before I was born.'

'But your father fell in love with the same woman as your uncle?'

'Yes, and he married her.'

The penny dropped, making Amy gasp. 'So this woman was your mother. Your uncle was in love with your mother.'

'Completely and hopelessly, I'm afraid.'

'The poor man.'

Amy could picture it all. Seth's uncle, this other Seth Reardon, must have been so upset when he lost the woman he loved, that he'd left his comfortable life in Sydney and travelled all the way up here to try to forget her. To start a new life.

'Did he have to start here from scratch?' she asked.

'More or less. It was hard work, but he took to the life like he was born and bred for it, and he soon toughened up. You know what they say? When the going gets tough, the tough get going. He pitched in with the fencing gangs. Joined in the mustering. Helped to build this house. He thrived on the life here.'

'But he never married?'

'No.' Seth's brow furrowed in a deep frown. 'When my father died, my mother brought me here, and I think my uncle had hoped that she'd stay.'

'But she went to America?'

'Chasing her dream.' His face darkened. 'This is no life for a woman.'

'Why couldn't a woman live here?' Amy asked. 'It's beautiful.'

'The house and garden might be beautiful,' Seth said tersely. 'But that's all there is here to keep a woman happy. There are no shops or cafés. No chance for catching up with girlfriends. The nearest hairdresser is in Cairns.'

Amy wanted to disagree. She knew Serenity was remote, but she suspected that a woman could be very happy here. She would have to be the right woman, of course, with the right man.

But if the two of them loved each other deeply, if the chemistry was right, why couldn't they be blissfully happy?

It wasn't a question she could ask when Seth's mother and Rachel and possibly the girl who'd broken his heart had not been prepared to stay.

Amy shivered at the thought of Seth's loneliness, which he seemed to accept as his fate. She longed to reach out and touch him tenderly, to cup her hand against the rugged line of his jaw, to brush his lips with the pad of her thumb, to show him that she cared.

She longed to rekindle the passion of their kiss, and now, with no Ming to interrupt them, who knew where it might lead? Amy didn't care. She wanted it, wanted him.

But that's crazy.

Oh, God. For an insane minute there, she'd almost forgotten Rachel, Bella, her job, her family… She'd almost been ready to throw every responsibility to the four winds…in exchange for a night with Seth.

Shaking, shocked by her foolishness, she reached across the table for his empty bowl. She spoke carefully. 'Thank you for the delicious meal. I'll take these things through to the kitchen.'

Instantly he was on his feet. 'No, you don't have to worry about the kitchen. You're a guest.'

Avoiding the fire in his gaze, she said, 'But I haven't performed a single helpful task since I arrived. Let me rinse these couple of bowls to keep my hand in.'

He gave her a puzzled smile. 'If you insist.'

'I insist,' she said quietly but emphatically. 'Goodnight, Seth.' She walked away swiftly, carrying the dishes, unable to return his smile.

A noise woke Amy, a sudden flapping of wings outside her room and the haunting call of a bird, which she thought must have been an owl. She rolled over and looked through the moon-streaked darkness to Bella's bed, hoping the sound hadn't woken her.

Fortunately, the little girl remained very still, undisturbed. Amy rolled onto her back again and closed her eyes. She crossed her fingers, hoping she would drift back to sleep.

She was tired. Really tired. She hadn't slept well since she'd left Melbourne and right now she wanted to stay drowsy and dopey. She needed to sleep, and not to think.

But already she could feel her brain whirring to fretful life, spinning thoughts…throwing up questions…

About…Seth.

And that kiss…

It was so easy now, in the middle of the night, to let her mind zoom in on the details of that kiss, to live it again in close focus.

She could feel again the intimate brush of his lips against hers, the imprint of his hand at the small of her back, the nerve-tingly pleasure and the rush of delicious heat that had flooded her, the astonishing need, the glorious, overwhelming longing…

Good grief. She was going mad, wasn't she? She had to be a little crazy to get into such a fever about one kiss.

From the start, she'd sensed she should be wary of Seth

Reardon. He was incredibly sexy, despite or perhaps because of his remote, brooding air, but she'd picked up all kinds of signals that he was dangerous, too.

Rachel had been so cagey about him. Even the woman at the Tamundra pub had hinted that he was trouble. And on reflection Amy had to admit she'd had difficulty thinking straight from the moment she'd met him.

Thank heavens she hadn't thrown herself at him tonight.

The man was a disturbing mystery.

He'd claimed that his heart had been broken, but it hadn't happened over Rachel.

And yet…he'd made love to Rachel and she'd thought he was *The One*…and he'd fathered Bella, and now Rachel was dead…but Seth wasn't particularly upset about it.

None of it made sense. Had the man no feelings?

Was there a cold unemotional side to him that Amy hadn't seen yet? Had Rachel known that, and sensibly kept her distance?

With a groan Amy rolled over to face the wall and thumped at her pillow. The Seth she'd seen over the past two days had given her the impression that he was warm and vulnerable—and wounded—but that didn't sit with the alternative image of him as cold and unfeeling.

Would the real Seth Reardon please stand up?

He was a jigsaw puzzle she couldn't solve unless she found the vital missing pieces.

She'd wanted to ask him about the woman who'd broken his heart, but she didn't know him well enough to ask such an intimate question. She'd known him for such a short time.

Heavens, had it really only been two days?

Sighing heavily, Amy rolled the other way again and pulled the sheet around her bare shoulders. She thought about Seth's uncle's sad story, and she wondered how the poor man had felt when Seth's mother—the woman he'd loved and lost—had given his name to her son.

And how had he felt years later, when his young nephew had been abandoned by that woman? He'd probably taken care of the younger Seth out of love for his brother, and a sense of duty, but it must have hurt deeply, if he'd still loved the boy's mother, in spite of her failings.

But fancy there being two Seth Reardons. That was a surprise. That was—

Oh, my God.

Amy shot upright in the bed, her heart racing.

It was a crazy thought, but…

Was it possible…was it even remotely possible that Seth's *uncle* had been Rachel's lover?

When Seth told her that his uncle had died, she'd pictured him as an elderly man, but he needn't have been *that* old.

At a guess, she would say that Seth was around thirty, and his uncle was younger than Seth's father, so he might have been only fifty or so when Rachel met him.

She tried to imagine Rachel falling for a fifty-year-old man. He'd need to have been a well-preserved and decidedly good-looking fifty-year-old man—but he was sure to be handsome if he was related to Seth.

It was possible, wasn't it?

Her friend had always been a little unconventional in her tastes, and the more Amy thought about it, the more it started to make sense.

Rachel was less likely to burden an older man with the

news that he was about to become a father. She'd confided to Amy that her schooldays had been blighted by the fact that her parents were so much older than everyone else's folks. Kids were cruel and their barbed comments had hurt.

And if Seth's uncle had fathered Bella, the younger Seth's apparent lack of grief for Rachel made more sense, too.

Slowly Amy sank back onto the pillow.

Wow!

Her head reeled with the thought that the Seth she knew, the Seth who'd kissed her and sent her to the moon, might not be Bella's father after all. It was ridiculous, but she *loved* the possibility that he hadn't been Rachel's lover.

But hang on, girl. Don't jump to too many conclusions.

This could be wishful thinking. If Seth wasn't Bella's father, why hadn't he just come out and said so? Was he trying to protect his uncle? His reputation? Was that why he'd been so negative about Rachel's book?

Or was her new theory total rubbish?

Amy groaned. She wouldn't be able to get any of these answers until morning, but the questions were going to keep her awake all night.

Seth woke, as he always did, at dawn and he lay very still, with his eyes closed, listening to the silence of the sleeping house and to the warbling songs of the honeyeaters in the rainforest, signalling the start of a new day.

Out of habit, he reached for the wristwatch on his bedside table and squinted at its dial. Yep. Five-twenty a.m. on the dot.

Normally he would leap out of bed. In summer, he liked to get any heavy work out of the way before the day got too hot. But in deference to his houseguests, he stayed put. They were just across the hall and the slightest sound might disturb them. No point in waking them too early.

It had made sense, he'd thought, to put Amy and Bella together in the room across the hall. If the little girl was scared during the night, Amy would be there for her.

But he couldn't help fantasising about Amy sleeping in a room on her own…

OK, lamebrain, what could you have done? Snuck into her room? Continued on where the kiss left off? Oh, yeah. Brilliant. Then you'd really make a dog's breakfast of this tricky situation.

If only he could stop thinking about her. Memories of their brief kiss had haunted him all night, reappearing and expanding out of all proportion in a string of X-rated dreams.

He wasn't sure that he could survive too many nights with Amy in his house, sleeping in her flimsy white night-dress just across the hallway. He'd be a pile of cinders before the time was up.

Problem was, the wanting wasn't only about physical desire.

He'd found himself enjoying simply *being* with Amy…hanging out…talking with her and listening to the warmth in her voice…watching the changing moods in her lovely brown eyes…admiring the sweet and tender way she cared for Bella.

For years, Seth had avoided this level of interest in any one woman, but Amy Ross had slipped quietly under his radar. She was so easy to be with and there was something delightfully refreshing about her. He liked her *and* he desired her, and he couldn't stop thinking about her.

Damn it… He had to stop.

He knew he and Amy had no future. Hadn't he learned anything from Jennifer?

His gaze flickered again to the nightstand and he saw the fancy wristwatch that had been Jennifer's last gift, the precious farewell gift she given him before she went back to New York.

She'd been so excited about finding the watch in a jewellery shop in Cairns.

'It tells two different time zones simultaneously, so you'll always know what time it is in New York. Isn't that neat, Seth? You'll know the right time to call, and you'll be able to picture what I'm doing. I won't be so far away.'

'But it can't change the facts, Jen,' he'd warned her. 'You'll still be on the other side of the world.'

'I'll come back. Soon. I promise.'

With that promise calming his fears, they'd made love for the last time, and if Seth closed his eyes he could still see the morning sunlight rimming Jennifer's auburn hair with fire…could still see the rainbow flashes from the diamond he'd put on her finger.

He'd let her go home.

To America.

She'd been so sure she would simply wind things up in New York and come hurrying back to marry him.

'I love you, Seth. I promise, darling. I don't need the city, when I'm with you.'

I promise…

She'd been sincere at the time—he'd give her that. Jennifer had never dreamed she would find the pull of her hometown impossible to resist. In all innocence, he'd let her go back and, inevitably, she'd been seduced by the exciting bustle and buzz of the Big Apple. She'd found herself clinging once more to the security of familiar faces, to the reassurance of well-loved sights and sounds, to the comfort of crowds.

It had only taken six weeks before she'd come to her senses. She'd cried so hard when she'd telephoned Seth that he'd barely been able to make out a word she was saying, but eventually he'd understood that she wasn't coming back, and, no, he shouldn't fly over there to be with her.

It couldn't work, she told him. Their worlds were too different.

For Seth, the lesson was clear.

Love, alone, was not enough.

The softest breath fanned Seth's cheek. Startled, he turned to find Bella's blue eyes half an inch from his.

'What are you doing here, little one?'

'Up!' the little girl demanded, and before he realised quite what was happening she gripped his bed sheets, slung one leg high and hauled herself, like a tiny commando, up into the bed beside him.

'Should you be here?' he asked as he flung one hand out to prevent her from tumbling back to the floor. 'Where's Amy?'

Bella didn't answer.

Somewhat alarmed, he scooted over to make room for her in his king-sized bed. She merely giggled and began to bounce on the mattress, sending her dark curls flying.

She was a cutie—no doubt about that—this tiny human being who was, amazingly, related to him.

Seth knelt on the bed, ready to catch her if she bounced

too high, and he marvelled at her incredible energy and enthusiasm. She was such a happy little thing, so full of life, and, thanks to Amy, she had no sense of the tragedies that had robbed her of her parents.

The word orphan had always horrified Seth.

When his father died and his mother disappeared to the far side of the world, he'd been haunted by visions of storybook orphans, starving and freezing in the snow.

But he'd had his mother's letters. Inadequate, but tangible, they'd arrived on his birthdays—and he'd had his uncle, whose kindness and love had saved him and kept him afloat.

Now, as he watched this giggling, bouncing little girl, he choked up, thinking about the man who'd fathered her.

I owe you one, mate. I owe you big time.

Except that Amy had picked up the baton. She'd assumed responsibility for her friend's daughter and, as far as Seth could tell, she loved the kid unreservedly, as if she were her own.

He supposed the security and stability of Amy's happy family had given her the grounding she needed to reach out without fear. Seemed she was doing damn fine splendid and she didn't need his help.

'You're a lucky kid,' he told Bella. 'You're much better off with her.'

Within seconds of waking, Amy saw that Bella's bed was empty.

She bounced out of bed in a panic. Bella usually climbed straight into Amy's bed for a morning cuddle and she'd never wandered off before.

Amy darted into the hallway. 'Bella!'

'She's in here.'

In mid-dash down the hallway, Amy skidded to a halt. Seth's voice had come from his bedroom.

Zap. Heart thumping, she turned in at his doorway.

Part of her brain must have registered that Bella was bouncing in the middle of Seth's huge bed, but almost all of her attention was caught by his bare chest.

Oh, help.

Amy had to stare; she simply *had* to. Seth's chest was so fabulously toned, so amazingly muscly and masculine and *naked.*

The sight of him now in his bedroom was such a different matter from seeing him by the pool yesterday. It was totally unexpected, for one thing. But now, after he'd kissed her… After her night of restless tossing and turning…

'Bella marched in here and took over my bed,' Seth explained, with an apologetic grin that didn't quite hide the fact that he was checking Amy out.

It was only when she saw the unmistakable spark of appreciation in his eyes that she remembered she was in her nightdress. Her thin white cotton nightdress. Again. Which meant she was even more scantily clad than he was.

This was becoming an embarrassing habit.

Surreptitiously, she attempted to cross her arms over her chest as she backed out of the room. 'Bella has so much energy first thing in the morning. Thanks for taking care of her.'

Frantically, she tried to beckon to the little girl. 'Come on, now, Bella. That's enough bouncing. Time to get dressed.'

Bella continued to bounce.

'Hey!' Seth caught the little girl in mid bounce and swept her so high she squealed with delight.

Amy watched the rippling sheen of his muscles and felt the oxygen sucked from her lungs.

Grinning, Seth turned to her, holding the giggling, wriggling child. 'Here you go. She's all yours.'

Struggling to breathe, she prepared to take Bella from him. Their forearms bumped, of course, and for a heady moment she found her hands squashed between Bella's squirming body and the solid wall of Seth's bare chest.

He was warm and satiny and hard…and touchable… She could feel his heat, smell his skin…

Pulling away, she blushed hotly, and turned to dash for the safety of her room, but she was distracted by a silver-framed photograph on the dresser near the door.

Clutching Bella, Amy took a second look. It was a close-up portrait of an incredibly handsome man approaching middle age.

His dark hair was feathered with silver and his face had the kind of tan that came from years of living in the outdoors. White creases showed at the corner of his eyes, but, despite the slightly weathered look, there was a breathtaking, film-star quality about him.

'Is this your uncle?' she asked.

Seth's eyes followed the direction of her gaze and she saw a flash of pain in their blue depths. 'Yes,' he said. 'That's Seth. Everyone around here called him Boss, so there was no confusion about our names.'

'He looks younger than I expected. When was the photo taken?'

'A few years ago. Not long before he died, actually.'

Cold shivers skittered down Amy's spine. So…Uncle Seth had been a hunk. A mature hunk certainly, but indisputably attractive.

Deep down, she sensed the truth as clearly as if the words had been spoken. This uncle had been Rachel's grand passion.

'Now's not the time, Seth, but you and I need to have a talk,' she said tightly. 'A serious talk.' Then she turned and fled from his room.

CHAPTER SEVEN

AMY arrived on the veranda, half an hour later, dressed for breakfast and ready for a showdown.

The questions about Bella's father had to be answered.

Today. Preferably, this morning. She had no idea why Seth had remained silent and mysterious about Bella's conception, but she was determined to have everything out in the open.

Perhaps he'd guessed what was on her mind. Despite his smooth smile, she could sense an extra tension in him. *Good,* she thought. It wouldn't hurt for him to stew for a while; a little discomfort might make him more cooperative.

Guiltily conscious that she was thinking like an interrogator, Amy turned her attention to breakfast, which was another of Ming's masterpieces.

While Amy helped Bella to dip toast soldiers into her softly boiled egg, she talked to Seth as any guest might, about the fruit trees scattered about the garden, and the hens in the coop at the back of the house.

'Perhaps Bella and I could collect the eggs,' she suggested. 'You'd like that, wouldn't you, poppet?'

'You're very welcome to collect them,' Seth told her. 'I'll warn Ming that the job's covered for the next few days.'

Playing his part as host, Seth talked politely and carefully about the scenic spots around the property. Amy was equally polite as she tried to pay attention, but she found it hard when her brain was boiling with seriously important questions.

As soon as Bella finished her breakfast Amy grabbed her chance. 'Seth, do you think Ming could keep Bella entertained, while we have half an hour to ourselves?'

He gave an unsmiling nod and stood. 'Ming's a good sport. I'll speak to him. I'm sure he'll oblige.'

In no time, Ming appeared, dark eyes sparkling as he flashed Amy a wide grin. 'Does Bella like to blow bubbles?'

She couldn't help laughing. 'Do kangaroos hop? Bella, would you like to blow bubbles?'

The little girl squealed, and as easily as that she was whisked away to the kitchen.

And Amy was alone with Seth.

'More tea?' he asked, smiling enigmatically as he lifted the teapot.

'Thanks.'

She had to concentrate hard, keeping her hand steady as Seth filled her teacup and his, then set the pot down. He regarded her steadily. 'You said we need to talk.'

'Yes, I did.' Amy took her time adding milk to her tea while she marshalled her thoughts. She had to get this right, had to get to the truth without making Seth angry.

Over the rim of his teacup, he watched her. 'Am I right in guessing you have questions?'

'Quite a few questions, actually,' she said. 'And I hope you'll give me straight answers.'

His expression remained impassive. 'Fire away.'

This was it. Time to hold her nose and jump in. 'Are you Bella's father?'

Seth looked her straight in the eyes. 'No, Amy. I'm not.'

Oh, boy. She felt as if she'd dived into a pool only to discover too late that it was the shallow end. Even though she'd guessed this possibility, it was still a shock to have it confirmed. 'You—you know that for sure?'

'Absolutely. I didn't sleep with Rachel. In fact, I had very little to do with her while she was here.'

I didn't sleep with Rachel.

Amy sat very still, trying to ignore the warm wave of relief that rippled through her. It was totally inappropriate to be pleased simply because this gorgeous man hadn't made love to her best friend.

She had to forget the way her body went into meltdown at his slightest touch. Her focus was Bella—Bella's parentage. Bella's future.

Bella was the only reason these questions were important. If Amy was going to take care of Bella for the next eighteen years or so, she wanted everything about Bella's family background out in the open. No murky secrets or skeletons in the cupboard.

'Rachel told me that Bella's father was Seth Reardon, so I assumed you were—'

'The culprit?'

'Yes.' With one finger, she traced the teacup's handle. 'But if it's not you I suppose Bella's father was—the other Seth.'

He nodded slowly. 'Your friend and my uncle were lovers. Neither my uncle nor I knew of Bella's existence, but if Rachel named Seth Reardon as her father, I can only assume Bella's their child.'

So there was the truth at last—or as close to the truth as she was ever going to get.

Amy folded her arms and hugged them against her, needing a little head space to adjust to this news. Rachel's lover was not *this* Seth Reardon, but a wonderfully attractive, older man. A man who, like Rachel, was no longer alive.

'Poor little Bella,' she said.

'She's fine, Amy.'

'But she has no mother or father.'

'She has you. You're a terrific mother. You're doing a fantastic job.'

She shrugged uneasily—disappointed that she couldn't feel happier now that she'd achieved her goal. 'Why didn't you tell me? Why did you let me think you were Bella's father?'

Seth switched his gaze to a distant spot in the garden. 'Would you like to go for a walk?'

A walk? He wanted to take a walk now?

'Are you trying to lead me up the garden path, Seth?'

He gave a soft laugh. 'No, but I can explain things better outside.'

She shrugged uncertainly. 'All right.' She supposed he mightn't want Ming to overhear them.

As they went down the short flight of timber steps the air was warm and humid and laden with the scent of frangipani. They followed a flagstone path past a bed of lush green plants with astonishing bright orange flowers shaped like lobster claws, and Amy stole a glance at Seth's frowning face.

She wasn't going to be put off. Now that she'd adjusted, she was getting increasingly angry that he'd let her think the wrong thing for so long. 'Were you ever going to tell me about your uncle?' she asked.

'I was planning to tell you the whole story.'

'When?' she snapped, annoyed by his coolness. 'When Bella turns twenty-one?'

His mouth tightened and, to her dismay, a distressing sheen brightened his cobalt eyes.

Sudden sympathy burned her throat and she stopped walking. She knew Seth had loved his uncle. 'I'm sorry,' she said gently. 'I should remember that this is difficult for you, too.'

They were at the top of a long flight of stone steps that led down to the very bottom of the garden. Below the steps, the tangle of scrub began, but right in front of them lay a breathtaking view of the beach below, curling like a slice of lemon peel at the edge of the sparkling, dancing sea.

'I always intended to tell you the truth,' Seth said. 'That's why I brought you back here. But I felt it was important to get to know you first, to make sure I was doing the right thing. And I wanted you to see this place, so you had the whole picture.'

Amy looked at the sea, shimmering like aquamarine silk. She looked at the moss-green islands floating silently, then she looked back to the beautiful house, the terraced gardens, the dark forest of trees. She thought about the hundreds of hectares beyond this, all of which had belonged to Bella's father.

'You're right,' she said. 'Seeing this place has certainly opened my eyes. It's nothing like I expected. I suppose you have to be wary of people turning up out of the blue and claiming some kind of connection. Like land rights. But that's not why I've come here, Seth. I simply wanted to find Bella's…family. Her roots.'

'I know,' he said quietly. 'And for my part, I'm very happy to have found Bella. I need family too and she's incredibly important to me. My relatives are rather thin on the ground.'

He flashed Amy a lopsided smile and her bones threatened to melt.

He said, 'Some time in the future, you'll be able to tell Bella all about this place.'

Some time in the future…

She thought about going back to Melbourne and resuming her old life…

Before she'd left the city, she'd wanted nothing more than to hurry back there as soon as this mission was accomplished. But from the moment she'd first set eyes on Seth in Tamundra, she'd been foolishly losing her sense of direction.

Even if they hadn't shared that sensational kiss last night, she'd still be in danger of swooning whenever he was near. Every moment she spent with him she was falling a little more deeply under his spell.

Newsflash, Amy. The enchantment is one sided.

Seth's kiss might have bowled her over, but it was a mere blip on *his* radar. He'd shown no interest in an encore.

It was time to be sensible. She had to stick to the original plan, which meant finding out as much as she could about Bella's father, then heading straight for home.

'There's something down here that I should show you while we're talking,' Seth said, and he began to descend the stone steps.

Amy kept pace beside him. 'Can you tell me more about your uncle and Rachel?'

His hesitation was momentary. 'I can tell you that he loved her. I didn't realise it straight away, but he was head over heels.'

Amy nodded, recognising the familiar story. Guys were often falling head over heels for Rachel—except that this time, Rachel hadn't remained immune.

'Apparently, this was the first time my uncle had been so deeply in love since he met my mother,' Seth said.

They'd reached the bottom of the steps and she saw a track winding through the untamed scrub. Seth slowed his pace.

'I think Rachel felt the same way,' Amy told him. 'For ages, she wouldn't talk about her baby's father, and that was highly unusual for her. Finally she admitted that she loved him, but she didn't think she could live here. Do you think your uncle tried to persuade her to stay?'

'I'm sure he must have. He certainly didn't want her to leave.'

'But he didn't try to come after her either.'

Seth stopped walking. His mouth was a pensive downward curve and he stood with his thumbs hooked through the belt loops of his jeans, not quite meeting Amy's gaze. 'I know he was worried that he couldn't make the relationship work, but he still wanted to jump on a plane and fly down to Rachel.'

His mouth twisted unhappily. 'I'm afraid I persuaded him that he shouldn't try to follow her.'

'Why?'

Her abrupt question seemed to anger him. 'Seth was a fifty-year-old man chasing after a girl almost half his age.'

'Stranger things have happened in the name of love.'

'Love?' He sent her a sharp glance.

'Why are you looking at me like that?'

'I don't want to bad-mouth your friend…'

He left the sentence dangling and now it was Amy who was angry. 'What?' she demanded. 'What are you not telling me?'

'I—I wasn't convinced that Rachel really cared for my uncle.' He looked away, eyes squinted against the bright morning sun. 'She was a flirt. A girl on the lookout for a holiday fling.'

Telltale wariness flickered in his eyes.

Amy gasped. 'Don't tell me she flirted with you, too?'

Seth sighed heavily.

'Seth?'

'She made it pretty obvious she was interested.'

Oh.

It was pathetic, but Amy couldn't hold back her next question. 'But you didn't sleep with her, did you?'

'I told you, no.'

With a pained grimace he kicked at a stone and sent it tumbling down the track. 'Rachel arrived here full of flirtatious smiles and ready for fun, but I must admit she changed her tune after she met my uncle. But I still didn't recognise how deeply he was involved. I kept trying to downplay the romance. We went through this weird kind of role reversal, where he was the reckless, love struck kid and I was the cautioning adult.'

Cords of tension stood out on Seth's neck, and when he shoved tightly fisted hands into his jeans' pockets, knotted veins showed in his forearms.

'Seth, I didn't mean to pry. You don't have to—'

He kept talking as if he hadn't heard her. 'He came to me one morning in the middle of the wet season. We'd had really heavy rain and the roads were cut and he demanded that I fly him to Cairns. Come hell or high water, he was going to Melbourne. He still hadn't heard from Rachel—no phone calls, letters, or emails.'

Seth gave a despairing shake of his head. 'I told him he was a hot-headed fool, that he hadn't thought everything through. I said he should wait till the wet season was over. If he still felt the same way about her then, he should go.'

Again, Seth looked unhappily out to the distant green islands. 'I forgot how stubborn and independent he could be, and there's no fool like an old fool. He took off alone in the flaming tinny to go to Cairns by sea—'

'What's a tinny?'

'An aluminium dinghy. We used it for fishing around the islands, but my uncle was planning to take it all the way to Cairns.' Seth's throat worked. 'A damn storm came up out of nowhere.'

Amy stared at him in dawning horror, guessing what would come next.

Grim-faced, Seth told her. 'A fishing trawler found the wreck three days later.'

The news rocked Amy. She'd never dreamed…

'I'm sure Rachel didn't know,' she whispered.

Appalled, she recognised Seth's grief, and felt his pain. It was there in the way he held himself stiffly, *so* stiffly, and his hurting was a live thing, reaching out to her and squeezing her heart.

'I blame myself,' Seth said softly. 'My uncle asked me

to do one simple thing for him and I turned him down. After everything he'd done for me.'

Again, he kicked at a stone and, with a gruff, anguished growl, he began to stride away from Amy. She hurried down the track to catch up.

'You mustn't blame yourself,' she said.

He whirled around. 'Why not? I should have seen how desperate he was. If I'd had any idea he'd take that bloody boat, I'd have flown him to Cairns in a heartbeat.'

Tears stung her eyes.

'I didn't know Rachel was pregnant.' His voice was rough and choked. 'I didn't know how to contact her after he died, but if I'd known she was pregnant, I would have made a bigger effort to find her.'

Blinking tears, Amy reached out and touched him on the arm.

He tensed as if she'd burned him.

'I do know how you feel, Seth.'

His eyes blazed with sudden anger. 'How could you possibly know?'

'I've been there. In that same place.'

She knew he didn't believe her, or care. His jaw hardened and a merciless light crept into his eyes. 'OK, so how do I feel?'

Amy's throat was tight, and it felt raw and fiery when she tried to swallow. 'You'd give anything to have that time over again, to make different choices.'

Seth continued to glare at her.

'Believe me, Seth, I know exactly what it feels like to be full of remorse, to feel responsible for what's happened. I've suffered all kinds of guilt over Rachel.'

In silence, he absorbed this news, and at last Amy saw his shoulders relax. He shook his head. 'But you weren't to blame for Rachel's accident.'

'I was,' she said, blinking back tears. 'I should have invited my boyfriend to a corporate launch, but I asked Rachel to come instead. If I hadn't invited her, if I'd asked Dominic and left Rachel safely at home with Bella, she'd still be alive.'

'But her accident was just bad luck. You told me that when you rang. Some fool ran a red light.'

Amy's stomach lurched unhappily and she couldn't look at him. She hated making this admission, but it had been eating at her for the past two months.

'I can't stop feeling guilty about that night because… because I wanted to show off to her. If I'm brutally honest, that was the real, the *only* reason I invited Rachel.'

Still she couldn't look at him, and she forced her eyes extra wide to hold her tears at bay. 'Rachel was always so amazingly clever and I finally had the chance to show her how good I was at *my* job. The launch party was going to be fabulous and I wanted her to see me in my finest hour. I—I can't believe I was so full of myself.'

She pressed her lips together tightly to hold back a sob.

'You're looking at this the wrong way,' Seth said, lifting his voice above the sudden noise of squabbling parrots in nearby trees. 'There's nothing wrong with inviting a best friend to a party.'

'But my motives were selfish.'

'So you wanted to show off? That's not exactly a crime, Amy. Half the parties in the world are about showing off.'

He snagged a stem of long grass and she found herself

watching the deft movements of his fingers as he wove the strip of green into a narrow plait. A sigh escaped her.

'Perhaps we're both being too hard on ourselves,' he said quietly.

Was he right? She felt a tenuous but amazingly deep connection to him in this moment. Here were the two of them—grieving and alone, lost and guilty—two strangers from different worlds linked by one tiny girl.

'I know one thing,' she said, at last. 'No matter how badly we want to, we can't change what's happened.'

Seth nodded. 'All we can do is look for a way to move forward again.'

His eyes regarded her warmly. 'Speaking of moving on, I still haven't shown you why I brought you down here.'

'Do we have time? Shouldn't we get back to Bella?'

'This will only take a moment.'

Ahead of them, the track narrowed and Seth led the way, holding back giant fern fronds so they didn't brush against Amy. She heard the sound of running water and when they rounded the next bend, the track opened up to reveal a picture-perfect, fern-fringed rock pool fed by a cascading waterfall.

'Oh, wow!'

'It's an alternative swimming hole,' Seth said with a grin. 'Better than the beach because it's too high up for crocodiles.'

'It's beautiful.' It was *truly* beautiful. Even so, at the mention of crocodiles, Amy sent a cautious glance over the tumble of rocks and she quickly scanned the massive over-hanging tree branches. 'Do snakes come here?'

'Not often.'

She edged closer to Seth. 'How often is not often?'

He grinned. 'I've seen the occasional harmless python sunning itself on a rock, but that's all.'

'But it wouldn't be safe to bring Bella here?'

'Why not? She'd be fine—as long as she was with a responsible adult. I wouldn't have brought you here if I thought it was dangerous.'

Amy turned from the pool to face him. 'You do understand how important Bella is to me, don't you? Rachel was my best friend and now you know how I feel about the accident—'

'You want to make amends by taking wonderful care of her daughter.'

'That's it exactly.' It was a relief to know that he finally understood. 'Bella's my responsibility now. I'm her legal guardian and I love her and I'm committed to watching out for her for the rest of my life.'

Seth nodded. 'It's a big thing to take on. Bella's very lucky to have you.' He looked down at the grass he'd been plaiting and tossed it away. 'I'd like to help, if I can. I know I can't offer much more than financial support. I have to stay here and run this place, but Bella's my family, and she's important to me, too.'

Without warning, he sent Amy a smouldering, half-lidded smile that awoke all kinds of unhelpful memories of last night's kiss.

I'm an idiot, she thought.

What was the point of thinking about another kiss when Seth was busily discussing their separate futures?

His thoughts were centred on practicalities, not kisses, and from the start she'd insisted that her future lay in

Melbourne with Bella. She'd made it very clear that she wanted to live miles and miles and miles away from here.

Her plans hadn't changed. She couldn't throw them away on the basis of one kiss.

OK, so maybe Seth's kiss had eclipsed all other kisses in Amy's experience, and maybe she was thinking far too much about the chances of a replay, and maybe now that she knew Seth hadn't slept with Rachel, she couldn't think of any reason to say no…

Except…if she was going back to Melbourne, the most she could hope for was a fling. And apparently, Seth didn't do flings. She was pretty sure he was the still-waters-run-deep type of man—which just happened to be Amy's favourite type.

Truth was, she wasn't into flings either, although she believed she could possibly make an exception for Seth Reardon.

Unhappily, she moved to the edge of the rock pool and looked down into the crystal-clear water. She watched the weeds swaying gracefully like thin green scarves anchored to the sandy bottom. She could see the sky reflected in the water and the overhead branches festooned with orchids and birds'-nest ferns like bracelets covering the arms of a belly-dancer.

The bright pink of her T-shirt looked strangely out of place amidst the greens and blues and browns…but as she stood there, watching the reflection, she saw Seth drifting closer, until he was standing right next to her…

Dangerous tingling sensations spread under her skin. She closed her eyes, wishing she could be more sensible about this man. She'd never been forward with guys, but right now she was fighting a shameless urge to turn and throw herself into his arms. *Kiss me, take me…*

'I guess we should go back,' he said, looking down at the water.

Amy let out the breath she'd been holding. 'I guess.'

Seth didn't move…and neither did she.

He was standing so close to her that she only had to sway towards him and their bodies would be touching.

'Amy,' he whispered hoarsely and she saw the movement of his reflection, saw his hand reach out to touch her hair.

When she turned to him, she bumped into his hand. He smiled; let his fingers trace the curve of her cheek, and her pulse began a hectic dance…

'You're so lovely,' he whispered.

Oh, man. She was wearing an old T-shirt and jeans. Her hair was in a ponytail and she hadn't a skerrick of make-up. And yet Seth was trembling as he touched her and was telling her she was lovely.

This incredibly attractive, gorgeous man thought she was lovely. This serious man who'd rejected Rachel's flirtations thought she, Amy, was lovely.

In a rocket-burst of confidence and overpowering need, she touched her finger to his lips. 'Just imagine I'm a female firefly and I'm flashing madly,' she whispered.

Seth smiled.

Beautifully.

His kiss started out tender and sweet, but within seconds it turned earthy and hot. His arms came around her, drawing her hard into his heat.

He broke the kiss for one pulse beat, maybe two…then

he began to seduce her slowly, slowly, teasing her lower lip, brushing it with his lips, with his tongue, with his teeth, wringing soft sighs from her, and tiny, tiny moans…before he took the kiss deeper, hungrier, wilder…making her feel like a goddess…

Goddess of the rock pool.

She felt this could go on for ever and getting wilder and wilder, spinning out of control, until she tumbled into the water with him, and swam naked. Made love beneath the waterfall.

'Do you fancy a swim?' Seth murmured into her mouth and his eyes were heavy-lidded and hot as he searched her face.

'You can read my mind,' she whispered, totally, totally lost in longing.

She reached for the hem of her T-shirt and hauled it over her head and Seth groaned softly. His hands were trembling as he touched her breasts.

With a cry, Amy began to tug his shirt free from his jeans. She'd never been so turned on, so drowning in desire.

But then, at the worst possible moment, like a distant echo from a past life, Seth said one word.

'Bella.'

What?

Her mind was too crazed to comprehend. Her eyes were closed, her breath trapped in desperate anticipation of his touch.

'What about Bella?' he said.

Oh, good grief.

She couldn't believe she'd been so carried away that she'd forgotten Bella. Completely.

Seth's groan morphed into a shaky laugh. 'I don't suppose we can leave her with Ming for a little longer?'

A little longer. *How long was that?*

Too long, surely.

If only…

With a heavy sigh, Seth gathered Amy close, pressed his lips to her forehead. His hands rubbed her bare arms, muddling her thoughts, making her yearn to throw off her responsibilities.

But how could she be so weak?

She sighed. 'Poor Ming will probably be demented by now. Bella has the attention span of a goldfish. I suppose we'd better head back and rescue him.'

'I was afraid you'd say that.'

His reluctance to leave was flattering, but with a good-humoured chuckle he released her and he bent down and retrieved her T-shirt from the rock at their feet.

He helped her into it, then enfolded her to him one more time, flooding her with happiness.

As they went back along the track and up the stone stairs the wild happiness strummed Amy's nerve endings and she had to stop herself from skipping.

She wasn't sure if this second kiss had been another reckless moment, or the start of something quite, quite wonderful…but exquisite thrills zapped through her like a riff on an electric guitar, and she was too happy to spoil the blissful sensations by analysing them too much.

Seth watched Amy disappear into the house to relieve Ming of his babysitting duties, and then, as sanity returned, let out his breath on an anguished sigh.

He'd totally lost it, lost himself in the sexy sweetness of Amy's kiss. He'd come within a hair's breadth of dragging her into that pool and taking things beyond the point of no return.

Kissing Amy was fast becoming a dangerous addiction.

But it was madness.

He should never have started this. He should have been stronger, should have had the sense to remember Bella before he made a move on Amy.

He'd set out this morning with the best of intentions, but he'd lost his perspective at some point during the conversation about Rachel and his uncle. He'd kept the details of their story to himself for so long, and it had been damned difficult to talk about what had happened, but Amy had been so incredibly sympathetic, so understanding.

She really did understand. She'd experienced the same black hole of grief. She'd been living there, in that same painful, guilty place.

She *knew*.

He'd felt a soul-deep connection, and when he'd told her she was lovely, he hadn't only been talking about her dark chocolate eyes, or her lovely smile, or her exceptionally lovely legs. Looking at Amy was a source of constant delight, but he couldn't ignore her warmth and sympathy, or her courage for taking on the responsibility of Bella.

The fact that these qualities all came wrapped in such a sweet, sexy package was a miracle.

Amy had looked so *right* standing there beside the rock pool and he'd almost hoodwinked himself into thinking that she belonged there.

Fool.

He shouldn't have started another kiss; should have been stronger. Amy hadn't been flirting. Hell, if she'd been flirting, the kiss could have been excused. But she'd been deadly serious when she'd turned to him.

She'd been asking him to take a leap of faith.

And Seth had no faith.

He'd lost his faith years ago in hard and bitter lessons, and he knew damn well that no amount of loving could overcome the problems posed by this remote lifestyle.

All faith in such rosy dreams had been shattered by his mother, by Jennifer, and by what had happened when Rachel turned up...

Seth's die had been cast then, just as Amy's had. They had separate responsibilities now. He had no choice but to keep Serenity going. He owed it to his uncle to stay here, and Amy had no choice but to return to Melbourne and to raise Rachel's daughter there, surrounded by family, schools, playgroups, ballet classes—everything a little girl needed.

He had no right to dally in kisses, or to toy with Amy's emotions.

For the rest of her stay, he had to remember that. Her sweetness and softness were out of bounds.

Hell, he'd already kissed her twice.

Twice.

Two mistakes.

He couldn't afford a third.

CHAPTER EIGHT

AMY was unhappily aware of how very quiet Seth was as they set off later that morning to explore Serenity in his four-wheel drive.

They were travelling west and ahead of them the sky was leaden and thick with grey clouds. 'Looks like the rain's coming back,' she said.

Seth merely nodded, but she told herself he was concentrating on the narrow, winding track that quite quickly emerged from lush rainforest into open eucalypt bushland and then to grassy plains.

Now, she could see big mobs of Serenity's cattle dotting the wide, flat paddocks. The animals were huge, pale cream and grey with droopy ears and humps on their shoulders.

'What kind of cows are they?' she asked.

'Brahmans. That's the best breed for the tropics.'

'So…do you ride horses and do all those wonderful cowboy stunts?'

'What cowboy stunts?' His eyes held a glint of amusement that suggested he was only pretending to be insulted.

'Oh, you know—throwing a lasso around some poor unsuspecting cow, or turning your horse on a five-cent piece.'

He spared her a small smile. 'You mean the incredibly valuable stock-handling skills that come after years and years of hard practice?'

'Well…yes. Have you been through all the years of practice?'

'Sure.'

'I'd love to see you on horseback.'

She wasn't sure why he frowned. She thought it would be so cool to see Seth thundering over grassy plains after a mob of cattle, or sending water flying as his horse cantered across a creek.

For a short stretch of silence, she let her thoughts play with these swoon-worthy images. She stole a glance at Seth's jeans-clad thighs, toned from all the hours he'd spent in the saddle, watched the competent way he drove over the rough ground, one hand on the steering wheel, the other smoothly shifting gears.

He was all hard-packed male and capable strength and every time she remembered the way he'd kissed her, the way his hands had touched her, her body caught fire.

Hugging the memories like happy secrets, she dug into her scanty understanding of the cattle industry to find more questions to put to him. When were the cattle mustered? When were calves born and weaned? Were the wet-season floods a problem? How often was a vet required? When did the stock go to market?

Seth answered politely and patiently, but she sensed his cautiousness, too, as if he didn't want to bore her with un-necessary details. His caution bothered her. Couldn't he guess that she would never be bored by anything to do with him? Or his lifestyle?

He pulled up at a group of cottages beside timber-railed stockyards. 'I thought you might like to meet one of the families who live here,' he said.

'I'd love that,' Amy replied with an eagerness that was totally sincere.

Seth frowned and she wondered what she'd said wrong.

Still frowning, he said, 'By the way, these folk know about you and Bella.'

Before she could ask him how much they knew, a tall, rather splendid-looking Aboriginal man came towards them, walking with a long-legged, easy stride.

Seth introduced him as Barney Prior, Serenity's head stockman.

As Amy shook hands with Barney the flyscreen door of the nearest cottage opened and a young woman, willow slender, with arresting green eyes and hair the colour of rich marmalade, waved to them.

She was wearing a colourful sarong and a sky-blue vest top. Her feet were bare, her toenails painted blue to match her clothes, and a silver chain twinkled at her ankle. Despite her fair complexion, she looked wonderfully at home in this tropical outpost.

Amy liked her at first sight, and her name, she soon learned, was Celia. She was Barney's wife. They'd met in Cairns, they happily explained, and they'd lived together on Serenity station for ten years.

Their two children appeared close behind Celia—a golden-skinned, bright-eyed boy of six and a shy little girl of three.

As soon as Bella was released from her seat belt she shot

out of the vehicle like a champagne cork from a bottle.
'Hello, kids! Hello, hello! My name's Bella.'

Luckily the children were charmed by her lavish enthusiasm for their company, and a mutual admiration society was quickly formed.

Within a matter of moments, Seth and Barney were lounging in squatters' chairs on the veranda, keeping watch over the giggling children, who were already climbing the railings on the stockyard fence.

'These guys are going to talk non-stop about the weather and the condition of the cattle,' Celia told Amy with a friendly wink. 'Why don't we go inside?'

Amy sniffed with delight as she caught delicious smells coming from the kitchen. 'You've been baking.'

'Scones.' Celia laughed. 'I knew Seth was coming.' She glanced at the stove. 'They won't be ready for a few more minutes. I left it a bit late, because I've been busy in the studio. Would you like to see my paintings while we wait?'

For a moment, Amy thought Celia was joking. Uncertain what to expect, she followed her onto a side veranda facing north, enclosed with glass louvres to let in the light. The area was filled with easels and paint pots, and it smelled of turps. Stacked against the inner walls were Celia's paintings.

And. They. Were. Amazing.

Bold, arresting, they completely captured every nuance of the wild beauty of the northern landscape. Amy saw scenes of the open country with straggly pandanus palms, red earth and anthills, scenes of the stockyards, of the main homestead and the gardens, glimpses of the tangled vines, the massive trees and the dark, secret magnificence of the rainforest. And views of the sea.

'These are stunning,' Amy murmured, full of genuine admiration. 'I'm sure they'd fetch a fortune in Melbourne.'

Celia smiled. 'They do.'

'So you've already sold your work?'

'Yes. I've sold several pieces through the Flinders Lane Gallery.'

'Goodness.' Amy laughed. 'Sorry for making assumptions. You're way ahead of me, aren't you?' And then she remembered. 'My friend Rachel brought back fabulous paintings from her trip up this way.'

'Rachel Tyler?'

'Yes.' Amy wondered how much Seth had revealed about her links to Rachel. Celia had shown no curiosity about the sudden arrival of a woman and small child on Serenity. Was she simply being polite?

'Rachel was a terrific help,' Celia said. 'She gave me my best contact down there, and, thanks to her efforts, I made enough money through sales to take the whole family to Italy last wet season.' She grinned. 'Can you believe I did an art course in Florence?'

'How fabulous.'

'I painted to my heart's content, while Barney and the kids ate pizza and gelato and explored the sights. They had a ball.' Abruptly, Celia's smile faded. 'I was so shocked to hear that Rachel died. I couldn't believe it.'

Amy nodded sadly.

'She seemed so happy when she was here,' Celia said. 'She should have stayed.' She shot Amy a rueful smile. 'A car accident. Just goes to show, those cities are dangerous places.'

'They certainly can be.'

Amy almost asked Celia if she was happy living here

in a place that had apparently frightened Rachel and would terrify most city women. But she'd already seen the way the other woman's eyes had glowed when she'd exchanged smiles with her husband, and she was sure she knew the answer without asking.

Morning tea was served on the veranda—strongly brewed and accompanied by Celia's scones with blackberry jam and cream.

'Ah.' Seth beamed a blissful smile as he swallowed the last mouthful of his second scone. 'Ming's a genius with a wok, but when it comes to scones he can't hold a candle to Celia.'

Amy bit her tongue before she made a hopeless fool of herself by announcing that she baked quite decent scones, too.

When it was time to say goodbye, Bella cried because she didn't want to be parted from her new friends and Seth took her for a ride on his shoulders to calm her down.

Celia hugged Amy and said how much she'd enjoyed her company. Amy was equally enthusiastic, but when she glanced Seth's way she saw the flare of dismay in his eyes and the sudden tight set of his mouth—and her spirits sank.

It was clear she'd done something to displease him, and she was terribly afraid he was upset because he'd kissed her. Again.

Big fat drops of rain began to fall as they drove back to the homestead. Amy caught the cindery smell of dampening earth, and wound up her window as the heavy drops splattered the dusty vehicle.

In no time the rain was torrential. Amy had never seen such heavy rain and she had to shout to be heard—and she also had to accept that it was not a good time to tackle Seth about his brooding tension and grimness.

When they reached the homestead, he parked as close as he could to the steps. He unbuckled Bella and took her in his arms as they made a dash through the rain. The distance was short, but they were soaked through by the time they reached the veranda.

Seth's pale blue cotton shirt was almost transparent and when Amy saw the way it clung to his powerful shoulders and chest and his tapered waist, she decided that statues of Greek gods looked weak and flabby by comparison.

It was only when he frowned at her that she remembered her clothing was similarly plastered to her skin.

'I'm sorry,' he said, clearly not pleased. 'I should keep umbrellas in the truck, but we don't have enough female company to remember the niceties.'

'Don't worry about it.' Amy almost snapped at him. Why did he have to look so unhappy about a little wet clothing? Hadn't he been on the brink of diving naked into the rock pool with her this morning?

'I don't need special treatment,' she said stiffly. 'There are lovely thick towels in the bathroom. Bella and I will soon dry off.'

Seth simply gave a curt, worried nod, and excused himself while he went to change into dry clothes, leaving Amy in no doubt that something most definitely had changed between them. The warmth had completely vanished from his eyes.

It was as if they'd never shared kisses, or laughter or painful confessions.

They were back to square one.

As if to confirm this, Seth was polite at lunch and then he disappeared again, muttering something about having to check beef prices on the Internet. Amy tried unsuccessfully to concentrate on a paperback novel while Bella napped.

When Bella woke the rain was still falling heavily, so they spent the afternoon on the veranda, listening to the steady drumming on the roof, thumbing through picture books, drawing, singing songs and playing hide and seek behind pot plants with Bella's pink pig.

The time was spent pleasantly enough and Amy wouldn't have minded at all, if she hadn't been so unable to stop thinking about Seth.

Try as she might to forget, she couldn't stop remembering the way they'd almost rocketed out of control this morning. The memory of that kiss by the rock pool made waves of longing roll through her, over and over, but it was obvious Seth wanted to pretend it had never happened.

Damn him. Why did he have to be so contrary? He'd been passionate and tender this morning, and withdrawn and moody ever since. Amy wished she hadn't been sensible.

The spell had been broken as far as Seth was concerned, but Amy was still dazzled. All she could think about was Seth and how much she wanted him again. She wanted his kisses, his touch. And if he kissed her again, she wouldn't be sensible.

No way.

There were times when a girl had to throw off responsibility and seize the moment.

By nightfall the rain hadn't stopped.

Bella ate her dinner in the kitchen again and afterwards she demanded that both Seth and Amy tuck her into bed. They took it in turns to read pages from her favourite bedtime book, and they gave her hugs and kisses, but Seth avoided any nonsense about kissing Amy afterwards.

Once again, Ming set the table on the veranda with a romantic candle under glass and floating flowers. The meal was superb—tandoori chicken, accompanied by salsa and a leafy salad, and a crisp white wine. Despite Seth's reserve, Amy couldn't help enjoying the novelty of dining, safe and dry, while the rain streamed past the veranda's wide eaves.

In the dancing candlelight the rain glittered like a silken curtain. Its steady rhythm drummed on Amy's senses. She felt its cool, refreshing breath on her skin, like the gentlest caress of a lover, and she found herself having fantasies about early nights beneath clean, finely textured linen sheets while the weather outside lashed at a dark window.

Of course, the fantasy would be so much more exciting if she weren't sleeping alone…but Seth's increasingly distanced politeness made it patently clear that her chances for romance were dwindling fast.

Seth was struggling.

All day he'd been struggling to put this morning's kiss behind him.

He'd tried to convince himself that he was proud of his restraint, but he was fast losing the battle. Tonight, Amy looked lovelier than ever. Her dark eyes shone in the candlelight and her soft pink dress hugged her figure and made her skin glow. Everything about her filled him with wanting.

As the meal progressed she bravely held up her end of the conversation while Seth did his best to behave like a polite host. He talked about books, and the movies he'd watched on DVD, and he asked more questions about Amy's work in Melbourne.

But he knew he was handling this situation badly. Really badly. And he was pretty sure that he hadn't fooled Amy. There was every chance he'd hurt her.

She was beginning to droop, like a rose in the rain. She didn't finish her food and she drank very little wine. Her fingers twisted the stem of her glass.

Hell. He had to say something, do something.

Ming took away the last of their dishes, and they were left alone to finish their wine without further interruption. Seth prised his tongue from the roof of his mouth. 'Amy, I think we should talk.'

Her eyes widened with surprise and a flicker of fear. 'We've been talking all evening.'

Seth swallowed. 'But we haven't talked about what happened this morning.'

The colour drained from her face. 'You wished you hadn't kissed me.'

Hell, no. Kissing her was the best move he'd ever made. It was incredible. She'd made him feel like a giddy youth madly in love for the very first time.

But he couldn't tell her that. 'I owe you an apology,' he said.

He saw her shoulders slump and he felt shame in the pit of his stomach. His apology was totally inadequate.

But Amy lifted her chin, as if she'd found sudden courage. 'You're confusing me, Seth. I'm not used to having a man kiss me as if he really likes me, then make me feel like a very bad mistake.'

Oh, God, he deserved this.

'It's not that I didn't want to kiss you. You must know that.' He dragged in a breath, forced himself to add, 'But I shouldn't have allowed it to happen.'

To his surprise, she narrowed her eyes at him and dropped her head to one side, watching him shrewdly.

'OK,' she said slowly. 'Tell me one thing. Why *did* you kiss me?'

It was a fair question, but for the life of him Seth couldn't think of a fair answer—not with Amy sitting there, looking like every kind of temptation he'd ever known. There was only one reason he'd kissed her. He'd wanted her, wanted her so badly he hadn't been able to think of anything else.

But he had to get his mind past all that now.

As if she'd guessed he wasn't going to give a straight answer, she let out a soft sigh. 'You know, there are all kinds of kisses, Seth. From my possibly limited experience, I know there are hello kisses and pleased-to-meet-you kisses, and I'd-like-to-do-that-again kisses.'

A deep pink blush crept into her cheeks and she dropped her gaze to the bowl of frangipani. 'And then there are kisses like your kiss this morning.' Her blush deepened. 'I've never been kissed like that before.'

She glanced up quickly and he saw the silver glitter of tears in her eyes and his heart felt as if it had shattered like glass.

'You kissed me as if you were making love to me. You showed me exactly what it would be like if you made love to me. And I'm afraid I haven't been able to think about anything else, ever since.'

Oh, Amy, Amy, Amy.

He couldn't bear that he'd hurt her…. She was so courageous and honest…and *lovely*.

If he thought he could make her happy, he would do so in an instant.

But if he weakened now…if he gave in…everything he'd been trying to protect would be destroyed. In a heart-beat he and Amy would be down the hallway and in his bed together, making fabulous, amazing, heartbreaking love. He would be lost in this sweet, courageous girl's kisses. His hands would be caressing her soft, smooth skin. Her lovely, warm body would be linked with his.

He wanted all of it. All of her. Now. He wanted to inhale her, to know every part of her intimately, to bind himself to her.

He'd spent three days battling this desire, and for Amy's sake he had to be strong. She wasn't a girl to be trifled with and he had to resist this last, terrible test.

'I'm sorry you feel that way,' he said, hating the lie, but knowing it had to be said. 'I gave in to an impulse when I should have known better.'

A tear spilled down her cheek and she hastily dashed it away.

Don't touch her.

Clenching his hands into tight fists, Seth said, 'I don't want to mess things up for you, Amy. You came here to find Bella's father, not to get involved with me.'

She took a small sip of wine as she considered this. After a bit, she said, 'Are you scared I might get too serious?'

'Perhaps,' he admitted reluctantly. 'I certainly don't want to send you back to Melbourne with emotional baggage. You have Bella to worry about. You don't need complications.'

'Why does a relationship have to be complicated?'

Something as hard and as spiky as coral lodged in Seth's throat. 'Our situations were already complicated, even before I kissed you. We're from two completely different worlds.'

She sat very still, as if she was thinking this through, and Seth prayed that she understood.

After the longest time, she shrugged her shoulders. 'You're scared I'll fall in love with you.'

'And vice versa,' he whispered.

Her mouth titled in a slow, knowing smile. 'I don't know, Seth. I think you're making a mountain out of a molehill. If you're worried about kissing me, maybe it would help if I kissed you instead.'

He tried to cover his groan with a laugh. 'How will that help? We'd both be in trouble.'

Clearly she wasn't put off. Her smile lingered. 'Wouldn't it be the honest way to find out what's going on between us?'

'Amy, don't play games.'

'Games?' Her smile faded. Painful seconds rode by, then she gave a bewildered shake of her head, let out a noisy sigh. 'OK, I'll behave, but I think you owe me a better explanation than that.'

So they ended up on the sofa, not in bed, as Amy had hoped. She sat sedately at one end, with her skirt smoothed over her knees, and Seth sat a discreet distance away from her, with his long legs stretched in front of him, crossed at the ankles.

With a theatrical flourish, she positioned a row of red and purple striped cushions between them. 'That's the no-go territory, right? It'll save us both from these complications you're so worried about.'

He smiled wryly.

OK. Problem was, now she'd got this far, she was so nervous she thought she might be sick. Had she really asked Seth Reardon to explain exactly why he couldn't risk falling in love with her? Did she need this depth of pain and humiliation?

She couldn't believe she'd been so pushy. The tropics must have melted her common sense.

'What exactly would you like me to explain?' he asked.

At that very moment, Amy wanted to turn tail and run. But where would that leave her?

A nerve-jangling wreck.

'I guess I'd like to get everything straight in my head,' she said. 'It seems we've both more or less agreed there's a mutual attraction, but you're saying we shouldn't do anything about it because—'

She nodded to him to take over.

'Because I live alone at the end of the earth and you live in Melbourne in the bosom of your family, with a great job and a small child and—'

'Wait a minute.' She made a sweeping gesture that took in the length of the lovely veranda. 'What if I actually liked this particular end of the earth?'

Seth rolled his eyes. 'You'd soon get sick of it here.'

'Other women live on Cape York.'

He didn't respond immediately, but she saw a flash of hurt in his eyes and she guessed.

She forced herself to ask. 'Is that what happened to the girl who—who broke your heart?'

After a beat he nodded. 'She went home for a short stay and never came back. She came to her senses instead.'

'But you really loved her?'

'I'd asked her to marry me. We were engaged.'

So, yes, he'd really loved her. Amy's throat tightened painfully. 'Where was her home?'

'New York City.'

A low whistle escaped her. 'Serenity would certainly be a culture shock for a girl from New York.'

'No more than it is for you, or for Bella,' Seth said tersely.

'Are you saying this is no place for a woman? Or there's no place for a woman in your life?'

He let out an impatient sigh. 'Look, I'm not warning you off because I'm still nursing a broken heart. This isn't about me and my tender ego. It's about trying to protect you. It wasn't easy for Jennifer to call off our engagement. She had a kind of breakdown. It was a really bad time for her.'

'I'm sorry.'

Amy's throat ached as she tried to hold back tears. She could feel the other woman's pain, as if it were her own. It would have been beyond terrible to have loved Seth, and to know that he returned her love, that he wanted to marry her, and then to discover, too late, that she couldn't cope with his remote lifestyle.

This Jennifer must have been devastated to give him up.

'Jennifer did the right thing, Amy. She knew she wouldn't be happy living here for ever.'

'Is she happy in Manhattan?'

'Married with two children the last I heard.'

He looked so grim Amy wondered if he was still in love with Jennifer. If that was the case, she also wondered why he hadn't thrown off his responsibilities here and gone after her.

She supposed the very fact that he hadn't gone showed how deeply he was anchored to this place.

But was he right? Couldn't a woman be happy here? The right woman?

She remembered the pain in Rachel's eyes when she'd talked about Bella's father. *I couldn't live there. It's so hot and wild and remote—I'd drive the poor man insane.*

Problem was, Amy couldn't really understand why Serenity was such a problem for Jennifer, or for Rachel. It was remote, sure. Seth had already explained that, and she'd seen for herself how long it had taken to drive from Cairns to Tamundra, and then from Tamundra to here.

But Seth flew a plane, and there were other people living here, and the house and gardens were absolutely beautiful…and if a couple really loved each other…

'What about Celia?' she asked.

Seth frowned. 'What's Celia got to do with this?'

'She lives here. Barney's house is just as remote as yours, and it isn't nearly as big or comfortable as your place, but Celia's blissfully happy.'

'Celia's different.'

'Of course she is. Everyone's different.' As Amy said this, she had a sudden burst of clarity, as if a knot in her thoughts had untangled. She wanted to punch the air in triumph. 'Seth, that's the point you're missing. You can't assume that every girl will be the same as Rachel and your American fiancée.' More gently, she added, 'Or your mother.'

She squeezed a smile. The logic of her argument seemed perfect to her, but after a stretch of silence Seth shook his head.

'Celia grew up in Far North Queensland,' he said. 'Coming here wasn't such a big change for her.'

Amy let out a heavy sigh. It was like talking to a brick wall and she had a terrible feeling that she could talk all night and not change Seth's mind. Even if she ripped off her clothes and lured him into bed, he would still want to send her back to Melbourne. The knowledge that he wasn't going to change sank inside her like a lead weight.

'OK,' she said softly. 'I've said my piece. Maybe I should shut up now.'

To her horror, her eyes flooded with tears.

No. Please, no. Don't let me cry. I have to retain a shred of dignity.

Quickly she jumped to her feet. 'You didn't ask for me to come barging up here, and I seem to be making life very difficult for you.'

When he didn't deny this, she cast a despairing glance at the rain. 'I'm sorry.'

Still he didn't speak and Amy couldn't bear to look at him.

'If the weather's not too bad in the morning, I'd be grateful if you'd take me back to Tamundra first thing,' she said, and, without waiting to see if he planned to respond, she turned and hurried away.

CHAPTER NINE

AMY slept in and when she woke she was groggy-headed and exhausted after another agonisingly restless night.

The first thing she remembered was asking Seth to take her back to Tamundra today, and she was swamped by a cold wave of misery. Oh, God. How could she feel so lost-in-a-black-hole dreadful over a man she'd known for a few days?

Desperate to feel better, she sat up quickly, and saw that Bella's bed was empty, just it had been yesterday.

But this morning Amy refused to panic—she knew Bella would be safe, playing with Seth in his room. Each day, the little girl was becoming more and more infatuated with him.

Funny about that.

Amy indulged in a huge yawn and slowly swung out of bed. She shuffled her feet into slippers and yawned again as she opened the wardrobe to get out her dressing gown. For once, she would be covered up when she said good morning to Mr Reardon.

The rain had stopped and the world outside was strangely quiet, but when she listened more carefully she could hear the now familiar birdcalls and the peep-peep-peeping of the tree frogs. She brushed her hair, tightened the knot in her dressing gown and went into the hallway and called to Bella.

There was no answering call from Seth's bedroom.

Amy winced. After last night's unhappy 'discussion', the last thing she wanted was to come face to face with Seth's bare chest and his pyjama bottoms, but she had to make sure Bella was safe.

Gingerly, she tiptoed forward. 'Bella, are you in there?'

Again, there was silence and another step showed her that the room was empty.

Amy stared at the huge unmade bed and rumpled sheets. Bella's pink pig was lying on the carpet beside the bed and Amy's heart swooped painfully. Where were they?

She told herself she wasn't going to panic. She'd slept in quite late, so Bella and Seth had probably started their breakfast without her. Tugging the lapels of her dressing gown higher, she went down the hall to the kitchen, and found Ming putting the final touches to a fruit platter.

He turned and grinned at her. 'You've had a good sleep in.'

'I hope I haven't held everyone up?'

He shook his head. 'You're the first to show up for breakfast.'

'Really?' She tried to ignore a spurt of fear. 'Where are Seth and Bella?'

Ming frowned. 'Seth's down at the hangar, checking over the plane.'

'The plane?'

'He said something about flying you to Cairns today.'

Oh, yes, he would want to get rid of her by the fastest means possible, she thought unhappily.

'I thought little Bella was with you,' Ming said.

Now tendrils of true fear snaked around Amy's heart. 'I haven't seen her. She's not in our bedroom, and I've already checked Seth's room. Do you think she could be at the hangar with him?'

'I'd be surprised.' Ming frowned. 'But I guess it's possible. There's a phone line to the hangar. I'll give him a call.'

'Thanks. While you do that, I'll start searching the rest of the house.'

Stomach churning, Amy went to the veranda first, checking behind furniture and pot plants and under the dining table in case Bella was playing hide and seek.

From the veranda railing she looked down into the fenced pool area, and was relieved to see that it was empty.

She was determined to remain calm and she went back to the bedroom she shared with Bella and checked beneath the beds and in the wardrobe. She checked the bathroom, then Seth's bedroom and bathroom, where she caught a lingering waft of his aftershave. Bella wasn't there.

In the hallway, she met Ming, looking worried. 'Seth hasn't seen Bella,' he said. 'He's coming back to the house straight away.'

'Have you checked any other rooms?' She was beginning to feel frantic now.

'I've checked my room and the study and the laundry,' Ming said.

'What about the pantry?'

'Yes, I've had a good look in there. No luck, I'm afraid.'

'I'll check the gardens, then.'

Amy began to run and every fear she'd ever felt in her life paled into insignificance compared with the terrible, suffocating fear that filled her now. She couldn't lose Bella. She simply couldn't.

She mustn't.

'I'll send Hans to start searching out the back,' Ming called after her.

Heart in mouth, Amy flew down the steps. Bella couldn't have disappeared. She had to be all right. She just *had* to.

'Bella!' she called as she rushed along wet paths between plants and shrubs still drooping after the rain. 'Bella, where are you? Come on, sweetie, it's time to stop hiding now.'

She kept telling herself that she would hear Bella's giggling laughter very soon now. She would find the little girl toddling up a pathway, grinning happily, arms outstretched.

As she rounded a tall hibiscus bush, however, it wasn't Bella she ran into, but Seth.

'Hey,' he said, gripping her arms to steady her. His blue eyes pierced her as he searched her face. 'You haven't found her yet?'

Amy shook her head and her mouth turned square as she tried not to cry. 'I slept in, and by the time I woke up she was gone. I thought she was with you. Her toy pig's in your room.'

He shook his head. 'I was up very early.'

'She must have gone looking for you, then. I don't know where she is.'

'Don't worry,' he said gently, and he pulled her against him and hugged her and she felt his heart beating hard above hers. 'She can't have got far. We'll find her.'

'She's so little,' she whispered, and to her horror she remembered the pythons out in the rainforest. Oh, it was too hard to be brave.

'I'll find her, Amy,' Seth murmured, and he pressed a warm kiss to her cheek. 'I promise.'

For a brief, thrilling instant, his big hand cradled her head against his shoulder and she closed her eyes, absorbing his strength and the musky warmth of his skin, the laundered cotton of his shirt, and she felt suddenly, wonderfully reassured.

'You should wait at the house,' he said as he released her. 'Bella might turn up there at any moment. Don't worry, Amy. Barney's on his way. He's a brilliant tracker, and Hans and Ming are already searching. We'll find her.'

'Good luck,' she whispered as she watched his retreating figure, tall, broad-shouldered, lean-hipped. Competent...

As Seth hurried away his stomach was in knots. Sweat trickled down his back, and his mouth was dry as bulldust.

He was facing terrible truths he hadn't fully acknowledged till this moment. He loved little Bella. Deeply, painfully.

She wasn't simply a cute, sweet, baby girl—she was his flesh and blood. His family. The daughter of the man he'd loved as a father.

And—he'd fallen in love with Amy...

The savage, inescapable truth tore at his heart.

Amy didn't deserve this worry. She'd turned her life upside down for Bella, and it was only because of Bella that she'd made this long journey north. He'd do anything to banish the awful fear from her eyes.

He'd told Amy that he'd find Bella and, by God, he would. He'd move heaven and earth to return the little girl safely into Amy's arms.

But the child was so tiny and this place was so wild, and he was gripped by the worst kind of terror.

Amy went back to the veranda and sat on the top step, hugging her knees. She tried to pray, but her fear kept getting in the way.

She kept picturing Bella's cheeky smiles and dancing blue eyes, kept hearing her high-pitched voice singing off-key, kept remembering the joy of Bella's little arms hugging her, the softness of her skin and the sweetness of her baby kisses.

How had she actually thought she could let her feelings for Seth get in the way of her responsibilities to Bella? How could she have been so sidetracked last night? So selfish?

Oh, heavens. Was Seth right when he'd said this was no place for a woman, or a child? There were snakes here, and crocodiles and dark, dangerous forests and—

She would go mad sitting still.

She jumped to her feet and began to pace. Appalling horrors crept into her thoughts, but she fought them back. She wouldn't allow herself to think the worst. There were four experienced men out there searching for Bella. The child was only two, and she had little short legs. Seth was right; she couldn't have gone far.

Could she?

She reached the end of the veranda for the third time, turned around for the third time, and was about to pace back when she heard a cry.

'Cooee!'

Her heart leapt.

Running to the top of the steps, she heard another cry.

It was Seth's voice and he sounded elated, but she couldn't make out the words.

Heart pounding, Amy gathered her dressing gown around her knees and flew down the steps, then dashed across the lawn in the direction of the voices.

Seth and Barney were coming towards her.

She saw a bundle in Seth's arms.

'Hi, Amy!'

Bella's voice called to her in the bright, happy, eager and innocent way that she greeted everyone.

With a sob of joy, Amy stumbled towards the little group and there were hugs all round, for Bella, for Barney, for Seth.

Seth's face was alight with laughter and Amy could sense his deep joy and relief, but when she looked into his eyes she saw something more—the dying glimmer of terror and pain and fear, mixed with a tenderness that pierced her heart. She burst into tears.

Breakfast was something of a celebration.

After Amy washed her face and changed into a T-shirt and jeans, she joined the others on the veranda. She was embarrassed by the way she'd cried all over Seth, but he'd been very sweet about it, offering her his handkerchief, and stroking her hair and trying to cheer her up by explaining that Bella had strayed only a little way down the main track.

Apparently, Bella had decided to go looking for 'the kids', as she called Barney and Celia's two youngsters.

Now there were six on the veranda for breakfast—Barney and Ming and Hans, as well as Seth and Bella and Amy.

The men ate their way through a mountain of bacon and

sausages and eggs, and they laughed and joked and fussed over Bella. Everyone, especially Seth, was trying to make light of the mishap now, but Amy knew she could never forget how horribly close they'd come to tragedy.

And sadly, Bella's misadventure had proved Seth right.

If ever there was an experience that proved they didn't belong here, this was it. She and Bella had caused all sorts of disruptions, and she didn't want to put any of these men through that level of worry again.

She accepted now that it was time to go.

All too soon, breakfast was over and Barney, Ming and Hans were heading off to work.

'I should say goodbye to you now,' Amy said, forcing a smile.

The men looked surprised. Ming sent a concerned glance in Seth's direction, but it was Barney who spoke. 'You're leaving already?'

Amy nodded, and avoided Seth's eyes. 'I'm afraid I have to get back to work, too.'

It should have been gratifying that these men appeared genuinely sorry to say goodbye, and Amy held onto her smile as she thanked them all again for their help in finding Bella. Hans offered to take Bella for a ride in his wheelbarrow, and he promised to keep a close eye on the little girl while Amy packed.

Seth waited until only he and Amy were left on the veranda before he said quietly, 'You know you don't have to rush away today.'

'But I think it's best, don't you? As long as it suits you to fly today, of course.' She turned to him and was dismayed by the bleak and lonely shadows in his eyes.

He looked so sad, and she thought, for one tingling, breath-robbing moment, that he was going to beg her to stay.

But almost immediately his air of sadness was replaced by nonchalance, and he shrugged. 'I've checked over the plane and the airstrip. It's not too boggy, and the sun's out now, so it should be fine for take-off.'

'What about the hire car I've left in Tamundra?'

'I'll get one of the men to run it down to Cairns when the rain stops.'

'Thank you. I guess I should pack, then,' she said in a small voice.

'Take your time,' Seth said coolly. 'There's no rush.'

But Amy had to rush. Her nerves were too frayed—she had no choice but to dash about her room, hunting for Bella's toys and books, folding clothes, slipping spare shoes into bags and swiftly stacking them into their suitcases.

If she stopped for a moment she might think.

She didn't want to think.

She'd done too much thinking here, and now it was time to hurry away before her mind—or her heart—imploded.

They set off midmorning, flying south into another bank of cloud. The hum of the motor and the steady vibration of the plane soon made Bella drowsy. Amy closed her eyes, too, and pretended to sleep.

It was cowardly, perhaps, to avoid conversation with Seth, but she was afraid she would become terribly emotional, and blurt out something that would embarrass them both.

Closing her eyes didn't help, of course. Her mind kept going over and over the events of the last few days. She couldn't believe it had been such a short time. She'd been through so much. She remembered her first meeting with Seth in the Tamundra pub, remembered the way Marie, the publican's wife, had warned her about him.

Eyes that make you wonder…Marie had said, and, oh, boy, was she right.

Amy flashed to their first night here at Serenity when she'd told Seth that Bella was Rachel's daughter, to the fire-flies in the heart of the rainforest, that one deliberate stroke on her hand, the meals on the veranda, the kisses… Oh, dear heaven, the kisses…

And then, this morning's drama.

Her chest ached when she remembered the depth of emotion she'd seen in Seth's eyes when he'd brought Bella to her, and the ache became unbearable when she thought about the sadness and loneliness she'd witnessed as well.

She'd wanted to throw her arms around him, to hold him and to tell him that it didn't have to be this way.

He could have them.

She and Bella would stay if he asked.

But she knew he wouldn't ask. He'd been through enough tragedy. He wasn't taking any more risks.

It was still raining in Cairns.

Apparently, it had been raining for days, and a blustery wind swept in from the sea, making Amy's umbrella dif-ficult to control as they ran across the tarmac in the general aviation area.

Seth had rung ahead and secured seats for her and Bella to fly direct to Melbourne, and they would be home by teatime.

Home. Already, Melbourne no longer felt like home.

With Seth in charge, everything proceeded like clock-work. He accompanied Amy and Bella to the domestic terminal, checked in their baggage and got their boarding passes.

He was especially attentive to Bella. When she spied a toy 'rocking' plane, he put two dollars in a coin slot and gave her a ride, and stood watching her with a smile that didn't quite reach his eyes.

He took them to a café and ordered apple juice and a cookie for Bella, and coffee with biscotti for Amy and himself. He was going out of his way to be helpful and Amy lost count of the number of times she said thank you.

Apart from thanking Seth, she said very little. Her tired-ness and the aftershock of this morning's crisis had taken their toll, and now the knowledge that very soon she would walk out of Seth's life brought her to the edge of tears. It was far safer not to speak…

And yet as she watched Seth entertain Bella with a magic thumb-sliding trick she knew there were things that needed to be said.

'Bella's going to miss you,' she told him.

He shrugged. 'Little kids have short memories.'

'I wouldn't bank on that, Seth. She's a bright little button. Besides, I won't let her forget you. You're her family.'

'She'll have you.'

Amy knew the flippancy in his voice was forced. He was putting on a brave face, pretending a coolness he didn't feel.

'Your family can provide her with all the aunts and uncles she needs,' he said. 'Grandparents, cousins. What more could she want?'

'A father.'

He scowled and shook his head. 'You know that's not possible.'

'But you've become her father figure, Seth. You're important to her, even after such a short time.'

His response was a sharply indrawn breath.

'I plan to keep in touch.' Amy wasn't sure how she managed to keep talking without breaking down. 'I—I'll make sure you don't miss the milestones.'

'When's her birthday?' he asked.

'March the fourteenth.'

He nodded and Amy watched a cold shadow of sadness slip over his face.

'But there'll be other milestones, Seth. Starting kindergarten, school, learning to play the cello.'

His eyebrows rose sharply. 'Cello?' For a scant moment, he almost looked amused.

Amy shrugged. 'Cello, ballet, pony club… Whatever. She's bound to have interests.'

'Yes,' he agreed quietly.

'As I said, I'll keep in touch.' Now her voice was definitely very scratchy and choked.

'You do that,' he said, 'and I'll come down for the special occasions.'

'Or I can bring her back here.'

'It's probably better if I come down. It would be too disruptive for you to try to come all this way.'

She suppressed an unhappy sigh.

'You'll send me a copy of Rachel's book, won't you?' he said.

'Yes, of course.' As she said this Amy realised with a nasty jolt that everything else that had happened had pushed Rachel's book clear out of her thoughts. She shook her head at him. 'Don't look so worried, Seth. I'm sure we can trust Rachel.'

Too soon, their flight was being called for boarding. The shimmer in Seth's eyes and the determined set of his mouth made Amy's throat ache more painfully than ever.

What was there left to say? *I've had a wonderful time* was pitifully inadequate.

Seth carried Bella to the boarding gate and he cracked a crooked smile as he rubbed his nose against hers.

Amy looked at the narrow walkway leading to the plane. Passengers were hurrying along it, eager to be on their journey. But they were going to something, looking forward to their destinations, whereas Amy could only think that she was leaving. Going away. For ever.

Unable to hold back the impulse, she said, 'You know, you could always put a fence around the homestead.'

The words tumbled out.

Seth looked stunned, and she felt foolish, but she was about to walk out of his life, so she had nothing to lose.

'If you want to keep a child safe, all you have to is put up a fence around the homestead,' she told him. 'Serenity could be as safe as a house in the suburbs.'

For a scant second Seth's eyes flashed with a hopeful light, but it disappeared so quickly Amy wondered if she'd imagined it. He shook his head and his smile was a happy-sad mix of amusement and despair. 'Amy, get on that plane.'

He gave Bella a kiss and then set her down, and as Amy took her chubby hand she was grateful that the little girl couldn't really understand the concept of goodbye.

Seth's eyes glittered too brightly. Amy felt the heat of

his skin as he leaned close. She felt the warm pressure of his lips, just once on the corner of her mouth.

'That kiss was goodbye and it was very nice to know you,' he said softly.

Her eyes stung and her throat was so painful she could scarcely speak.

She couldn't bear this. How was it possible to fall so deeply and completely in love with a man and still walk away from him?

'One last thing, Seth.' She tried for a smile and missed. 'Just remember that we're not the ones who are dead. We still have long lives to live. You, me and Bella.'

And then she turned, showed their boarding passes to the waiting flight attendant, and she held Bella's hand very tightly as they went through the exit doors.

CHAPTER TEN

AMY tried to convince herself that she and Bella were better off in suburban Melbourne with its rows of safe brick cottages behind neat brick fences. She knew she should feel secure and reassured by the familiar sights of Melbourne's trams and skyscrapers, and its umbrella-carrying businessmen in dark, serious suits.

Here in this great southern city the gardens were pleasantly tidy and manicured and the grass didn't grow six inches overnight. The hedges here were soft green, carefully clipped and well behaved.

Now that she was safely back in Melbourne she could put the lush and shiny extravagance of the tropics out of her thoughts. She could slowly forget the spicy fragrance of ginger flowers and cardamom, the delicate scent of frangipani.

And surely, in time, she would stop thinking about a tall, rangy cattleman who wore battered jeans and faded shirts, and who strode through the tropical rain without a coat or an umbrella.

Like Rachel, she would put those heady days she'd spent in the tropics down to experience. She would get on with the life she was meant to live, in the south, in the city that was famous for having four seasons in one day, rather than long, intense and endless summers and glorious, balmy non-winters.

She told herself that she'd been happy enough before she set off for the north and she could be happy again. She'd find fulfilment in her work, in taking care of Bella. She and Bella would once again be a special little unit, facing the world together.

Who needed guys anyway? Dominic and Seth had used up every last drop of her romantic blood. She was over men. From now on, the most important days on her social calendar would be Bella's play dates and her family's get-togethers.

After all, she'd only known Seth for four days, so this ghastly gaping hole inside her couldn't possibly be love. If she distracted herself with hard work and with taking very special care of Bella, the wound would eventually heal.

At least that was the theory.

Six weeks later, however, as Amy organised the finishing touches for Rachel's book launch she still felt a painful, distressing longing for Seth Reardon and it remained lodged in her heart like the dart of a poisoned arrow.

Seth stalked Amy's thoughts during the day and she dreamed about him every night. His name was a constant ache in her throat. She'd lost weight and people—notably, her family—were beginning to worry about her.

Her mother tried to talk to her about it and Amy would have liked to pour her troubles into her mum's sympathetic ear. Really, she would have spoken up, but she'd known Seth for such a short time she was sure her mother wouldn't believe that she could possibly know him well enough to truly love him.

Anyone with common sense knew that you needed time to get to know a man properly before you could be sure you loved him.

Until she met Seth, Amy had been brimful with common sense, but now it seemed to have deserted her. Common sense couldn't explain the deep, shattering yet exhilarating certainty that her life belonged with Seth Reardon.

There were times when Amy thought about that other woman—Seth's fiancée, who'd gone back to New York and found she couldn't give up her lifestyle. Amy wished she could find the same certainty and security in Melbourne. She wished she could feel that she would, in time, be cured of Seth, but she feared it was impossible.

She blamed herself for losing him. She'd been too pushy, asking far too many probing questions.

In her stronger moments, she was determined to be stoic about the whole thing, to stop being selfishly maudlin and to be grateful that Bella had one important link to her flesh-and-blood family.

During this time, there was only one good piece of news. Rachel's book turned out to be a lovely, heartwarming romance, and, as Amy had expected, it was beautifully written. Rachel had used her poetic skills and sensitivity to perfectly capture the story of a couple falling in love in the tropical north.

She'd made the world of Cape York come alive on the page, and as Amy read late into the night she could once again see the tapestry of the clouds, the movements of the butterflies, the strident colours of the parrots and the flowers. She could smell the rainforest, could hear the birdsongs, feel the tinkling crunch of coral underfoot.

But while Rachel's setting was authentic, her characters bore no resemblance to the people who'd lived on Serenity.

For one thing, their love story ended happily.

Amy sent a copy to Seth and included a note to say that she hoped he was as pleased as she was that his family's privacy had been respected. She was disappointed, but not surprised, when Seth didn't reply.

It was patently and painfully clear that he was determined to keep his distance.

Seth dreamed of Amy.

Together, they were hosting a party at Serenity and the verandas were filled with the sounds of their friends' laughter and a jaunty jazz CD playing in the background. Children were running on the lawn. Bella was there, as well as Barney's two, and another little fellow, a chubby toddler. In the dream, Seth had been sure the child was his son and he'd felt a rush of astonishing love and tenderness for the cheeky little chap.

He woke to the smell of burning gum leaves, rolled in his swag and squinted through the creamy dawn. Barney was crouched over a small fire, using his Akubra hat to fan it to life. Soon the billy would be boiling and they would make tea. They'd fry up a couple of snags and toast slices of bread over the coals. Before the sun was properly up, they'd be in the saddle again, continuing their cattle muster.

It was time to shake off the lingering effects of the dream and his restless night—*another* restless and miserable night.

Seth rose and stretched his arms high, then bent down and fished his wristwatch from inside one of his dusty riding boots, the safe spot where he kept it every night when he was out in the bush.

In the faint early light, the watch glinted as he slipped it over his wrist, and he found himself suddenly staring at it as if he'd never seen it before.

The metal band was unnecessarily fancy and he hadn't bothered for years with adjusting the intricate dials that simultaneously told the time in two parts of the world.

Why hadn't he noticed before that out here in the bush, surrounded by red dirt, anthills, straggling pandanus and mobs of cattle, the watch looked totally wrong? It was too citified, like the woman who'd bought it for him, a relic from an unhappy past.

'Why am I still wearing this thing?' he muttered out loud.

Hell. Only a fool carried a constant reminder of unhappiness. All the time he'd worn it he'd been blinkered, with his eyes fixed on everything that had gone wrong in his life. *Crazy.*

Seth took the watch off again and hooked it on a tree branch while he rolled up his swag. After breakfast, he and Barney watered their horses, loaded their saddle packs and stamped out the fire. With luck, they'd have the mob back in the home paddocks in two days' time.

'Hey,' Barney called as Seth swung one leg high over his horse's back. 'Don't forget your watch.'

Seth looked back and saw it hanging on the branch, gleaming like a weird kind of Christmas-tree ornament, and he shrugged. 'You want it?'

Barney frowned, rode over to the tree, and snagged the

watch. 'What's the matter with you? You're not going to leave this here, are you? It must be worth a bit.'

'Maybe your young Sam would like it,' Seth said. 'He's old enough now for a watch.'

Barney sent him a puzzled smile. 'Sam would love this, but why? What's got into you?'

Seth grinned at him. With a flick of his reins, his horse took off in a canter and he called over his shoulder. 'Maybe I've come to my senses at last.'

Amy's close links to the author and her background in marketing made her the perfect choice to organise the launch of *Northern Sunsets*, and she worked on the fine details with the publishers and the bookstore proprietor to make sure it was a huge success.

The launch was to be a Friday-evening cocktail party in a trendy bookstore in the heart of the city. Huge posters of the book's stunning cover and a portrait of Rachel, looking gorgeous and Bohemian, had been hung from the ceilings.

A display filled a big front window with the photos Amy had taken at Serenity as well as books, and there was also a tiered stand of books just inside the store's entrance. A barman had been hired to serve cocktails with tropical names such as Mangolicious, Coral Sea Breeze and Pineapple Passion.

Amy had almost given in to the accepted law that black was de rigueur for a cocktail dress in Melbourne, but at the last minute she scoured boutiques until she found a cute strapless number in coral pink. She added silver sandals and a frangipani behind her ear.

When she looked in the mirror, she felt a catch in her

breathing. She was back on the veranda at Serenity, where a table was set with bamboo mats, and a candle beneath a glass cover. Flowers floated in a pink bowl and the fragrant smell of simmering curry drifted from the kitchen.

When she closed her eyes, she could hear Seth's footsteps coming towards her, could feel the brush of his lips on the nape of her neck, and the thrill of his arms enfolding her.

Yeah, right.

She shook her head to clear it of the nonsense. Each day she was a step closer to getting over Seth Reardon. OK, so maybe she still had a few thousand steps ahead of her before the mission was accomplished, but his continuing silence left her with little choice. She was determined to move on. If it killed her.

On Friday evening, Amy stood to one side of the main display and watched with growing delight as the shop filled with booklovers enticed by the ads she'd placed in the media. There weren't going to be any follow-up books, so it was really important that this launch went well. The publishers were super keen for *Northern Sunsets* to sell squillions.

Amy allowed herself one sad moment, when she fervently wished that Rachel could have been there to enjoy the glory and the fame and excitement that was due to her, but she couldn't afford to think about that for too long, or she'd be a mess. Anyway, despite Rachel's outgoing nature, she'd never liked to big-note herself.

Once Amy was sure that everything was going to plan, she began to circulate, smile pinned in place, chatting with enthusiasm. At first, when the woman she was talking to appeared a little distracted, she took no notice. She was trying to describe her initial impressions of Cape York.

But then the woman said, 'Oh, my! Does that man know you?'

'What man?' Amy turned to follow the direction of the woman's gaze.

'The tall fellow there with the amazing blue eyes and—'

Amy didn't hear the rest.

Her ears had filled with the deafening roar of her galloping heartbeats.

Seth.

Was here.

He was standing alone, dressed like every other man in the room, in a conservative dark suit with a white shirt and dark tie, but even in city clothes he was stop-and-stare gorgeous. All sorts of people were turning to take a second look at him, almost as if they thought he was a celebrity they should recognise.

Across the busy bookstore he sent a smile to Amy, and she felt her eyes well with tears. He began to thread his way through the sea of people, and she wasn't sure her legs would support her.

Dimly, she was aware that the woman she'd been talking to muttered something about getting a drink.

And then Seth was standing in front of her.

He was smiling as he greeted her. 'Hello, Amy.'

It was a moment or two before she could speak. 'Hello,' she said at last and she was shaky and nervous and breathless all at once. 'What—what a surprise.'

His smile deepened, making beautiful creases in the corners of his eyes. 'It was a spur-of-the-moment decision.'

'So you got the book I sent?'

He nodded. 'I found it yesterday when I got back from mustering. It was in the pile of mail.'

'Mustering?'

'We've been rounding up the cattle after the wet season, and I've been out bush for quite a few weeks.'

Well, of course it made sense, didn't it? She hadn't seen Seth working with his cattle, so she hadn't given them a second thought, but now she was ridiculously pleased that he had such a credible reason for not writing back to her.

She wanted to stare and stare at him. He looked so wonderfully refined and handsome in his suit. She loved the way his collar sat so neatly against his suntanned neck, loved the way his shoulders filled his jacket so beautifully. Compared with the city fellows with their pale complexions and pudding-soft stomachs, he carried an indefinable air of belonging to a different breed.

He'd come all this way.

Why?

At last she remembered her manners and she held up her cocktail glass. 'Would you like a drink?'

Seth cast a dubious eye at the contents of her glass, the colour of a tropical sunset.

'Not now, thank you.' And then he asked, 'How's Bella?'

'Oh, she's fabulous. She's talking in proper sentences now, and I can't shut her up. She loves learning new words. Her latest is upside down.'

Amy knew she was gabbling, but Seth was making her dreadfully nervous, even though he looked genuinely interested in hearing about Bella.

The bookstore was filled to capacity now and people

were squeezing past them, holding their drinks high so they didn't spill.

'How did you know about this launch?' she asked, lifting her voice above the buzz of conversation.

'You sent a brochure.'

'Oh, of course.' She'd sent him all the promotional material with the book, as a courtesy. And here he was twenty-four hours after receiving it.

Nervously, she asked, 'So…what did you think of the book?'

'It's very good. Not the sort of thing I usually read, but I was really impressed.'

'You must have been relieved to see that the characters were entirely fictitious.'

'Absolutely. I must admit I feared the worst.' His mouth twisted in a self-deprecating smile. 'Seems I was brewing a storm in my own teacup.'

Amy let this pass. 'I thought the descriptions were fabulous. The landscape seemed so real.'

Seth nodded. 'Rachel certainly had a gift.'

She drew a quick breath. All week she'd been talking intelligently to strangers about the book, but now, with Seth, it was suddenly difficult.

She tried again. 'Most people I know have loved the ending.'

As soon as she said this she winced. How crass could she get? The book's ending was wonderfully happy and romantic. Why had she mentioned it to *this* man?

She was shaking.

Seth was looking directly into her eyes. 'The ending's perfect,' he said.

The warmth in his smile melted every bone in Amy's body and she was in danger of dissolving into a puddle on the bookstore's carpet, but she was saved by a loud tap-tap-tap on the microphone.

'Excuse me, ladies and gentlemen. Can I have your attention, please?'

It was time for the formal speeches, and the buzz in the room died.

Amy found a place to set her drink down and she took several deep, steadying breaths, bracing herself for the bittersweet emotions that always came when tributes were paid to her friend.

As Rachel's talent was praised in glowing terms Amy was grateful for Seth's tall, strong presence beside her. After the first speech, Rachel's literary agent, her publisher, the bookstore owner, and a librarian all wanted their five minutes in the spotlight, and although Amy tried, *really* tried to concentrate on every word, her mind buzzed back to her unanswered questions.

Why had Seth come? *Really?* Why was he smiling at her so—so warmly?

As soon as the speeches were over, he jumped in with questions of his own.

'What are your commitments here, Amy? Do you have to stay till the bitter end? Do you need to help with stacking things away?'

Dazed, she shook her head. 'Why do you ask?'

'I was hoping we could slip away.'

Her heart did a backwards somersault.

'I'd like to talk, Amy.' His smile wavered.

'Talk?'

As she watched him his face changed. His smile slipped away and his features grew tight and serious. For a moment, his eyes had that shadowy, hopeless look that she'd seen on that final morning at Serenity, and it scared her, because she didn't know how to make it go away.

'I'd like to talk about us,' he said. 'Unless I've frightened you off completely, and you'd rather not.'

She pressed a hand to the leaping pulse in her throat and told herself that she mustn't read too much into this. 'I— I think it would be OK to leave now. I just need to say goodbye to a couple of people.'

Rachel's agent accepted Amy's apology with a knowing wink. 'I can't blame you for wanting to run away with that man.'

Amy pretended she hadn't a clue what she meant.

The other woman smiled. 'Off you go, honey. Run, before someone else nabs him. He's frighteningly gorgeous.'

Amy went.

Outside in Bourke Street the air had quite a nip and she drew her shimmering silver pashmina around her.

Seth eyed it with concern. 'Will those cobwebs keep you warm?'

'Oh, yes,' she assured him. 'This is cashmere.' As she said this she realised that a shrewder woman might have been less honest, so that Seth felt compelled to put his arm around her.

Then again, how could she be sure that Seth wanted to put his arm around her? He'd made it very clear that he wasn't looking for romance. Not with her, at any rate.

But he wanted to *talk* and she was almost sick with worry. What if he didn't plan to tell her any of the things she needed him to say? What if she was misreading his sudden appearance in Melbourne completely? She so wanted him to tell her that he'd missed her, but she was equally scared she'd make a fool of herself.

His gaze flashed down to her high-heeled silver sandals. 'I don't suppose you'll want to walk too far in those glass slippers.'

She gave a shaky laugh. 'They're not too bad, actually. I can manage a couple of blocks.' After all, she thought, it might help her to calm down if they walked while they talked. 'Would you like to go down to the Yarra River?'

'Yes. Good idea.'

Together they set off, with Amy's high heels clicking on the concrete, while Seth measured his steps to match hers.

'How long will you be staying in Melbourne?' she asked.

He sent her a tense smile. 'For as long as it takes.'

She stumbled and his hand gripped her elbow. 'Careful, there.'

For as long as *what* took? She was too nervous to ask.

'How have you been, Amy?' His voice sounded strangled and tight.

'I've been very well, thanks. Life has been good.'

Seth shot her a sharp glance. 'Is that an honest answer?'

In spite of her warm wrap, Amy shivered. 'I'm not sure you'd want honesty.'

'But I do.' His eyes were deadly serious. 'I want to know exactly how you feel.'

Exactly…

The fierceness in Seth's eyes told her that this was important.

Oh, boy. Amy took a deep breath. If she was going to be exact, she would tell Seth that she'd missed him every minute of the past six weeks. She would tell him that she'd almost been flattened by heartache. But she'd exposed her feelings to this man before, and he'd rejected her soundly.

If she sacrificed her pride again she feared she might not recover.

She also knew, however, that if she tried to lie, her face would give her away.

'Well, if you must know,' she began bravely, 'I've been trying very hard to get over you.'

'Have you been successful?'

'I thought I was making reasonable progress.'

In the light cast by an overhead lamp she saw the jerky movement of Seth's throat, and wondered if he felt as she did: as if he were walking along a knife edge.

'What about you?' she asked. 'Why have you come here, Seth?'

'I had to see you, to see if you were OK now.'

'Do you mean you wanted to reassure yourself that I like being back in Melbourne? Were you expecting me to be relieved now that I'm safely away from you and Serenity?'

He stopped walking. Amy stopped, too, and they stood facing each other.

A group of young people went past, couples arm in arm.

'Don't you like being back in Melbourne?' Seth asked.

'Not especially.'

His intense blue eyes searched Amy's face, but he didn't speak and that maddened her. She knew there were very good reasons why he doubted her—his mother's defection, Jennifer's rejection, Rachel's denial of his uncle. But why couldn't he believe she was different from those other women?

Amy might have set him straight, might have told him that Melbourne wasn't much fun when she was pining to be somewhere else, but to confess that was like launching off a cliff into thin air. How could she be sure Seth was ready to catch her?

Tears burned her eyes.

'Amy,' Seth said softly. 'Can't you guess?'

She blinked. 'Guess what?'

'How much I've missed you.'

He took another step towards her and his eyes shimmered. 'Saying goodbye to you at the airport was the most painful experience of my life. The minute you'd gone, I knew I'd done the wrong thing.'

He gave her a sad, lopsided smile. 'I thought going away on the cattle muster would help. It would give me some distance and I could get my head straight. But each night, as soon as the work stopped, all I could think about was you.'

Amy felt her mouth wobble, as if she was trying to smile, but she was still too scared, too terrified that she might be dreaming this.

'I wanted to rush down here and sweep you off your feet,' Seth said, 'but I knew it wouldn't be fair to you.'

'Because I might have already lost interest in you?'

'Yes,' he admitted unhappily. 'But then I realised I had no choice. I had to come and look you in the eyes and ask—'

The entire city seemed to stop as the air solidified around Amy.

'I wanted to ask how you feel now about—' Seth swallowed '—about everything.'

'Everything?'

'Me. Serenity.'

'Oh.' A fat tear spilled onto her cheek. 'You're an impossible man.'

Seth stood very still, eyes too shiny, throat working, then he smiled shakily and held out his arms to her.

Next breath, they were together, clasping each other tightly. 'Amy, Amy… Amy.'

She was laughing and crying.

Seth kissed her cheek and then her eyelids and he wiped away her tears with his thumbs. He drew her into the alcove of a shopfront so he could kiss her properly.

Oh, man.

When they'd been at Serenity, Seth had told her that he couldn't risk another kiss, but now he was kissing her as if his life depended on it, and Amy knew, deep in her heart she could tell…

He was risking all that he had.

Later, much later, they pulled apart, but only a little apart.

'So…' Seth looked happy as he touched her cheek. 'Where's this river of yours?'

'Oh, it's just another block away.'

'Let's go there.'

Linking arms, they began to walk on, past shops with beautifully lit window displays, which Amy couldn't normally resist, but this evening blissfully ignored. She still wondered if her feet were actually on the ground. She was sure she must have been visibly glowing.

At the pedestrian crossing they waited impatiently for the lights to change, and ahead of them lay the Yarra River, dark and silent, gleaming like an unrolled bolt of black satin.

'This is more like it,' Seth said when they reached the bridge.

It made perfect sense, she thought, that even in the middle of a big city like Melbourne Seth sought out a river, the one natural element amidst all the concrete and steel and glass. They stood together, forearms resting on the bridge's smooth stone balustrade, watching the way the lights from the buildings on the Southbank made fat yellow stripes on the dark, silky water.

Amy remembered another time when they'd stood together, looking out at the sparkling Coral Sea while they shared heartbreaking confessions. It was the morning she'd decided that she loved this man, and in that moment her love had felt like a beautiful gift, something bright and wonderful resurrected out of tragedy.

For the past six weeks she'd tried to tell herself that she'd been wrong—foolishly so—but now Seth was here, miraculously, beside her in Melbourne.

She had to ask. 'You said you're here for as long as it takes. What do you mean? As long as *what* takes?'

He gave her a tender smile and touched the frangipani behind her ear. 'As long as it takes to fix the damage.'

'Damage?'

He traced the curve of her cheek. 'I hurt you, Amy. I know I did.'

She couldn't respond without crying, so she bit her lip.

Seth said, 'I was holding back from you, because I

didn't want to start something, only to end up hurting you. But then I watched you walk onto that damn plane, and I knew that I'd hurt you anyway. So I'm here to make amends, to try again.'

A cool breeze rippled the water's surface, bringing a faint smell of mud, and breaking up the stripes of light on the water. The wind played with Amy's hair.

Seth leaned a little closer. 'I mean it, Amy. I don't think you've any idea how much I've missed you.'

He looked serious and scared, and Amy loved him for it.

'Probably not as much as I've missed you,' she said.

He reached for her hand, enfolding it in his warmth.

'If it's OK with you, I'm not planning to hurry away.'

'That's very OK,' she assured him. 'How long can you stay?'

Seth shrugged. 'I've left Barney in charge at Serenity. He's breaking his neck to have a crack at running the place.' His face broke into a grin. 'I should be honest and tell you that everyone's missed you and Bella—Ming, Hans, Barney, Celia and the kids.'

He chuckled softly. 'As soon as I got back from the muster, they were pestering me blind to know when you're coming back to Serenity.'

'What did you tell them?'

'That I was going to Melbourne to ask you that very question.' Seth drew her into his arms and his warm lips grazed her jaw.

A delicious shiver scampered over her skin.

'You're cold,' he said.

'Just a little.'

'Let me take you somewhere warmer.'

Amy said softly, 'Perhaps you could take me home.' A bright blush flared in her cheeks. 'So you could see Bella,' she added, 'although she's sound asleep.'

She watched the slow unravelling of his smile.

'I'd love to see Bella,' he said.

And just like that, holding hands and laughing, they ran as fast as Amy's high heels would allow to the nearest taxi rank.

From the tiny front porch of Amy's flat, they watched the young babysitter safely negotiate the footpath and turn in at her gate two doors away.

Amy had to pinch herself. She still couldn't quite believe that Seth was here in her flat—all six feet plus of him, looking gorgeous in his dark suit, and quite possibly planning to stay the night.

'Bella's this way,' she whispered.

Light from the hallway spilled into the small bedroom, illuminating the sleeping child. Seth stood behind Amy and they both looked down at Bella's dark ringlets, at her eyelashes curling like black little commas against her flushed pink cheeks, at the familiar fat pig clutched in her chubby hand.

'My uncle would have loved her,' Seth whispered, and his voice was rough around the edges.

Amy swiped at her eyes with the backs of her hands as Seth followed her outside into the hallway.

Reaching for her wrists, he drew her close enough to kiss her damp cheeks. 'The thing to remember is that Bella's a very lucky little girl to have you, Amy.'

Gently, his hands cradled her face and he smiled into her

teary eyes. 'Let me tell you something a very wise woman once told me.'

'What's that?' she sniffled.

'You and I are the ones who still have lives to live.'

Her heart seemed to swell inside her as Seth's lips traced a dreamy path over her jaw. 'Do remember telling me that?'

'Of course.'

'Ever since, I've been thinking about the way I want to live the rest of my life.'

'H-have you found an answer?'

'I'm working on it.' He rubbed his lips softly against hers and she thought she might explode with wanting him. 'That's why I'm here,' he said. 'I was hoping maybe we could work something out. Together.'

Now she was smiling. In fact she was grinning so hard she thought her face might grow stretchmarks. 'That sounds like a plan.'

EPILOGUE

THE trail of frangipani and gardenia petals was Hans's idea. The flowers led along the garden path and up the steps to Serenity's big veranda, where the wedding would take place.

For many weeks Hans had spent every waking moment working hard to make sure that Serenity's garden was at its best. Now, pots of romantic, trailing wisteria adorned the veranda. Chinese paper lanterns glowed warmly in the grape-purple twilight, and the romantic strains of a string quartet drifted into the gathering dusk.

Flowers trailed along the edges of the long trestle tables that would soon groan beneath the weight of the fabulous food that Ming and two friends from Cairns had prepared.

Wedding guests were gathered on the veranda, talking in hushed whispers.

At a nod from the visiting bush padre, Seth, who was waiting in the wings, turned to his best man. 'That's our cue, mate.'

Barney's white teeth flashed in his dark face as he grinned. 'I've been waiting a long time for this day.'

Minutes earlier, Celia had pinned tiny orchids on their

lapels and told the men they looked 'seriously dashing' in their dark formal suits.

Now, the men stepped together onto the veranda, and there was an audible collective gasp. Seth smiled at his guests—at Amy's family, at Celia and her children and the various friends from both Melbourne and the Far North. They'd all been accommodated right here on Serenity, either at the homestead, or in the stockmen's quarters.

'Hi, Daddy,' called Barney's little daughter, and everyone laughed, breaking the tension.

The padre, the same sympathetic and worldly-wise man who'd come here to bury Seth's uncle, smiled at Seth now, then he gave Seth a kindly wink. 'Your bride is on her way.'

Your bride.

The two words set off happy explosions inside Seth.

Amy, his bride, his warm-hearted, lovely bride, his friend, his lover was coming to him.

Truth be told, she was only coming from the back of the house, making her way on her father's arm, through the garden, following the trail of flower petals, but Seth was impatient to see her.

Over the past three months they'd spent as much time together as possible. In Melbourne they'd enjoyed trips to the theatre, and to restaurants. They'd taken Bella to the zoo, and the three of them had driven up to the Dandenong mountains for picnics.

They'd spent a weekend at Queenscliff, enjoying the cold southerly sea breezes as much as the seals and fairy penguins. Seth had been to dinner with Amy's parents, and to a Ross family barbecue, where he'd been given the once-over by Amy's brothers and apparently had passed muster—no easy thing to achieve.

Back on Serenity, both Amy and Bella had started riding lessons. Amy was keen to learn every last thing about Seth's cattle business, and she'd hatched all sorts of exciting plans.

Each day, Seth had grown happier and surer that he and Amy and Bella were meant to be together as a little family, and he'd felt the certainty and rightness take root deep inside him.

Now, his heart gave a lift as he saw Bella coming along the path that wound between the shrubs and ferns. Her dark curls shone in the light of the lanterns and her dress was of palest pink tulle, and she looked like something from a fairy tale. His smile widened as every so often she stopped to pick up flower petals, which she solemnly placed in the tiny white straw basket she carried.

Behind her, in elegant pearl-grey silk, came Amy's bridesmaid, Jane, and then, on her father's arm, was Amy.

Misty-eyed and smiling Amy.

Beautiful in white.

Seth remembered the first time he'd seen her in the Tamundra pub, hurrying after Bella, and his heart gave the same unexpected lift he'd felt that day.

Now she reached him, and with a smiling nod her father stepped back.

Amy slipped her arm through Seth's and smiled at him. He smelled the delicate scent of the flowers in her bouquet, saw her love shining in her warm, dark eyes and he was terrified he might cry with happiness.

'Hi, Sef,' called a small voice.

He looked down and there was Bella, reaching up to hold his free hand.

To have and to hold.

Seth grinned, and Amy laughed, and he felt his tension melt away.

The ceremony began, and the reassuring clasp of a small, warm and slightly sticky hand remained with Seth as he and his bride promised to be together for ever.

THE SOLDIER'S
HOMECOMING
DONNA ALWARD

This book is dedicated to the men and women of our Armed Forces and their families—who put their lives on the line for our freedom every day.

We can never thank you enough.

Donna Alward can't remember a time when she didn't love books. When her mother took her to town, her 'treat' wasn't clothes or candy but a trip to the bookstore. This continued through university, where she studied English literature, writing short stories and poetry but never attempting full-length fiction.

In 2001 her sister told her to just get out there and do it and after completing her first manuscript she was hooked. She lives in Alberta, Canada, with her husband and children, and when not writing is involved in music and volunteering at her children's school.

To find out more about Donna, visit her web page at www.donnaalward.com or her blog at www.donnaalward.blogspot.com, and sign up for her newsletter.

CHAPTER ONE

SHANNYN SMITH heard the door open but didn't dare tear her eyes from the column she was adjusting. "Good morning," she said to the figure she knew was in front of the reception counter. There was a glimpse of muted green in her peripheral vision as she input the last series of numbers. "I'll be right with you."

She turned in her office chair, put a stack of patient files on the desk and clicked the mouse, minimizing the table and bringing up today's appointment schedule. Of all days for their receptionist to call in sick, forcing her to fill in. She had monthly reports due. "And you are?"

When no one answered, she lifted her eyes. And the world started to spin dangerously. Dark hair. Green eyes. The khaki color of army combats.

Jonas.

"Sgt. Kirkpatrick to see Ms. Malloy," he answered brusquely. But she knew he recognized her too when his Adam's apple bobbed up, then down as he swallowed hard.

"Jonas," she whispered. That was all. She couldn't bring herself to say more, not with him standing in front of her as if he'd materialized from a dream.

Six long years. Six years since he'd said goodbye to her. Six years since he'd been transferred to Edmonton, leaving her behind here, in Fredericton, New Brunswick, and never looking back.

"Hello, Shannyn."

His words were cold and impersonal. Shannyn knew she couldn't expect anything different, nor did she want to. It had been so long since they'd seen each other. He'd moved on. Perhaps even married. Just because the shock of seeing him made *her* heart give a little flutter, didn't mean it did the same for him. And simply seeing him now suddenly complicated *everything*.

A counter separated them, which was a good thing, Shannyn realized. On the heels of her shock came an irrational spurt of pure joy in knowing he was alive. Despite how things had ended, she'd wondered at times where he was, or if he'd been killed or wounded. The elation of seeing him in the flesh shot through her veins. Yes, it was good that the reception counter was there. If not, she'd have been tempted to jump up and give him an impetuous hug of relief. That would be vastly inappropriate. They were old lovers, a flash from the past. And that was all they would remain. She'd worked too hard to build her life after he'd moved on, so she remained firmly in her seat. He certainly hadn't cared enough to keep in touch, had he? Not a single letter or phone call. Right now it shouldn't matter in the least that he was standing in front of her.

Except it did.

"You look well," she managed, trying a professional smile that fell a little flat as it encountered his stern expression.

He looked amazing, in fact. His hair was military short, but still thick and sable colored. His eyes were large, a beautiful shade of moss green with thick black lashes. When they'd met, it had been his eyes that had been the clincher. It had been his eyes that had stayed with her all this time, making it impossible for her to forget completely.

His tall, firm body was dressed in everyday combats, nothing special, even though he was neat as a pin. She noticed the three stripes on his sleeve. When he'd gone back to Edmonton, Alberta, he'd been a private with his eyes set on being an elite soldier. The best of the best. Obviously his career had progressed. Time had passed.

"Is Ms. Malloy running behind?"

Her weak smile faded and she recoiled. That was all? She hadn't expected old-home week or anything, and didn't want it, either, but pleasantries would have been appropriate under the circumstances. Some acknowledgment that he remembered her.

Clearing her throat, she looked up at the screen. "About ten minutes, that's all. You can have a seat in the waiting room."

He turned from the counter without a word, walked toward the blue padded chairs, and Shannyn stared, her stomach tumbling.

He was limping.

A million thoughts flooded her brain all at once. The overriding one was that he'd been injured, and momentarily all her resentment at his nonexistent reception evaporated. Somehow, somewhere he'd taken "fire and blood", and *his* blood had been spilled. In that split second she imagined it leaking out of his body and soaking into the dry desert earth. Where had he been? In the Middle East, like so many of the Canadian troops? It seemed all they heard of nowadays were the small skirmishes that had devastating results.

On automatic pilot she let Geneva Molloy know that her next appointment had arrived. And what was he doing back here? The last she'd heard, he'd been stationed in Edmonton with his battalion of the Princess Pats. So why was he back at Base Gagetown, after all this time?

She stared at the back of his head, her earlier work forgotten.

She could hardly go up and ask him about it, could she? He'd already been cold and dismissive. Hardly inspiring a heart-to-heart between them.

She discovered it was a conversation she didn't want to have. After years of wondering what it would be like to see him again, to tell him the truth…it was surprising to discover it was not what she wanted. Uppermost in her mind was simply the preservation of the life she'd built for herself.

She'd done what she had for good reasons. To forget that, to be tempted to engage with him, would mean everything would change. The shock of seeing him face-to-face made that abundantly clear. Everything she'd done in the past six years—her silence, her going to night school, running this office—it had been for the best of reasons. She owed nothing to the cold stranger who had suddenly appeared today. Injured or not. He was the one who'd left her behind. He was the one who had decided his career was more important than what they had together.

"Shannyn. You okay?" Carrie Morehouse, one of the therapists, put a hand on Shannyn's shoulder. "You're in another world."

"I'm so sorry." Shannyn straightened and exhaled. "What do you need, Carrie?"

"Mrs. Gilmore's file. Are you sure you're okay? You look like you've seen a ghost."

At that moment Geneva Malloy's voice came through the far door. "Sgt. Kirkpatrick? I'm ready for you now."

Jonas stood, and without a backward glance at Shannyn's desk, went through the door with his physiotherapist.

"Hey…'Kirkpatrick'." Carrie paused, then pierced Shannyn with a questioning look. "Isn't Kirkpatrick the name of—"

Shannyn confirmed it with a twitch of her eyebrow.

Carrie grabbed a nearby chair and pulled it close, plopping down. "Then it is a ghost."

"He's very real, I'm afraid." Shannyn took Mrs. Gilmore's file and handed it over, torn between wanting to talk about it and wanting to pretend he wasn't back at all.

"Did he even recognize you?" The file went forgotten in Carrie's hand.

Maybe it would have been easier if he hadn't recognized her, although after all they'd shared there was little chance of it. It might have been easier to take, though, than the cold reception she'd been given.

"Oh, he knows who I am. He just doesn't seem to care. Which is just as it should be." She tried hard to be glad Jonas had been so cold. If he wasn't interested in her now, it made her life a whole lot easier.

Carrie looked at her watch. "I wish we could talk. I've got to run or I'll be behind. We'll chat later, okay?" Carrie reached over and gave Shannyn's hand a reassuring squeeze.

There was nothing for them to talk about, not really. Jonas would move along soon enough, and she'd still be left behind. After his impersonal greeting this morning, it was very clear he didn't hold any lingering feelings for her at all. That was for the best. Dreams were well and good, but reality was a whole other ball game. She'd learned that the hard way a long time ago. Everything would be much easier this way in the end.

Shannyn sighed. Anything with Jonas would be temporary, no matter how much she'd never been able to completely let go, no matter how tempted she was to go there again. But temporary wasn't good enough. Not anymore.

Shannyn attempted to go back to her monthly reports but her heart wasn't in her work. She kept picturing Jonas's limp and wondered what he was going through with his therapy. Wondered what had brought him to this point in his life.

Questions she had no right to ask.

After an hour had passed, Jonas reappeared at her desk. She looked up at him over the counter. Goodness, he was tall. It was one of the things she'd always really liked about him. Jonas was easily six-one, and seemed to stand even taller after his physio session.

"I need to book my next appointment."

"How frequently are you supposed to have sessions?" Shannyn tried to keep her voice professional and light.

"Once a week, for now."

She opened up the schedule. This was ridiculous. They were talking over appointments as if they were complete strangers. Yet she'd tried already to bridge the gap, make it personal, and he'd been cool and dismissive. She straightened her shoulders. "Next Thursday, two-thirty in the afternoon is all I've got."

"That's fine."

She wrote it on a card for him and started to hand it over the gray counter. But when his fingers closed on it, she knew she couldn't let him go without asking one question.

"Jonas…your leg. It's all right?"

"My leg's fine."

"How long are you on base, then?" Her heart stopped as she finished her second question, unable to help herself.

For a moment, just the space of a breath, his eyes spoke to her, delving in, acknowledging that he wasn't as cold as he seemed. But then he shuttered them. Shannyn knew she hadn't imagined the look. There was still a connection. Perhaps only the memory of what had been, but it was there, and she wished it wasn't. Her life would be much easier if she felt nothing at all.

"This is my station. I have no plans to be going elsewhere in the foreseeable future."

Here, for good? She swallowed. A short visit would have been better. Certainly less risky. But she also knew that "for good" was a relative term. No one in the military was ever in one place for long.

"All right, then," she replied dumbly.

He turned crisply and went to the door, his limp slightly less pronounced than it had been before his appointment.

He left without looking back.

He was really good at that. And she'd do well to remember it.

Shannyn left work on Friday and stopped for pizza. Every payday she stopped for a takeout meal, a biweekly extravagance. Last payday it had been chicken strips and fries. Tonight was Hawaiian pizza, with extra cheese.

She was leaning against the takeout counter when a door slammed just outside and she saw Jonas getting out of a battered four-by-four truck.

What were the chances?

Obviously pretty good. She took a deep breath and turned her attention to the teen behind the counter who was getting her change. As the glass door opened, she tucked the money in her wallet and slid to the side to wait for her order.

"Pickup for Kirkpatrick," he said to the girl in the red-and-white visor.

He dug out his wallet and turned with the box in his hands, stopping short when he saw her waiting to the side.

"Shannyn."

"Small world, huh?" She attempted a faint but cool smile.

"Bachelor's supper," he replied civilly, lifting the box a little to illustrate.

"Friday-night treat," she replied. Perhaps the initial shock of seeing each other was over, or the casual atmosphere of the pizza place helped, but he seemed slightly more approachable now than he had at his appointment. Which still didn't say very much.

"Ham and pineapple?"

"Still my favorite," she replied, feeling ridiculously flattered that he'd remembered that tidbit of information.

They stood there like statues, exchanging the most basic of pleasantries, an air of discomfort between them.

"Miss? Your order is ready."

She took the box, shifting her hands from the hot bottom to the sides. "Fresh from the oven."

And still they stood awkwardly, until Jonas chuckled.

She hadn't realized she'd been holding her breath until she let it out at the sound of his soft laughter.

"This is a hell of a thing, isn't it."

"It is." She started for the door and he followed her. It was easier for him to relax, she reasoned, her forehead wrinkling as she frowned. He wasn't the one carrying a secret around.

"There was a time when we weren't uncomfortable with each other at all. I don't know why we are now. That's all in the past. I didn't even know you'd still be here after all this time."

His words contradicted his cold manner of their first meeting and she wondered at it. "I stayed," she answered, hitting the door with her hip to push it open.

Jonas held the door and then followed her out, putting his white pizza box down on the hood of his truck. "I just go where they tell me."

Shannyn paused, the heat from the pizza warming her fingers. That had always been the problem. He was at the mercy of wherever his superiors sent him next. He'd done his training here, at Base Gagetown, finished when he was twenty-two. Still so young, full of energy and determination to be the best shot in the Army. Then he'd gone to Edmonton, and who knew where he'd been since then. Who knew how long he'd be stationed here? Despite his injury, it was obvious he was staying in the military, not looking to be discharged. That meant more moving around.

"And where would that be?"

He smiled but it seemed grim, a thin line. "Here and there. Doing what I do…what I did," he corrected himself. "I went where I was needed."

The very level of danger she'd worried so much about lent a sense of the mysterious to him, and Shannyn felt a glimmer of awe. He would have performed each task as it was assigned, no questions. For some strange reason, despite his aloofness, she knew what she'd always known. There was something heroic about Jonas Kirkpatrick. Something that made her feel safe. That was odd, because right now he was her biggest threat and he didn't even know it.

"What are you doing on base now? When you left you'd just finished sniper school." She looked up into his eyes. That had been a bone of contention in the end, too. An extra degree of danger that he'd relished and she'd feared. And it looked as though she'd had good reason to worry. He was only wounded. How many hadn't come back alive?

His jaw hardened, only slightly but enough that she saw it. Saw his eyes cool until they seemed to shut her out completely. In a matter of a few seconds, he had fully withdrawn into himself.

"I'm back at the school."

"More courses?" She couldn't imagine what else they would want him to do; he'd already accelerated through basic and had set his eyes on Special Forces. He'd obviously done his job and done it well.

"I'm instructing, sniping and small arms."

Her eyebrows lifted. Now he was in charge of training the next generation of sharpshooters? No more active duty? Had his injury caused that? How had it happened? She had so many questions and no right to ask. No right to pry. They were exes only, as far as he was concerned.

And truth be told, curious as she was, even though she still felt that *pull* to him, she knew it would be better for everyone if they kept things very impersonal. Getting involved in his life meant he'd get involved in hers, and she couldn't let that happen. For all she knew instructing was a temporary position until he could return to active duty. The last thing she needed was Jonas temporarily involved in anything and then leaving. She'd been through that enough in her lifetime.

"Do you like the new job?" She asked the question to fill up the awkward silence that had fallen.

His eyes didn't warm, just seemed to assess her distantly.

When they'd met six years ago, he'd been outgoing, fun, ebullient and full of life. It was hard to reconcile that energetic youth to the hardened man before her. The gulf between them now was wider than it had ever been.

"It has its good points."

Despite his earlier attempt at lightening the atmosphere, it was clear Jonas wasn't in a social chitchat sort of mood anymore, and it was just as well.

"Then I'm glad. I should get home."

"See you around."

She gripped the pizza box with one hand and looped her key ring around the index finger of her other. "Goodbye," she replied, surprised to feel her throat tighten.

It would have been easier if he'd just stayed away. She could have kept the memories of their idyllic months together untarnished. Now they were bookended with an image of a colder, harder man who seemed familiar yet a stranger.

She didn't need a man. She'd proven that. But if she were to choose one, it would be someone devoted, dedicated and, above all, present. Committed.

She couldn't imagine Jonas as any of those things.

* * *

The leg press moved smoothly, up, down, up, down. Jonas grimaced at the weight on the bar. Ridiculous. It was half of what he'd been able to press only a year ago. He had enough reminders of what had happened to him without dealing with his body giving out.

He set his teeth and stubbornly added five more reps to his set, until the muscles quivered all the way up to his hip.

Tomorrow was his next physio appointment, and he was determined to have made progress. Everyone said his expertise and experience were beneficial to the training program here. But he knew the real reason he was back. He could no longer work out in the field. People called him a hero. He knew better.

He knew it was his fault.

Jonas slid off the black vinyl seat and sat on the mat, his legs spread out in a vee. Slowly he leaned forward, stretching out the muscles he'd just worked, gritting his teeth against the pain.

He hadn't expected to see Shannyn, that was for sure. Even so, he'd done nothing but think of her as the transport flight came in on final approach. He'd only been here in the Fredericton area for basic training, then sniper school. A small wedge of his life so far. But during that time…Shannyn had been a big part of that, and he wasn't immune to remembering happier days. She'd never been far from his mind.

But that was before. Before war, before deployment, before everything. Before the pervading taste of dust and blood. He could offer her nothing now, and he didn't want to. That part of his life was over, and he was moving on in the only direction he knew how. Within the Army. His home.

He lay down on his back, crossed one ankle over his knee, and drew the knee in, stretching out his hip. They'd run into each other twice already, and he'd been back less than two weeks.

Switching legs, he sighed. Tomorrow he'd go to his appointment, and then he'd see about switching therapists, go to another office. The less they saw of each other the better. For both of them.

CHAPTER TWO

JONAS arrived for his appointment a few minutes early, provid-
ing the blond receptionist, who wasn't Shannyn, with a letter
before seating himself in the waiting room.

"Shannyn?"

Shannyn, just entering reception, shook her head, diverting
her gaze from the back of Jonas's head to the cheerful face of
their receptionist, Melanie. "What is it?"

"It's Sgt. Kirkpatrick's letter. He wants his file sent to another
clinic. He wants to switch therapists."

Shannyn took the file. "Thank you, Melanie. I'll take care of it."

Her even tone betrayed nothing of what she felt. Truthfully,
she wasn't sure of it herself. Part of her was disappointed he
wanted to go somewhere else, but mostly she felt relief that she
wouldn't have to see him on a regular basis. The more she saw
him, the more likely she was to be reminded of how she'd cared
about him. Cutting down the risk of bumping into him could only
be a good thing, right?

Then why did she suddenly feel so disappointed?

Shannyn unfolded the paper and stared at the writing. When
she reached the end she looked over at him in the waiting area.
He turned, meeting her eyes, his face unreadable. She wondered
if they taught them how to perfect that look in the Army. In his

letter, he hadn't offered any explanation for the switch. But then he didn't need to, did he. She got the message loud and clear. He didn't want to be anywhere near her.

The question she did have, however, was the one that she couldn't seem to get out of her mind. What had happened that made him only a whisper of the man he'd been six years ago? Where had that gung-ho, save-the-world optimist gone? Where had Jonas left him behind?

His file was already pulled for his appointment, and she went to retrieve it. It might be her only chance to discover what had really happened to him, and more than anything, before their brief contact was cut off, she wanted to know.

She opened the beige cover, staring at the documentation. So little information, just facts and figures and terminology that said very little about what had happened to the man.

He'd sustained his injury eleven months ago, but his file didn't say where or under what circumstances. The absence of data only made her more curious. He'd been stabilized, but the location had been blacked out. She'd had no idea there'd be such secrecy, and she looked up again at him sitting in the waiting room.

Where have you been, and what have you been doing that's so dangerous it has to be classified?

She continued reading. The file only stated that he'd been airlifted to Germany where he'd had surgery for a broken femur. Spent time there before being sent home to Canada for recuperation and rehab.

She read further, absorbing notations about the complicated operation to repair the bone and also about an infection that had delayed recovery.

He hadn't had an easy go of it.

It was probably enough to change a man. If combat hadn't

changed him first. She couldn't shake that nagging thought from her mind.

"Sgt. Kirkpatrick?" Even now the name seemed that of a stranger. She took a deep breath. "May I see you for a moment?"

His uneven gait carried him back to the counter. "Yes?"

Shannyn forced her voice to remain professional, even as she looked up into his face. He looked the same as he had last week. That inherent neatness and military bearing, despite his disability. She had the irrational longing to reach out and lay her hands on his lapels, straightening an imaginary crease. She shook off the silly urge. It would serve no purpose. If she were sure of one thing, it was that Jonas wouldn't stay around. She'd been burned by him before. There was no way she'd let him do it to her again.

She gripped the papers in her hand. "There are a few things I need you to authorize before I can sign off on your file and send it to the office you've specified."

She handed over the proper papers and a pen. "You should be fine there, although I think Ms. Malloy is the best physiotherapist in the city. Still, once this is taken care of, all you'll have to do is call and set up your first appointment at the new clinic."

Jonas's hand paused over the papers.

"Why you? I thought you were the receptionist."

She smiled thinly. When he'd been sent to Edmonton, she'd just enrolled in business school. "I started out that way. Now I'm the office manager. Any paperwork needs to be signed off by your therapist and by me."

"Sgt. Kirkpatrick? I'm ready for you now." Geneva Malloy called him in.

His eyes darted up to Shannyn's but she didn't let her gaze waver. She wanted him to sign the papers and be free to go on his way. On the other hand, they were running behind schedule and she didn't want to keep Geneva waiting. "I'll hold on to these," she said brusquely. "You can sign them after your session."

He handed her back the pen. She tapped the papers into an orderly stack and laid them on top of his file.

"Thank you," he replied politely. For a flash, his eyes betrayed him and she felt he wanted to say something more. Why, after all this time, did her heart still leap every time her gaze met his?

Then the look was gone and he limped his way to the facilities in the back.

She left his paperwork on the desk behind the counter and turned her attention back to her computer. This was her job, and had been for a long time. She'd done just fine, going to school, making a new life. She'd told him the truth—she'd started by answering phones and had gone on to manage the entire office. It was a good life. It was real and it was permanent and those were two things that Shannyn rated highly.

She turned her attention to her work while he was with Geneva. Checking her watch, she realized he'd been in there nearly an hour and her spreadsheet was complete. She sat back in her chair and sighed. Shortly he'd come back out, walk out the door and unless fate was unkind, she probably wouldn't meet him again. Being near him at all stirred up too many feelings she'd tried hard to bury.

Switching physiotherapists was a godsend. She could get on with her life, and he'd never know the difference. Even as she thought it, a slick line of guilt crawled through her. Most of the time she was successful in not thinking about what she'd done. But deep down she felt some remorse at keeping her secret.

The door to the back opened and she heard Jonas's voice talking to Geneva, thanking her politely. Shannyn turned her head toward the sound, only to snap it back abruptly as the front office door swung open carrying laughter with it.

"Mommy!"

A charged bundle in jeans and a red T-shirt barreled across the floor towards Shannyn's desk, bouncing to a halt and grinning up precociously. "Surprise! I came from kindergarten!"

Jonas released Geneva's hand as he turned, his heart stopping for a brief moment as the girl wrapped her chubby arms around Shannyn's neck.

I have a daughter. The thought struck him like the sure aim of a bullet.

As if she sensed something was off, the girl turned her head and their eyes met, green to green. Every muscle in his body tightened with the impact of the truth. *This is Shannyn's daughter. She's in school. I left six years ago. She has my eyes.*

Shannyn's cheeks colored; the blatant guilt on her face and the way she shifted in her chair seemed to confirm his suspicion. This was his daughter, one Shannyn had kept hidden from him all this time. A tiny poppet who looked eerily like the pictures of himself he remembered from his grandmother's photo album.

All of it left him gutted. How much more could he lose? He clenched his fingers. It wasn't enough to have the life he'd made for himself ripped away in the space of a moment. Now he had to find out he had another, separate life that he hadn't even known existed.

It took every ounce of his self-control to not go to the little girl, to kneel before her and demand to see her eyes again. Moss green eyes. His eyes in a miniature of Shannyn's delicate features. But what would that accomplish beyond frightening the child? She wouldn't understand. *He* didn't understand. No, it was Shannyn who owed him an explanation.

That overriding thought filled him with tense rage. And explain she would. She'd known. Known all this time and hadn't told him he had a daughter. For six years he'd been a father. She'd deliberately kept it a secret, and then when he did return to town, she'd said nothing, even though she'd had opportunity. This was the third time they'd met and still she hadn't breathed a single word of it to him.

Shannyn felt as if her head was moving in slow motion. Her daughter's happy, smiling face looked up at her. Then, turning her head a few degrees, she caught Jonas watching her with a startled expression blanking his face. Emma turned to see what she was looking at and lifted moss-green eyes to the man standing across the room.

Her heart raced even as the moment froze. He would know now for sure. There was no mistaking those eyes. Her own were aqua blue, and the only reason her lashes were dark was because she'd put on mascara that morning. Emma's eyes were his. Green with lovely thick dark lashes that curled naturally. Just like the brown curls that rested on the tips of her shoulders, the same sable color as his short spikes. She could almost see him mentally counting back six years.

Emma looked from Shannyn to Jonas and then to her baby-sitter, who stood in the doorway looking confused.

"Why's everyone standing so still?" Emma's voice piped up curiously in the silence that had fallen.

Shannyn shook herself out of her stupor. She forced a cheery smile to her face, the skin tightly stretched under the false expression. Right now she had to ignore Jonas and deal with Emma. Lord knew Jonas would have to be dealt with later.

"What brings you here in the middle of the day, pumpkin?"

"I told Melissa that I wanted to see you when she picked me up from school."

Shannyn reached down and lifted Emma up so that she was

on her knee, aware of Jonas's eyes on them unwaveringly. "And how *was* kindergarten today? Did you have fun? Learn the secret of moonbeams? Solve the mystery of the dinosaur?"

She made jokes, but her stomach churned with anxiety. He must have put two and two together by now. If not, he would have left the office. No, he knew exactly what the deal was. That they had a child and she hadn't told him.

He would hate her. This wasn't how things were supposed to happen at all. He was supposed to be switching therapists. Out of her sphere of existence. So she and Emma could live their lives as they always had.

"Mommy, that's silly."

She forced a smile as Emma's bright voice brought her back to the present. "And so are you, girly-girl."

"Can you come home?"

Melissa, Emma's sitter, stepped forward, holding out her hand for Emma to take. "I thought you were coming to run errands with me? We need to let your mom finish work." Melissa had sized up the situation, and had ascertained something was wrong. "We'll meet her at home later."

"Give me a hug, honey," Shannyn said, squeezing the tiny waist tightly against her. She blinked back the tears that threatened, already sorry for the changes she knew were coming to Emma's life. She'd hated the upheaval she'd experienced as a child; had tried to protect Emma from going through the same thing. Now, in the space of a few minutes, all her intentions were blown to smithereens. She gave Emma a little squeeze, wanting to hold on to her and keep the inevitable from happening. "Thanks for coming to see me. I'll be home soon, okay?"

The response was a smacking kiss on the cheek. "See you later, alligator."

It was Emma's latest funny and she never seemed to grow

tired of it. "In a while, crocodile," Shannyn called back, her throat tight.

When the whirlwind had departed again, Shannyn braved a look up at Jonas.

"We need to talk." She heard his voice and the tight quiver of anger it carried. Trembling, she made her gaze remain on his, no matter how his tone intimidated her. He ignored the other faces in the waiting room, his eyes piercing hers, accusing. She'd lied to him, and right now she knew that was all he could see.

"We need to talk, Shannyn, *right now*."

Shannyn's heart quaked. It would have been too much to ask that he not see the resemblance. She'd spent so much time telling herself that he'd never find out that she wasn't prepared for this conversation.

"I'm working. We can talk later, Jonas."

His voice was nail hard as it bit back. "We can do this here, with all these people around, or we can go somewhere more private, but Shannyn—we're talking *now*."

Carrie stood behind her, and Melanie picked up the phone that jangled in the stillness, shattering Shannyn's nerves. There was no way on earth she and Jonas could talk here. And by the way his lips were thinned, she knew prevaricating further would be a mistake. Plain, unvarnished truth would be the only way to explain. They had to get out of here, somewhere neutral. She looked into his face, all hard angles and unrelenting anger. He was furious, and she knew she didn't want to be completely alone for this conversation. She needed the protection of somewhere public if she were going to make him listen to her.

"I'm taking the rest of the afternoon off," she said to Carrie in an undertone. "If you need anything over the weekend, e-mail me."

"You go," Carrie murmured back. "And call if *you* need

anything. I mean it, Shan. Anything." She looked over her glasses meaningfully at Shannyn.

Shannyn grabbed her purse and nodded at Jonas. "I'm taking the rest of the afternoon off."

He followed her out the door.

They stepped out into the June sun, and Shannyn squinted against the glare. She'd left her sunglasses on her desk, and she could really use them now, both to cover her eyes and to put some distance between her and Jonas. Hostility was fairly emanating from him, and she had no idea how to defuse the situation so they could actually have a conversation. One where he might understand why she'd done what she had.

When they reached the sidewalk, he grabbed her arm none too gently and guided her across the street, past the old barracks and down to the Green.

Shannyn shook his hand off when they reached the grassy expanse, taking a few steps away from him. He hadn't hurt her. But her hopes at an amicable conversation had evaporated when the firm grip of his fingers dug into her skin. Even though he wasn't holding her arm anymore, she felt his animosity. His jaw was clenched tightly and he walked—no, marched—across the grass, assuming she'd keep up with him.

He was angry, and had every right to be. Right now she had to pick her battles. How she dealt with him now would affect everything that happened from this moment on.

He stopped beneath an elm, shoved his hands into his pockets and stared out over the glittering water of the river. Shannyn held her breath, waiting for the explosion, not knowing what to say, wondering what his first words would be. She was grateful that they were in a public place. It would preclude a shouting match, and perhaps the presence of others would make him more willing to listen. If she were lucky.

But the words wouldn't come. When she remained silent, he spoke. Not with anger, not with a shout. With a quiet certainty.

"She's mine."

Shannyn nodded, surprised at the sting of tears that filled her eyes at the simple statement, the moment of truth. This was the father of her baby. A man she'd once loved. A man who was all but a stranger now. She tried to focus on the sailboat gliding down the river, but the image blurred.

"What's her name?"

"Emma."

She made herself turn and look at him, face this conversation head-on. The time of evading was done. His Adam's apple bobbed as he swallowed. But he wouldn't look at her. His face remained stoic, expressionless.

"Emma is my grandmother's name."

"I know."

"Why did you do that?"

Finally he turned his head from the river. His eyes glowed like polished jade in the shade of the elm.

How could she explain without it seeming more than it was? The truth was she knew how much the Army meant to him. His grandfather had fought in World War II and died. If Emma had been a boy, Shannyn had been going to name him after Jonas's grandfather Charles. Paying tribute to the wife Charles left behind seemed the next best thing. At the time, it had been the one and only way she planned on connecting her child to her father. Making sure a little bit of Jonas lived on in his daughter. Perhaps she had also done it to assuage what guilt she had at her silence.

"I know how much you love your gram." She went with the simple explanation.

"Loved. She died two years ago."

The lump in Shannyn's throat grew, making it difficult to

swallow. So many changes, for everyone. Time didn't stand still. "I'm sorry."

Jonas walked away, finding a nearby bench under the elm and bracing his elbows on his knees.

She gave him a few minutes, taking the time to calm herself so she could control the conversation. If that were possible.

She'd done what she thought was best. She also knew Jonas wouldn't see it that way. She'd wanted to protect Emma. Emma deserved more than a part-time father. More than a dad who would only be around when it worked out with his schedule. She didn't need a dad out of obligation. They'd been dating when Emma was conceived. She'd known the moment he'd said he was shipping out that he wasn't interested in a lasting relationship. If he had been, he would have asked her to wait, or asked her to come with him. When she'd discovered she was pregnant, two weeks after he was gone, she knew she couldn't tell him. He'd already qualified as a sniper. He'd be in danger every day.

Jonas hadn't wanted more with her, and she hadn't wanted a man who stayed only because he'd been trapped into a role he hadn't expected. She'd been a product of that sort of relationship and had seen the devastating consequences of pretending. She'd known from experience that eventually it would have crumbled, and Emma would pay the biggest price. Shannyn had vowed then and there to never put her daughter through that sort of pain.

CHAPTER THREE

JONAS looked over at Shannyn, watching her bite her lip, worrying it. She'd changed. He hadn't realized how much when they first re-met. But she was a mother now. A mother to a child. A child he'd never known existed. His child. It was hard to reconcile the fun-loving girl he remembered with this woman who seemed so remote and unfeeling. Because her not having told him was cold, and she would never convince him otherwise.

How could she have done that to him? He wanted to reach out and shake her, demand to know what she'd been thinking. Hear her paltry justifications.

Instead he rubbed a hand over his face, struck once more by the image of a curly haired poppet with his eyes, vibrant and excited. A huge argument wouldn't accomplish anything, and he knew it. But keeping his cool outwardly didn't stop the shock or the anger pulsing through him.

He'd never wanted to be a father. But finding out he was one, knowing she'd kept it a secret, made his blood boil. What had he ever done that was so bad she thought to punish him in this way? The fact that she wouldn't have said anything if she hadn't been caught only fueled his anger.

"You shouldn't have done it," he finally ground out through his teeth. He kept his voice as level as he could; too many people were around and he didn't want to make a huge spectacle. "You had no right to deny me my own child."

Shannyn moved a step or two closer. "I can explain."

Jonas stared out over the river. How much time had he spent in this very water during his training? How many times had they gone boating or swimming, feeling the cold slickness of the water on each other's skin? How had things gotten to this point? How could it be that they were in this place again, strangers dealing with something as intimate as a shared child?

His heart pounded as memories flooded back, unfaded by time. When had Emma been conceived? On a day like today? Years ago, on an afternoon like this, he would have found a secluded spot downriver. He would have made love to her there in the heat of the afternoon. Things had burned hot between them from the very beginning. And fires that burned hot usually were extinguished just as quickly.

Only it hadn't. It had smoldered all this time in his memories of her.

He had good memories. Memories of the two of them together during a summer that had been more than a fling. Memories he'd kept tucked away, bringing them out only when the pressure got to be too much. Memories that were now suddenly tarnished by a gigantic lie.

"Nothing you can say will justify keeping this from me."

"Please Jonas, just hear me out."

"Hear you out? What can you possibly say that will make this right? I left for Edmonton six years ago. And you knew you were carrying my child and let me go anyway, none the wiser."

His hand automatically found his thigh, rubbing it absently as he'd had a way of doing since his injury.

"I didn't know I was pregnant when you left."

The defense rang false. "Don't give me that. You would have

found out within a few weeks. You knew where I was stationed, knew my battalion. You could have gotten in touch if you'd wanted."

She came closer and sat on the opposite end of the bench. "You're right. It was my choice not to tell you."

"Why?" He thought briefly of how his grandmother would have loved seeing her great-granddaughter, her namesake, and the single word came out thick with emotion as anger and loss poured through him in waves. It was a struggle to keep his voice steady and low. He was glad she was sitting closer, so not every person wandering the walking path could hear the sordid details.

"There were lots of reasons. For one, you left me. You never once said you wanted me with you. I knew if I told you and you came back, it would be out of obligation and not a...deeper emotion."

"I had my reasons," he bit out. He knew she was referring to love. He hadn't said it back then, hadn't wanted to.

"I'm not saying you were wrong. I'm saying what I based my decision on. Let's face it. If you'd wanted more from me, you could have called. Or sent a letter. You left and I never heard from you again."

"You're blaming me?" He couldn't keep the incredulity out of his voice. Somehow she was making this his fault? Just because he hadn't said *I love you*? He'd lost his daughter for five years because she felt *spurned*?

"No, Jonas, of course not." Her words came faster, and he sensed her desperation. "But what I am saying is that our situation, our personal status, wasn't one that supported the idea of us and a baby. I knew you didn't want marriage and a family. And I wasn't about to put Emma through what I went through as a kid. Divorce sucks."

She sighed and softened her tone. "But that wasn't the only factor."

"Go on."

He met her eyes as she folded her hands in her lap. Good Lord, she was beautiful. Maybe even more so now than she'd been then. Her blond, streaked hair was gathered up in a clip, the ends falling in artful disarray. Her eyes were blue and clear as a morning sky over the Arabian Sea. Her skin was sun kissed and dotted with light freckles.

He'd been enchanted back then, not knowing she'd have the ability to do something like this to him. It irked him to find that he still responded to her girl-next-door sort of beauty, even when he was as angry as he'd ever been in his life.

"Oh, Jonas, look at you," she lamented, her lips downturned as she struggled to explain. "You were young, we both were. You were in the military, on the fast track to Special Forces. I knew it. You would be moving around all the time or deployed. And what would we do when you were gone for months at a time? Wait for you to come back, perhaps more of a stranger each time? A part-time father for a daughter who didn't understand why Daddy wasn't around? Or worse—what if you didn't come back at all? I didn't want to give my daughter a father only to have him ripped away from her in some foreign country."

"So you took her away from me. Denied me the chance to know my own flesh and blood."

"I protected her!"

"From me! From her father!"

"Not from *who* you were. From *what* you were."

Heads turned in their direction as their voices rose. She took a deep breath, spoke more calmly and tried a different tack. "Did you want to be a father then? Be honest."

He paused, clamping his lips together. Of course he hadn't. He'd been twenty-two, at a brand-new posting with a new stripe on his sleeve. He'd been well on his way to becoming the best shot in the regiment. He'd had his eye set on deployment and making his mark. And as much as he'd cared for Shannyn, the last thing he'd wanted was to be tied to a wife. A family. He'd had things to accomplish first. A wife and children had no place in that world.

"That doesn't mean I didn't have a right to know."

She turned away so she was staring at the lighthouse in the distance. "I did what I thought was best for my daughter."

"Our daughter."

Even saying it felt foreign on his tongue.

How had his life come to this? Back where he started? He stretched out his leg, trying to relieve the ache that settled in his quadricep. Why couldn't things have just stayed the same? Being with the battalion. Doing what he did best. Being the best.

He stared ahead. He could see Chris's face before him still, wide and smiling after cracking some joke. The two of them running laps around the compound before the desert got too hot to breathe. The quiet, reassuring sound of his voice while Jonas stared through the scope.

Their last mission:

The taste of dust was everywhere.

Parker's voice was low beside him telling him to hold his shot. The midday sun beat down harshly, and Jonas wondered if it was possible to bake in one's own skin. He held his position; sweat trickled down his neck, sticking to his skin, but he didn't move a single muscle. Hadn't moved for the past three hours, twenty-seven minutes and fifteen seconds. "We've got someone at the door, Park."

"It's not him. Not yet."

Godforsaken desert, *Jonas thought, biding his time. He'd been in the desert long enough that he was sick and tired of it. There were nights when he lay awake for hours, thinking of home. Of cold beer in a sports bar and a bacon cheeseburger, instead of army chow and warm water from his canteen. Instead of dusty roads and the same unending landscape as he traveled from assignment to assignment. At least he had Chris Parker to keep him from going crazy.*

"Jonas? Jonas, are you okay?"

Shannyn's voice broke through, and he turned his head slowly, surprised to see her sitting there beside him. She reached out to touch his arm, and he flinched. She drew her hand back automatically, her blue eyes suddenly troubled.

"I'm fine," he answered roughly. The flashes of memory were happening more and more frequently, and always at the strangest times. He couldn't seem to control them. They were always, always of that one day. Bits and pieces here and there that hit without warning, leaving him feeling raw and exposed. It always took him some time to reestablish himself with his surroundings.

"You don't look fine." Her voice was low with concern. He hated that tone. Hated it every time someone looked at him the way Shannyn was looking at him now. As if he didn't quite make sense.

"I said I'm fine," he snapped, rising to his feet and taking a half-dozen steps to get away from her. Faces turned again in his direction, and he took deep breaths to try to get his heart rate to return to normal. He wished the memories would all go away so he could get on with what was left of his life. Only, now that too was thrown into chaos by learning he was somebody's father.

Shannyn stared after him, warning bells pealing madly in her head. What was going on?

They'd been talking and then suddenly he'd gone. His eyes had blanked and every muscle in his body had stilled. It had been eerie, watching him disassociate, until she realized his breathing was accelerating.

She'd tried to call him back, and the empty stare she'd seen before he came to frightened her more than anything else.

What in the world had happened to him?

She was getting in far deeper than she cared to. Now that he knew Emma was his, naturally he'd assert his rights and demand to see her. She couldn't deny him that. And seeing him this way, knowing something was horribly wrong, she could already feel herself being drawn in. Wanting to help him almost as much as she wanted him gone.

What if he shouted this way at Emma?

When he turned back, she fortified herself with all the courage she could muster. "This is a perfect example of why I didn't tell you. Emma is five years old, Jonas. She's not going to understand if you blank out and then shout at her. She's not equipped for that."

She wanted to say that, even as an adult, she didn't understand him either, but right now the focus had to be off her own feelings and on keeping Emma safe and happy.

"I have a right to see her. She has a right to know me."

"Why is this so important to you? Why can't you just let it go?"

"Because she's my daughter. My responsibility." His former control reasserted itself. "I'm not the kind of man who shirks responsibility. I thought you understood that much about me."

"That's what I'm saying." Shannyn implored him with her hands. She did understand. As much as she was hurt that he'd left her, she'd admired him for his dedication to what he considered his duty. And he would have been dutiful to Emma too and it would have broken her heart little by little to know that he was staying for that reason and not of his own free will. Would have destroyed her to come home one day to a man who wanted out. Who wanted a life away from her and Emma. She never wanted Emma to feel abandoned and unloved the way she had felt growing up.

"You would have stayed involved out of responsibility, not out of any lasting affection."

Jonas looked around them. Now that the shouting was over, no one seemed particularly interested in their exchange, no one noticed anything out of the ordinary. People simply walked along the path, enjoying the early-summer day, the mellow heat, the fresh green of the grass and leaves. Everything seemed to spin in a slow circle. The desert, Germany, the base, all spiraling outside of *here*. A perfect world around him while he felt trapped in chaos. His whole world was changing. It didn't seem real.

He clung to the one thing he hoped she might understand, searching for common ground that would anchor him to this unreal situation. "Shannyn, you've brought her up alone. I could have helped."

"With child support." Her lips thinned to a straight line.

"Well, yes."

Her short laugh surprised him. "And your money would have made it all right."

"It might have lessened your financial strain. It couldn't have been easy."

"We've done just fine, thank you."

Jonas stared hard at her—dismissive. Her tone, her body language…it was all dismissive. He wasn't wanted or required here. God, he wasn't really wanted or required anywhere anymore. In a world of doers, he was now redundant. What had once been his purpose was gone. And he'd never thought about what he'd do when it was over. He'd always thought he'd keep doing what he was doing until he died on some battlefield. He certainly hadn't expected to come home with a gimp leg, leaving him good for next to nothing.

He saw the talent in the next wave of elite soldiers and hated that he wasn't one of them anymore. Put out to pasture at the ripe old age of twenty-eight. It didn't seem fair. He'd lost his career, and now he discovered he'd lost a family he hadn't even known he had.

"I want to see her."

"I'm not sure that's a good idea."

His eyes blazed. "Shannyn, you can't keep me from my own daughter."

"I'll do what I have to, to keep her safe and happy."

"And you think I'd threaten that?"

"She doesn't need a temporary dad who'll leave once he satisfies his curiosity."

That was what she thought of him, then. It showed how little she knew. How far apart they were.

"Look at me," he whispered stridently. "Does it look like I'm going anywhere? You've seen my file, right? Active duty is a long shot at best, out of my realm of possibility, more likely, according to the doctors."

He stepped closer, close enough that she had to tilt her neck sharply to look into his eyes. Her chest rose and fell rapidly, so close he could almost feel it against his. His gaze fell to her lips, and they opened slightly. How he could despise her so much right now and still want to kiss her was beyond him.

"I'm obviously not in danger anymore. So tell me, Shannyn. What is it you're really afraid of?"

CHAPTER FOUR

SHANNYN took a step back. "You're invading my personal space."

Jonas laughed, a brittle sound as he stared at her with accusation in his eyes. "I beg your pardon." He affected a small bow, mocking her, and put more distance between them.

"You can't keep me from my daughter anymore," he argued firmly. "And you know it."

Shannyn's heart sank. He was right. Now that he knew about Emma, she had no right to keep him from her. Legally she had no reason to deny him visitation. All she had were her own reservations, which would matter very little in the overall scheme of things if he pressed his case. She decided to appeal to whatever sense of fatherly concern he might possess.

"I don't want her upset."

He put his hand into his trousers pocket and tilted his head, watching her closely. "Neither do I. I'm willing to let you name the terms of how we do this. Within reason."

"You are?" It was the last thing she'd expected from him and she couldn't keep the surprise from her voice.

"You can tell her about me by yourself, if you wish. And we'll meet wherever you think she'll be most comfortable." He balanced his weight on one leg and smiled thinly, a smile that seemed forced and manufactured for the moment.

"Thank you," Shannyn breathed with relief.

"I don't have any desire to traumatize her, Shannyn." His jaw softened slightly. "I'm not in the habit of terrorizing children."

"Of course not." She dropped her eyes. After the initial blowout, he was suddenly being remarkably reasonable. Appealing to him from Emma's point of view had been the right course. He was exerting his rights, but at least he wasn't blind to how this would affect Emma.

"You have the weekend." He straightened, putting his weight equally on his feet once more. "I'll be in touch Monday, and we'll talk then about how to move forward."

She met his gaze again and clenched her fingers. He was making it sound like a business transaction, or an assignment.

"For someone who says I can handle this how I want, you're being awfully dictatorial. It's not some battle plan you've concocted."

"I just want to make sure you don't drag this out. It's been six years. I think I have a right to have doubts about your...*expediency.*"

Shannyn felt as if they were right back to the beginning of the argument again, and she didn't want to rehash everything that had been said—and unsaid.

"Fine. But just so you know," she lifted her chin, "bossing me around really isn't going to help your case any."

Jonas stared down into her eyes, and she struggled not to feel intimidated. In front of her now was a man accustomed to getting what he wanted. One who gave orders and had them followed. One way or another. But she *was* going to do this on her terms. It didn't matter what it took, she'd go toe-to-toe with him, for Emma's sake. Protecting herself right now came second to making sure Emma remained unhurt through everything.

She got the feeling the battle was going to be draining. In more ways than one.

"The weekend, Shannyn." The words were softly spoken, but she was left in no doubt of the ultimatum they contained. "I'll be in touch on Monday."

He spun on his heel and walked away, his gait lopsided from his injury.

Shannyn went back to the bench and sat down heavily. How on earth was she going to find the words to tell her baby that she had a daddy after all?

She chose the backyard because that was the place Emma was most comfortable and happy. They didn't have a huge yard, but what they did have was lush with green grass and a perfect place to play. A white fence separated them from the neighbours, and in one corner Shannyn had put a small flower bed and herb garden, as well as Emma's outdoor toys.

Today Shannyn felt the need to be outside in the fresh air, not cooped up in a room where she found it hard to breathe. Every time she thought of what she'd say to Emma, her heart faltered. In her mind she'd gone over and over the questions Emma might have, and how she'd answer them so a five-year-old would under-stand. She'd thought about it so much that here it was Sunday afternoon and still she hadn't done it.

But Jonas would call tomorrow. She was sure of it. And if she hadn't told Emma by the time he did, she knew Jonas would make things very difficult.

"Honey, you want a Popsicle?" Shannyn called out to Emma who was pumping her legs and swinging on the secondhand swing set Shannyn had bought at a yard sale last spring.

"Okay." The legs stopped pumping, and the swing slowed until Emma popped off and landed on the grass.

It felt more like August than June today. Mellow warmth soaked through Shannyn's T-shirt and heated her legs. It was the kind of day that made her wish she were out boating on the river, or lying on the beach at the lake. For a minute she got caught in memories of Jonas, a Jonas who was less jaded and more carefree, squidging his toes in the sand at the beach as she lay in his arms.

But reality was that she was supposed to be having a life-altering discussion with her baby, who wasn't so much of a baby anymore.

She handed over the Popsicle and patted the seat of the picnic table.

Emma hopped up and Shannyn smiled down on her dark head as she licked the Popsicle. Everything she'd done in these past years had been for Emma. To give her the kind of life every child deserved. One filled with love and fun and, most of all, stability. Different from the one she'd had. Her number-one priority had been to protect Emma. To do what she thought was best. Now she had to undo everything with a simple conversation. Turn her little girl's life upside down.

How did she even begin?

She hadn't said anything at all until Emma started preschool and began noticing her friends had mommies and daddies. Or that they lived with their mommy and saw their daddies on weekends. When the question arose, she had given Emma the short version. That her daddy didn't know that she was born and that Shannyn didn't know where he was right now. And then she'd reinforced how happy and good their life was. It had never been her intention that Emma would find her life lacking in any way. And Emma had accepted her answers like any young child would. With trust.

How could she now explain that her father was here and wanted to see her? In her heart, Shannyn knew he would leave again. Maybe not next week or next month, but eventually he would leave and Emma would be fatherless again. How was that fair? She put her hand on Emma's curls, feeling the warmth radiating from her scalp. Every single decision she had made had been to protect Emma from upheaval.

"Mama? Can I play on the slide now?"

Shannyn looked into her daughter's eyes. They were so like Jonas's and since she'd seen him again they seemed even more so. Being with him, even through their arguments, only served to remind her how much she'd invested in him so long ago. And how much she'd invested in their daughter in the years since.

In the end she couldn't give the words voice. "Yes, you go play, honey." She took the empty Popsicle stick from Emma's sticky hands and kissed her cheek. Emma went back to playing, and Shannyn watched from the table. And for the first time since she'd found out she was pregnant, she really had no idea what she was going to do.

"What time's your lunch?"

Shannyn knew the voice even though the words were clipped and economical. He didn't waste any time. Nine-fifteen and he was calling already.

"I get a break from twelve until one."

"Meet me at the lighthouse at noon."

"But, Jonas, I…"

She heard loud noises slamming in the background as he cut her off. "I've got to go now, but twelve o'clock at the lighthouse." Shannyn heard a voice shout in the background before the line went dead.

Her hands trembled, not with fear but with anger. He said he was going to let her handle this, but all he did was make demands left and right. When to tell Emma. When to meet. She should ignore his latest order and stay right where she was. But that meant he might come to the office and confront her there, and a public scene was unacceptable for their clients. Damn him for putting her in such a position.

He was expecting her to tell him that Emma knew about him and plan the next step. It would have been easier to tell him over the phone rather than face-to-face. There was no way she could explain it so that he would understand, but she was going to have to try.

She was waiting outside the white-and-red structure, looking over the water when he stepped up behind her.

"We're in for some showers."

She turned and caught her breath.

He was wearing his trousers but his shirt was missing and he stood before her in an Army-issue T-shirt. And, oh, he filled out every cotton inch. Flat where everything should be flat, a wide chest and broad shoulders that led to arms with muscles that dipped and curved. His boots gave his six-foot-plus frame even more height. His size made him more attractive to her, not less. She wished she didn't find him attractive at all. All that lean fitness, paired with his handsome, if uncompromising, face, was a tempting combination. Not tempting enough to make her forget how he'd hurt her, though. Thankfully his interest at the moment was focused on Emma and not her. One complication was enough.

She swallowed, chilled by the sudden puff of cool air preceding the dark cloud coming down the river. Goose bumps shivered up her arms and she folded them around herself as thunder rumbled low, still miles away. Even though the sky directly above was blue, the water seemed discolored and white caps dotted the surface.

"Yes, it looks that way," she managed to reply.

He held out a brown paper bag. "I know I hijacked your lunch break, so I grabbed something on the way."

Shannyn stared at the bag, recognizing the familiar logo. "You didn't."

A smile crept up his face and she realized it was the first time he'd really smiled at her, a smile that connected. It moved from his lips and thawed the ice in his eyes as he admitted, "Of course I did. You can't get a hamburger like this overseas, heck, not even in Edmonton. And I brought lots of napkins." He held out his other hand, revealing the white stack.

He led her up the steps to one of the benches that lined the perimeter of the lighthouse, then reached into the bag and handed her the foil-wrapped sandwich. "I got extra cheese on yours."

Shannyn smiled back, secretly pleased that he remembered another one of her favorites. She hadn't had one in ages. Sliding the foil pocket back slightly, she took her first bite and sighed in appreciation at the juicy beef and tang of the condiments.

"Mmm." She let the sound vibrate through her lips as she swallowed and put the sandwich down on her lap. "I haven't had one of these in a long time."

"We used to eat a lot of them, way back when."

She used her napkin to dab at her lips; it was a tasty but messy business. She wrinkled her eyebrows. She was surprised he'd made such a casual reference to their past after the resentful tone of their last meeting. For a brief moment as their eyes caught and held, she got that tumbling in her stomach, a lifting and turning that she'd almost forgotten. Perhaps it was brought on by nostalgia of what had been, but not completely. Part of it was a pull to the man beside her now. Tall and strong and more than a little enigmatic. A man who made her wonder what was simmering underneath.

"Yes, we did," she responded, the words coming out slightly breathy.

"It was a good summer."

That summer had changed her life. And not just because she'd gotten pregnant. But because it was the first—and only—time she'd been in love.

They'd met through mutual friends at an outdoor concert in Officers' Square. Right away she'd been attracted to the lean, dark-haired boy who seemed to have so much energy.

They'd started dating, and things had progressed rapidly. It had been a whirlwind, magical.

But the young man who had captivated her heart and enjoyed life to the full and made her laugh, was gone. She supposed they'd both grown up. But his smile and the brief memory took her back. Made her wonder what it would take to bring that smile back again.

She watched him as they ate for a few minutes in silence. He was more relaxed right now. Perhaps it would be a good time to get some answers to her questions. And not just for Emma. For herself. She wanted to know what had happened in the years since that summer. What made him tick. When her curiosity got the better of her, she asked the question that had been plaguing her.

"What have you been doing the past six years?"

His chewing slowed. He looked away as he admitted, "I made Special Forces. I was there until nearly a year ago."

"Where were you stationed?"

"I moved around a lot. Wherever I was needed."

"You won't tell me."

He looked back at her then, and she realized the soldier was once again in control. "I can't tell you. Sometimes I was sent with a regular Recce platoon."

He saw her confusion and elaborated. "Reconnaissance. We'd offer support to operations, that sort of thing. Other times…" He paused, his gaze slipping from hers again. "It doesn't matter now, anyway. Those days are gone."

Shannyn folded her hands and watched his head turn away from her. She got the feeling it mattered a great deal. "It changed you, Jonas."

"Being in combat changes everyone." He still refused to look at her, instead appeared to be people watching.

She didn't know why he felt the need to generalize everything so much. "I'm sure it does. But I'm interested in how it changed *you*."

"Why?"

Ah, a question with several answers, some she'd acknowledge, some she wouldn't. She picked the only one that was relevant. "Because you are Emma's father."

Whatever was left of his lunch he wrapped up and put back in the bag.

"Whatever it was I thought I knew that summer, I was wrong."

"Wrong how?"

He balled up the bag and got up, taking a small hop on his good leg to right himself before depositing everything in the trash can. "I was full of myself and what I was going to do. I was indestructible. I thought I knew everything." He sighed heavily. "And I really had no idea."

"You hardened." Shannyn held her breath waiting for his response. She could sense his stubborn withdrawal and couldn't help but see the resemblance between him and Emma, especially now when he seemed so unhappy. His lips seemed fuller; the bow shape of his mouth so much like her daughter when she'd had a rough day at school or got overtired. He'd passed on his fair share of traits whether he knew it or not, and it drew her to him. How could she hate the man who had given her such a precious gift?

When his answer came it was not what she expected.

"I know I've probably seemed hard and demanding. I'm sorry. I've lived in a world where you give and receive orders."

The small confession touched her. "You don't smile anymore. Or at least not like you used to."

His eyes pierced her and she wondered if he was trying to see her thoughts.

"You've changed, too. You're cautious. Reserved. And for what it's worth, you don't smile much, either."

"Maybe we just don't smile at each other." It was out before she could think about what she was saying, and she bit her lip.

"Perhaps we should try." He sat down again at the table. "I'm trying to look past my resentment of you for lying to me. For Emma's sake. What did she say when you told her?"

Another gust of cold air hit them, and Shannyn brushed a piece of her hair away from her face, lowering her eyes. The thunder that had been creeping up the river rumbled closer, and the first lightning pierced the gray sky.

"I didn't tell her."

"You what?"

His earlier geniality evaporated. The hard edge of his voice was matched only by the thunder that boomed. The first cold droplets hit her skin, and Shannyn looked at the path of the storm. She could only see perhaps half a kilometer away; farther than that was a gray curtain of rain.

"We've got to get inside," she exclaimed, thankful for the temporary diversion.

"Are you kidding?" Everyone who'd been outdoors was suddenly scrambling for shelter. The lighthouse, really a museum, was already filling up with tourists. "My truck's parked on the street. We can make it if we run."

Heavy drops of rain marked the path as they jogged toward his pickup. Jonas reached the vehicle first and unlocked her door before running around the hood to the driver's side and clambering in just as the skies opened up.

For a few seconds the only sound was the drumming of rain on the roof of the truck and their heavy breathing.

Jonas rested his hands on the wheel, picking up the conversation where it had left off, much to her dismay.

"You didn't tell her. We agreed."

"No, you demanded. You said I could do this my way and then you ordered me about like one of your privates. Which I am not."

His only response was the use of a very indelicate word.

Shannyn straightened her back and half turned on the seat. "I'm the mother of your child and perhaps you should remember that."

"You're right. How could I possibly forget something that has happened so *recently*."

Embarrassment bloomed in her cheeks at the acid in his tone. He was never going to forgive her. "Look. I tried, I really did. But I just didn't know how to tell her. How to answer the questions she's sure to have. Can't you understand that?"

"You had no trouble with the decision not to tell me. What have you told her about her father, anyway?"

Shannyn looked at the windshield, but saw nothing but water streaming down the glass. "I told her you didn't know that she was born and that I didn't know where you were."

She felt his eyes on her, condemning.

"Now that was a bit of a lie, wasn't it. Because you could have found me quite easily if you'd tried."

"Does it really matter now?" She sighed. "There is no point belaboring what has or hasn't been done."

"Convenient for you."

Shannyn snapped her head around at the contempt in his tone. "I beg your pardon, for trying to find the best way to tell our daughter that you are here now. For trying to find the way to explain things that will cause the least hurt and confusion. She's five, Jonas. Five. If I need an extra day or two to do that, then you're going to have to deal with it. What if she asks why you left me in the first place? Why you didn't care enough to stay?

What am I supposed to tell her then? That your precious Army was more important than we were."

Her lower lip trembled slightly as emotion overwhelmed her. Her cheeks flamed hotly at what she'd revealed in her outburst. It didn't take great powers of deduction to realize that a good part of her decision had been based on her own feelings of abandonment.

"I don't know what you tell her," he answered. "But you know as well as I do that your last statement isn't quite accurate."

She didn't know what he meant. Whether it was the part about the Army being more important or the fact that he couldn't have chosen the army over them because he didn't know there was a "them." The straightness of his body, the way his eyes blazed at her, kept any thought of clarifying it at bay.

"But I know two things," he continued after a moment. "I know you want to be the one to tell her, and I know that you're the one who got us into this whole situation and you are going to have to work it out."

"Why do you even want to be involved in her life?"

Jonas gripped the steering wheel. Why indeed? He wasn't happy; he knew that. He had a permanent limp, and he was a single man in the military.

But none of that mattered because he was now also a father. And surprisingly, that seemed to carry more weight than anything else. He stared at the rain streaming down the window as he answered.

"Because I am her father. Because I missed out on her first five years. I didn't get to see her as a baby, or watch her first steps, or hear her first words. I didn't get to help her on the school bus on her first day of school or put a Band-Aid on her bumps and bruises."

He stopped, turned his head and met her eyes. The aqua-blue eyes of the woman he'd once loved, who now didn't understand anything about him at all. "I missed all of that, Shannyn, and I missed it because you thought it was 'best' not to tell me. And I'm sure about one thing. I am not going to miss out on any more of her life. She is my daughter. I am her father. She is a part of me whether you like it or not. And I agreed to let you tell her in your own way. I *trusted* you to do that. It appears I misplaced my trust."

Shannyn lifted her chin. "You haven't inspired a whole lot of trust yourself, Jonas."

He took his hands off the wheel, turning his body so he was angled on the seat. He winced against the sudden spurt of pain in his thigh. She thought he'd betrayed her in some way when he'd left her. Maybe that was just as well. They were certainly miles apart now.

"I will see Emma. You will tell her about me and we will, together, come up with a time and place for me to meet her. Because if that doesn't happen, Shannyn, you'll force me to take legal action."

All the color dropped from her face, and he regretted that he'd had to resort to such tactics. He wasn't sure if he could even go through with such a thing. He knew it made him sound cold and unfeeling. And he wasn't. The problem was he felt too much these days. Felt so much that at times it overwhelmed him. He pushed away the emotion. She was the one forcing his hand, not the other way around.

"You wouldn't," she breathed.

"I would," he returned. "Don't test me on this, Shannyn. I want to do this amicably. I really do. But that's up to you now."

The windows had steamed up, and he started the engine, cranking up the defrost button. Within seconds a circle of clear glass expanded until he could see outside. The rain was moving downriver and he turned on the wipers, clearing off the windshield.

"Buckle your seat belt. I'll drop you off at the office."

When he pulled in front of her building, he put the truck into Park but left the engine running.

"I'll expect your call very soon, Shannyn. If I don't hear from you by the end of the week, you'll be hearing from my lawyer."

She got out and slammed the door without saying anything.

He pulled away from the curb, heading back to base. He was determined to get to know his daughter, and he was willing to threaten her with lawyers and judges to do it.

But he hadn't counted on how much it would hurt—not just to fight with Shannyn but to spend time in her company.

CHAPTER FIVE

"HONEY, remember the man at my office the other day?"

Shannyn closed the book she'd been reading to Emma and snuggled the pajama-clad body close. She couldn't put this off anymore. She had no doubt that Jonas would find a way to see Emma, and it was her job to make sure Emma was okay with it. More than okay.

"The tall one that looked at me funny, right?"

"Yes, pumpkin, that man." Shannyn wasn't surprised Emma remembered; she had a sharp memory. "I have something to tell you."

Emma turned her face up at Shannyn expectantly. Shannyn didn't know whether to smile or cry. How could she make Emma understand something that she herself did not? This perfect little face, the creamy skin of youth, devoid of the lines of worry that came with age and a loss of innocence. Lines like the ones she'd seen around the corners of her own eyes lately.

Shannyn had done everything she could to protect Emma, and yet here they were.

"Emma, that man…" She paused, tucking Emma close. Her voice caught on the rest of the sentence. "That man is your daddy."

Emma pulled away slightly and her mouth opened. "My daddy?"

Oh, honey. Shannyn took a deep breath, willing the right words to come.

"Yes, pumpkin. He didn't know that you were born, so seeing you…well it was a surprise to him."

"He didn't know I was a baby?"

"No, sugar. His job took him away before you were born. But—" and this was the hard part "—he wants to know you now."

"Mama," Emma whispered, a smile broadening her face at the brilliant news. "I thought he forgot."

Shannyn wrinkled her brows. "Who forgot what, honey?"

"Santa. Last year I asked him for a daddy but I didn't get one and so I thought he forgot."

If ever there were a moment that Shannyn truly regretted what she'd done, this was it. She'd thought she'd done such a good job as a single mother, but knowing that her precious baby had asked Santa Claus for a daddy broke her heart. She only hoped that somehow Jonas could live up to Emma's expectations.

"He wants to meet you, Emma. But I don't want you to get your hopes up too high. Jonas doesn't know what it's like to be a dad, and I don't think he's been around kids much." Shannyn paused, wondering what sorts of people Jonas *had* been around over the years. "I don't want you to think this is going to be perfect, okay? We need to take it one day at a time."

But Emma's joy was undiminished. Her eyes shone as she rose up on her knees to give Shannyn a kiss. "I can't wait!" she said before falling back on the couch and hugging her arms around herself. "A mama *and* a daddy," she murmured, fully pleased.

The tears and questions Shannyn had anticipated never came, but Emma's blatant, unvarnished enthusiasm worried her even more. What if it all went wrong? Where would Emma be then?

Shannyn rotated her neck, trying to work out the nervous kinks that had settled there. All her careful planning and her years of justifying her decision to herself were about to become reconciled in the next half hour.

She fussed with a tray on the breakfast nook table. Thankfully the showers of the week before had moved on and the skies were clear and pure. Today had been the last day of school for Emma; she'd been done at noon, and Shannyn had taken the afternoon off. She was so nervous enough about tonight that she wouldn't have been able to focus at the office anyway. Jonas was due any moment. And she was going to introduce him to his daughter.

She looked through the patio doors at their picnic table, the red vinyl tablecloth flapping gently in the light breeze. Metal clips anchored at the corners kept the cloth from blowing away. An end-of-school barbecue had seemed the best idea.

"Mama?"

Shannyn looked away from the window and down at Emma. Her little girl was dressed cutely in a denim skort and red T-shirt, her curls pulled up in a bouncy ponytail.

"Yes, pumpkin?"

"Does my daddy like hamburgers?"

Shannyn's heart caught. Emma's wide eyes looked genuinely concerned that perhaps her new father wouldn't like what was for dinner, and Shannyn's returning smile was slightly wobbly as she knelt down before her.

"Don't you worry. Jonas—" she still couldn't seem to bring herself to say "your daddy" "—loves burgers." She tipped Emma's nose with her finger. "I think he even likes pickles almost as much as you do."

Emma's smile was bright as she skipped away outside to play on her slide. Shannyn, however, couldn't help but frown. As rational as Shannyn had tried to be with her, she hadn't been able to contain Emma's innocent enthusiasm. There was so much potential for Emma to be hurt when she had such expectations.

"Shan?"

She started at the sound of her name. When she spun in response, they both froze. The absurd impulse to rush forward to his arms sluiced through her. Years past they would have done just that. He would have pulled her close and kissed her, let his hands…

But not now. It was only the surprise of his sudden appearance that made her fancy such things. Now he kept his distance, his very presence larger than life as he stood in her kitchen.

"I knocked but no one answered. I let myself in."

She took a fortifying breath. She'd been so lost in her worry she hadn't even heard him drive up. "Sorry…"

Whatever she was going to say evaporated from her mind. Gone was the military-issue clothing. In its place he'd worn jeans and a T-shirt in a gray-blue color. Out of politeness he'd removed his shoes at the front door and was in stockingfeet. His hair was always the same, but the relaxed dress brought him down to a level of greater familiarity, and Shannyn remembered all too vividly the times they'd spent together when he'd been out of uniform. Walking the beach, he'd dressed in board shorts and T-shirts, or going to clubs he'd worn jeans that hugged him and made every woman in the room thank the good Lord for the rear view.

"Are you okay?"

She tried a light laugh that came out as a nervous twitter. "I'm fine."

He looked down at himself and back up at her. He had yet to smile, and she hoped he could muster one up for Emma's sake.

"I thought this would be better than the uniform. More approachable."

He'd been right on that score. Shannyn wondered what kind of shape he'd been in *before* his injury, if he still remained this lean and fit now, a year later. His casual clothes emphasized his slim hips and muscled upper body.

"Just be careful with her," Shannyn warned. She had to put some distance between them because seeing him in civvies was affecting her more than she liked. It was bad enough that Emma had her heart set on a new, perfect daddy. Shannyn had to be the voice of reason in all of this and couldn't afford to forget that, just because simply seeing him cranked up her pulse a notch or two. In the end it changed nothing.

"Of course I will. I would never hurt her, Shannyn. You must know that."

Maybe not intentionally, Shannyn thought, but pursed her lips together.

Jonas was nervous, Shannyn realized, seeing how stiffly he held his body. It would probably be better for everyone if they got the introductions over with and dealt with whatever came next.

"Why don't you get your shoes? Emma's in the backyard, and we've planned a barbecue." When he'd departed for the front door again, Shannyn pressed a hand to her belly.

Jonas had no idea what it meant to be a father. He certainly wasn't prepared for what Emma would throw at him. Despite Shannyn's best efforts, Emma was expecting a ready-made, perfect dad. One that perhaps smiled once in a while. And what did Shannyn expect out of this? If it didn't work out, she'd have to deal with Emma's disappointment. And if it did, she'd have to deal with Jonas on a permanent basis. Neither option held a lot of appeal. Seeing him was a constant reminder of how much he'd hurt her.

When Jonas came back grim-faced, shoes in hand, Shannyn let out a huff.

"For God's sake, Jonas, could you muster up a smile? You don't need to frighten her half to death."

He stilled, sucking in his lips and letting them roll out again to their natural shape. She couldn't help but watch the movement, struck by a memory of how soft yet firm they had been years ago when he'd kissed her. When she let her gaze roam upward, his eyes had darkened from their usual green to a deeper hazel color.

They only did that when he was upset, she remembered.

"I'm sorry," he replied gruffly. "I'm…I'm just nervous."

"You're scared of a little girl." Shannyn couldn't help the smile that curved her lips. "You, the big bad soldier."

But her teasing didn't help banish the anxiety from his face. "This is different," he said simply.

It made her feel a bit better. At least he wasn't treating this cavalierly. "I'm just saying—" She tempered her sarcasm, keeping her tone even and gentle."—Emma is a very open, loving child. She's not going to understand if you're cold and distant."

Jonas stared down at Shannyn. Sometimes she seemed almost the same as she'd been…like the other day when they'd eaten lunch together. Approachable, warm. At those times he remembered all too well what it had been like with her before. When her smile had been just for him, making him feel ten feet tall and bulletproof.

At other times, like right now, he felt he didn't know her at all. And while he wanted to meet Emma, he felt totally un-equipped to handle the challenge being thrown his way—to be a happy, loving father. How was he supposed to do that when he'd all but forgotten what love felt like?

"I don't know what to do," he admitted.

Her face softened, and the gentle way she laid her hand on his arm felt foreign. But good. Suddenly they were connected again, and as his eyes met hers he was shocked to realize that he wasn't imagining the link between them. The one that would have been there, Emma or no Emma. It almost felt uncompli-cated. But that was crazy. There were scads of complications between them. Those she knew about and those she didn't. Hopefully never would.

"Just say hello. Smile. Tell her you're pleased to meet her. She'll help you with the rest."

Jonas figured Shannyn knew Emma better than anyone, and he pulled away, already missing the feel of her hand on his skin. "Let's go." He slid his shoes onto his feet while Shannyn opened the patio doors.

The heat hit him first, the steamy humidity of a June after-noon. Inside the cool house, he'd momentarily forgotten how hot it was outside until the wall of it hit him. He thought for a moment how it was a very different kind of heat from that in the Middle East.

It was a lifetime ago; it was yesterday.

He shook himself from his thoughts to hear her calling Emma from the swing set.

The bundle that came running was the liveliest picture he'd seen in years. A flawless vision of life and innocence, and the purity of it struck him square in the chest. She ran across the grass, a bouncing tail of curls and arms and legs that had not quite lost all their baby chubbiness, still perfect in their youth.

His heart stopped when she smiled and called out, "Daddy!" as she ran directly for him.

He wasn't prepared, and she hit him full force in his bad leg.

Her tiny arms were wrapped around his hips as the muscle quivered and buckled completely, taking him to his knees on the grass. Tears stung the backs of his eyes as Emma let go and stepped backward, shocked—the big, strong man brought to utter humiliation by a tiny squirt of a thing. The pain was nothing, nothing compared to the shame he felt.

"Oh my God, Jonas, are you all right?"

Shannyn's worried voice reached his ears and he inhaled deeply, nodding. Emma was staring at him with something like fear and guilt paling her tiny face. When he looked up at her, she choked a little and started to run to the other side of the yard, to the pint-size playhouse by the far fence.

"Emma." Shannyn started toward her but Jonas stopped her.

"No. Let me."

He got to his feet, hopping a bit on his good leg so he could get steadied. *Introduce himself and pleased to meet you, indeed.* All the good intentions for a smooth transition were annihilated. He ignored the pain radiating from his thigh up through his groin and even to the pit of his stomach. Taking a deep breath, he took the first painful steps toward making things right with his daughter.

When he got to the playhouse, he looked inside and saw her sitting on a small bench, her knees pulled up to her chest and her delicate lips turned down in a perfectly inverted *u*. Tears glimmered like emerald drops in her eyes.

"Emma?"

She looked up. The playhouse was too small for him to go inside. He tried squatting by the door and the pain took his breath away. He finally rested his weight on his knees, bracing his hands on the miniature wood door frame.

"Emma, I'm so sorry for what just happened. It's not your fault."

"I hurt you," the words came, tiny and contrite.

The knowledge that she blamed herself touched him. He knew how that felt, only in his case, the self-blame was deserved. But Emma hadn't known of his wound, he was sure of it.

"No, honey, you didn't. I was hurt a long time ago, and you didn't know. It was bad luck that you grabbed the wrong spot."

"How did you get hurt?"

Jonas swallowed against all the pain that came with that

question. Being here now was heart wrenching enough. How did he explain it all to an innocent girl? One who deserved a more perfect world than the one she was inheriting?

"I was in an accident about a year ago. It was a long way away from here and I was in the hospital for a few months. And it is getting better. Now I just have to exercise and keep seeing the therapist. That's why you saw me at your mommy's office."

"Oh."

"I'm the one who's sorry, Emma. I think you feel bad and that makes me sad. I wanted us to meet and be happy."

Emma's eyes cleared and her knees came down from her chest. "Me, too."

He held out his right hand as if introducing himself. "Let's start over. Hi, Emma. My name's Jonas and I'm your daddy."

He hadn't known how those words would actually make him feel until he said them. They cracked the shell he'd constructed around his heart, letting in little beams of love. He was someone's father. She was a part of him. And she was beautiful.

She rose from the bench and took his large, callused hand in her smaller soft one. "I'm Emma. I'm pleased to meet you, Daddy."

When she smiled she looked like Shannyn. So much of him was in her looks, but the smile and the freckles were all Shannyn. He shook her hand gently.

"I think if you were to try hugging me again, you wouldn't hurt me."

When her arms went around his neck he put his around her and squeezed.

So much over the past few years had convinced him that life was devoid of hope. Of beauty. Of tenderness. Somehow, by some miracle, one hug from his unknown daughter changed all that. Because in her embrace he knew beauty and tenderness and most of all, the elusive glimmer of hope.

When they released each other his smile was genuine. "That was a first-class hug," he praised. "Now, I think your mom is probably worried about us. Let's go back and get this barbecue underway. I think I saw hamburgers."

He pushed himself to his feet, took her hand in his, marveling at the innocent trust in the simple clasp, especially after he'd frightened her so. Together they walked back across the lawn toward Shannyn.

Shannyn had waited for them to return from the playhouse. She must have decided not to come after them, because as they turned the corner of the playhouse she took only a few steps forward and halted. Emma held his hand, walking slower than usual in deference to his contracted gait.

Shannyn's fingers lifted to her lips. He could see the tremble there, could see the soft shine of tears on her lashes, and for a moment he forgot about his injury and all the reasons why it was wrong. For a few blissful seconds he was the man he'd wanted to be for her, all those years ago.

For a brief flash, the bitterness of the past disintegrated and he felt larger than life. Like a man coming home to his family. A child's pure handclasp and a waiting woman.

It wasn't just Emma who was bringing back to life the feelings he'd locked away. It was Shannyn. He understood her wariness and fear. He'd experienced his share of it. Right or wrong, she'd made her choices and now she was having to deal with the consequences, and the strain showed on her. But in those moments when she forgot, she was the Shan he remembered. There'd been times when their eyes met that he felt sure their connection was still strong.

He had no clue how he was going to maintain a relationship with his daughter while keeping Shannyn at arm's length. He wasn't the man for her. Not anymore. He'd made his choice and to change his mind would only be unfair to her. He wouldn't make promises he couldn't keep.

What woman would want half a man? He couldn't help the limp that took him closer to her with every step. What woman would choose such a man? Even one who had never forgotten what it was like to love her?

As they reached the patio, he wished for the first time that they could go back. But there would be no going back. She'd broken faith with him with her lies.

He looked down at Emma, holding his hand with the simple trust of innocence. Somehow he and Shannyn would have to find a way to work through this. He was here now.

Shannyn blinked back the tears that had gathered as they approached. She'd been wrong, she realized. Jonas had said it but somehow she hadn't believed him. She'd thought her reasons had been justified. But seeing them together now, their hands joined, the beam of pure bliss on Emma's face, only slightly brighter than the one on Jonas's... She shouldn't have kept Emma from him all these years. She should have told him and dealt with the consequences, then and there, instead of putting it off, pretending it would never happen.

"Mama, this is my daddy," Emma announced as they met Shannyn in front of the patio blocks.

"We've met." Shannyn tried a smile, but it quivered.

"He was hurt and I didn't know, so that's why I hurt his leg."

Shannyn got the meaning behind the strange five-year-old logic and nodded. "I know, sweetie. I should have told you; warned you to be careful."

Emma held his hand firmly in his. "That's okay, Mama," she responded. "Daddy 'n' me? We're good."

Shannyn couldn't help but laugh, even through the emotion

thickening her throat. At times Emma sounded so much like the
toddler she'd left behind, and at other times the adult tone told
Shannyn she was growing up fast.

"I'm glad. I think we can start cooking the burgers now. Do
you want to set the table, Emma?"

"If Daddy helps me."

It was going to take a very long time for Shannyn to get used
to the word *Daddy* coming out of Emma's mouth. "Maybe Jonas
can pour the drinks while you put out the plates."

For several minutes dinner preparations were ongoing, and
Shannyn was thankful for Emma's happy chatter, telling Jonas
about school and her friends and what her favorite toys were. It
filled up the awkward silences that would have happened. When
they finally sat down to eat, Emma passed Jonas the plate of
sliced pickles first thing.

"Mama said that you like pickles almost as much as me."

Jonas took the plate and raised an eyebrow at Shannyn. A slow
smile flirted with the edges of his mouth. "I do. I'm surprised
she remembers."

Emma brushed it off. "Oh, Mama, she remembers *everything*."

Shannyn felt Jonas's eyes on her, and heat infused her cheeks.

"Does she now," his soft, knowing voice answered.

Oh, she did. She remembered things she knew would be far
best forgotten, no matter how his smile or the sultry sound of his
voice played havoc with her good intentions. Just because Jonas
was back and involved with Emma, didn't mean there was room
in her personal life for him.

Perhaps she'd been wrong in deciding not to tell him he had
a child, but the reasons she'd done it were still there. He hadn't
loved her then. He hadn't once contacted her after he'd transferred. Nothing between them had changed since then. She

hadn't been enough, and they were even farther apart now. Nothing he'd said or done since coming back gave her the impression that anything would be different a second time around.

And she knew she wouldn't survive a second time.

But it didn't stop the remembering. She remembered how it felt to lie in his arms and look up at the stars. The touch of his lips on hers, the feel of his hard muscles beneath her fingertips.

When she shook herself from her reverie, Jonas was looking at her strangely.

It would be best if he didn't know the direction of her thoughts. Because somehow she had to keep him at a safe distance.

CHAPTER SIX

WHEN dinner was over, Shannyn sent Emma inside to change into her pajamas while she cleared the table. To her surprise, Jonas wordlessly gathered plates and took them into the kitchen.

Shannyn came back through the patio doors, folding the red-and-white tablecloth as she went. Everything had its place here. But then, she'd always felt the need for order. Perhaps it was the lack of structure she'd had growing up, once her mother left and her father had raised her alone. She'd had to take it upon herself to provide some sort of home life, but she'd only been a child. Her father hadn't put in much effort, either.

By the time adulthood came around, Shannyn had known what she'd always sensed during those difficult years. She wanted a home. A stable, secure, consistent environment. She'd been ready to settle down as Jonas had been getting ready to explore what he'd thought were bigger, brighter horizons.

She watched Jonas open the dishwasher, loading it with the dirty dishes from the counter. Quietly she passed by him and tucked the tablecloth into a drawer. Jonas might look the picture of domesticity right now, but she knew he'd been carted from pillar to post as a child as the son of an army major. It had never seemed to bother him, moving around from one place to another.

Shannyn had made a home for herself and Emma, something permanent, and it was yet another thing that kept them apart.

He put the last plate in the rack, added detergent from the cupboard beneath the kitchen sink and started the cycle. Shannyn wondered how he felt about it now, knowing he probably wouldn't face deployment again. Was he looking forward to less travel, or would he miss it terribly? Did he dread being sent from base to base for the remainder of his career and missing out on the action?

When he finished and turned back around, she avoided his eyes, keeping her hands busy by fussing with a dish towel. Jonas wouldn't stay; she knew that. But for Emma's sake she was glad he didn't face the same level of danger he always had. At least she should be able to avoid *that* conversation with her daughter.

In the quiet of early evening, with the mess tidied up, Jonas's next words were a surprise.

"She's a wonder, Shannyn. You've been a great mom. I can see that."

All her senses seemed to tingle as she tried to exit the intimate working area of the kitchen. "Thank you."

His hand caught hers as she passed by.

Shannyn looked up, her blue eyes pleading with him not to make this more than it was. "Don't. Don't do that."

She tugged her hand free, but he didn't let the matter drop.

"Do what?"

"Pretend this is something it's not."

"I only spoke the truth."

He dismissed her concern, and Shannyn tried to tell herself it had been a compliment and a casual touch. But her cheeks flamed as his eyes remained steadily on her face. She hadn't been mistaken about the connection she'd felt earlier. A part of her wanted to explore it, to see if it was still as strong as she remembered.

A bigger part, the broken part of her, told her to leave it alone.

That they were all better off if he went his own way. Or at least kept his contact with her in reference to their daughter only. She wasn't prepared for more from Jonas. She couldn't harden her heart and enter into something she knew ahead of time was temporary. It would be a huge mistake, and she needed to keep both eyes open. Even she understood that much.

"I'm just being honest. She is a bright, happy little girl and I have you to thank for it."

"Even though I kept her from you."

"Yes, even though." He shoved his hands into his pockets.

"You're not angry anymore that I lied to you."

"I didn't say that."

Shannyn sighed, going to the table and resting her hands on the back of a chair. She couldn't expect him to forgive her just like that. The fact that they could even discuss it now without argument was progress. Progress she didn't want to sabotage by throwing blame back and forth. It would accomplish nothing, and Emma would be in the crossfire. After listening to her parents argue for years, she refused to repeat that pattern with her own child.

"You…you were great with her. Thank you."

He took a few steps closer, so that his voice rumbled, the seductive sound raising the fine hairs along her arms. "She made it easy. I'm sorry about how things started out." His apology was genuine. "If I had have anticipated…"

His words trailed off but she picked up where he'd finished. "I didn't see it coming, either. I knew she was excited. I should have been more prepared."

"I don't know how we could have been prepared for this."

His words hung in the air between them. "This" meant more than coparenting. She'd be a fool to think that it didn't also mean the growing attraction between them. If she was feeling it, it was possible he was, too. Despite all the reasons they were angry and resentful toward each other.

"Me, neither. I should have thought of it. I'm awfully sorry, Jonas."

Shannyn kept the topic on track but couldn't help but think how odd it was that they were discussing their child's welfare while she was upstairs changing into her nightgown. To do so after six years of no contact whatsoever. To see him, hear his voice, feel the brief touch of his fingers after thinking he was gone forever.

"She's not going to understand when you have to leave again." Shannyn grabbed the stack of paper napkins from the holder and started folding them into triangles. Anything to keep her hands busy. "She doesn't understand how the military works like I do."

"What do you expect from me? I can't help that assignments change. I go where I'm needed. And in my current condition, that's here." He pointed to his leg. "I have a constant reminder of where my life has led. It doesn't stop me from being her father. It's not my fault we're in this mess."

She heard the bitter tone in his voice and wished he didn't feel so angry all the time. It was becoming clearer that he wasn't just mad at her. She was sure there was something deeper, something to do with what had happened to him. Perhaps it was how he'd received his wound. She didn't know and refused to ask. She only knew she couldn't shoulder all the blame.

"It's not exactly mine, either," she snapped.

"If you'd told me from the beginning…"

"Are you saying you'd have left the Special Forces? Stopped being a sniper? You'd have come home to change diapers?"

"I was deployed. The decision of where I'm stationed isn't usually up to me, Shannyn. Whether I like it or not."

Jonas clamped his jaw shut and stared past her shoulder. It had never bothered him before, going where he was told. Yet in the past few months he'd started to resent the choice being taken away from him. "Let's just say I don't know what the future holds for me and I'll deal with it when it happens," he finally ground out.

"That really doesn't help me prepare Emma, now, does it." She stopped her folding and finally faced him dead-on.

"It's the best I can do." He pursed his lips, resenting the fact that somehow they'd ended up arguing anyway, even though he had only wanted to pay her a compliment.

"And it's why I didn't tell you about her in the first place." Her eyes narrowed with accusation. "Did you know she asked for a daddy for Christmas?"

Of course he hadn't, but he couldn't help but warm at the thought. It fit with the impression he'd gathered of her today. He made another attempt at defusing the situation.

"Shannyn, we're all feeling our way around here. I've only just met her today. I don't have a fatherhood instruction book telling me what step to take next. And believe me…I have enough to deal with already."

But Shannyn was undeterred. It was as if she was pushing him to admit something. "Like what? You're working as an instructor now. That seems a pretty choice assignment for someone your age."

The simple mention of having to deal with things made his heart pound harder, faster. It wasn't a choice assignment. It was all he was able to do after having his leg mangled on a nameless battlefield no one was supposed to know about. He wasn't fit to do anything else.

"That doesn't mean I necessarily earned that spot. What do you want me to say, Shannyn? That I miss active duty? I'll admit it, freely. I was damned good at what I did and at least there I didn't feel…redundant."

"Passing your expertise on to others makes you redundant?"

"It's what they do when you can't do your job anymore." He spread his arm wide. "They find a place for you somewhere else. Reassign you to something in an office. Because you're not fit to serve your purpose."

It was out before he had a chance to think, and he realized how angry he sounded.

"You do that a lot. Say things but leave it so ambiguous it seems like a riddle. Why don't you explain what you mean."

That was the one thing he couldn't do. She looked at him differently now, and it would be even worse if she knew the truth. A sheen of cold sweat popped out on his forehead. He'd let his unit down. He'd let Parker down. And they'd given him a medal and called him a hero for it. But no one understood what he'd been through.

"Jonas?"

Shannyn put her hand on his arm. He'd gone again, just the way he had that other time on the Green. One second engaged in conversation, the next completely disassociated and so very, very still. Except for the nearly imperceptible trembling beneath her hand.

She didn't know what she'd said to prompt his withdrawal, but it was becoming clearer to her that there was something else going on with Jonas. Watching him disappear from the present was frightening enough. She didn't know if he blanked out or if he actually went somewhere else. To a memory maybe, one so potent it couldn't exist in the same space as the present. Despite her warnings to herself to stay uninvolved, it wasn't in her not to care.

Besides, it was in Emma's best interest. If there were something more going on with him, she had to know. If it frightened her, she couldn't expect a five-year-old to understand.

"Jonas. Are you all right?"

Slowly his eyes focused on her again. "What?"

"Where did you go just now?"

He slid his gaze away and she knew he was evading.

"Nowhere."

"Jonas." She refused to let him turn away when he would have, and she reached up to cup his chin. "Jonas, please let me help you."

Green eyes settled on hers as he pulled his head away from her touch. There was something different about him just at this moment, she realized. He seemed almost vulnerable, so different from the aloof hostility he normally used to armor himself. Perhaps now she'd be able to take advantage of a window of opportunity. Gain some understanding of what was really going on with him.

"You don't want to help me, Shan. Trust me."

But he used the shortened version of her name for the first time since returning, and it tethered them together. They both knew it. It didn't matter how many years were between them. Once his gaze connected with hers, it held. Clung. Like a lifeline between them.

"You should talk about it," she persisted. "You're so angry. I know there's more going on than just discovering Emma is yours. More than you being angry with me for keeping her from you. Not talking about it isn't going to make it go away."

"I wouldn't know where to begin."

Shannyn sighed and leaned against the front side of the counter, forgetting all about napkins and tablecloths and focusing solely on him. Jonas was weary, she realized. And not just from his injury. It wasn't physical. But inside, where it really mattered. And he was holding it all inside where it festered like an infection. He would only balk at tenderness. But a more logical approach…

"You need to talk about it, because right now I get the feeling you're having a hard enough time by yourself, let alone parenting a five-year-old girl." She folded her arms. "Now that you've met,

I know you're going to ask for time with her. What happens, Jonas, if you have her and you lose time the way you did just now?"

"I don't lose time."

"I just watched you. For nearly five minutes."

His jaw hardened, a muscle twitching beneath his ear. "You're using her to deny me access now."

Shannyn shook her head. "No, I would never do that. You know that. The last thing I want is to put her in the middle of some ridiculous struggle between you and me. For her sake, I want to help you."

She pushed away from the counter and went to him, laying a hand on his arm. His lack of response didn't faze her. "I'm her mother. Before you decide you're going to be a father, you need to act like one. And that means getting help for yourself when you need it, whether you want to or not."

Jonas heaved an exasperated sigh, and his chin jutted out stubbornly. It was a look Shannyn recognized in Emma and if she weren't so worried, the resemblance would have made her smile.

"What's it going to take to make you happy with this?"

The answers that raced through Shannyn's mind were varied and surprising in their complexity. She'd thought she was happy before he came back, but sometimes now it seemed as though he'd never gone, as silly as that sounded. She wanted Emma to be happy. She wanted Jonas to be a part of Emma's life, now that the truth was out. And she realized she might even want him to be a part of *her* life, even though she didn't see how that could ever happen.

He would always be the kind of man to run off chasing a new assignment, a new adventure. And she'd be the one left behind again. Wanting to be a part of his life and allowing it were two very different things. Knowing what she knew about him, and what would inevitably happen, made being attracted to him utter nonsense.

But they had to build some sort of bridge.

"A good start would be telling me how you were injured."

He shook his head, his chin jutting out farther. "No, I can't."

She raised her eyebrows, pulling her hand off his arm. "Can't or won't?"

"Right now it's the same thing."

"You're going to tell me it's classified, right?" She blew out a puff of air, lifting her hair from her forehead. "Convenient."

"The location is classified. The…incident…is a matter of record."

She watched him swallow, look at his shoes and then look up again. "I just can't, okay?"

She accepted it because it was obvious that pressing him would get her nowhere. Perhaps it would be better to work their way there gradually. "Okay, then, how about telling me about what happened when you left me and went to Edmonton?"

She instantly regretted her choice of words. His face closed off completely, all vulnerability wiped away until he had all the openness of a classified document.

"You make it sound like I chose the Army over you."

"Didn't you?" She asked the question without hostility. She already knew the answer. She turned to get the kettle, feeling the sudden need for the soothing effects of tea.

At that moment Emma reappeared, dressed in a soft pink nightie, her face scrubbed.

"You ready for bed, pumpkin?" Shannyn put the kettle aside and forced a smile.

Emma nodded. "My story first, please."

Shannyn took her by the hand and led her to the stairs, taking the first steps.

"Aren't you coming, Daddy?" Emma paused and asked the question over her shoulder.

The plea was heartfelt, and Shannyn let her gaze fall on Jonas, still standing by the kitchen counter. He looked so lost, a great giant without a country. But that was ridiculous. Jonas had always been the strongest man she'd known. She wondered what his answer would have been—about choosing the Army over her. The way he sometimes looked at her made her believe that he'd cared after all. That maybe he still cared a little. Just not enough.

The bigger question was, did she want him to care at all? Even if she had loved him then, his answer to her earlier question was of the greatest importance. If he hadn't cared enough to choose her then, what made her think he'd be any different this time? And could she take that risk with her heart after letting him break it once already?

He smiled but kept his gaze on Shannyn. Before her eyes he went from looking lost to having a purpose, and she knew it was Emma that made the difference. Her body warmed beneath his appraisal.

"I'd be honored, Emma. If your mama doesn't mind."

"It's all right."

His steps sounded behind hers as they climbed the stairs. It was an intimate sound. How many nights had she climbed these stairs alone, wishing for another's to echo behind her?

She tucked Emma in, all the while aware of his body filling the doorway, blocking the light from the bathroom. Standing guard as she read Emma's favourite book, *Love You Forever.* Waiting quietly as she tucked Emma in snugly and kissed her good-night.

She'd nearly made it to the door when Emma's voice stopped her.

"Aren't you going to tuck me in, Daddy?"

Shannyn made the mistake of looking up at him. His eyes widened with the wonder of being asked such a thing, as if he'd been given the moon.

"Okay." Hesitantly he stepped forward, smoothed the blankets about her, and leaned down to place a kiss on her forehead. "Good night, Emma."

"Good night," she whispered back.

Shannyn watched, swallowing against tears gathering in her throat. She'd missed him so when he went away, and had often wondered what it would have been like for him to know Emma, even while doing her best to protect her daughter. She still wasn't sure Jonas wouldn't hurt them in the end, but the tender way he was with Emma touched her deeply. It was like he put everything aside and focused on her alone.

He was here now. The more she saw of Jonas, the more convinced she was that he was dealing with something bigger than she realized. Perhaps Emma with her guileless ways could help with some of that healing. Perhaps in a way Shannyn couldn't seem to.

He turned from the bedside and Shannyn saw the glimmer of tears on his cheeks before he cleared his throat. When he passed by her, his hand squeezed hers.

She turned and followed him downstairs, expecting to talk. But when they got there, he merely mumbled a thank you and left before she could say anything.

Leaving her with more questions than she'd had when he'd arrived.

On Sunday, Jonas called on the fly, saying he was heading across the river on an errand and would Emma like to go for lunch.

Shannyn paused. On his first visit they hadn't even broached the topic of visitation—when and where he could expect to visit. Yet after his episodes, she wasn't comfortable in letting Emma go with him alone. He'd only met her once, after all. The alternative was that in order to say yes, she'd have to go, too.

She held the receiver close to her ear, knowing he was waiting for her answer. And wasn't this a slippery slope? If she wanted to keep her perspective, seeing Jonas should be the last thing she wanted. Instead, her heart leaped at the sound of his voice.

"I'm not sure that's a good idea," she explained. "Emma has only seen you once. I think it might be too soon."

"Then you come, too. I have to drop something off on Main Street, and I was going to grab some fast food. I thought I could use some company."

She didn't know what to say.

"Shannyn, you told me that you wanted me to be present in Emma's life, not in and out. That's all I'm trying to do."

Now he was using her own words against her. Keeping him at arm's length was proving more difficult than she'd imagined. "I don't know, Jonas, it's awfully sudden."

"Come on, Shan. It's only lunch. What else have you got going on today? It's Sunday. It's raining."

"I'm cleaning the house." She looked around at the living room, dusted and polished. A tiny white lie wasn't going to kill her.

"It's an hour out of the afternoon. I'd really like to see her."

Shannyn couldn't come up with a more-logical argument. "Oh, all right. Lunch, but that's it."

"I'll pick you up in half an hour."

Shannyn hung up the phone and frowned. The sudden urge to change into neater clothes came over her and she resisted. There was nothing wrong with her jeans or the cotton pullover she'd put on this morning. Her hair was up in a ponytail and she left it that way as a point of defiance. She was not going to make an effort to be *pretty* for Jonas Kirkpatrick!

Emma, on the other hand, decided primping was necessary, and the minutes leading to his arrival were spent picking out "the" right shirt and brushing Emma's hair until it shone. Shannyn tucked it back with a headband and couldn't help but smile at the pixie face grinning up at her.

"Where're we going to eat?" Emma asked.

"I don't know. You'll have to ask Jonas."

Emma held on to the stair railing as she bounced down the stairs. "I hope it's Wendy's. I'm going to have chicken nuggets and fries and root beer."

Shannyn only shook her head. Some days she wished she had a fraction of Emma's energy and enthusiasm.

"Put your coat on, Emma. It's raining."

She was helping with the zipper when she heard the slam of the truck door. "He's here. Best manners, now."

"Oh, Mama," Emma lamented at the reminder, making Shannyn laugh.

That was how Jonas saw them when she opened the door. Giggling like two girls sharing a secret. Shannyn's hair was pulled straight back into a ponytail and the remembrance of wrapping that tail around his hand and pulling her close slammed into him, making him catch his breath. Emma looked up at him expectantly as she stepped outside and on impulse he reached down and scooped her up.

He held her on one arm as he smiled at Shannyn. "Let's go. First one to the truck gets extra large fries." He shamelessly used the old taunt from their dating days.

Shannyn shut the door and took off at a run. He couldn't follow, and they both knew it. He was handicapped twice over, once with his leg and the other with the extra weight of Emma on his arm. She reached the vehicle and placed one pointed finger on the hood before snapping open the door and hopping in out of the rain.

Jonas leaned his head close to Emma's and whispered, "Your mama was always a pig about French fries."

Emma giggled and Jonas bounced her on his arm. It was probably wrong to tease Shannyn so, but he couldn't resist. Not when she opened the door looking exactly like the girl he'd fallen for long ago.

His heart told him that a date with his daughter and her mother was the perfect way to spend a lonely Sunday.

His head was another matter. Because it came through his consciousness loud and clear that spending time with Shannyn was a big mistake for both of them.

CHAPTER SEVEN

THE buzzer sounded for the second time. Jonas lowered the towel from his head and anchored it around his waist with a hand. Whoever it was wasn't going away. He might as well answer it.

"Yeah," he barked into the intercom.

"It's Shannyn."

He paused, sighed. He'd thought the voice mail he left was clear enough. There was an air show this weekend and he wanted to take Emma. Shannyn too for that matter, if she still wasn't comfortable with him taking Emma on his own.

Their lunch had been fun, devoid of all the loaded atmosphere of his first meeting with Emma. Perhaps it was getting away from home, being in a neutral location. Or the fact that it was a brief outing with no purpose beyond lunch. Whatever it was, he'd enjoyed it. Enough that the air show seemed like a great opportunity. He could show them some of the birds he'd flown in.

Apparently his message hadn't been clear enough, because she was here now.

Shannyn would press him about things he didn't want to talk about. She wouldn't have forgotten his last episode. But it wasn't something he cared to discuss—ever.

He had to expect to talk to Shannyn now and again if he planned on being a part of Emma's life. He had to keep his thoughts away from what had been between them, because letting their past spill over into the present would only cause complications. If he could keep the topic of conversation away from his past, they might be able to come to some sort of understanding on how to navigate their way through co-parenting.

He pressed the white button when it rang again, telegraphing her impatience. "Yeah, sorry. Come on up."

Shannyn stomped up the stairs to his apartment. Jonas didn't have any right to simply make demands where Emma was concerned. He hadn't even asked if they were busy on Saturday. He'd just left that infernal message stating he would be picking them up. She didn't take orders. It was time to set him straight on that.

Jonas held the door open, only his arm visible as she approached from the stairwell. When she came around the corner, everything in her body froze.

He was naked except for a white scrap of cloth that might, in some circles, have passed for a towel. It hung low, delineating the hollows of his hips and leading to tapered abs all the way up to deliciously muscled arms and shoulders.

There was no way she could hide the shock or frank admiration from her face. Jonas Kirkpatrick was physically stunning. Full stop.

"Sorry I took so long. I was in the shower."

"So I see." Shannyn halted in the doorway, avoiding his gaze. Her eyes remained firmly fixed on the center of his chest. The sight of the narrow band of white was arousing at the very least. As she stared at his pecs, he inhaled, and they expanded before her eyes. She had to do something besides gawk like a nitwit!

"Come on in." He finally stood aside, leaving her room to pass by him into the apartment.

Compared to her house, the living arrangements were sparse. The living room held a small drop-leaf table and two chairs, a home gym and a battered sofa in front of a stand holding a thirteen-inch TV/DVD combo. It was meager accommodation, even for a bachelor. She glanced around the corner, seeing doors to what presumably was a bathroom and bedroom, and she'd passed the tiny galley kitchen on the way in. She'd stayed in hotel suites bigger than his apartment.

"It's not very big. But with only me here…" His voice trailed off and he shrugged, making no move to excuse himself to get dressed.

"It's fine." She tried a bland smile. She knew he hadn't missed her initial reaction, from the smug expression on his face. She ignored it and tried to find a place for her gaze to land. She couldn't lose sight of the reason for her visit. He had no right to assume anything.

Jonas adjusted the towel with one hand. Shannyn's nerves were shot and she wasn't sure if it was still the cause of her visit creating such a reaction or the fact that he was standing before her nearly naked. She was struck by a memory—a good one for once—of herself and a hot shower after a particularly nasty walk in the rain when his truck had broken down. They hadn't slept together yet, so he'd let her have the bathroom first, and when he came out later after his shower with his towel wrapped around his hips, one thing had led to another.

His smile seemed to flirt with her, and on top of the potent memory, it wreaked havoc with her intentions.

"How are you, Shan?"

And damned if she didn't blush like a schoolgirl. She inhaled, shoring up her defenses against his unwitting charm. "I'm fine."

"Is Emma okay?"

She spun, again avoiding looking at him. "Emma's fine. How are you?"

"I'm *fine*." He deliberately parroted the word they'd already used several times, and her consternation grew as she realized he was still awfully good at getting around her without even intending it. "Right as rain."

He spread his hands to demonstrate, and the towel slipped. He caught it quickly, revealing nothing beyond the hollow of his hip, but her eyes followed the direction and in that split second she saw the scar, long and angry and jagged, big enough she couldn't possibly miss it.

"Jonas," she whispered, unable to tear her eyes away from the towel that hid his wound once more.

His lips thinned to a hard line, all the earlier teasing wiped clean from his expression. "Stop. I don't want your pity."

She met his gaze evenly. "Of course you don't, and that's not what I meant. But it does look horrible, and I'm sorry for what you went through."

"I'm alive, and there's a hell of a lot more who aren't."

Shannyn paused as his eyes skittered away from hers. Any cockiness he'd exhibited had evaporated. But with his last sentence, things became crystal clear. Survivor's guilt. She didn't know why she hadn't thought of it before. But it all made sense now. He'd been hurt, but he'd gotten out. Who hadn't? And why did he feel so guilty about it?

He turned away, disappearing into a room on the right, she presumed to get dressed. She'd be a liar if she didn't admit to herself that the sight of him nearly naked wasn't an extreme pleasure. She'd been right about what she'd guessed was beneath those lovely T-shirts he was so fond of wearing. Injury or not, his physique was splendid. Her fingers had fairly itched to caress the skin of his ribs.

But that wasn't her place anymore. It was a physical reaction. It had nothing to do with the reality of their situation.

When he returned, he had covered his scar with denim and was buttoning up a light shirt.

"The scar is why you don't wear shorts."

"I don't want questions. Or sympathy. Or revulsion." He finished buttoning his shirt, and his hands dropped to his sides.

"I wondered, when you wore jeans the other night and it so hot."

She put her purse down on the small dining table, wanting to sit but waiting to be invited to do so.

"Meeting Emma was hard enough. I didn't want to have to answer questions about my scar. Although I ended up talking to her about it, anyway."

He stood several feet away, not inviting her to make herself comfortable, and she felt more awkward with each passing moment.

"She had a wonderful time." Shannyn's lips curved a little, a slight invitation to make things more comfortable. Most of her temper had dissipated once she'd seen his scar. "Despite any mishaps. And she enjoyed our lunch out a lot."

"Then why are you here?"

Her smile vanished at his blunt tone, bringing back her motive with distinct clarity. "I think we need to work out a visitation schedule."

"A what?"

Shannyn blinked at his incredulous tone. She'd heard his voice on her answering machine and didn't know what to think. She'd thought that he would come over now and then, spend some time with Emma. But after their first meeting, he'd called with that lunch invitation, and now it was a plan for an air show. She didn't quite know how to feel about that. She wasn't sure Emma was ready for a one-on-one outing with Jonas. Wasn't sure Jonas was ready for that, either. And there was no rhyme or reason to his invitations. It made it awfully difficult to say no.

"Don't you think we should? Set up boundaries, I mean?"

He ran a hand over his cropped hair and shook his head. "You're serious."

Shannyn folded her hands in front of her. "Yes, I am. For one, Emma asks questions like a normal five-year-old. Like when you're coming over again. When she'll see you. What you'll do together. I don't know how to answer her, and that's not fair. It's confusing to her."

"But you must have gotten my message. About this weekend."

Shannyn nodded, wary of rushing the conversation, wanting to make sure she got it right. It was good that Jonas was excited about spending time with Emma, but she couldn't shake the nagging feeling that Jonas was facing his own demons right now and that it would be better if they spent time together with Shannyn around. If they set up boundaries, it would help her as much as it helped Emma. It would be easier if she knew and could prepare, rather than be hit with seeing him out of the blue.

"Yes, of course I got your message. And it was a reminder to me that we should talk this out, decide how we're going to proceed. I think your visitation should have structure."

"You're setting restrictions."

She bit down on her lip. Perhaps she was, but that wasn't exactly how she meant it to be. "I'm not trying to stiff you on time with her, Jonas. It's just…I'm not sure I'm comfortable with your plans for this weekend. I think it should be—"

"Supervised time." He finished the sentence flatly.

She sighed. "Can we sit down and talk about this? All this standing and gawking and I feel like we're going head to head or something."

He motioned towards the single item of furniture—the battered couch—and she sat down, comfortable until he took the cushion farthest away from her.

"Like I said—supervised time." He didn't let go of his point. "Unless you can show me that I can trust you with her."

She held her breath for a moment, expecting him to lose his

cool. Her fingers dug into the edge of the cushions. This wasn't going at all the way she'd hoped.

"You don't trust me. God, Shan. You should know I'd never do anything to hurt Emma." His eyes pinned her, hotly accusing. "Is that really what you think of me?"

Her fingers relaxed slightly, but she wasn't sure how to proceed. It wasn't a matter of trusting him, per se. She knew he'd never do anything to hurt Emma, not intentionally. Some of her doubts had to do with the changes in him, and she knew to broach the topic was to push a hot button.

But she also knew that many of her reservations had to do with herself and how she felt about being near him so often. It had been difficult enough, having Emma as a constant reminder of how much she'd loved him. Now to see him in the flesh on a regular basis—each time cut her a little deeper. It didn't get easier. Quite the opposite. Being with him reminded her both of how she'd felt about him and how little had changed.

"If you were in my shoes, would you let her go so easily? Look at this rationally. I don't doubt your intentions, not at all." She angled herself on the couch, scared to face him yet knowing she must. Knowing she had to say the hard words. "Six years ago you left and never looked back. And now you're here. You've discovered you have a daughter. I don't doubt your motives with regard to Emma. But you hate me for keeping her from you, and you are a different man. You can deny it all you want. But it's true. Something has changed you, and until I understand what and how it will affect Emma, the visits will be supervised."

He got up from the couch. "So what, I get to visit her at your house a few nights a week? What kind of father would that make me?"

"What kind of father do you want to be?"

She'd asked herself that same question all day. His message

hadn't even asked for a reply. He'd just said he would be there Saturday at one o'clock. It had sounded like an order, not an invitation. She'd been tempted to call, but decided talking to him in person would be better.

How *did* he see himself as a father? She'd wondered about it all the while she'd been at work and had gotten his address from his file. What did he want out of his relationship with his daughter? Wondered even as she'd stopped at home to change into her favorite jeans and top, knowing she was going to see him again. Asked it as she'd dropped Emma off for a play date at Lisa's and as she'd stood in the foyer of his apartment building for a full ten minutes before ringing the security buzzer.

What kind of father did Jonas want to be? A part-time one? Full time? She remembered the way he'd looked at her as he'd come across the lawn with Emma's hand in his. Did he want to be a father that sent presents on birthdays and Christmas or one-half of the set that included a wife and mother?

It was the last that caught her every time. Six years ago she might have accepted an offer like that. But she looked at him and could honestly say she didn't think she could trust him not to break her heart all over again. She didn't know how to compete with his career.

"Are you serious? What kind of father do I want to be?" He got up and started to pace, his gait only slightly uneven. "You're asking questions I don't know how to answer. I just go through this day to day, trying to make sense of everything. I'm sorry but my 'big picture' is slightly myopic right now!"

Shannyn took a deep breath, trying not to rise to the bait. "That's what I want to find out. How do you see this playing out? How involved do you want to be in Emma's life?"

He faced her squarely. "I want to be her father and everything that entails."

"It's not all bedtime stories and barbecues. Sometimes it's really hard. So you need to decide what sort of a commitment you can make to her. I don't want to get her hopes up only to have you decide it's too much and back away."

"You think I'd do that?"

"Your commitment record is a little shaky."

"Say what you mean. My commitment record is shaky with *you*."

Heat bloomed in her neck, making its way up to her cheeks. He was right. He'd never had a problem committing to the Army or his unit. He'd run from *her*. She needed to remember that.

"We need to settle this, Jonas."

"Shannyn, there is no 'we.' It's better that way and we both know it." He resumed pacing. "I cannot believe you are honestly sitting there thinking about there being a you and me."

Shannyn felt as though she'd been struck. Whether or not Jonas had been thinking it or not, she had, and it was clear to her now that any atmosphere she'd detected between them earlier, any flirting he'd promoted, had been misinterpreted.

She didn't trust him. She didn't know him. He was a different man but in some ways nothing had changed. For all her intentions today, Jonas was the one making the first real step to setting boundaries. It should have been a relief. Instead she found herself irrationally blinking back tears that she didn't want him to see.

"I'm sorry if that's harsh." His voice gentled slightly. "I just think we have to be honest here. You are still furious with me for not taking you with me. And I'm still angry with you for keeping Emma from me. To start anything between us would be foolish at the very least."

It sounded so perfectly reasonable.

She lifted her chin. She had been thinking it. How could she not, when the only man she'd ever loved was back and had landed smack-dab in her business? He was right about them being angry at each other, but it wasn't quite so easy for her to ignore the feelings she'd always had for him.

"You're right, of course," she responded, as coolly as she could. Somehow she had to get the topic back on track. "Regardless, we have to resolve the visitation issue."

He ran a hand over his head in frustration. "In the Army we just move on and leave the past behind."

She pointed at his leg. "That's a lie and you know it. There's a lot you haven't left behind."

"Let it go."

"I can't. I have to know."

"Know what?"

Her breath strangled her as she tried to straighten her shoulders. All these years she'd wondered, and now she had the opportunity to ask him and fear held her captive. No, she had to ask. She couldn't leave this time without knowing the truth.

"Why you left me without a word. Why *did* you do it, Jonas? You transferred out and never spoke to me again. Just like that. And I was left here with a baby on the way and no one to rely on but myself."

"You think it was easy to leave you?"

She was surprised at how he raised his voice. Somehow this was developing into an argument, but she kept it going because she thought perhaps it was the only way to get to the truth.

"That's exactly what I think. I think that you had your fun with me, but when the call came to go, you were ready. More than ready. I think you thought of nothing more than what was in your sights. Being a sharpshooter."

"You're wrong!"

She stood up, angry now because he'd never said a single word to make her think anything different. "How on earth would I know?"

The words hung in the air between them, crackling with hostility and something darker, something persuasive.

"Because of this."

Before she could breathe, he stepped up to her, gripped her waist with his right hand and pulled her close, pressing his lips to hers.

No warning. No prelude. Just mouth-to-mouth pent-up passion that made her knees turn watery and her heart pound ridiculously.

She wound her arms around his neck, kissing him back as if he were her lifeline.

The kiss gentled, grew fuller as their tongues twined and meshed. When he needed breath, he pulled away and rested his forehead against hers. She opened her eyes, marveling at seeing his lashes against his cheeks.

"Jonas," she whispered.

He pushed her away, stepping back, in control once more.

"You came here for answers, Shan. And I don't have answers. I don't have a plan or a schedule for this. You think I left you without a thought, and that's far from the truth. But you want more of me than I can give. You always have."

"No, I…"

"I'm Emma's father and I won't abandon her. But there's not enough of me for you, too. Don't you understand that?"

"Maybe if you helped me understand…"

"I can't. You'd better go."

Her thoughts, her senses, were all jumbled up and she couldn't make heads or tails of what had just happened. "About Saturday…I'm not comfortable with you taking Emma to the air show on your own. I think it's too soon."

"I never meant to take her by myself. The invitation was for both of you. Although that seems to be a mistake now, considering what just happened."

Shannyn paused, still trying to regain her balance. Maybe if she could get him in another setting. One that was more like the life he was comfortable with. Maybe then he'd open up a little, help her understand.

"It's a simple outing. Let's not make it more complicated than it has to be. If Emma agrees, we'll both go with you."

"If I'm going to build a relationship with her, we need to spend time together."

"I'm sorry if me coming with the package makes it difficult."

He smiled at her but it wasn't warm. "Don't worry about it. It's not my feelings that matter. She'll be more secure with you there with her, too."

Shannyn blinked. Somehow Jonas still had the ability to surprise her. His insight into Emma's feelings, even after their argument, was incredibly thoughtful.

"In the future, it might be good if you *asked* if we were busy or if it's a good time to visit. And I'll do my best to accommodate."

Jonas nodded. "I appreciate it."

"We're both feeling our way, Jonas. Let's just give it time."

"Time," he echoed, going to the door and opening it for her.

She'd had six years of time. Six years of resenting him for leaving and six years of remembering what it was to love him.

Now he was back—possibly for good.

Dealing with that wasn't anything time could cure.

"I'll see you Saturday," she offered weakly, grabbing her purse.

"One o'clock," he reminded her.

When the door shut behind her, she pressed her fingers to her lips. And knew that despite her best intentions, she was leaving with more questions than answers.

CHAPTER EIGHT

SHE'D forgotten about his physiotherapy appointment. After Jonas had discovered Emma was his, it had seemed pointless to change therapists, and when she'd reminded him briefly about the paperwork not being completed, he'd answered with a terse "never mind." Avoiding each other was no longer an option.

Thursday, when she checked the morning's files, his name was there—"Jonas Kirkpatrick"—and just seeing it sent a little thrill through her. A flutter in her tummy, a smile on her lips.

Oh no, she cautioned herself. Remembering the past was one thing, but getting fluttery and silly after a kiss was another matter altogether.

That kiss had been shocking. Not because he'd done it—there was enough chemistry sizzling between them lately it seemed inevitable now that she looked at it in hindsight—but the way the brief contact had affected her threw her for a loop. Her fingers ran possessively over the white label on his file.

She couldn't help but wonder what it had meant. In one breath they'd been arguing. Her words—"How on earth would I know?"—had precipitated it. Did it mean he hadn't been as flippant about leaving as she'd thought? Did he have regrets of his own? Or had it just been the frustration of the moment bubbling over?

She put the file back on the stack of morning appointments, letting her fingers linger over the brown material. His kiss was exactly the same as it had been years before. He tasted the same. The feel of his lips on hers ached with familiarity. She'd tried to dismiss all the signs. Credit the past for the long looks they'd shared or her reaction to his brief touches. Blaming the flutters on simple nostalgia and the fact that they shared a daughter. But actually kissing him again had been a turning point that she couldn't ignore.

Kissing him felt right in a way that nothing had been right since he'd gone away. With one kiss she started longing for things she hadn't let herself long for since Emma had been born.

With one kiss, it had stopped being about what had been between them in the past. And had moved firmly into the territory of what Shannyn wanted for the future.

And what she wanted terrified her. Loving Jonas would be a risk, and she wasn't a risk taker. He was still in the Army. He would still work where they told him to work. And she knew that he would still go, rather than choose her, choose them. She closed the appointment book firmly.

At that same moment the door opened and he walked through it, larger than life in his regular work clothes. His bearing—so straight, so tall and confident—garnered looks of approval.

Then his eyes met hers and she felt it clear to her core. The kiss that had been present in her memory now seemed to tingle on her lips. She could feel the way his fingers had dug into her arms as he pulled her close. The way his breath had fluttered against her cheeks as he pressed his forehead to hers.

He paused longer than necessary, the door handle forgotten in his hand. The longing to cross the room and find his arms again was crazy, but strong. Her breath caught. It wasn't that she hadn't moved on after Jonas. It wasn't that being a single mom made it hard to date, even though that's how she'd explained it for years.

Suddenly seeing him again, for the first time since they'd kissed, she realized that what she'd done all these years was waited. She'd been waiting for him.

And now here he was, a little older and with a lot more baggage, unwilling to let her in. And she was unwilling to ask him to.

Jonas must have realized how they were staring because he finally let the door handle go. It took its lazy time shutting behind him. He approached the desk, his eyes only leaving Shannyn's briefly as he gave his name to the receptionist.

Shannyn stepped forward. "Hello, Jonas." The words seemed strangled and forced. Yet to say more, here in public, seemed too intimate, inappropriate.

"Shan."

She swallowed at the warm tone of the single syllable. Was she just imagining it? Or did he seem less aloof now than he had before?

"I forgot about your appointment today."

"I didn't."

He put one hand in his pocket and balanced his weight on his good hip. Had he thought about that kiss as much as she had?

They had to stop staring at each other.

"I told Emma about Saturday. She's very excited."

His lips tipped up and her heart did a slow turnover. Simply knowing that he'd pleased their daughter made him smile and his eyes light, and that touched her.

"I'm excited, too. I've got to be on base in the morning, otherwise I could have taken you both to the static display."

"Don't worry." She dipped her head, suddenly shy. "We're both looking forward to the afternoon."

His eyebrows came together a bit, and she licked her lips nervously.

"Me, too," was his simple reply. His forehead relaxed and she thought for a moment he was going to come toward her.

She turned her head slightly at the sound of a door opening. "It looks like Geneva is ready for you now."

He turned toward the door leading to the treatment area.

"Jonas?"

He stopped, turning only his head to look at her.

The words stuck in her throat. "Nothing, never mind," she muttered. "I'll see you when you're done."

He was gone several minutes when curiosity got the better of her. She rarely interrupted a therapy session, but today she wanted to see—to really see—what had happened to his leg. More than an accidental glimpse of the angry scar marring the skin of his thigh. He had been so self-conscious about it the other day. And she knew if she were to ask to see it, he'd find an excuse.

She knocked on the door to the exercise room. Inside she saw Jonas on a blue mat on the floor, Geneva kneeling beside him, her touch gentle on his leg as he bent at the waist, stretching the stiff muscles.

"Hi," she offered quietly.

Jonas looked up. "Shannyn."

He was wearing gray shorts, the line of his incision clear and imprecise. His eyes darted away from hers, the twist of his mouth communicating his consternation. She probably wasn't playing fair. He couldn't hide his injury from her here.

But he needed to know she accepted him with it, so she stepped into the room and moved ahead to a bench a few feet away.

"We're just finishing up," Geneva explained, smiling at Shannyn. By now the staff all pretty much knew that Jonas was Emma's father; it was difficult to keep very much a secret in such a small group. "You want some privacy?"

Jonas colored while Shannyn smiled, shaking her head. "No, that's okay. I just wanted to see how he was making out."

She turned her attention fully to Jonas. He lengthened out his leg, his foot nearly reaching the end of the mat. "Soooo." She drew the word out. "How are you?"

"Not bad, besides having a gimp leg," he grumbled.

"You're hardly limping anymore."

"That's right," Geneva added. "Your range of motion and strength are really coming along."

He finished stretching out his quadriceps, and Shannyn heard the small gasp as he reached the point where he could go no further. When Geneva let him relax the pose, she got to her feet. "Good work today, Jonas. I'll see you next week. Don't forget to work on those stretches every day."

She left, leaving Jonas on the mat and Shannyn on the bench beside him.

"Why are you here?" He folded his legs, partially covering the scar with his arm.

"Because here it's harder for you to hide. You reveal all to your PT but the moment I catch a glimpse of your leg, you run and cover up. I wanted to see it."

His lips thinned. "Why? It's just a scar."

Shannyn tucked her hair behind her ears, then shook her head in disagreement. "It's more than a scar. It's more than a physical injury, Jonas, and you know it."

"But it's my problem, not yours."

"What if I said I wanted to help you?"

He'd been avoiding her gentle gaze, but now he faced her head-on, frustration a dark spark in his eyes. "I'd say you're crazy."

Shannyn slid off the bench and onto her knees on the mat. Maybe she was crazy. But now they were bound by the link of their daughter. Her lingering feelings for him meant that when he was hurting, she was, too, even if she didn't understand exactly why. His kiss said he wasn't immune to her, either.

"We have a past, Jonas. And now we have a daughter. That ties us, don't you see?" She looked straight into his eyes. "We may not be together anymore, but I still care about what happens to you."

Her heart pounded as she put a cool hand on his knee. "Let me help you."

Verbally she'd denied their attraction, but the touch of her fingers on his skin belied the message. With her index finger she gently traced the incision line, noticing how the skin felt different there, thrilling as the muscle beneath her finger contracted at her touch. "I want to help you."

"What if I don't want you to?"

She stopped her finger and let her palm fall. She realized that the scar was longer than the length of her hand. The fact that he could do as much as he could now was a miracle.

"Are you saying you *don't* want me to?"

She leaned forward, moving closer to him. He was balanced on his palms, but when he lifted his right hand, the balance shifted, pushing him closer to her. His fingers reached behind her ear, pulling the hair taut and cupping her neck.

"What if I wanted to kiss you and that's all?"

Her pounding heart shifted into overdrive. The idea was seductive even as she realized by saying it he was refusing to let her in for more than a kiss. Still…if kissing him could break down barriers…help her understand…

She didn't wait but leaned the rest of the way and touched his mouth with hers.

He pushed further forward, taking his other hand off the mat and sliding it behind her other ear, forming a perfect cradle for her head as he opened his mouth, letting her in.

It was sweet perfection, better than the one in his living room. That kiss had been fast, new and fueled by anger and frustration. This time they were both going into it knowing what was coming, and it showed. No rushing, but a willing coming together, soft and accepting. Soon her knees ached and she leaned slightly, curling into his lap while his hands adjusted her head to the right fit.

And still the kiss went on.

He moaned into her mouth, the sound vibrating through her like a string that had been plucked. Her arms curled around his neck and her weight shifted.

He stiffened, going perfectly still before letting her go and resting back on his hands again.

His eyes closed, his mouth no longer soft with passion but tight with pain.

"Oh, Jonas, I'm so sorry," Shannyn gasped, sliding off his lap and kneeling beside him. "I didn't mean to hurt you."

"It's okay."

"What can I do to help?"

"You've done enough."

She recoiled as if slapped, sliding backward and sitting back up on the bench.

Jonas pushed away and got up, less than graceful after the bump to his injury.

"I need to get changed."

Sitting on the low bench, his scar was nearly at Shannyn's eye level. She dragged her eyes away and looked up at him. "Why does it sound like you're blaming me?"

"Maybe I am." He started to walk away.

"We need to talk about this."

"You're awfully fond of talking." His words came back to her as he kept going toward the door.

She ignored his bitter tone. "We can't just leave things this way, Jonas."

He stopped, didn't turn around, but she saw his shoulders rise and fall in a frustrated sigh. They both knew that avoiding each other wouldn't work. They had to clear the air.

"A cup of coffee. That's all I have time for this morning."

A cup of coffee would do if that's all he'd give. At least it would get them out of the office and somewhere neutral. So much of their time lately had been on his turf or hers.

"Sold. I'll meet you out in reception when you're ready."

When he came out minutes later, she grabbed her purse and hustled from behind her desk. She didn't trust him not to leave without waiting for her.

"There's a Timmy's around the corner," he said as they emerged on to the sidewalk. He thumbed in the general direction of a popular coffee chain.

But it would be too easy to get a coffee there and go their separate ways, and Shannyn wanted to hold on to him a little bit longer.

"There's a place I know on Queen that makes great iced cappuccino."

He paused, looking again at the familiar coffee shop and back at her.

"All right."

Jonas followed along, this once. Kissing her had been a mistake, he realized. Both times. The first time he'd been angry and frustrated and remembering all too clearly what it had been like to leave her at the end of that summer. And this morning…this morning had been madness. He knew what folly it was to kiss her again and he'd gone ahead and done it anyway. Slid his hands into that soft hair and pulled her close.

He knew better. He should be putting more distance between them, not kissing her. No matter how he felt about her, the one thing he was sure of was that this would all end badly. It would be better for everyone to stop it all right now. She knew it too, and he was angry with her for putting him in such a position.

She'd initiated the contact, the kiss. And now he was going to have to put a stop to this sort of thing ever happening again.

She stopped before a coffee shop and opened the door, her hair swinging in the breeze as she looked over her shoulder. "You coming?"

He followed her inside and looked around. It certainly wasn't his normal type of establishment. Trendy decor, drinks with long, nearly unpronounceable names. It looked to be a place more suited to poetry readings than a quick cup of joe.

"Jonas? Aren't you going to order?"

He stepped up to the counter, looked at the woman in the plain apron and dared, "Large coffee. Black."

A minute later they picked up their drinks, and Shannyn led them to a table in the corner.

"This wasn't what I had in mind when I said a quick cup of coffee."

She smiled at him but it seemed frail around the edges. "I know."

Not knowing how to respond to that, he took a sip from his cup. For all that the atmosphere wasn't his style, they did know how to brew a good cup of coffee. Shannyn dropped her eyes and sipped on her iced drink, then made circles with her straw.

"Jonas, I wanted to talk because…because something is obviously happening between us and we owe it to Emma to make sure there's as little confusion as possible."

Her logic made sense, but he saw through it. She looked a little too earnest, too innocent. He never should have kissed her the other day. It had sent the wrong message and he'd been foolish to act so impulsively. She wanted more. He could sense it.

"This isn't about pinning me down to some sort of expectation, then."

She had the grace to look uncomfortable. She shifted in her seat and looked down at her cup again.

"Shan, I told you the other day. You want answers and I don't have them. Kissing you was a mistake." He folded his hands on the table before him. "Both times. Because there can't be anything between us."

"But there is something between us. Emma." Shannyn leaned forward, imploring.

"And I want to do the right thing by her, and be a good father. But you and me…it wouldn't work. I hurt you badly when I left. And you destroyed my faith in you when you lied to me. We can't pretend that doesn't exist."

Jonas had to look away after he said it. He wasn't good at lying to her face. Whether or not there should be more to their relationship was irrelevant. There already was. The kisses proved it.

She studied her straw for a few moments. "I knew you were going to say that."

How could he make her understand without telling her more than he should? There was so much inside of him, and it was all so jumbled together that to even attempt anything would be like trying to untangle a ball of string. One complication would get sorted and another knot would present itself. How could he put them all through it?

He knew the things he'd done, the regrets he had. There was no way he wanted to put those on Shannyn or Emma. Even if Shannyn didn't understand it, he knew it was the right thing.

"You have to understand, I'm not the same person I was then. I'm…I've seen and done a lot of things over the years. Things that mean I'll never be the same. It wouldn't be fair to you to bring all that to the table in addition to everything else."

She looked up at him, sipping her drink. He wished she'd say something so he could rid himself of the feeling that he was hanging himself. But she stayed quiet, forcing him to keep talking to avoid empty silence.

"And what would happen if we took things further and then it all fell apart? Who's the real casualty going to be then? Emma."

He felt momentarily guilty for that statement. Shannyn had used Emma's existence as protection only moments before and now he was doing the same thing. The truth of the matter was that he knew *he'd* end up hurt. Worse, he would hurt Shannyn again and that was the last thing he wanted. It had hurt badly enough the first time.

"I think it would be better for everyone if we were just friends."

He was finished. To his mind there was nothing more to say.

She pushed the drink aside, studied her fingers for a few seconds before looking up. She was so beautiful. Gazing into her youthful, hopeful face he felt old and world-weary. He could see what she wanted, even if she denied it to herself. She wanted the fairy tale. The happily-ever-after. And he was the last person on earth to give it to her.

Fairy tales were just that. Tales. They didn't exist. They were there to give false hope in a world that was darker than even she realized.

"What about the kisses?" Her voice ached with sweetness and he wished things were different. That he could just forget it all and love her like she wanted.

"An echo from the past, that's all."

It had the desired effect: her eyes dropped and her shoulders relaxed.

He should let it end there, but he hated knowing he'd hurt her in any way.

"I still want you to come to the air show on Saturday. We're still going to parent Emma, and I meant what I said. We should be friends."

"Friends would be the mature thing to do," she agreed, but the light had gone out of her eyes.

It was better now, he reasoned. A small disappointment now versus a big one later.

"I need to get back to the base."

"I need to get back to work, too. I've probably taken too much time as it is."

Shannyn picked up her cup. The mocha-flavored mixture had lost its appeal. She'd obviously misread his signals from before. Foolishly she'd let herself hope that maybe she still meant something to him. This morning his touch had been so tender, so gentle. And fantasy had gotten the best of her and she'd allowed herself to picture the three of them—herself, Jonas, Emma—all together, happy and strong.

What she'd done was let herself be foolish and forget all the reasons why she and Jonas wouldn't work. He was right. She still resented him for leaving, and despite moments of accord, she knew he couldn't put aside the fact that she'd kept Emma hidden from him.

Apparently he hadn't had the same vision of familial bliss. She wasn't surprised. He hadn't wanted those things before, either. It wasn't his fault she'd let silly fancy sweep her away after a few kisses. She needed to do what she'd always done. Make sure Emma was safe, secure and happy.

If being friends with Jonas was the way to do that, she'd do it. Even if it killed her.

They were outside in the glaring brilliance of late morning when a call interrupted their steps.

"Sgt. Kirkpatrick!"

Jonas and Shannyn turned as a fresh-faced young man jogged up. Like Jonas, he was dressed in ordinary combats, only two stripes on his sleeve instead of the three that Jonas sported.

"Good morning, Corporal." Jonas smiled.

"I'm glad I ran into you." The young soldier grinned. "I'm sorting a few things before I leave tomorrow."

"You're shipping out?" Shannyn interjected.

He looked at her, the smile never leaving his face. "Yes ma'am. Sgt. Kirkpatrick was my instructor. I'm headed for Base Petawawa in the morning."

"I see."

"Good luck to you, Cpl. Benner." Jonas held out his hand. "Give 'em hell."

"Count on it."

Shannyn realized that the effusive youth before her was a man ready to do a man's job, with an infectious enthusiasm she recalled seeing on Jonas's face that same summer he'd gone to Edmonton. When she looked up at Jonas, she was surprised to see a mixture of pride, enthusiasm and longing beaming from his features.

He hadn't changed. Not that much.

"You look like you wish you could go with him," she teased.

The men broke hands and Jonas looked down at her. "Maybe I do…but those days seem to be over."

"Oh, I don't know," Corporal Benner joked. "I saw you running on the course the other day, and the leg's looking great." The young man turned his attention to Shannyn. "Sgt. Kirkpatrick is something of a hero on base, ma'am. Best shot in the country, if the rumors are true."

"Benner," Jonas started to protest.

"Not many men do what he's done and live to tell about it, ma'am, and that's the truth. It's too bad he's not still out in the field. We all count ourselves the luckiest bast…fellas in the Army to have him as a teacher."

"Cpl. Benner," Jonas said more firmly.

"Sorry, Sarge." Benner looked a little sheepish, but not enough to resist throwing Shannyn a wink. "But it's true."

He held out his hand to Jonas again. "I've got to get going, but thanks again, Sgt. Kirkpatrick."

"Good luck, Benner."

"Thanks. Ma'am." He nodded at Shannyn before jogging away.

"He's had his caffeine this morning," Shannyn laughed lightly. She was still reeling from all that the young soldier had said. Jonas was a hero. He'd done great things. Things he refused to talk about.

"He's young, and full of the belief he can make the world a better place," Jonas responded, his face clouding. "Give him a few weeks in combat and that'll all change."

"Like it did for you?"

He didn't answer. They resumed their steps, walking back to the clinic.

"Jonas? Are you really a hero?"

He snorted, a humorless chuckle of irony. "Hardly."

"Then why would Cpl. Benner say it?"

He wouldn't look at her. "I have no idea."

He was hiding something, but she didn't know what. She wondered what he might have done that constituted hero status.

She tried a different tack. "Are you really the best shot in the Army?"

He kept walking, his gait even and steady. "There's an official sniping record in place. My name ain't on it."

"But unofficially?"

He angled his head in her direction, a wry smile cracking his stony expression at her tenacity and insight. "Unofficially is another story."

She couldn't stop the beam of pride that shot through her at his admission. It was what he'd wanted, when he'd been younger and idealistic like Benner. It made her proud to know he'd accomplished his goal.

"And you really did run the other day?"

"Yeah."

They were back at the parking lot, and their steps slowed as they reached his truck.

"Thanks for the coffee," she said.

"You're welcome. I'm…I'm glad we got things straightened out. I think it'll be better for everyone if we keep things clear. If we keep things friendly between us. Consistent for Emma."

He wanted to be friends.

Shannyn looked up into his eyes, wishing he'd look at her again the way he had once. Free of shutters and caution. Hungry to drink in the sight of her face the same way she was his. She was more certain than ever that Jonas had done great things, even if he refused to talk about it. Every day, as his recovery progressed, she sensed a greater strength in him. It was hard not to be attracted to that. Even harder to resist a man who was concerned about her daughter. It was all she'd ever wanted. It was hard to hate him for pushing her aside, when it was clearly to Emma's benefit.

"We're still good for Saturday?"

"We're good." He smiled. "Tell Emma I'm looking forward to it."

"I will."

Their gazes clung for a few seconds and her heart lifted. Because no matter what came out of his mouth, his eyes said there was something more.

He climbed into the truck and started the engine. As she watched him drive away, she wished she weren't looking forward to it quite so much.

CHAPTER NINE

WHEN Shannyn answered the doorbell, Jonas was surprised to see that both she and Emma were dressed in red and white.

Shannyn's hair was plaited in an intricate braid, revealing the pale curve of her neck. For a brief second, he remembered how she'd felt in his arms just a few days ago. Her long legs extended beneath the hem of her shorts and ended with cute white tennis shoes. Legs that had been folded up into his lap as she'd pressed her chest to his. He longed to run his fingers over the smooth length of them.

This was ridiculous. He was here for an outing, nothing more. He'd made it perfectly clear during their coffee date that more wasn't possible. No matter what he truly felt. Protecting her was more important than his attraction.

"I didn't realize you'd take the festivities quite this seriously," he joked, looking down at Emma. Despite their similar dress of white shorts and red T-shirts, he realized again how much Emma resembled him, and it filled him with paternal joy. He remembered seeing pictures of himself as a small boy. The eyes, the curls, the shape of the lips...there was no doubt Emma was his daughter, and he felt a shaft of pride knowing it.

"It's Canada Day. If ever there were a day to be patriotic..."

"Then it's today," he agreed. Being in the forces, much of his identity and pride was wrapped up in his nationality. It was more than a long weekend to him. Spending it with Shannyn was probably not the smartest move, but he was determined to enjoy this one last indulgence. Soon she'd see that Emma could spend time with him alone, and these family scenes would come to an end. It would be the smart thing to do.

"You look great. I didn't realize you'd dress up, so I brought something for you to put on before we go." He held out a small bag, handed it to Emma. She reached inside and pulled out a flat package covered in plastic.

"Tattoos!"

He smiled. He hadn't been able to resist the temporary, maple leaf tattoos at the store where he'd stopped for snacks on his way to the house.

"Should we put them on?"

"Mama?"

Jonas smiled at the indulgent way Shannyn looked at Emma. When she turned her warm gaze back to him, his grin broadened. It would be a different sort of Canada Day than they'd spent together before, but he was no less happy with it. Maybe there wouldn't be swimming followed by fireworks on a blanket…but he could see she hadn't lost her sense of fun. He had worried about there being tension between them today. So much had happened since his last visit with Emma. Perhaps Shannyn had taken his plea to heart to stay friends for Emma's sake.

Shannyn held open the door. "Why not. Come on in."

Emma went first, choosing to have her maple leaf emblazoned on her cheek. "Very cool," Jonas complimented. Emma spun to rush to the bathroom and check the mirror. When Jonas looked back, Shannyn was waiting for him with tattoo and sponge at the ready.

"Where do you want it?"

He met her eyes. The kitchen was strangely quiet without Emma's vivacity. "On my cheek, too, I guess. I didn't have time to change after working this morning, so it won't be visible anywhere else."

Shannyn took one from the packet that was shaped like a rippling flag. Suddenly his combat jacket seemed tight, constricting. When her cool fingers touched his skin he held his breath. She was so gentle. Standing so close, the tip of her tongue between her teeth as she concentrated, rubbing the temporary sticker with the damp sponge.

He wondered what it would be like to kiss her again. *Stop thinking about it, you fool,* he fretted to himself. Two kisses had been more than enough to tell him he was in dangerous territory. He'd been the one to put on the brakes, and he'd do well to remember it. It had been the right decision. No matter how she made him feel, he knew it was better all around this way. He wasn't capable of more. There could be no kisses or meaningful touches.

Before he could think about it further, she stepped away. "There you go. All done."

Shannyn put the sponge down on the counter. What had started out as a fun game had suddenly changed. As soon as she'd touched the smooth skin of his cheek, she'd been reminded of the way he'd kissed her at his apartment. Without prelude, without apology. Like the years between them hadn't happened. The way he'd cupped her neck and she'd crawled into his lap on Thursday.

"What about you?" he asked hoarsely.

She swallowed. The last thing she needed right now was him touching her, in any way. She took the last tattoo and pressed it against her arm. "I can do my own. Why don't you take Emma out and buckle her in?"

"Shannyn, I…"

She looked up from her arm, holding the paper against the skin. "I know. I get it. Friends, Jonas."

He paused, his eyes unsure. Shannyn made herself hold her ground. It was tempting to want to know what he'd meant to say, but the boundaries had been set, and the more she thought about it, the more she realized it was the right approach.

"I'm glad you're coming," he finished, looking away.

She was glad, too. Too glad. At first, seeing him had been a shock, then a complication she didn't want. And then something had changed. She'd stopped resenting him quite so much. Had started thinking of him while she lay in bed at night.

But now there was Emma to consider, and Shannyn had been hurt badly enough that there was some comfort in being friends. It was safer. It was still complicated, maybe even more than it had been in the beginning. But it was because the more she saw him the more she was reminded of how much there had been between them. How much there still *was* between them. She'd promised herself she'd be strong. It was proving more difficult with each day. She had such a weakness for him. Nothing had changed for her, except now she was unwilling to risk her heart. She'd jumped in recklessly the first time and it was a lesson well learned. She'd tested those waters the other day over coffee, and it had reinforced her knowledge that she couldn't go through a full-fledged breakup with him again. Not ever.

Nothing had changed for Jonas, either, and that was the sticking point. He hadn't cared enough to make a life with her before, and he'd made it clear on Thursday that he still didn't. Only as Emma's parents, and that was the sum of their relationship.

But it didn't stop her from caring, not when he looked at her the way he was looking at her right now.

"I'll be right out," she whispered, not trusting herself to say more.

Jonas took Emma to the truck. When Shannyn joined them

a few minutes later, she couldn't help but smile at Emma's chatter. She threw out questions at a mile a minute. Where were they going to watch from? What sorts of planes would there be? Would it be noisy? Had he flown in any of them? Jonas happily answered all her questions, and Shannyn listened to his answers, with Emma sandwiched snugly between them.

Emma's nonstop talking kept the truck from being too quiet and within a few minutes they had crossed the bridge and found parking on the north side of the river.

"I thought the crowd would be smaller on this side," he explained, reaching behind the bench seat for an army blanket and the grocery bag of snacks.

"This is fine," Shannyn answered, and they made their way to an empty space on the grass.

Jonas spread the blanket, and Shannyn felt strangely as if they were on a regular family outing. It didn't matter that their family wasn't a "normal" family unit. Looking around, the scene was much the same. Parents out with children, spreading blankets and handing out water bottles and juice boxes. Others sat in couples, but all waited to see the aircraft fly one by one up the river's path. Some would perform stunts; others would simply showcase their aeronautical abilities and impressive structures. Sitting down on the blanket, she watched Jonas strip his jacket. He leaned back on his arms and soaked up the summer sun.

"You look rested," Shannyn commented, assuming a similar pose.

"I feel rested. Better than I have in a long time."

"Mama! There's a hot dog cart." Emma bounded over and tugged on Shannyn's finger. "Can I get one?"

Jonas sat back up and reached into his jacket for keys. "I can't believe I forgot. I brought a bag of food and left it in the truck."

Shannyn put a hand on his arm. "You stay and enjoy the sun. Emma and I will go." She took the keys from his hand.

He watched them go with a smile. Looking across the green, his eyes fell on a young couple. The man was in combats, like Jonas. He had blond hair and an easy way about him that reminded him of Chris Parker.

The muscles in Jonas's shoulders tightened. He was torn, being here with Shannyn and their daughter, enjoying a summer's afternoon. He wanted it both ways. He kept insisting there could be nothing between them, but at the first opportunity he was with her enjoying her company. He listened to the birds in the elms and maples, his eyes staring up into the cloudless blue sky. What really wasn't fair was that Parker wouldn't ever feel the sun on his face again. And yet Jonas was here. Free. Healthy. With a family he never knew he had. It didn't seem right to him.

Didn't seem right without his best friend.

Dust. Everywhere, on his skin, in his hair, in his mouth.

"I've got him at the door." Chris's hushed murmur came from beside him.

"I've got him, Park."

"You're clear. Take the shot."

The midafternoon sun was unrelenting and he blinked against a bead of sweat that trickled into his eye.

He squeezed the trigger, heard the echo of the shot. Seconds later he saw the body fall through his scope.

"Damn," Parker murmured, still keeping his voice low. "Over twenty-six hundred. How's it feel to hold the new record?"

Jonas angled a wry look over his shoulder. "It feels classified."

He laughed quietly and they slid back down the embankment, efficiently folding their gear and packing it.

"Good job today. Make sure you've got your canteen. We've got five miles to hike before we're picked up, and we're already behind."

Two hours later they were back with the company they'd been assigned to. And thirty minutes after that they were all heading back to the airfield where they'd meet up with the platoon.

"Daddy. We got the bag."

Jonas came out of the memory with a start and struggled to appear normal. Normal. That was a joke.

Shannyn reached the blanket, and he knew he hadn't covered up his lapse completely because her expression clearly said she knew something was up.

"Emma, why don't you go look at the ducks for a moment while I talk to Jonas. We'll have a snack soon."

Emma went closer to the bank, creeping up on the ducks and gulls that were in the grass. Her giggles reached Jonas's ears and he took long breaths, forcing himself to relax.

"You okay?"

"Yeah." She didn't need to know what he'd been remembering. Besides, it was over now. And this time the memory had been shorter, and he'd snapped back quickly. Maybe it was getting better after all.

"Your leg's all right?"

"Seriously, Shan. I'm fine. I'm just glad to be here."

She took her place back on the blanket, stretching out her legs and drinking in the summer sun. "Your physiotherapy is helping. I noticed at your appointment, and watching you walk today."

Jonas squinted through the sun to look at her, her blond hair gleaming, her slim legs crossed at the ankles. She'd painted her toenails a patriotic red. It helped to rid himself of the memory of Chris Parker. "Emma is helping more."

Just as he said it, Emma plopped down on the blanket next to his knee. "I'm thirsty."

Jonas slapped his leg, ridding himself of the glumness. "By George, so am I. I wonder what's in this bag anyway."

He handed Emma the bag and let her root through it. "Mama! There's lemonade! The pink kind!"

He grinned as Emma pulled out a bottle. "We'd better open it before it gets warm."

Shannyn watched the two of them with a lump in her throat. His fingers unscrewed the cap on the bottle before handing it to Emma and then ruffling her hair. Jonas frightened her on so many levels, but seeing how he responded to Emma touched her deeply. He'd come back and had started making demands, never asking, always expecting his orders to be followed. He'd been cold and autocratic. She supposed his training had taught him that. And naturally she balked at being told what to do. She'd been doing the parent thing single-handedly for years.

Emma reached into the bag and pulled out a paper-wrapped package before plunking herself back on Jonas's lap.

Jonas's penchant for bossiness wasn't what scared her. What scared her most were moments like these. Normal family moments. Moments she deeply wanted for Emma, but ones that were dangerous for her. She couldn't let fancy get the best of her. Like now, when his low laugh reached her ears. The way the muscles corded when Emma tripped and he caught her in his arms. Remembering those arms wrapped around her.

"Shan?"

Jonas held out his hand to her, even that simple gesture tying them together. "I brought sandwiches."

"You mean, you brought a picnic," she teased, but her smile was weak. Jonas had thought of everything, it seemed. It pleased her but threw her off her stride. Usually she was the one looking after details like snacks and blankets.

"I came prepared." He flashed a grin at her.

His grin was like a bolt of lightning, reaching into her and bringing her to life. It made it seem like Jonas had never been

away. Even though she knew that being friends was absolutely
the right thing to do, she also recognized that it wouldn't take
much for her heart to be completely lost all over again. And that
terrified her. There were still so many questions between them
that were unanswered. Answers she wanted to share with him but
that he was unwilling to give. And a niggling fear that if she knew
the truth, maybe he was right. Maybe she wouldn't look at him
in the same way.

He still held out the sandwich and wiggled his eyebrows at
her. In all the times she'd seen him since he'd returned, never had
he been this mellow, this approachable. Maybe he was feeling
as comfortable in their new "friend" capacity as she was uncomfortable. She took the paper packet from his hand and unwrapped
it. "You sure did."

For minutes they munched quietly. Emma sat in the vee of
Jonas's outstretched legs, her head leaning back against his chest.
He lifted one arm and pointed out over the river at a duck taking
off; Emma raised a finger and followed the same path. When
Emma's glowing face turned to say something, he leaned forward
and kissed her forehead as laughter shook his chest.

There was no denying it now. He was a part of Emma's life
and by extension, hers, too. And somehow she would have to find
a way to fortify her heart against him. Keep the status quo. Make
sure nobody got hurt. Establish themselves as friends, the way
he wanted. For Shannyn the way to her heart had never been with
pretty speeches or flowers or any of the traditional trappings. She
found that seeing him with Emma, seeing how he naturally responded to her, touched her in a profound way.

But he didn't love her. Perhaps he never had. So she'd have
to bury her own emotions if it came to that.

The very thought seemed laughable. She could never be just
friends with Jonas. Feelings would always get in the way.

The loudspeaker crackled and an unseen emcee's voice echoed over the riverbank.

Shannyn watched the show quietly, absorbing the way Jonas put his arm around Emma to point out features of the different aircraft. There were small biplanes and single-engine private craft. A pair of old WWII bombers flew up the river in formation, their engines rumbling loudly. Jonas laughed when Emma put her hands over her ears as the CF-18s did a fly-by and when she laughed at the painted nose of the A-10 as it screamed past.

"Do you know what they call that?" he asked her.

She shook her head and he grinned. "A warthog."

She giggled. Shannyn caught his eye. "She's having a wonderful time."

"So am I." His gaze held hers, making the simple words mean more.

"Me, too," Shannyn replied, and meant it. She was glad she'd come along, although from the way Jonas and Emma were getting along, she needn't have worried about them spending time alone. She'd never seen him so relaxed, and it was clear Emma trusted him completely.

The river quieted as the announcer told everyone to listen. An aircraft was approaching. Still, there was no sound. Jonas's smile grew with each passing second. He nodded to Shannyn, then pointed at a speck behind them in the distance. It took her a few seconds to find it, but his trained eye had picked it up right away.

Still there was no sound, until suddenly the plane passed in front of them and the boom followed. Jonas's voice echoed the announcer—"That's a B1B stealth bomber."

When the words were out of his mouth, his face clouded over. His jaw tensed slightly and his eyes lost all their warmth. Shannyn could tell he was remembering something. She wished he'd tell her what. What was so painful that the memory kept haunting him over and over? What was it he couldn't get past?

After the bomber, they looked up high and saw a parachute team jump. Emma's finger pointed and her mouth made an O as the jumpers got closer and closer, their chutes billowing in the wind as they steered themselves toward the ground. Shannyn looked away from the parachute team and examined Jonas instead. Something was wrong. Emma was talking to him, but his face looked as if it had been carved in stone. His eyes, clear green, focused on nothing in particular and his chest barely rose and fell as he breathed. He was pulling away again but this time something was different, and Shannyn couldn't put her finger on it.

One by one the parachutes landed in a wide circle that had been marked off, and the audience clapped enthusiastically. The speaker started again, remarking on the team's accuracy and telling the crowd to look downriver. As the team divested themselves of their chutes, a helicopter wound its way up and toward the wide white-marked circumference—waiting to extract the team.

As the announcer droned on about the challenges of a quick extraction in a combat situation, Shannyn never took her eyes off Jonas. Her heart pounded as his face paled and his hands started to visibly shake. In a matter of a few seconds, he'd gone from vibrant father to a marble statue.

"Emma," she said quietly, tugging on the little girl's sleeve. "Emma, come sit with Mama for a moment."

At Shannyn's quiet, commanding tone, Emma did what she was told. Shannyn put Emma by her right hip, so that she was between Emma and Jonas. The helicopter came closer, closer, the syncopated rhythm filling her ears while Jonas remained deathly calm.

One by one the parachute team was loaded into the waiting helicopter, the end of the performance. But Shannyn felt real fear when she saw a single tear trickle down Jonas's pale cheek. His eyes never blinked, his lips never moved, but that one tear crawled its way down his cheek and dropped off his jaw.

CHAPTER TEN

NOTHING existed beyond the sound.

Heavy rotor blades cut through the air as the Chinook hovered a few feet from the ground. Jonas could see the pilot, the helicopter close enough that he could see the headset over his ears and his lips moving as he spoke into the mike, the deafening noise of the helo drowning out the nearby voices.

"Let's clear these men out!" The announcer crowed with enthusiasm.

"Let's clear out, eh, Parker? Or that fiancée of yours'll get bored and find someone else," Jonas teased his partner as they bounced along the dirt road.

"Yeah, well it sure won't be you," Parker shot back with a wide grin.

Jonas laughed.

The Iltis hit a rut, jostling the soldiers sitting in the back. "Hey, Sgt. Kirkpatrick. There's something up ahead."

Jonas leaned forward, peering through the windshield of the Iltis. Before he could open his mouth, everything shifted. He felt himself thrown into the air, out of the back of the vehicle. For a moment he was weightless. And everything went black.

At first he was only aware of sounds. Shouts and skids as the rest of the vehicles in their small convoy ground to a halt behind them. Then it was smells.

The heavy, coppery scent of blood mingled with dust filled his nostrils in the desert heat, but he saw nothing. Sudden weakness caused his eyes to close against the blinding sun. Gunfire echoed, tinny and thin, along with the dry crackle of fire—the charred, mangled pieces of the Iltis.

Everything was fuzzy, like being underwater.

With huge effort, Jonas turned his head to the left, opening his eyes enough to squint. What he saw was a narrow radius of carnage. Parker was dead, his mangled form sprawled motionless on the hard gravel of the road. Jonas blindly touched his leg, drawing his shaking fingers up and seeing the blood staining the tips as he fought the nausea curling through his stomach. Behind him he heard the shouts of his comrades; rifle fire popping over the ridge.

He heard a shout for a medic. He heard someone calling to get on the radio for an extraction. His eyes slid closed, trying to keep things linear and logical in his mind. Confused shouts echoed all around him.

"Hold on, Sarge." A steady voice was at his right side, but he couldn't distinguish who it was. Hands pressed against his leg and he gritted his teeth. "Help's coming. Hang in there."

The syncopated whomp-whomp of helo blades reached his ears. He squinted into the sun, enough to see the dark hulking shape of a Chinook hovering several meters away. The feeling was leaving his leg, the cold numbness crawling up the rest of his body, and he knew it was too late.

"Jonas," Shannyn said, reaching over and gripping his arm.

He turned his head, his eyes unfocused.

"Park! No!" He gave a mighty shout and leaped to his feet.

He paused and then without saying a single word, he ran up the embankment toward the truck.

Shannyn pulled back as if burned, shocked by his outburst and frightened, not for herself but for him. She knew without a doubt that he hadn't seen *her* when he'd looked into her eyes. She wanted to race after him, but she had Emma to worry about. "Honey, you pack up the food and I'll get the blanket, okay?" She ignored the stares of people around them and hastily folded the green blanket, gathering it and Jonas's jacket in her arms.

"What's wrong with Daddy?"

Shannyn gripped Emma's hand tightly. This was what she'd wanted to avoid. Putting Emma through any sort of stress. Shannyn should have known at their first meeting, when Emma had hit his leg. She should have known when he had those moments when time seemed to stop completely. Now Emma's face mirrored her own—concerned and frightened. Shannyn was torn between concern for Emma and worry for Jonas.

She paused a moment, squatted before Emma because she didn't know what frame of mind he'd be in when they got to the truck.

"I don't know for sure, Emma. But I think your daddy has some very bad memories. And I think that helicopter today reminded him of something bad, and he got scared."

"Daddies don't get scared."

Shannyn pulled her into a quick hug.

"Yes, honey, they sometimes do." She pulled away and held Emma by the arms, fighting to keep her own hands from trembling. "Mommies *and* daddies. Now, when we get back to the truck, Daddy might still be upset. So you're going to do exactly what I tell you, okay?"

"Yes, Mama," Emma replied meekly.

When Shannyn got there, Jonas was hanging on to the tailgate with one hand, his other hand braced on his thigh and his head hanging.

She approached carefully. "Jonas?"

When he looked up at her, all the color was drained from his face. Somehow he looked smaller. But he was reachable, she realized. She let out the breath she'd been holding.

"Emma, Daddy's fine. I'm going to talk to him, so you sit up in the truck, okay?"

She got Emma settled with the remainder of the lemonade.

"What happened?"

Jonas took long, restorative breaths, but they didn't help. Fear and shame overwhelmed him. Each day he went to work he told himself he was getting better. Even today, after the first flash, he'd convinced himself it was all fine. But it was a lie.

He'd told himself the debriefing he'd had with the shrink in Germany had been enough. Another lie. Never before had he had two episodes in the same day. Not even dealing with live fire exercises on base. It was something else and he couldn't put his finger on what was different now. It had been almost a year. Things were supposed to get better, not worse.

It had been easier when he hadn't felt anything. But lately…seeing Shannyn, remembering how he'd loved her, and now becoming involved with his daughter…he was feeling again. And feeling *something* meant feeling *everything*. Not just the here and now, and not just trying to fight his attraction to Shannyn. But everything he'd denied himself for nearly a year. Guilt, grief, resentment. Love.

Now she was waiting for him to explain, and he had no idea what to tell her.

"I need a minute." He took more breaths, willing his heart rate to calm completely as he searched for words.

"All right."

She couldn't understand. Didn't know what it was like out there. No one did unless they'd been through it. And who could he talk to? The only one who understood him was Parker. And

Parker was gone. Jonas closed his eyes, flooded with guilt and without the will to fight it.

She waited patiently for him, leaning against the door of the truck, and slowly he felt control slipping back, giving him enough strength to move out of the moment. He couldn't believe she was still standing there and not running. He remembered the feeling of thinking he was going to bleed to death and how his last thought had been that maybe he'd made a mistake leaving her. It was selfish. It had been selfish then and it was selfish now, but as the paralyzing fear drained away, all he was left with was need. For her.

When he looked into her face, it was with apology in every fiber.

"I am so sorry. What you must think…"

"We can worry about what I think later." She dismissed his apology with a hand. "We need to worry about you right now."

It was a fresh wound. He didn't want to be anyone's worry. It was his job to worry about others. To protect them. It was something he used to do very well, but lately he had done nothing but fail at it.

"I'm fine."

Her laugh was sharp with disbelief. "You can't possibly expect me to believe that. Oh, Jonas, you are so far from all right. You've slipped away before, but it's more than that, isn't it. More than you've let on."

He bristled. What did she know about it, anyway? She hadn't lived through it. She hadn't seen her best friend die. And he wouldn't wish that pain on anyone. As much as he wished he could lay his burden down, he knew that it wasn't fair for Shannyn and Emma to pay the price for his problems. He'd done a horrible job so far. The best thing he could do for them was protect them from the ugliness.

"It's for me to deal with."

Her lips formed a firm line and she waited five long seconds before speaking again.

"Not if you expect to have any sort of relationship with your daughter."

He was in no shape for her to be giving ultimatums. Sudden anger piled on top of the confusion left in the wake of his vivid flashback. It overrode the longing for her and the self-loathing he felt at his weakness, propelling him into action. He let go of the tailgate and squared his shoulders. "Don't threaten me, Shannyn."

She glanced into the truck and back at him. "Let me make it easy for you, Jonas. If you want to see Emma, you're going to have to let me help you. Even if it kills you."

Shannyn watched his fingers on the wheel, gripping as if his life depended on it. His jaw was set firmly; he gritted his teeth. He was furious with her. It came off him in angry waves.

She didn't care. Emma sat between them, her animated chatter of earlier silenced. She might only be five but Shannyn knew Emma got that something was wrong. It wasn't fair of them to put her in the middle of all their problems. From the first moment he'd shown up, Shannyn had a feeling that there would be nothing but trouble. But she hadn't anticipated it being this bad.

This wasn't just about them and their past relationship, although that was far from resolved. It was about Jonas and his health. And he could deny it all he wanted, but he needed help. She couldn't just wash her hands of him and send him away. There was Emma to consider. Despite knowing it would be simpler if she pushed him away, her heart couldn't let her do it. Not when he needed someone.

She sighed, licked her lips nervously. Who was she fooling? She wanted to help him, needed to. She cared what happened to him. She'd never really stopped caring for him. Today she'd had a glimpse of how good it could have been for all of them. And it had surprised her how natural it had felt, even after all these years. It was no longer a question of whether she'd done the right thing by keeping Emma a secret. They were a family of sorts now. Families stood by each other. Even when it hurt.

Just before they reached the house, she motioned to a small brick bungalow. "Pull in here," she said.

She took Emma with her and rang the bell.

When her neighbour, Patty, answered, Shannyn didn't beat around the bush. "Could Emma stay and play for a bit?"

Patty knit her brows. "You okay?"

"Yeah, but something came up. If it's too much of a bother…"

Patty looked down at Emma and back at Shannyn with a smile. "We're just having a Canada Day barbecue. Lisa's in the back playing by herself, so the company would be welcome."

"Thanks, Patty. I hope it won't be for long."

She knelt before Emma. "I'll be back to get you later, honey."

"Are you going to make Daddy feel better?"

Shannyn's smile wobbled at the concern on Emma's face. Her baby shouldn't have to worry about things like this. "I'm going to try. We need to talk about some things, that's all."

She stood and ruffled Emma's hair. "Thanks again," she said to Patty. She lifted a hand in farewell and jogged back to the truck where Jonas waited. Climbing into the cab, she knew he'd built a wall around himself. She could sense his isolation, see it in the cold, stony expression molding his features, the stiff way his hands gripped the steering wheel. Breaking through that wall wasn't going to be easy.

She unlocked the front door and led them into the quiet house.

"Shannyn, I'm sorry. I frightened Emma and upset you and ruined our day." The apology was perfunctory, devoid this time of true remorse. He was still behind that wall, giving her what he thought she needed to hear.

She turned at the kitchen counter. If she wanted answers, real ones, she was going to have to come at it strong, push her way through. "Yes, you did. And I want to know why."

He looked past her, through the window at the empty backyard. "It's complicated."

"I think I got that."

He turned his head a little and met her gaze. She knew he didn't want to talk about it. She also knew he had to let it out if they were going to move forward and establish some sort of status quo.

"Shannyn, you don't know what you're asking."

"I'm willing to take that chance."

"Maybe I'm not. Maybe I'm not willing to put you and Emma through this." He spun away, running his hand over the stubble on his jaw. But the veneer was starting to crack.

Shannyn looked at him. Why did he mean so much to her? It went so much deeper than the fact that he was Emma's father. She stared at his broad shoulders, the way his combat trousers sat on his hips. It was more than attraction to his physical perfection. She remembered the sight of the jagged scar running down his thigh, now marring that perfection. It wasn't sympathy, either.

The truth of the matter was, six years ago he'd been the first man she'd ever loved. She hadn't loved one since. And she knew she hadn't imagined their connection, no matter how he'd gone off and left her. There was something elemental between them, something tethering them together, and as much as she'd denied it to herself over the years, being with him again changed everything. It was his energy, the glimpses she got of it now and then. It was his sense of honor and his strength. It hurt her to see that strength tested; to see the battle he was waging with himself.

Their connection was as strong as ever. Perhaps even stronger. Too bad she'd already learned that the happily-ever-after she'd dreamed of as a child didn't really exist.

"Jonas, please look at me."

When he turned back around, her heart wept for the broken man before her. Whatever had happened, it was more than his leg being wounded. Something that would explain why he didn't consider himself a hero. Or why he kept distancing himself from her. Why he kept disappearing into himself.

"It's about time you trusted someone with it. And you know you can trust me."

"You'll look at me differently." His throat bobbed as he swallowed.

"Don't you know me better than that by now? I know you." She went forward, touched the hairline just above his ear with a tender hand. "I know you better than anyone. We might not like it, but it's true. Please let me in."

"Let's go outside. I need…I need space. And air."

She opened the patio doors and they went out, taking chairs on the tiny deck overlooking the yard.

"I don't know where to start." He leaned forward in the chair, resting his elbows on his knees, hands clasped.

Shannyn reached over and took his hand in hers. Somehow the simple contact linked them, more than just a handclasp. It was trust. Acceptance. A bond that went far deeper than attraction.

"Why don't you start with what it was like serving in Special Forces? We'll take it from there."

Jonas looked down at their joined hands. His was wide and scarred, hers slender, dainty. They were so different. Shannyn was being more than understanding. How much of that would change when he told her the truth? Would she look at him with shock, or derision? Yet, after today and his outburst at the air show, he knew he had to do something. It had been too long and the past was still stuck in the present. He had to move forward, somehow.

He pulled his hand away and started to get up. "Maybe it would be better if I talked to someone on base," he said, prevaricating. It was a weak argument and he knew it. But somehow he had to spare her the details. He didn't care what she said. When she knew what he'd done, she'd be disappointed at best. Disgusted, more likely.

"You don't need to protect me, Jonas. I grew a hard shell the day I realized I was pregnant and alone."

He sat back down. She didn't understand, not at all. Perhaps she would always hate him for leaving her behind. And he couldn't tell her the real reason why he'd left as he had. Maybe she was right. Maybe he did need to tell her what had happened. Once she knew what kind of man he really was, he wouldn't have to worry about protecting her in the future. Or worry about her getting ideas about them that wouldn't work. She'd send him packing and they could just move on to working out a visitation schedule.

She was strong. He got that. She had pulled herself up and had done a fine job of making a life for herself and Emma. But her lifestyle was far removed from the places he'd been or the things he'd seen. Even now, still dressed in her Canada Day colors, she was a picture of unspoiled beauty. He was anything but unspoiled. He was more convinced than ever that it wouldn't work between them.

Flirting had been fun. Kissing had been great. But today's episode reminded him very clearly why being with Shannyn was impossible, and why he'd insisted on being friends only. He'd allowed himself to forget. Telling her about Chris would create the distance he needed so he wouldn't have the power to hurt her again.

"You want to hear about what it was like?" His voice came out stronger than he thought possible. "I loved my job. Sure, it had its downside. In the Middle East it was hot and dusty, and there is a lot less glory to being a sniper than you'd imagine. You spend a lot of time waiting. And a lot of time isolated."

"But you had friends."

"Yeah."

He stopped, surprised at the lump that appeared in his throat. "You probably don't remember Chris Parker."

"The one from basic. Sandy-blond hair and devilish blue eyes."

He closed his eyes. She did remember him. And her description put a picture in his mind, one of Chris in full camouflage gear, his head tilted back and laughing. They'd constantly teased each other about nothing at all. It had been their one saving grace to get through the monotony of life there.

"Yes, that's him. He was my partner. Snipers work in pairs. Being with Chris…it was the closest I felt to being home. He was like a brother."

"Was?"

He couldn't look at her. "Yes, was. He was killed the day I was wounded."

He didn't know what he expected, but she simply said, "I'm sorry."

Shannyn angled her chair so she could see him and rested her arms on her knees, inviting him to continue. "Tell me."

A muscle in his jaw twitched, moving the tattoo on his cheek. The moment of fun, the touch of her fingers on his skin as she applied the sticker was far removed from their conversation now. The silence drew out for several beats.

"We were on assignment, nearly a year ago now. It was so hot it was like the sun had teeth. We were behind a knoll, over a mile from a village."

"Where?"

He chanced a look in her eyes before his gaze skittered away. "It doesn't matter where."

She translated it easily. "Covert."

"We waited over three hours for our mark to be in position. That day Chris was the spotter, I was the shooter."

Again he paused, taking his time, deciding what to tell. "When it was done, we hiked back to our rendezvous point and met up with the convoy that was to take us to the airfield."

He stopped, and at his silence she prodded gently, "What happened?"

He stared at a point somewhere past the back fence of the yard. "It had taken longer than we expected. There were… children involved. Children, Shan."

His haunted eyes probed hers, asking her to understand. "There were children there, holding guns. What kind of person gives a child a gun and gives them the burden of killing another human being?"

"I don't know."

He shook his head, as if he still couldn't believe it. "So we waited until the perfect time. But our delay meant the convoy was late getting out. I convinced them to take a shortcut, a different route. Chris and I were in the first vehicle, joking and laughing when we hit a landmine."

The picture threatened to take over again but he focused on her eyes, determined to go on with the story. "You have to understand…an Iltis is a light vehicle. It isn't built to withstand that sort of blast. We were thrown clear. The driver and the private beside him were wounded. My thigh was shattered, but Chris…Chris was dead."

When she looked at him, his eyes were filled with unshed tears. What she saw inside the shimmering depths cut her deeply. It wasn't just the loss of his best friend. The wound went so much deeper than simple grief. There was blame, regret, all pointed directly at himself.

"Seconds before, we'd been joking about his fiancée finding someone else. And because I insisted on a shortcut, he's gone. If I hadn't suggested that route, we never would have hit that mine and we'd both still be out there. My arrogance and impatience cost him his life."

Shannyn took her time answering, because she knew she had to get the words right. Oh, it was all so clear to her now. She could tell he was wearing guilt like a heavy shroud, carrying its weight every day. Feeling like he'd failed not only his friend but himself.

Quiet settled over the deck and birds sang. Shannyn wondered if birds still chirped in the places he'd been. How difficult it must be for him to come back to a place with such simple pleasures, to people who understood nothing of what he'd faced. She was one of those people. The least she could do was try.

Again she reached over and took his hand in hers.

"*You* didn't kill him, Jonas. It wasn't your fault."

"But it was. It was my decision. I wanted us to get a move on, get to the airfield and get out."

"And would there have been any guarantees that nothing would have happened if you'd gone the other way? Done things differently? Who's to say there wouldn't have been someone waiting to ambush you? The news is full of stories like that."

He shook his head stubbornly. "That's not the point. The point is, it was my decision, I made it, and now he's dead."

"You make it sound like you pulled the trigger."

"In a way I did."

She grabbed his other hand in hers and squeezed. "You look at me."

When he did, resistance masked his face. Oh, he was going to be a stubborn nut to crack. But now that she had an idea of what he was dealing with, she could at least help him move forward.

"You've been carrying this around ever since, haven't you."

When he didn't reply, she persisted. "This is eating you up inside, Jonas. I've been so focused on you and Emma that I didn't notice enough. I saw you were troubled but passed it off. But after today…I know it's not something you can ignore anymore. I think it's time you did something about it."

He sat up straighter, pulled his hands away, his brow wrinkling a bit in the middle. "What are you talking about, Shannyn?"

"What I'm talking about is getting you some professional help."

CHAPTER ELEVEN

"A SHRINK? Don't be absurd."

Jonas got up from his chair and stalked to the door, sliding it open and escaping away from her, into the kitchen. She wished he wouldn't run away. Why couldn't he see that she was only trying to help him?

He had to know she was right. Shannyn got up and followed him.

"Jonas, you can't deal with this alone, and I'm pretty sure I can't help you the way you need. I had no idea it was this big. I knew you were different somehow. I could feel it. But you obviously can't go on this way."

"I can manage." He folded his arms in front of his chest.

"Jonas, for God's sake, put your pride away. I know you, remember? You're blaming yourself and it's tearing you apart. What would it hurt to talk to someone who deals with this sort of thing?" She went to a drawer and pulled out a phone book. She longed to reach out and touch him, but held back, knowing she had to stay focused on the issue at hand.

"Look, we can go through the yellow pages. Or maybe there's someone on base you can talk to. This has to be pretty common after a tough tour of duty, don't you think?"

She handed him the book, but to her frustration, he held it in his hands without looking at it. She reached out and grabbed his wrist, the contact sending a current to her toes.

Tears stung her eyes as she felt more torn than before. Wanting to be free of his hold on her and needing to help him was all mixed up with what was best for Emma. He could be so stubborn. "Please, Jonas," she whispered, squeezing his hand. "You need to get help. Your leg is nearly healed. But you're still hurting inside."

"I can't go there, I'm sorry." He pulled away and put the book down on the counter. But she noticed his hands were shaking.

"You're scared." She shook her head at him. "Don't worry, I'm not going to take out a billboard or put an announcement in the paper. I'm just saying you should talk to someone who knows how to help you the way I can't."

"And let it get around the base?"

Obstinate. For a moment she wondered how many soldiers came back to the same thing and were too proud or ashamed to get the help they needed. Tough guys that thought they could handle it alone. But she couldn't be concerned about others. She needed to help this man. The father of her child. The man she'd once loved.

"Then go off base. Find an independent doctor."

He started pacing, his hands braced on his hips. His gait was stiff, like he'd suddenly tensed everything in his body. Now that she knew about Chris Parker everything fit. And that was only one incident over the course of several years. How many other demons haunted him? It would be naive to think that he hadn't had other experiences that affected him deeply. Perhaps not as much as that of the death of his friend, but cumulatively…no wonder he was a mess. She wanted to take the pain away for him, but knew she was helpless to do so. Her only hope was to make him see that he needed it for himself.

He stopped pacing and looked at her. Every one of his features held some measure of pain.

"Why are you doing this? To keep me away from Emma? Are you angry about the other day? Why are you punishing me?" His arm swept wide, anger his new armor.

"Of course I'm not punishing you. You're doing a fine job of punishing yourself."

"I don't believe you. You wanted to keep Emma from me all along. And when you couldn't anymore, you decided to…"

His gaze changed suddenly, calculating, assessing her. "That's it, isn't it. You're angry about what I said Thursday. About being just friends."

The abrupt change in him threw her off balance. What did he mean? This was about him and the disturbing flashbacks. It had nothing to do with her.

"What are you talking about?"

"You came on to me during my session. And when that didn't work, you kept it up during coffee. Only it didn't turn out the way you wanted."

Her mouth dropped open. "That's ridiculous. I'd never do something so manipulative."

"You don't think keeping Emma from me was manipulative? Why in the world would I trust you?"

Shannyn's lip quivered. Didn't he understand how important this was? She could barely get the words out. "How did this suddenly become about me?"

"You're the one who had a secret. If I hadn't shown up, I still wouldn't know about Emma. So don't pretend my problems matter to you." He braced his hands on his hips, looking satisfied with himself.

"Of course you matter to me!"

"Because of Emma."

"Not only because of Emma!"

"Now we're getting somewhere. Why don't you just admit what you want, Shannyn."

"I don't understand."

"I'm talking about this."

He took three giant strides, swept her up and pressed his lips to hers.

And, oh, he felt good. Tasted good. Like tart lemon and sweet sugar blended with a flavor that was simply Jonas. Her arms were pinned against her sides as he crushed her close, kissing her and making every nerve ending in her body thrum with hope.

Hope.

Hope would be the worst mistake she could make.

"Stop." She pulled her way out of his arms, walking backward until she was blocked by the stove. "Stop this. This doesn't change anything."

His lips curved craftily. "Oh, I think it does. I know how you felt just now." His voice was silky, seductive. "What you were feeling. You wanted me."

A shiver teased over her body. But she knew now that it was his way of diverting the topic. And she had to press on. It was too important.

"No, Jonas. Not like this. We have issues to work out. I know that. But today is not the time. Today is about something bigger."

The sexy smile disappeared as quickly as it had appeared.

"Jonas, no one can go through what you did without having some sort of lingering effect." She put the topic back on track. "You need to put it behind you. You do."

"I just want to forget about it. I didn't misread what happened just now. You can help me forget." His eyes communicated tacit suggestions on how that might be accomplished.

Shannyn wanted to cry. If he only knew how desperately she

wanted to make love with him. Knowing the reality of their situation had nothing to do with longings, and she had those aplenty. She remembered how it had been between them. Had imagined how it could be again, to her growing consternation.

If only healing were that simple. But damage had been done and she didn't see how it could be fixed. And to use it as a method of running away…she wasn't so naive. She knew it would only lead to more hurt. What she secretly wanted…the three of them together…that would never happen.

"You'll never forget, Jonas, and you know that. You need to find a way to make peace with it, not make it disappear." If only she could take her own advice.

She knew she'd gotten through to him when he exhaled and put a hand over his face.

She went to him. For right now the rest didn't matter. She laid her fingers on his shoulder and softly put her other hand over his and drew it down so his face was uncovered once more. "Please let me help you. Don't you know you're safe with me?"

The shoulder beneath her hand trembled and she struggled to hold back tears, longing for him to trust her this much. She let her fingers soothe their way down his arm, feeling the firm muscle beneath the warm skin.

"I care about what happens to you, Jonas. Not for Emma. Not for myself. For you." She halted, afraid of the next words but saying them, anyway. "Can't you see you're still in my heart?"

His breath caught. She felt him hold it in. She was so close to getting the rest of the way through. "If you can't do it yourself, then let me be the strong one. You've fought for so long. Please, let me fight for you this one time. All you have to do is hold on."

"I don't know how to do that," he admitted quietly.

"Just trust in me for once. Let go and start at the beginning and we'll do it together, I promise."

His arms snaked around her, pulling her close, cinching her tightly against him. She wrapped her arms around his ribs and held on, feeling their strength coming together. Accepting that together they were so much stronger than they were individually.

The sun had moved and was shining through the side window of the kitchen when Jonas stepped back and out of her arms.

"I'm sorry," he murmured, not looking at her.

"No," she answered strongly. "No more sorry. You needed to get it out."

"I wanted to spare you the ugly parts. I didn't want you to know."

Shannyn rested her hand on his cheek and peered into his face. "But I wanted to share them with you. I'm glad you told me, Jonas. It explains so much. It's going to get better now, you'll see."

He put his hand over hers, and she smiled up at him. "I can't promise to understand all of it. I wasn't there. But I'll do my best. It's going to get better," she repeated. "That I *can* promise."

He sighed, pursing his lips and looking away. "It already it is better. I'm the one who's alive. He isn't."

"And punishing yourself won't bring him back." She put her right hand on his other cheek, forcing him to look into her eyes. "I still think you need to talk to a professional. Someone who knows how to deal in this particular area of trauma."

"I don't need a shrink to tell me what I need, Shan. Spouting a bunch of touchy-feely gobbledygook."

"Do you want to live like this for the rest of your life, then?"

He pulled away from her hands. "You know what? I can't think of that now. It's been such a roller-coaster day. Right now I'm just tired."

Shannyn suppressed a sigh. One conversation was not going to fix this and make everything all right for him. It would take time. He needed time. She knew that sharing as much as he had must have been exhausting. She merely nodded.

"Of course you are."

"I should talk to Emma, though. I don't want her last memory of today being that of me flipping out." He sighed. "You and me…we've talked about it. You understand. But Emma doesn't."

Shannyn was glad. Not only for Emma—it was good that he was considering their daughter's feelings—but for herself. It would be a way to keep him close a little longer today. To perhaps convince him to get the help he needed.

"Why don't you lie down in the living room and rest? I'll go get Emma from Patty's in a bit, and we'll have a quiet dinner together. The three of us." She put her hands in the pockets of her shorts and tried to sound normal.

"That sounds good. More than good." He attempted a small smile and nearly succeeded.

"It's the least I can do. And I agree. I think it's important for Emma to see you again, to see that you're okay." She hesitated. "Jonas…you promise you won't leave?" She didn't quite trust him. She could very well go to pick up Emma and come home to an empty house.

"Are you kidding? If I tried to pull that, you'd be at my door in ten minutes."

Shannyn laughed. "Yes, I would. Besides, I think we could both use a regular evening after the events of the day."

"You're probably right. I'll lie down for a bit and then we'll have dinner and I'll make it up to Emma for ruining her afternoon."

When Shannyn came back with Emma, Jonas was asleep on the couch, his body so long that his feet hung over the curved arm at the end. One arm was bent and under his head, the opposite hand resting on the cushions in front of his abdomen.

When he slept, his troubles all seemed to vanish from his face. Like when they'd met Corporal Benner, he seemed younger. Freer.

"Daddy's sleeping," she whispered to Emma, holding her hand. For some reason, the word *Daddy* no longer seemed foreign on her tongue. It belonged. Like Jonas did.

She knelt down before Emma and squeezed her hand. "Let's make him a special supper, okay? And we'll all eat together and have ice cream sandwiches for dessert."

Emma nodded enthusiastically. "Can we make hot dogs?"

Shannyn laughed. To a five-year-old, hot dogs *did* constitute a special meal. "Sure, pumpkin. Hot dogs it is. And maybe a potato salad and your favorite veggies and dip."

At Emma's broad smile Shannyn put on her mock stern face. "But this is a team effort, young lady. You've got to pull your weight."

"Yes, ma'am," Emma replied. She giggled. "That's what Daddy says."

Shannyn pulled Emma in for a hug. Jonas, with all his problems, was already becoming a part of the family, an influence on Emma's life. And this was only the beginning. She had no idea where things were going to lead with him. No matter how he denied it, his kisses didn't lie. The connection she felt didn't lie. The fact that he trusted her with the truth, and that she was beginning to trust him more every day, brought them closer together. It complicated *everything*.

A sigh escaped as she released Emma and turned to the refrigerator. She didn't want to care, didn't want to need him. It would be so much simpler if she didn't. If only they could agree to parent Emma separately. If only she could turn her residual feelings off.

She put potatoes on to boil for salad and as she cut vegetables, Emma arranged them on a pretty plate. Together they mixed the potatoes and dressing and she let Emma sprinkle the paprika on the top. She lit the barbecue and got out a pack of hot dogs, leaving Emma to carry out the condiments and plastic dishes.

Emma came back inside for plates and cutlery and slid the patio door shut with far too much force than necessary. It banged loudly against the frame, the harsh slam echoing through the house.

Shannyn jumped, then jumped again as a horrific shout and crash came from the living room. Without thinking, she rushed around the corner, Emma on her heels, and the sight that greeted her froze her to the spot.

Jonas stood in the middle of the floor, his chest pumping heavily and the coffee table overturned. Picture frames and her favorite vase lay scattered on the floor.

"Jonas! My God, what happened?"

His head turned, nothing else. Shannyn took a step backward at the sight of his cold eyes. Now she knew what he'd meant when he'd said he wanted to spare her the details. There was a dark side he hadn't wanted her to see. The Jonas before her now wasn't the same man she'd held in her arms earlier. At Emma's whimper, she automatically put her arm out, pulling Emma close to her side, comforting her.

Jonas stared at them blankly. The dream was still so real. Vignettes and faces that made little sense, and then cut to the hospital in Germany. He'd been shouting to the doctor about Chris's body and then suddenly he'd been screaming that it was Shannyn's body and he'd broken his promise…

Now, slowly, slowly her face registered. As the fog cleared, he realized he was standing in Shannyn's living room. She was staring at him with horror etched on every feature. Eyes wide, mouth open, face pale.

Behind her right hip stood Emma, wearing the same expression but with an added emotion he recognized. He'd seen it before. More than he cared to recall.

She was afraid. Not just frightened but afraid of *him*.

He looked away, only to register the chaos created by his

outburst. The silk flowers in the vase were scattered in a tangle of red, orange and green. The coffee table was on its side. A picture frame lay facedown, but bits of broken glass peeked from beneath the wooden frame. He didn't remember jumping up. Didn't remember knocking the table over.

He turned back to Shannyn and Emma. This was so wrong. They both deserved so much better. But especially Emma. She didn't understand any of this. "I'm sorry," he tried, but the words came out choked. He cleared his throat. "Emma…"

But Emma spun around and ran from the room. Her footsteps pounded on the stairs, and moments later her bedroom door slammed.

Shannyn glanced at the stairs and then back at Jonas, undecided.

"You were right, Shan. About everything." His voice was quiet and broken in the silent aftermath of his outburst. "Go to Emma while I clean up this mess. While I get my head on straight. I need to talk to both of you."

Shannyn quietly did what he asked. She turned and walked away from him, up the stairs to Emma. It was the right thing for her to do. Emma needed her mother now more than anything.

He squatted and picked up the picture, careful of the broken glass. It was a five by seven of Shannyn and Emma together. Shannyn's arms were looped around Emma's neck, both of them smiling. A set of blue eyes and a set of green, both with a dusting of freckles on their noses.

Carefully he righted the table and then placed the pieces of glass on it gently. He'd broken their family as surely as he'd broken the picture, just by being here.

This was why Shannyn hadn't told him about Emma. He understood that now. And he knew that somehow he had to make it right. It was too late for him to walk away. Emma wouldn't understand him leaving now.

Hell, he wouldn't understand, if it came to that.

He'd made a promise to be a father, and he wasn't going to break it. And Shannyn… Somehow he had to find a way to fix it for all of them. No more running away.

He picked up the vase, held it gingerly in his hands before placing it precisely in the middle of the table. The nightmares weren't going away any more than the flashes of memory were. Today had been the worst day since it had happened.

In this one he'd dreamed it was Shannyn at the end and he'd overturned a doctor's trolley trying to find her. It didn't take a rocket scientist to realize that she was there because he'd started caring about her again. He could bluster and protest all he wanted, the truth was he cared about her. In his heart he knew he wasn't coping very well. With losing Chris or with losing Shannyn.

Shannyn's footsteps came back down the stairs and he straightened, his hand full of silk flowers. He put them on the table too when she came back in the room.

She'd put everything on the line for him today, even though he'd been a complete jerk, using whatever feelings she had for him against her. No matter where they ended up, at the very minimum she would always be a part of his life because of Emma. And he'd hurt her enough over the years. He knew that. He was done with hurting her. It was time for him to attempt to make things right.

"You were right." He began the conversation by taking responsibility for all of it. "I can't do this by myself. I need help and I'm going to get it. I can't do this to you and Emma."

Shannyn crossed the floor in quick steps, wrapping her arms around his neck and pressing her cheek to his chest. Slowly he put his arms around her, unsure of what to do. She was crying. He could tell by the irregular jolt of her chest against his, the hint of wetness that clung to his shirt. It wasn't what he'd expected.

She should be shouting at him, kicking him out after what he'd done! Instead she was giving him acceptance and comfort.

"Why aren't you afraid?" he whispered into her ear, overcome. "God, Shan, you should be afraid."

Her head shook against him. "No. I'm not afraid *of* you, Jonas. I'm afraid *for* you. If you mean it about getting help, I'm relieved. It kills me to see you in so much pain."

"But I scared you both so much."

"We'll be fine. And you will, too."

She was so strong, so willing to give of herself. She always had been. In some strange way, it made him proud. At that moment he couldn't think of a woman he'd rather have as a mother to his daughter.

Shannyn stepped back, sniffing and swiping a finger beneath her lashes.

"Don't you see, Jonas? This is a beginning. A new one for you. Why would I be upset about that?"

CHAPTER TWELVE

WHEN the hot dogs were almost ready, Shannyn called Emma down for supper.

Jonas was waiting for Emma outside, nervously bouncing his knee as he sat at the picnic table. He'd spoken to Shannyn, but she was glad he felt he owed Emma an explanation, too. His respect for her feelings, and for Emma's, told her he meant what he said about getting help.

Shannyn was relieved to find Emma subdued but not afraid when she came downstairs. "Your dad wants to talk to you, honey. Do you think you can do that?"

Emma nodded, looking suddenly far older than her five years.

Shannyn watched the scene outside unfold with a lump in her throat. Dinner was ready, but Emma and Jonas needed this time together. Hot dogs and potato salad could wait.

Jonas talked to Emma, his face sober and honest. For a minute they remained a few feet apart. Then Emma held out her bear— the one she called Mr. Huggins—and he took it into his hands.

Emma's arms went around her father and Shannyn pressed a hand to her mouth. Children were so forgiving. Seeing Jonas come apart at the seams had frightened her to death. But her fear had instantly become secondary once she realized he'd been trapped in his own personal hell.

And Emma had been crying when she'd gone upstairs to check on her. Explaining hadn't been easy, but Shannyn had tried to keep it simple. Daddy had nightmares sometimes, and he'd had one today. He wasn't angry at her, or at Shannyn. It wasn't Emma's fault.

She ran her fingertips over her lips, unable to forget the passion in his kiss.

When Jonas and Emma pulled apart, Shannyn saw Jonas turn his head to wipe his eyes privately before turning a smile on Emma. He'd made everything right. She was surprised to find tears in her own eyes, and wiped her lashes. Clearing her throat, she picked up the tray holding their food and went to the patio door. When she knocked on the window, Emma bounced up to open it. Even though Jonas was awake, Shannyn noticed how gently Emma closed the door behind her.

"Supper's ready, guys," she called out, and had to work to paste on a smile. What a topsy-turvy day it had turned out to be.

Jonas got up to help her, taking the tray from her hands, his warm fingers brushing over hers. "Is there more?"

"Yes, there are a few more things on the counter."

He placed the tray on the picnic table and then followed her inside. She grabbed the pitcher of lemonade but before she could go back out, he put his hand on her arm.

"Thank you," he said, his voice low. It sent shivers up her spine. "Whatever you said to Emma upstairs, it worked. She's strong, Shan. She gets that from you."

Shannyn closed her eyes. Every time he touched her now it seemed all her senses kicked in. Each touch, each caress seemed loaded with deeper meaning. He'd verbally thrown a lot of things at her this afternoon, but she was smart enough to know they had only been a smokescreen. Now every moment, every revelation into his character, drew her closer. Intertwined their lives. It elated her almost as much as it frightened her.

"Don't credit me. I saw you through the window. You clearly said the right thing. She *never* shares Mr. Huggins."

He let her arm go, and she turned to open the door.

"Shan?"

When she faced him again, he was holding glasses in his hands. For a second she got an intuitive feeling, as if he were going to say something she wouldn't like. He looked almost apologetic.

"I know what I've got to do."

He slid past her out into the yard before she could ask him what he meant.

They sat at the table, reminiscent of a regular family ritual. Plates were filled, chatter ensued. Shannyn stole glances at Jonas. He acted as if he was fine; he laughed and smiled and ate like all was normal. But Shannyn couldn't shake the feeling that somehow something was wrong. What did he feel he had to do? And why was he waiting to tell her?

The evening was waning, settling into mellow sunset when they unwrapped ice cream sandwiches. Shannyn handed around napkins as chins sported dribbles of vanilla and chocolate. Jonas sighed.

"What is it?"

Jonas looked into her eyes. She wondered again if she saw remorse in his hazel depths or if she only imagined it. He held her gaze for a long time, reached out and squeezed her free hand, then pulled away and cleared his throat.

"I want you both to know that I might not be around as much for a while."

Shannyn put down what was left of her sandwich, blindly wiping her fingers on a paper napkin. What was left of her appetite had diminished completely. This was it, then. She'd overstepped after all, and he was backing away. After all that had happened, he was clearing out. Just like last time.

"Why, Daddy?" Emma voiced the question for both of them.

Jonas smiled at Emma, a wistful turn of his lips. "You know my dream today? I get them a lot. And your mom and I think it would be good if I got some help."

"Help from who?" Emma took a bite of her sandwich, her eyebrows raised in innocent curiosity.

"Help from a doctor, sweetheart."

Shannyn's heart gave a solid thump. He had meant it, then. He was going to get help. She was glad. Glad for him, but selfishly couldn't help but think that if she were interpreting right, he was doing it alone. She'd begged him to do it, but now couldn't help but feel left behind.

They'd come so far, and they'd done it together. Sometimes fighting, sometimes crying, but he'd shared it with her. She didn't quite understand why he was withdrawing from them now. Perhaps her heart would be safer, but not Emma's. She balled up the napkin, fussing with it, wanting to ask the questions but knowing they needed to be voiced in private, not in front of Emma.

"Do you have to go away for that? Will he give you a needle?"

Jonas laughed. "No, and I hope not."

"Then why are not going to be here?" Her lips formed a tiny pout. "I start soccer this week. I wanted you to come."

Thank you, Emma, Shannyn thought. She was wondering the same thing. Why did getting help preclude him being with them? She knew that if *she* were to ask, he'd find a way to avoid answering. It was harder for him to put off Emma's innocent questions.

Jonas got up from his side of the table and moved over to sit beside Emma. He took her sticky hand in his. "I'm not going to be gone completely. I just won't be here regularly. I need some time to figure things out, that's all. So I can get better, and be a better daddy to you." He halted, then lifted his hand and grazed her cheek with a finger. "I don't want what happened today to happen again. It hurt me to see you scared." His eyes darted up to Shannyn's. "To see you both scared."

Shannyn saw the logic in what he was saying even as her heart rebelled against it. It was the responsible thing to do, she supposed. She wanted him well, she truly did. But she didn't understand his need to avoid them while he was doing it. They could help him, she was sure of it. He'd already said that Emma helped him. What she'd feared would come true. He would withdraw and she'd be left to answer Emma's questions about why Daddy wasn't around.

Emma wasn't the only one who would miss him. Shannyn admitted to herself what she wouldn't to another soul. She would miss Jonas; the sound of his voice, the way he bounced his knee without realizing he was doing it. The way he ran his hand over the stubble of his military cut or rubbed his bad leg when he got upset.

"I'm sure your daddy will come for visits, honey." Her eyes fell on Jonas, telegraphing a look that said, *You'd better.*

She wished she could read his thoughts. When his gaze locked with hers, they seemed to acknowledge what she'd said. And when he spoke, he spoke to her, even though the words were meant for Emma.

"I'm not leaving you. That I promise."

Her heart lifted. He meant it. She was suddenly sure of it.

There was still so much to say. She longed to know what he was going to do, when she would see him again.

"Let's take this stuff inside and run you a bath, Emma. You're sticky from one end to the other."

"I'll get it," Jonas offered. He stood and began piling dishes on the tray. "You get Emma in the tub." He smiled at Emma. "Then I'll read you a story before bed."

When Shannyn came back downstairs, he was putting the supper mess away. It felt right, having him there in her kitchen.

She smiled a little, remembering how she'd first considered him an intruder into their lives. But now…now she was beginning to believe she could trust him to keep his word. He was getting the help he needed. He was taking a genuine interest in Emma. She couldn't ask for more than that.

"Thanks for tidying up."

He turned from the sink. "You're welcome. It's the least I could do after the day I put you through."

"What are you going to do now, Jonas?" She leaned against the breakfast nook.

"I don't know."

That made her frown. "But you think withdrawing from us is a good idea?"

Jonas put down the dishcloth and rested his hips against the counter so that they were facing each other in the contained space. "How can you ask that, after today?"

"I think today has shown you that we're tougher than we look." She stood straighter, her back coming off the resting spot. Why couldn't he see that it wasn't she and Emma that needed to be protected here?

Jonas folded his arms. "Today taught me that it's not fair for me to expect you to deal with my problems. Today it was a nightmare. A broken picture, an overturned table. What if it had been different? What if you'd come in and had shaken me to wake me up?

"I don't trust myself, Shan. And I never want to see that look on Emma's face again. I realized I'm unpredictable. I don't know what will trigger a memory, a flash. Today is the worst day I've had. Twice at the air show I lost time. I'll admit it now. And then after all that, the nightmare. Until I know it's okay, I don't want to chance scaring her again." His face softened. "Scaring you."

"Going away is hurting us. Emma won't understand." She let

her gaze skitter away, as she admitted, "I…I don't understand. I thought I helped you. I thought…I thought we'd agreed that we'd be friends." The idea sounded so odd from her lips. They meant more to each other than friends, yet somehow even friendship seemed elusive between them. They'd built a tenuous truce, that was all.

"You did help me. But you were right about one thing. I need more than time and a friendly shoulder. I promise I'll make time for some contact. I'll pick Emma up and we'll go for an ice cream. I'll come to a soccer game. But not…not a scheduled, prolonged thing. Please try to understand. I need to do this. I need to get things clear, and you…you complicate things."

After what they'd been through together today, all she'd wanted was some quiet time for them to just *be*. To maybe sit quietly in the shade of the maple tree and unwind, to let the day settle and drift away on the evening breeze. To be held in his arms, secure. Safe. Instead he was talking about walking away. Putting *more* distance between them rather than drawing closer.

Shannyn felt the quiver in her stomach, a little sliver of fear. She'd already begun to rely on him, to get too involved. Even tonight she'd started to trust him again. Longing to be held in his arms. He'd never given the impression he truly wanted more. A few kisses and a whole lot of arguments did not translate into rebuilding a relationship.

The last time she'd trusted him he'd gone away for good. Perhaps he was right. Maybe a little distance would let everyone regain their balance. Moving slower wouldn't hurt. She was wrong about not needing protection. Maybe she did need it, but not from him. From herself. From letting herself feel more than was prudent. It was for the best.

Except that it already hurt. Each time she felt them get closer, the fear that he'd eventually leave her again was like a crack that spread under pressure.

Emma's footsteps came down the stairs. She was shiny-faced and in a blue-and-white nightdress, a brush in her hands.

"Mommy. I'm ready for you to brush my hair."

Shannyn looked back at Jonas. "Do what you have to do," she murmured, then moved to take the brush from Emma's hand.

Jonas picked up the paper cups and opened the truck door with a finger. One year. Exactly one year had passed since they'd driven over the landmine, and it was time to face a few things.

He shut the truck door with a jut of his hip, holding the hot coffee in shaking hands. His therapist had said this would be a good idea. The doc had also said he was making progress. Right now, with his stomach churning and his body trembling, he wasn't so sure of that. But he'd promised Shannyn he'd get help, and so here he was. Four hours from home in a small town in Nova Scotia.

He put one foot in front of the other until he reached the gate, swinging it open with a rusty creak.

It wasn't hard to find the headstone. It was slightly larger than the others, with a maple leaf adorning the top. For a minute he stood staring at it, at the words carved in gray stone.

He took one of the coffees and put it down beside the monument. "I brought you a double-double," he said quietly, referring to the familiar term for two cream and two sugars from Tim Hortons. Feeling awkward, he flipped back the plastic on his own cup to reveal the drinking spout and took a hesitant sip.

He'd been afraid that seeing Chris's name here, seeing the date, he'd be inundated with memories and painful flashes. But there was none of it. Only a deep sorrow that he'd lost his best friend.

"I'm sorry, Park," he whispered. He squatted down so he was

at eye level with the epitaph. "I'm sorry. And I miss you." He smiled a little. "That's all."

"Sgt. Kirkpatrick."

He rose and spun, coffee flying out of the small hole in the lid. "Nessa."

She smiled sadly. "You know who I am."

"Park carried your picture everywhere." She was even more beautiful in person, he realized. Creamy skin, dark hair flowing around her shoulders, brown eyes that seemed to really see him and held a note of sorrow he recognized.

"How are you holding up, Sgt.?"

Jonas looked back at the headstone. "I'm here. I'm fine."

She came forward, putting down a handful of mixed flowers. She caught sight of the cup and covered her mouth, suddenly laughing.

"Oh, how he loved his morning coffee with you. What a lovely tribute, Jonas."

It was odd, feeling so connected to someone he'd never met. "I've had some trouble getting over what happened," he admitted, surprised he was able to talk about it without feeling like he was strangling. "So I drove down to see him. To apologize. That sounds stupid," he finished.

Nessa put her hand on his arm. "Not at all. You never got to say goodbye. I can't imagine what you went through. If this is what you need to move on…"

"But you lost a fiancé. A future. I'm so sorry for that." Despite counseling, he still couldn't completely erase the feeling of responsibility that haunted him for denying this woman a husband.

She smiled at him then, a soft understanding. "It wasn't your fault. I know that. It was what happened and he's gone. He lived for the Army. I knew it and wanted him, not even despite it, but maybe even because of it. It was so much of who he was." Her soft eyes shone with the love she still felt. "I've accepted it, Jonas."

"But knowing what you know now, would you have done it? Would you have been with him knowing he would be killed?"

The question had been on his mind a lot lately. Being with Shannyn, and experiencing all the old feelings, had made him wonder about the woman Chris had left behind. Nessa was a living example of exactly what Jonas had tried to protect Shannyn from. He'd done what he thought he had to do, what was best. But now he was more involved in Shannyn's life than before. He had a daughter, and he was beginning to doubt everything he'd believed. Was starting to think he'd had it all wrong in the first place.

She hugged her arms around herself. "Yes, I would. Even with the pain…loving him was beautiful. I'm grateful for the time we had. I wouldn't trade a second of it. He made me a better person."

She faced the grave, a wistful smile curving her lips. "He was the most *alive* person I ever knew. Yes, it hurts. It still does and I think of him every day. But my life was better for having him in it. And I know he wouldn't want me to grieve forever. He'd want me to go on and have a fabulous life. To be happy. So I try to spend every day living up to that."

Jonas swallowed. It was simple and the most beautiful tribute he'd ever heard. It fit his memories of Chris perfectly.

Nessa reached down and took his hand, lifting it up between them. "Do you think he'd want anything less for you, Jonas? You, his best friend? Do you think he'd want you to spend your life blaming yourself? Denying yourself happiness because you feel guilty that you're here and he's not?"

Jonas choked on a laugh while tears filled his eyes. "He'd tell me to shut up and get on with it. And probably a few other choice words."

"Then why aren't you?"

He stared into her eyes. Why wasn't he? She was right. She

was absolutely right. What sort of tribute was *he* paying his friend? Chris would say he was alive but not living and he'd be right.

There were two girls back in Fredericton who deserved more than he'd been giving. He'd been foolish to try to engineer things in the first place. He'd played God with Shannyn's life thinking he was doing the right thing, but he knew now he'd been wrong. He had held on to the anger about Emma's paternity to avoid facing the fact that his feelings for her hadn't changed at all. Tried putting all the blame on her to keep her at arm's length. But the truth was, he wasn't really that mad about it anymore. They'd both spent so long being afraid that it was all they knew.

He had to see her. Had to tell her what he'd really done six years ago when he'd left for Edmonton, and tell her he was sorry. Knowing it, and for once *not* being afraid of it gave him a sense of freedom he hadn't known for many years.

He turned to Nessa, who was watching him with a broad smile.

As everything became crystal clear, his lips curved up in response. "You are one hell of a woman. Chris always said so and now I know he was right. You have no idea what you've just done for me." He let out a giant breath. "Thank you. Thank you so much."

"Be happy, Jonas," she replied, leaning up and kissing his cheek. "Chris would want that for you."

Jonas turned back to the monument and lifted his hand in salute. His chest filled, his back straightened, his chin lifted.

When he passed Nessa, he put a hand on her shoulder, then broke into a jog as he headed out the gate and back to the woman he loved.

CHAPTER THIRTEEN

AMIDST the happy shouts and whistles, he saw Shannyn. On the sidelines of the field, clapping her hands, engrossed in the game. The dying sun gleamed off her hair, warmed the skin of her arms to an amber glow. For a few moments Jonas watched, saw Emma running up the field in her yellow-and-white shirt, following the ball, joined by a handful of identically dressed children.

He'd made so many mistakes. So many decisions based on fear and not enough based on faith. And in the face of it all she'd somehow found the strength to help him when she thought he needed it.

What made him qualified to decide what was best for Shannyn? He'd loved her all along and had pushed her away out of fear. Not anymore. He'd been gone for too long. Six long years they'd wasted.

He was home. They were his. It was time he started taking the steps to claim them.

As if she could read his thoughts, she turned, her body suddenly backlit by the sunset, golden and gorgeous.

He had so much to tell her. About what he'd been doing over the past weeks. About what he'd done earlier today. About what he envisioned for the future.

Shannyn turned, her heart catching at the sight of Jonas

staring. He was all long legs and broad shoulders in faded jeans and a green T-shirt with a small crest on the chest. When he started walking toward her, his limp was indiscernible.

She stepped off the sidelines, retreating from the cheering crowd a little. His eyes locked with hers, his strides purposeful.

In that moment it became very clear. She loved Jonas. She always had, even when he'd come back and turned her life upside down with demands. Even when she'd seen him struggle with demons that frightened her. And especially now, watching him walk toward her. For her it would always be him.

He stopped in front of her, and it took everything she possessed not to launch herself into his arms. Blood rushed into her cheeks and she covered them with her hands, laughing softly. What was she thinking? There were at least twenty impressionable children around as well as parents and coaches. She'd never been much into public displays of affection. As much as she wanted to, she held back. This wasn't the place, even if it did feel like the right time.

"We didn't expect you tonight." Her words came out on a soft rush of breath. "Emma will be ecstatic."

"I hope it's okay that I came." Her eyes were drawn to his lips as they formed the words. "I have so much to tell you. So much to explain."

Shannyn lifted her chin and held his hands tightly as she looked deeply into his eyes. "I'm glad. I've been waiting…"

"I know. And I'm sorry I've made you wait so long."

"It's all right. I knew you were trying to get better."

"No." He shook his head. "I don't mean just now. This is so much bigger than me dealing with grief and stress. I mean from the beginning. I shouldn't have made you wait." The pressure of his fingers on hers tightened. "I…oh, hell. I need to tell you some things, things I should have said a long time ago."

He *had* done some serious soul searching, then. Shannyn kept her hands within his.

She thought back to the rare times over the past weeks that he'd carved out time to spend with them. He'd kept it simple then, too. An ice-cream cone, watching one of Emma's games. She'd known he was getting help, but he had distanced himself as he said he would.

But tonight…something had changed. Tonight he looked like a man set free. There was something more. Hope slammed into her. She wasn't imagining their connection. Could it be he felt the same way and he wanted to tell her? What was it that had happened that had caused this transformation?

"Each time I've seen you, you've seemed taller. Stronger. And I've wanted to ask you so many times…"

The shriek of a whistle cut through the air, ending the game and halting their conversation.

"Mama, Mama! Did you see me?" Emma came barreling off the field, ponytail bobbing, a streak of dirt gracing the sleeve of her shirt. Then she saw Jonas and squealed, "Daddy!"

Shannyn didn't have time to caution her to slow down. Emma raced straight at Jonas.

She needn't have worried. Jonas hefted her in the air, dirt and all, laughing. "Hey, angel! How was the game?"

"It was great. I almost scored."

"Good for you." He plopped a kiss on her nose, grinning broadly.

Shannyn's eyes widened. He was so open tonight, so giving. Without the wall he'd put around himself. Seeing him this way was like waking up. Like seeing the first crocuses blooming in the midst of the late-winter snow. Defiant beauty through cold ice. He'd always warmed to Emma, but this was more than that.

This was the Jonas she remembered. The man she'd fallen in love with. Having him back only made the feelings more intense.

"You ready to go home?"

Emma's face fell. "Aren't you coming?"

His eyes softened as he smiled tenderly at his daughter.

"Of course I'm coming. I'll tuck you in tonight and then I'm going to have a talk with your mom."

"Goody!"

Shannyn laughed even as her heart skipped. "We'd better get going, then. I promised Em a treat after the game. And then it's bedtime for you, silly girl."

Shannyn looked at Jonas, a secret thrill rushing through her as his eyes warmed on her. They would talk. She knew she should keep the topic away from their personal relationship. As happy as she was to see the old Jonas new again, so many things hadn't changed. They would need time to talk about what had just happened. About what was changing inside him. About what needed to happen in the future, for all of them. They had work to do, but for the first time, she knew that somehow they'd find a way.

Emma ran ahead to Shannyn's car, but Jonas stayed with Shannyn, his hand a warm anchor on her back. She wasn't sure she could trust herself to stay on topic if he kept up with the little meaningful touches.

"I've got the truck. I'll meet you there."

"Okay."

Before he changed direction, he leaned over and kissed her temple.

The warmth on the spot lasted long after he was gone.

"I bought some potato chips and pop for a treat," Shannyn said in an undertone as Emma spun around the kitchen, still pumped up from her soccer game. "I'm going to run a bath for Em, but if you want you can get those things out."

Jonas leaned casually against the kitchen counter, legs crossed at the ankle. "I can do that."

She paused. "I'll be back in a bit. Emma's going to need a scrubbing."

"I'll be here."

And he would, she realized. For the first time she knew he'd be exactly where he said he'd be. Wondering what had changed was driving her crazy, but Emma had to be tended to first. Normally this was a time of night she enjoyed, but tonight she was impatient to get Emma safely tucked in bed. He was waiting for her.

When they came back downstairs, Jonas was unloading the dishwasher, putting the dishes back on their shelves. Shannyn halted at the bottom of the stairs and stared. He looked so much as though he belonged there. Briefly she got a flash of what life would be like if he were here every day, and it shot straight to her core. She had to be careful. The plain fact was that he was still in the Army, and now that he was nearly recovered, the chance of reassignment was suddenly a possibility. She couldn't allow herself to get used to him when there was a good chance he would be gone again.

Still, the simple action of being here gave her hope that somehow they could compromise, to make it work.

"I smell like bubble gum," Emma announced, letting go of Shannyn's hand and marching over to her father. "Smell my hair."

Dutifully he lifted her up and buried his nose in her curls. "Bubble gum? Smells like blueberries to me."

"Nope. Bubble gum." Her face was a picture of seriousness. "*Pink* bubble gum."

Jonas laughed. "I hope you didn't brush your teeth yet. Your treat's on the table."

Emma scrambled down and ran for her chair and the bowl of chips he'd set out. He followed her and poured her glass half-full of root beer.

He was so good with her, Shannyn realized. For a man who hadn't wanted children, he was a natural. Decisive but fun, willing to play a little. She'd been wrong in keeping Emma from him. When she'd realized she was pregnant, she should have told him somehow. And for that she owed him an apology. A real one, not one out of guilt that came from being caught. And she needed to apologize for depriving him of what should have been his all along—the joy of being Emma's father.

"Penny for your thoughts." He smiled and her heart turned over.

"Later," she replied, her cheeks blooming. It was almost as though she was transported back six years to the man she remembered—the young man filled with optimism and energy. Knowing now what he'd been through, all that he'd faced, how he'd suffered and how he was bouncing back, made him into so much more in her eyes. A dangerous, potent combination of charm and manliness.

She turned away, feigning attention to Emma. Relaxed mood or not, it frightened her to realize how deep her feelings ran for him. She loved him more now than she ever had, she realized. Suddenly her earlier joy and hope faded. She'd had her heart broken once; she was afraid to give him the power to do it again.

Nothing made sense. She wanted him, loved him, admired his parental instincts. Yet she still felt she had to hold back, to protect herself on some level. Fool me once, shame on you. Fool me twice…she didn't want to be that woman.

Emma finished her snack and Jonas took her up to bed, storybook in hand. When he came down several minutes later, Shannyn was just finishing tidying the mess left over from the snack.

Suddenly, now that they were alone, it felt awkward. Shannyn wasn't sure what to say, and Jonas stood in the kitchen looking as if he felt the same way. Saying they needed to talk, and then putting it off for over an hour had put everything off-kilter.

"Would you like a drink?"

"I'd love one. Especially if it means I can sit in the shadows with you and drink it."

Her heart gave a heavy thump as she reached into the fridge for two bottles of beer. The flirtatious response did funny things to her insides and she cautioned herself to remain objective. Seeing him walk across the soccer field had filled her with optimism. But now…now she wasn't so sure. Reality was beginning to settle in and there were a lot of things to tackle. Including her own insecurities.

She twisted off the top and handed him the bottle. "Bumps," she said, and they tilted their bottles so that the bottoms knocked gently.

It was a movement so familiar, yet one long forgotten. Without warning, memory upon memory seemed to be coming back to her about their time together. Trying to isolate how she felt then and how she felt now. It was becoming more difficult as her feelings escalated. They all seemed to blend together, as though it had only been yesterday rather than years.

Outside, the air had cooled, the summer evening breeze fluttering over her skin. Shannyn sat in a chair and leaned back, stretching her legs. She knew he had something on his mind. She forced herself to be patient and wait for him. It would be better that way, if she let him take the lead. She took a deep breath of air softly perfumed by the blooms in her flower bed.

Jonas paused, then turned the opposite chair so that it was at a ninety-degree angle to her and likewise, sat.

After a moment or two of silence, his voice cut through the night sounds of the breeze flickering the leaves and a mourning dove just finishing its song.

"I have a lot to explain to you, Shan. I didn't fully realize it until today, so bear with me okay?"

She nodded. Any trace of flippancy he'd shown inside was totally gone. Now his face was completely earnest.

"I did as you suggested, as you know. I started seeing a therapist after Canada Day. It…it hasn't been easy. Sometimes—" He stopped, swallowed. "Sometimes it's been like living through it all over again. But it was the right thing to do. I'm getting better."

Shannyn encouraged him softly. "I know you are. I can see it. You're less on edge. Relaxed, freer with your smiles." She recalled the chaos of July First, then the few times he'd been in contact since. "I think not seeing you as much made the difference stand out more each time you *were* around. You were more changed each time. More grounded."

"I didn't realize it was noticeable."

"I noticed." She touched his knee gently, then took another drink from her bottle.

The mourning dove's cry faded away. "Today is one year since the accident."

"I know."

His gaze met hers then. "You do?"

She nodded. "I saw the date on your chart." She hadn't forgotten it. It was a day that had changed his life forever. When she'd first read it, she'd had no idea how much. She'd been so absorbed with herself and protecting Emma. She hadn't known how much more there really was.

"Was it difficult? How did you deal?" She'd thought of him often today, wondered how he was coping, wanting to call but unsure of whether or not she should.

"Today I drove to Nova Scotia, to Chris's hometown. And I went to visit him."

Shannyn put down her bottle. "That's a huge step for you." It had obviously been a good choice. If not, he wouldn't be here now.

"I was scared. Facing him…seeing his grave…I didn't know how I'd react. I've been such a loose cannon. But I stopped and bought us each a coffee." He looked up, a shy smile teasing the corners of his mouth. "Sounds stupid, I know, but in basic we had this thing about coffee in the morning. So I took one to him, and I just talked to him. It was good."

Shannyn's eyes misted. She doubted Jonas realized how much strength he was exhibiting right now. Facing the past took courage, and in her eyes, letting himself be vulnerable made him more of a man than any war he'd fought.

She reached over and laid her hand on his thigh. It was nearly healed, the muscle firm and sure beneath her fingers.

"Oh, Jonas, that's wonderful."

"I needed to do it. I'd made him a promise, you see. We always said that if something happened to one of us, the other one would escort the body home. I broke that vow. I didn't come back with him. Hell, I didn't even make his funeral. By the time I was stabilized and conscious, it was all over. Today I apologized for that."

Shannyn smiled. "You do realize that he forgave you long ago. You needed to forgive yourself."

He pulled his leg away from hers. "That's one of the things I'm beginning to see."

"You couldn't have known what would happen, and you couldn't have stopped it." She halted, unsure how much to reveal to him right now. He'd asked for space and she'd said she'd give it, but tonight seemed to be about honesty. Could she be honest with her feelings? Or was it too soon?

"You don't know how thankful I am that you weren't the one killed." She offered a compromise.

"But I came back and complicated everything for you."

"Maybe at first." She smiled sadly. "I was afraid. Fear is a powerful motivator."

Jonas rubbed a hand over his face. "I know. I wrote the book on it. Which brings me to what happened next." He studied his hands, rubbing the fingers together. "Someone else was visiting him, too. Nessa."

"Nessa?"

"His fiancée. He was planning on marrying her after that last deployment. We were only supposed to have another month or so before coming home for a while. The day we hit the mine, he'd told me she'd just bought her dress. I'd never met her, but I met her today."

"How is she?"

Shannyn studied him closely. Jonas smiled a little. In the trees at the edge of the yard, bats flitted in and out as darkness settled over them. The light over the kitchen stove filtered through the patio doors and threw his face in shadow.

"She's amazing. Resilient. And when I saw her today I knew I'd made a huge mistake.

"Even though Chris is gone, she is determined to honor him by living her life and being happy. She cherishes their time together, instead of being bitter and resentful. Nessa is grateful, Shan." His tone was incredulous, reverent. "She's simply grateful that she had the chance to love him. Even though that love was cut short."

He put his bottle down. "And that's where you come in, Shan."

Nerves skittered along her arms. "Me?"

"I owe you an apology. I did what I thought was right all those years ago. I went to become an elite soldier in an uncertain world. I thought that I was right in leaving you behind. I was afraid to have you care for me too much. What would have happened to you if I'd died in action? If I never came home again? Or if I came home crippled and you had to look after me? How could I ask you to waste your life like that? And now I'm telling you that I was wrong. I'm sorry. More sorry than you know that it's too late to take it back."

Shannyn closed her eyes against the pain searing her heart, only to have the tears that had shimmered there escape and trickle down her cheeks. Not *I'm sorry but I'll make things right*. His closing words echoed in her mind— *It's too late*. She'd been right to keep her feelings to herself just now. He saw her as a mistake he couldn't undo. And as happy as she was for him that he was finding his way back, the bitter taste of regret was on her tongue. He'd hurt her then and he was hurting her now.

"You say now that you did what you thought was best for me," she whispered through the pain. "But you never asked me." Her throat ached, raw. "You took away my choice. How could you do that?"

"I thought I was protecting you."

One of his hands rose to touch her cheek, the pad of his thumb caressing her cheekbone. He could be so tender, so caring, and it ripped her apart. She pulled her cheek away from his touch as the hurt spilled out with the truth. "You broke my heart, Jonas. Don't you realize that?"

She opened her eyes. Jonas didn't know that the words were as true tonight as they'd been six years ago. His face was a mixture of regret and surprise.

"No, I didn't. I thought we cared about each other but that you'd get over it. We were young, foolish."

"Foolish or not, I fell in love with you that summer."

Jonas slid forward so that their knees were touching. "So did I."

Shannyn sat up straighter. He'd what? Her heart pounded heavily, her throat convulsing against the tears she kept fighting back. All this time she'd thought that summer had been fun for him, nothing more. He'd loved her? Her head spun. How things could have been different if she'd only known. She would have fought harder, instead of accepting his disappearance from her life. If only he'd said something, all this time might not have been wasted. How stupid they'd been. How much they'd lost.

"But you never said it," she whispered.

"Neither did you."

"I was waiting for you to say it first."

It sounded juvenile now, and made her angry, knowing that perhaps if they'd just been honest back then things might have turned out differently.

"It was a test, then?"

Jonas said the words quietly but there was an edge to his voice that made her look away. Had she been testing him? She'd been young and in love and unsure of everything. She hadn't wanted to beg for his feelings, and perhaps her pride had gotten in the way. Pride and fear had kept her from contacting him once she'd known she was pregnant. Fear that the worst would happen. That he wouldn't love her as she loved him. Fear that he'd come home in a box. Fear that he'd be wounded. In that, she hadn't been wrong. It was small consolation.

"If it was, it wasn't intentional."

Her response sounded flimsy and she bit her lip. Would she have wanted him to choose her over the Army? Is that what she wanted now?

She didn't like the answer that came back.

"We both made mistakes." He was still apologizing, as though he was the only one carrying any responsibility around. "I took the choice away from you, Shannyn. I wasn't honest with my feelings. I wanted to ask you to come with me. But then I thought of all the service men who never came home and I knew I'd hate myself for hurting you. I made my decision based on fear, not on faith. Faith in you, faith in us. I realized that today. I took that choice away and I'm sorry. More sorry than you'll ever know."

His hand squeezed her wrist, warming the skin with a gentle touch before letting go. All these years she'd thought he hadn't cared enough to stay, or to ask her to wait for him. But he had cared. He'd made a mistake, yes. He'd taken the choice away from her. But he'd done it for the right reasons. Not out of concern for himself, but for her. He'd done it out of love. Could she say the same? She knew she couldn't, and it made her own admission sting that much more.

"I'm sorry, too, Jonas. I thought you hadn't loved me at all, so when I found out I was pregnant with Emma I knew I couldn't ask you to come back out of obligation. It would hurt too much to know you didn't love me the way I loved you. So I kept it from you. I denied you your daughter and denied her a father who clearly loves her. And I denied us the chance at a future. You're not the only one with regrets and with apologies." If only he knew.

"It's over now." He sat up a bit, holding her hand between both of his and chafing it. "No more looking back. No more regrets. What's done is done and we go from here."

Where exactly was that, though? Shannyn realized that while Jonas had said that he'd loved her then, he hadn't said that he still did now. There was something between them, certainly. But neither of them had said the word *love* and referred to it in the present tense. Once again she was waiting for him to say it first, too afraid to take the first step. Too afraid that they were repeating the same pattern. Could she bear for him to stay in the service, knowing how quickly their lives could change? Could she risk putting Emma through it, as well as herself? It wasn't just her to consider anymore.

"Where do we go from here?" she asked quietly, withdrawing her hands. "What do *you* see happening between us, Jonas?"

"I don't know." Jonas sighed and rested his elbows on his knees. "I've spent so much time living in the past that I'm not even in the future yet. I'm still taking things one day at a time. I'm going to have some decisions to make soon about where my future lies. I…"

He stopped midsentence, turned his head and looked out over the backyard.

"You what?"

"Tonight I had to tell you the truth about why I left. And for the first time, today I actually started thinking about the future rather than just being in crisis mode, taking things one day at a time. I've been there for so long, it's hard to get out."

His gaze met hers. Even, honest. "I still need time. Time to figure everything out. I'm going away for a few days. To talk to some people. Figure out my options."

Shannyn sat back in her chair, putting some distance between them. She wanted to say, *You've had six years to figure it out,* but knew it would be unfair. He was making progress. It was good he was moving forward. It wasn't up to her to approve of the direction he chose. The longer they talked, the clearer that became.

Perhaps that was why his next words shook her to the core.

"I'm not sure what the future holds, Shannyn. But I am clear on one thing. I never should have left you six years ago."

After all these years, finally hearing the words didn't feel the way she'd expected. It made her deeply mourn the time they'd wasted. Made her resent the choice he'd made. If only he'd stayed. Perhaps they could have worked it out. If he'd just asked her to go with him…

But she imagined hearing that knock on her door in the middle of the night. Imagined what it must have been like for Nessa. She didn't want to be a young woman standing beside a grave.

"You don't seem happy."

His voice, flat and expressionless, reached her and she snapped her head up to meet his gaze.

"It's not that…it's just…why are you telling me this today?"

"It doesn't matter."

She started to panic. He was taking her reaction as rejection, and she desperately needed to understand. "It does matter, Jonas. It matters a great deal." When he made to get out of the chair, she reached out and stopped him with a hand on his arm.

He sat back. "You want to know why today? Because I'm not afraid anymore. I needed to come clean. It's that simple."

Shannyn inhaled, the air trembling on its way to her lungs. "Nothing between us has ever been simple."

"No."

He needed to make a clean break. It was all making sense now. The words hung in the air as the silence grew thick around them. She couldn't bring herself to answer. She couldn't imagine delineating all the reasons why they couldn't be together. He'd made a mistake in the past, he'd made that clear. And she forgave him for it. What good would it do to talk about it now? It would change nothing.

Her eyes stung. So much for taking that leap of faith.

Jonas pushed back his chair and stood. His weight was even over both feet, and again Shannyn was reminded of how far he'd come over the past few months with his recovery. Jonas was putting his body and his life back together. She needed to do the same. She couldn't live her life waiting for him to make decisions. She'd learned that the hard way, and she and Emma had been okay. Having him around again, she'd started to think of him as part of their lives. Now she realized she had to stand on her own two feet again.

"Come here," he murmured in the dark.

She went to him, the evening breeze chilling her, raising goose bumps on her flesh. He pulled her lightly into his arms, resting his temple against her hair.

"You've given me strength, Shannyn Smith. You've given me the strength and the courage to get through this. Don't you think I'll ever forget that. I owe you everything."

She sighed, drank in his scent one last time. Imprinted on her heart every sensation of his body against hers. Then she pushed away.

"I'm happy for you."

Shannyn was surprised at how strong she sounded. She instantly missed the warmth of his arms around her. But as much as she knew she loved him, she also knew what he was saying. He was still who he was...*what* he was. He hadn't made promises, or proclaimed any feelings. The very strength that she'd wished for him was now driving him away, and she couldn't find the will to voice her feelings. She was too afraid. Afraid of losing him. Afraid of growing farther apart during his absences rather than closer together. Afraid that despite their renewed relationship, she'd always be the one that loved more. That hurt more.

She reached up and ran her fingers over his shoulders, imagining him in his uniform. She smiled sadly. "You are still a soldier. And now a healthy one. I don't doubt for a minute that this job posting will end and you'll be off on some new adventure. It's who you are, Jonas."

"You're still scared."

"Of course I am. I don't think I could survive losing you again. It's good that it's stopping here."

Everything in her wanted him to fight now. Fight for her like he hadn't six years earlier. Instead he remained silent and what little hope she'd held on to died a quiet death.

"You think my life is too what, transient? Dangerous and uncertain?"

"Something like that."

He wasn't fighting, then. It was over. Really over. It was the ending perhaps they'd never had, but there was no relief in it. All Shannyn felt was cold resignation at the way things had turned out.

She didn't want him to leave but understood now that it was exactly what he was doing. He had made her fall in love with him again, and now he was walking away. Just like before.

When he pulled away, his hand on the railing of the deck, she didn't stop him.

"We covered a lot of ground this evening," he acknowledged. "Maybe it's better to let the dust settle. Then we can meet and talk about where we go from here. We need to talk about Emma. We need to stay consistent for her, no matter what."

"That will be fine." It sounded forced and she knew it.

"I'm not sure when I'll be back. But I'll call you," he said softly. "Give Emma a kiss for me."

"I will," she replied, trying to hold back the tears that suddenly threatened. They were done. Reduced to talking about visitation schedules and what was best for their daughter. Knowing that every time she saw him she'd die a little more inside from loving him so hopelessly.

He hopped off the porch and lifted his hand in a wave before skirting around the house. Moments later his truck started and she heard his tires on the gravel of the drive.

Worn-out and overwhelmed, she sat back down on the chair, letting the sobs finally come. And tried to put together the pieces of what had just happened.

You've given me the strength and the courage to get through this. Don't you think I'll ever forget that.

She'd wanted him better, had wanted him to stop suffering, had wanted to help him through it. She just hadn't thought the cost to herself would be so high.

CHAPTER FOURTEEN

SHANNYN looked at the phone for the umpteenth time that afternoon. Each time it rang and Melanie answered it, her heart skipped a beat. Monday was the same, as was yesterday. Patients came and went; she did spreadsheets and payroll.

There was no reason for her to look for his call, but he was never far from her mind.

He'd been up-front about telling her that he was going away to discuss future options. Who knew what he'd be doing, or where. She remembered the gleam in his eyes as he'd spoken to Cpl. Benner outside the coffee shop. There's nothing he'd love more than to be back with the men of his unit. She knew that.

She should have known things would only grow more complicated. Emma had asked about him on Sunday, and again yesterday. Shannyn had no answers for her. He'd said they needed to talk about Emma, but now he wasn't making himself available. It was what she'd always feared. Shannyn was a grown-up and could deal somehow. But a child didn't understand why Daddy was suddenly *just gone*. Finally, last night, she'd broken down and tried calling his apartment, but there'd been no answer.

She played with a pen sitting on her desk, clicking the tip over and over. Jonas had admitted his mistake of years past. As hard as she tried, she couldn't forget that, even though she had forgiven him for it. Maybe he'd made a mistake leaving her, but the truth of the matter was if he'd loved her so very much, it wouldn't have mattered. He'd have asked her to go with him. No doubt. She realized now she probably *had* been testing him. And she'd punished him by keeping Emma from him.

She ran a hand through her hair. She loved him; she wouldn't lie to herself and attempt to deny it. But loving someone and making it work were two very different things. Now there was Emma in the middle, ensuring he'd always be linked to her somehow. She set her lips and went to the stacks to take out his chart. They needed to talk regardless. She wouldn't let Emma be pushed aside the way she'd been.

With a fortifying breath, she picked up the receiver of her phone and dialed the work number from his file.

When she asked for him, the polite woman on the other end apologized. "I'm sorry, ma'am, he's on base in Petawawa."

On base? Being out of town explained why he hadn't called, and she relaxed. "Do you know when he'll be back?"

The line was silent as the woman hesitated for a moment. "That will depend ma'am, on if he starts his new posting."

Shannyn sat down in her chair, suddenly numb. *New posting?* Jonas was going to a new posting? And he hadn't told her, or Emma? When had he decided? After they'd talked? Or had he known that night when he'd shown up at the soccer game?

Emma. Oh, no. Her heart sank to her toes. Shannyn had her own disappointments, but Emma was different. She was too small to understand a father coming and going, always in and out of her life. Realizing she still loved him had provoked all the old fears. Shannyn had known in the beginning that no one in the military stayed in one place for long. Over the past few weeks she'd conveniently forgotten it. How could she ever tell Emma that her dad had been killed in action? She'd almost wanted him to retain some of his injury so returning to active duty wouldn't be an option. It was purely selfish, she knew. And she truly was glad for him that his leg was healed and he felt whole again. Oh, what a mess she was in.

"Ma'am? Do you want to leave a message?"

"No," Shannyn muttered hoarsely. "No, thank you."

She hung up the phone heavily. Suddenly things he'd said became clear. Thanking her for being strong for him. Saying he'd never forget it. No more looking back and no regrets. She'd felt it was goodbye and it looked like her intuition had been right on the money. His file still lay on her desk. She hadn't given him a reason to stay. She had no one to blame but herself.

Nausea rolled through her stomach. She'd done it again. She'd lost her heart to him only to have him leave her without asking her opinion. He'd made decisions already and left her in the dark. Just like then, he'd charted out a life for himself and hadn't asked for her input. Only now there wasn't just her. There was Emma who was going to get hurt.

She let the cold anger roll in, and stacked the items on the top of her desk with terrifying precision. Anger was easier to deal with than the hurt. At least last time she'd known where he was going. It had always been a given. She'd just hoped he would ask her to go along, or leave her with some sort of assurance of keeping their relationship going. This time he was making changes and not even keeping her in the loop. After the way he'd seemingly bonded with Emma, it was hard to believe he'd do something like this without considering their daughter. She thought he'd changed.

She took his chart and shoved it back onto the shelf. She deserved better. Emma deserved better. The way he'd held her, the way he'd won Emma's heart told her he owed them more.

She made it through the remainder of the afternoon simply

by going into automatic pilot. She picked up Emma at the sitter's, chatted mindlessly with her about painting and grape Popsicles, all the while stewing about how she'd ended up in this place again. Vulnerable to him. Waiting for him. Waiting for a man who wasn't coming.

Shannyn took the key out of the ignition with a sigh. She felt used. Now that he was better physically, and making great strides emotionally, she felt that she was no longer needed. She'd been there while he'd been struggling, but now that he was moving on with his life, she was forgettable. The woman who had helped him through his *rough time*. Someone he'd once loved.

She'd promised herself she'd never let herself be vulnerable again, but here she was. Left behind. Again.

Emma bounced into the house ahead of her mother. "What's for dinner?" She skidded to a stop in the kitchen, her day care backpack dropping to the floor. Shannyn bit back her irritation; it wasn't Emma's fault she was in such a tumult.

"I don't know."

"Can we have mac and cheese? Can we?"

Shannyn's eyes caught the red blinking light of the answering machine. Holding up a finger to silence Emma for a moment, she hit the button.

The first message was from Patty, saying that she was taking Lisa to the diner around six and asking if Emma would like to go along.

"Yes, yes, yes!" Emma called out, dragging her backpack through the kitchen to the table. "The diner beats macaroni and cheese!" She started pulling things out of her pack.

The second message was from Jonas.

"Shan, it's me. I need to see you. I know it's short notice, but could you come by tonight? Anytime after five-thirty is great."

It was ridiculous, how she was affected by the mere sound of him on an answering machine. Even knowing what she did now, the husky timbre of his voice reached inside of her. She steeled herself. Likely he was going to break the news to her tonight. A new posting meant moving on. After what she'd said, she knew it meant moving on without her.

"Can I come see Daddy, too?"

Shannyn hated to say no but this was one time she knew she and Jonas would be better off alone. "I thought you were going to the diner."

"Oh, yeah."

"Daddy and I need to discuss some grown-up things anyway. You'd be bored." Shannyn paused, wanting to be encouraging to Emma but not giving her false guarantees that she couldn't deliver. "I'll talk to him, though, and see when he plans on visiting again, okay?"

Emma nodded, not too upset, apparently. Shannyn exhaled slowly. If he *were* going away, she'd make sure he spent time with Emma before he went. That was nonnegotiable.

She called Patty and accepted the invitation, then asked if Emma could stay there until she got back from an errand. But that left her with the problem of time on her hands and trying to keep occupied until Emma was picked up. She sorted the laundry and put a load in the washer, vacuumed the living room. Sat with Emma and read a few stories. When six finally arrived, she heaved a great sigh of relief.

Once Emma was gone Shannyn considered revamping her appearance. She changed into a pretty skirt and blouse, then looked in the mirror and frowned. This was ridiculous. She was bracing herself for a breakup, which was funny because they weren't really together in the first place. It was silly to dress up and look extraspecial. She changed out of the skirt and slid back into her comfy jeans and T-shirt. Again she met her own gaze in the mirror. If he were truly going to destroy her world, she was at least going to be in comfortable clothes.

Tucking her hair behind her ears one last time, she took her purse, got in her car, and drove toward the end.

Jonas answered the buzzer, a smile of relief breaking out on his face. He smoothed his hands down his shirt, making sure it was tucked neatly into his waistband. He hadn't even changed out of the dress uniform he'd worn today when he'd met the Minister of Defence. He'd removed his tie and red beret, but that was it. Somehow, tonight required more than jeans and a ratty T-shirt.

When five-thirty had passed, he'd started to worry. Had considered calling again but decided against it. Perhaps she was running late or couldn't get a sitter for Emma. Finally he'd given in and dialled the phone again.

The door buzzed when he was hearing the third ring, and he hung up.

Tonight was going to change everything.

He held the door open for her, surprised when she breezed past him coolly. He frowned. Her dander was up about something, although he couldn't imagine what.

"Thank you for coming," he started, his head turning to follow her as she sailed through the small foyer. There was so much he had to say. To explain.

"So, when do you start?"

"I beg your pardon?" His steps halted behind her.

Shannyn zipped straight through to the living room, planting her hands on her hips. After a momentary lapse, he followed her, confused. What was she talking about? And why in the world was she acting as if he was the villain? Her eyes met his, full of a challenge he didn't understand.

"Your new job? When do you start? Where is it this time?"

Staccato words, so harsh. She raised one eyebrow at him, her lips set in a firm, unpleasant line. All his well-thought-out speeches evaporated. How could she possibly know? He'd only been offered the position this morning, and he'd caught the first hop back to Gagetown. He'd been home all of three hours.

"Shannyn, I can explain. All of it." He folded his hands behind his back, trying to remain rational and not take the bait for an all-out argument. Even if her aggressive stance did try his temper.

"Oh, there's no need. I heard all about it today. Petawawa, right? Is that where you're going next? Or back with the Princess Pats in Edmonton? Where are you *needed* this time?"

"Why are you acting like this? You're so angry!" He stepped further into the room, shoving his hands into the pockets of his trousers. If she'd only give him a chance to explain. Instead she was treating him as though he'd done something unforgivable. "You sent me away, remember?"

Damn. He'd told himself she wouldn't draw him into an argument, and here he was, rising to the bait.

She folded her arms with defiance. "Maybe I'm angry because I finally trusted you. I trusted you to be honest, Jonas. If not for me, for Emma. And now I find out from someone else that you're taking a new job." She held up her hand when he started to protest. "No, don't bother. I know a new job means a new posting and a new base. I've enough experience with the Army to know *that* much. This is exactly why I didn't tell you about Emma in the first place, Jonas. Because I didn't want her to know—to love— a father who was only in her life when his schedule permitted."

"Only Emma?" He smiled a little. She was covering her misgivings with blame. He took it as a good sign. Their parting last week had been surprisingly cold. But now the thought of him going away had her panicking. "Or are you afraid I'll only let *you* in my life when I can pencil you in?"

"That's ridiculous. And it doesn't matter. You're obviously leaving again."

"You're wrong." His voice was firm but sure. He could see what was happening. He recognized the fear, knew it was much more promising than not caring at all. He knew she was remembering how he'd left her before, and it kept him from getting too angry with her. If she would only listen to him, she'd understand everything.

"Oh, please. Don't insult me," she retorted.

"Don't insult *me*, Shannyn." He kept his voice even. "I don't know what you think you know, but perhaps you'd be interested in hearing the actual truth."

Her brazen sneer faltered just a little.

"This isn't about Emma. Not really. It's about you, and you being afraid that I'll leave you again."

Her mouth dropped open.

"You think I don't get it? After we talked last week? I know now how I hurt you the last time. I don't blame you for being scared. You don't want to go through it again. You don't want to go through what Nessa has gone through. And believe me, I've no desire to put you through it."

"Why would you, when you clearly said goodbye?"

"Is that what you think?"

"Isn't it true?"

He smiled a little. She was more afraid than he'd thought. He thought back to their conversation. He hadn't meant it as goodbye at all. He'd thought they'd been finding their feet. Setting the groundwork upon which to build something great.

And she thought he'd been preparing to leave for good.

He could see the vulnerability through her aggressive stance, and softened his voice, trying to draw her in, make her understand.

He tilted her chin, lifting it so that his eyes burned into hers. "Do. You. Love. Me. It's that simple, Shan."

"Nothing is ever that simple. You know that."

"I know I love you. Do you love me back?"

Tears burned the backs of her eyes. He was standing here saying it after all, and she hated how much she wanted to hope. To believe. Damn him. Damn him for making her feel so much all over again.

"Please," he murmured. Her eyelids fluttered closed as he dropped tiny kisses on them, the light touch making her sway. "Please tell me the truth."

She nodded, her forehead brushing his cheek as the answer came out in a strangled whisper— "Yes."

"Yes, you love me?"

She blinked, and two tears ran silently over her cheeks. "Yes, I love you."

Instead of the heated kiss of earlier, he drew her tenderly into his arms, resting his chin against her hair.

"Think about this for a moment. Would I have told you I loved you if I were going to give up on us?"

"I don't know." The vigor deflated out of her argument, the vulnerability creeping closer to the surface. She pulled out of his arms and away, where she could think clearly. "I…I'm not sure of anything where you're concerned."

"And that scares you." He took a step closer.

Shannyn inhaled, trying to stop the shaking, trying to keep up the bravado. He was being so steady. Looking so tall and heroic and handsome in his uniform.

She'd thought that just laying it all on the table would be less painful, like ripping off a bandage. She'd come in here with both barrels blazing, taking the offensive to cover her concerns and hurt. Full of resolve, knowing it was over between them. But, damn him, he'd seen right through it. She'd felt strong in her righteous indignation. Now here he was telling her she was wrong. Recognizing she was scared. And, oh, she was so sick of living in fear. With his words, she'd gone from being on the offensive to being left with very little defense.

"Shan," he continued. Another step. "Tell me what scares you. Trust me with it. I trusted you."

"This is different," she murmured. "Because *you* scare me. I'm scared to love you."

Jonas came all the way to where she was standing. Close enough it would only take a breath and she would feel him against her. Only inches separated them. But still he did not touch her.

"Faith, not fear," he murmured. If only he'd realized it sooner. "I hurt you so badly the first time. I know that now. And because of it you doubt me."

"Maybe I need a reason not to."

He lifted her chin with a finger, touching her skin there but nowhere else. "Then how's this for starters. I loved you then. I love you more now. Even more today than I did last week. And I want to spend the rest of my life proving it."

Tears sprung into her eyes and she blinked them away. She couldn't breathe.

She couldn't let herself be placated so easily, not when the simple words did splendid things to her insides.

"Then why didn't you tell me what you were doing?" She challenged him, pulling her chin away from his caress. "A phone call, or even an e-mail to let me know your plans. Instead you walked away. For all I knew it was for good."

He smiled. "I can see that you think that, and I'm sorry. It's not what I intended. I wanted to be honest with you about the past so we could put it behind us. I didn't mean to give you the impression that I was putting *us* behind *me*. I told you I was exploring some options, remember? But nothing was definite, so I didn't want to tell you prematurely and get your hopes up. I had meetings with some men in Ontario, it's true. About my future."

There were still too many blanks to fill in. "What sorts of options?" The earlier thought of active duty leaped to front and center. The thought of him going back out in the field, to the front line of danger...the threat of losing him always present...she couldn't lie; she wished he'd do something other than rejoin his unit. Something safer.

"There's something I have to know first."

"What?"

They stood only inches apart, a standoff. Yet Shannyn felt inexorably tied to him. Like there was a cord binding them together, even when they were coming from different places.

"If my life were more settled, would you give us a chance?"

All the air seemed to squeeze out of her chest. "How can you ask that, without giving me details?"

"It's easy. Don't make it more complicated than it is. Forget my job. Forget the past. Forget Emma. Ask yourself if you are willing to take the risk now. If you trust me to do the right thing."

His eyes softened, her gaze was drawn to his full lips as he formed the words.

How could she do it? Walk blindly into a life of uncertainty? Live with the danger, knowing he could be taken away from her at any time?

She'd only wanted him to ask her the last time, but it was much more than that. Loving him meant accepting the possibility of being hurt.

"Faith, not fear." He whispered the gentle reminder.

She watched his mouth form the words. It didn't matter. She was hurting right now. And he was standing before her, the strongest man she'd ever known, asking her to share his life. Without guarantees.

She knew the answer as it shot out of her heart.

"Yes." The words choked out on a near sob. "I need you, Jonas. It's what scares me more than anything."

Letting the words out, confessing her feelings and her fears, felt like complete surrender, and for a moment she reveled in the freedom of it. Her eyes slid closed as he came closer, dropping his lips to touch hers gently.

"That's really good news," he murmured against her lips. "Because I thought I was alone in that particular area."

Her lips followed his, eager to taste more, now that they'd said the words. "Loving you comes naturally. Dealing with it is the hard part."

She was suddenly reminded of his new posting and she drew back. "But you're leaving, aren't you? Are you going back into active duty? Being stationed at another base?" Dread at losing him, anyway, curled darkly through her.

"If I were transferred, would you come with me? You and Emma?"

This, then, was the question he'd never asked the first time, and even though she couldn't help the thread of anxiety at the thought of leaving her home and job behind, she knew this time she couldn't back away.

"Yes. Yes, Jonas, I would come with you this time."

"Why?"

She looked up at him. Over the time she'd known him, he'd been three men. The first was the carefree, indestructible warrior. The second a hard, uncompromising man broken by the things he'd seen and done. The third, though, the third was a mixture of those two men. A man so much stronger than the two parts that made him who he was. In his eyes she saw not only shades of his youth but a wisdom and gravity that only experience could bring. A man who felt deeply, loved his job, loved his daughter. Loved her. How could she ever let that get away? How could she give up the chance to love him? Maybe he would be back in the line of fire. But she knew that if she passed up the chance to try, she'd regret it always, and she told him so.

"Because I love you. Because I'm tired of being scared, too. I let you leave before because I thought you didn't love me. I didn't tell you about Emma because I was afraid you'd be with us for the wrong reasons and so I built a wall around my heart, told myself I was doing the right thing. I came here tonight, ready to tear into you because I was afraid to love you more than you loved me. But I do love you, I always have and being *without* you now is more terrifying than any of those things."

His hand cupped the back of her neck, roughly pulling her close and cradling her head against his chest. His pulse thudded against her temple, steady and strong. She felt him swallow, press a kiss against her hair.

"I promise I won't give you reason to regret it. I know the risk you're taking, and I love you more for it. But I don't have to leave, Shan."

She pulled out of his arms. "You don't? But what about Petawawa? The new posting?"

His teeth flashed as he smiled. "I did go to Petawawa. And I did have meetings, and I've been offered a position. But I haven't accepted it yet."

"Why not?"

"Because I needed to talk it over with you first. It wouldn't be fair to make that sort of decision without finding out how you and Emma feel about it."

Suddenly the tears came, great consuming ones that surprised her as much as they surprised Jonas. She hadn't even realized she'd been testing him again or that this had been part of it, but his consulting her meant more than he could ever know.

"Shhh," he murmured, cupping her face and wiping away tears. "You haven't even heard what it is yet."

A bubble of laughter rose up through the sobs. "That's not why." She pressed a hand to her chest and regained control. "How can I tell you what I think about it if you don't tell me what it is?"

He grinned. "You'll be pleased to know the job is right here. At Base Gagetown."

"No active duty?"

He gripped her arms. "Is that what you thought?"

She nodded, flooded with relief that he wasn't going to be back in the field after all.

"No, baby, no active duty. An opportunity came up. One so good I didn't want to jinx it by saying anything prematurely. You and Emma…I didn't want to uproot you from the lives you've worked so hard to build. I can see how you've created a real home for her. I want to be a part of that, Shan, not take her away from it."

She blinked slowly. He was doing a fine job of building his case. Right now she was spellbound, hanging on his every word with breathless anticipation.

"I was offered a contract through the SAS to train Special Forces. Everything's being spearheaded out of Petawawa, but the majority of training will be at the Combat Arms Center here. Included in that is a chance to be a liaison with the government for antiterrorism."

"Oh, Jonas. You must be so proud. Of course you must take it."

"It's a choice assignment. I couldn't ask for better. I couldn't answer, though, until I knew what you wanted. All I knew is that it could keep me where I belong—with you and Emma. If…"

"If…"

She held her breath.

He reached into his trousers and pulled out a ring, the platinum and single diamond catching the dying sunbeams in the fading light. "I should have done this years ago, but better late than never." He gripped her left hand in his strong right one. "If you'll marry me. Give me a chance to be the husband and father you both deserve. Let us build a family together." His eyes twinkled at her. "Maybe even a bigger family."

She put the fingers of her right hand over her lips, unsure of whether to laugh or cry. She'd come here tonight prepared for a standoff, not a proposal. Not the answer to all her hopes and dreams. And she'd come in her ratty jeans, she thought. A spurt of laughter crept up and out her lips.

"You haven't said yes yet," he reminded her.

"It's about time I made that leap of faith, don't you think?" Her fingers trembled but her smile was wide. "Put it on, Jonas. Put on the ring and make us a family."

He slid the ring over her knuckle, the diamond winking as she wiggled her fingers.

She lifted both her hands to cup his face.

"I love you. No matter what, you'll always be a hero to me. You just remember that, Sgt. Kirkpatrick."

"I'm not a hero, Shan. I'm just a man. A man who loves you. Always have, always will."

He sealed the covenant with a kiss. "Hey, Shan?"

"Hmmm?"

"Let's go tell Emma."

Sharing conspiratorial smiles, she tugged him by the hand to the door.

"I think we're about to make her day," Shannyn said, laughing.

MARRIAGE FOR BABY

MELISSA McCLONE

For Virginia Kantra and Tiffany Talbott,
talented writers and friends extraordinaire.
Special thanks to Ceci and Robert Kramer.

With a degree in mechanical engineering from Stanford University, the last thing **Melissa McClone** ever thought she would be doing was writing romance novels. But analysing engines for a major US airline just couldn't compete with her 'happily-ever-afters'. When she isn't writing, caring for her three young children or doing laundry, Melissa loves to curl up on the couch with a cup of tea, her cats and a good book. She enjoys watching home-decorating shows to get ideas for her house—a 1939 cottage that is slowly being renovated. Melissa lives in Lake Oswego, Oregon, with her own real-life hero husband, two daughters, a son, two lovable but oh-so-spoiled indoor cats and a no-longer-stray outdoor kitty that decided to call the garage home. Melissa loves to hear from her readers. You can write to her at PO Box 63, Lake Oswego, OR 97034, USA.

CHAPTER ONE

STANDING on the sidewalk outside the lawyer's office, Kate Malone stared at the double glass doors. She still had a few minutes until her appointment. No reason to rush inside.

She raised her face to the cloudless, blue sky. The spring sunshine heated her cheeks. Sun kisses. That's what Susan called them.

Susan.

The unusually warm April temperature reminded Kate of their college graduation eight years ago. She had approached the proceedings as a necessary step, one more thing to mark off her To Do List on the way to the top, but not her best friend, Susan. Unlike Kate, Susan had relished every moment of the drawn-out ceremony in the sweltering ninety-degree heat. She'd bounced across the stage, tossed her University of Oregon diploma box in the air and twirled around.

A smiled tugged on Kate's lips. Susan always lived life to the fullest. Or rather…

Had lived.

Until a driver fell asleep at the wheel and collided head-on with Susan's car two days ago here in Boise, Idaho.

Tears stung Kate's eyes. Grief slashed through her. How could Susan be dead? Susan, so full of life, so full of love. Susan, with her adoring husband, Brady, and their cute baby, Cassidy...

All three had died in the crash.

Kate swallowed, hard.

No. She couldn't lose control now.

She didn't have a tissue. Or the time.

She needed to hold herself together during the meeting with Susan and Brady's attorney. Once Kate checked into her hotel, she could fall apart, but not until then.

Squaring her shoulders, she pushed open one of the doors to the law office and stepped inside. A blast of cool air hit her. Goose bumps prickled on her arms. The sight of the empty receptionist desk deflated her resolve. Her composure slipped a notch. Now that she was inside, she wanted to get this over with.

"Kate?"

The familiar male voice made her stiffen. Jared. She wasn't ready to face him. Not now. Possibly not ever. And yet she found herself turning in the direction of his voice.

As Jared rose from a leather club chair, her breath caught in her throat. He wore a tailored gray suit and the multicolored silk tie she'd given him for his thirty-first birthday.

Five years ago when Brady and Susan had introduced them, Jared Reed had been a twenty-something single woman's fantasy. He'd gotten only more handsome. Kate's heart thudded. She wished she still didn't find him so attractive.

His square jaw and slightly crooked nose—from a snowboarding accident when he was a teenager—gave his face the right amount of rugged character to offset his long lashes and lush lips. She couldn't believe how much his hair had grown in the last three months. Normally he went for the short, corporate cut, but the wavy, carefree style suited him better.

Not that she cared.

Much.

His hazel-green eyes met hers. "How are you?"

"I-I'm—" Her voice cracked. Tears blurred her vision. Oh, no. She didn't want him to see her like this.

Kate blinked. Once, twice.

"I'm so sorry, Katie." He was at her side in an instant and brushed his lips across her forehead. "So very sorry."

At the best of times, she struggled to remain indifferent to him, but his tender gesture and simple, yet sincere words shattered her defenses. She sunk against him, breathing in his familiar soap and water scent, drawing in the welcome comfort of his hard chest.

Stop…now, logic shouted.

Get away…now, common sense cried.

But Kate didn't want to listen. She didn't care if her actions went against rational thought. Jared understood what she was going through. He was going through the same thing.

"I'm sorry, too," she choked out. "It's so…"

He wrapped his arms around her. "Horrible."

She hugged him. "I keep thinking it's a mistake or I'm going to wake up and it's all been a bad dream."

"Me, too," he admitted. "As soon as I heard, I called your office. They said you were out of town."

"Boston."

"I didn't want to leave a message."

"I wouldn't have gotten it." She closed her eyes. Not being alone felt so good. "After my assistant phoned me with the news, I turned off my phone."

"A first."

"I hope I never have to do it again."

He gave her shoulder a reassuring squeeze. "So do I."

She stared at him. "I'm sorry I didn't think to call you."

"You wouldn't have been able to reach me. I was in San Francisco. My boss had me pulled out of a meeting and relayed the message." A corner of Jared's mouth lifted. "Besides, I didn't expect you to call, Kate."

She flinched. "Why not? Brady was your best friend."

"Susan was like a sister to you. How old were you when you met?

"Seven." In a foster home. Kate's first. Susan's third. That had been so long ago. They had come so far.

"Seven," he repeated. "You have to be devastated."

Devastated didn't begin to describe the anguish ripping Kate apart. She felt as if a part of her had died, too. She inhaled slowly.

Jared's arms tightened around her, and she found herself resting her head against his chest, a foreign yet familiar position. "It's okay to cry, Katie."

She fought the urge to pull away. But she couldn't. Not when she relished the feel of him, of the steady beat of his heart beneath her cheek.

"I've cried." Kate didn't want to sound defensive. It was the truth. She had cried. More than she would ever admit. She just didn't like crying in front of others.

"I spoke to Brady a couple of weeks ago," Jared said.

"Susan e-mailed me a picture of Cassidy on Thursday. She promised to send more." But those pictures would never arrive. The baby girl would never grow any bigger. Kate smothered a sob. "I can't believe they're gone. Why them? Why now?"

"I wish I knew."

"Me, too."

But thinking about what she'd lost hurt so much. Too much. She'd rather think about something else. Someone else. Jared.

Kate curled the ends of his hair with her finger. It had never been long enough to do this before, and she liked the extra length. He brushed his hand through her hair, his fingers sifting through the strands, the way he always had. She nearly sighed.

It was as if nothing had changed between them. Kate knew that wasn't true, but she wasn't ready to back out of his arms.

For now she could pretend the past didn't matter and ignore the future. She could do that because she needed Jared. She needed his warmth, his strength, him. And a part of her hoped he needed her, too.

He cupped her face with his left hand. She noticed the gold band on his fourth finger. Her ring finger felt conspicuously bare. She curled her hand into a fist.

"Mr. and Mrs. Reed?" a female voice asked.

Jared turned his head. "Yes?"

A cute brunette with short, curly hair and dangling gold earrings stood next to the receptionist's desk.

Kate backed out of his embrace. "Actually I'm—"

"My wife. Kate Malone," he interrupted, a slight edge to his voice. "I'm Jared Reed."

Kate recalled the long discussions about her not taking his name. He had claimed to understand, to accept her decision. But he hadn't. Not really. She shifted uncomfortably.

"I'm sorry, Ms. Malone. Mr. Reed." The woman picked up a thick manila file from the receptionist's desk. "Don Phillips is running a few minutes late. I'll show you to his office once I drop off this folder."

"Thank you," Jared said.

As the woman walked away, Kate bit her lip. "Why didn't you tell her the truth?"

"Because with or without your wedding band, you are still my wife." His gaze hardened. "At least until the divorce is finalized."

The receptionist led them down a hallway and motioned to an office at the end. "Don will be right with you."

"Thanks." Jared hoped the atmosphere in the office would be more comfortable than that of the lobby. But knowing Kate, he wasn't going to hold his breath.

The woman smiled. "Let me know if you need anything."

"We will." He was tempted to ask the friendly receptionist to stay until the lawyer joined them. That might ease the tension between him and Kate. Not to mention the silence. Kate hadn't spoken to him since he'd mentioned the word divorce. His jaw clamped. Maybe she'd forgotten she was the one who filed.

No. That wasn't fair.

She'd lost her best friend and goddaughter. She was in tremendous pain. Who knew what was going through her beautiful, blond head?

Kate sat in one of the chairs opposite a large mahogany desk. With a posture that would make a charm school proud, she looked poised and in control as she studied the diploma hanging behind the desk. Not surprising really. Kate kept her emotions under a tight lid, and hated showing any sign of weakness.

Or at least had until today when she entered the law office on the verge of tears. She had looked so lost and alone. The sadness on her face had clawed at his heart.

Jared sat in the chair next to her and extended his hand. "You okay?"

She nodded once, not meeting his gaze. Maybe she didn't see his hand, either.

At least he'd tried. Jared rested his arm on the chair. No one could say he hadn't tried to save his marriage or hadn't wanted to give the relationship another go. He had, and he would. If she would give him the chance.

Ironic, Jared thought. Brady and Susan had introduced him to Kate. Now their deaths were bringing them back together after almost three months apart.

The seconds turned into minutes. The only sound was the ticking of a vintage Felix the Cat clock. At least one thing hadn't changed since the last time he saw Kate. The same stone-cold silence. They had been in Boise three months ago for Cassidy's baptism. The weekend hadn't gone well. Separation and divorce had been mentioned, but he hadn't expected the call from her lawyer the next week. Ever since then lawyers had handled the communication between them. And that seemed…strange. Wrong. Yet Kate wouldn't consider another option. He brushed his hand through his hair. "Kate—"

"There's a reason I'm not wearing my wedding rings."

Uh-oh. Jared drew a cautious breath. Words and actions could easily be misconstrued with emotions running so high. He and Kate were both hurting enough, but he couldn't deny how seeing her ringless finger had affected him. "You don't owe me any explanations."

"I was afraid the ring would fall off," she said anyway, still not meeting his eyes. "I lost some weight."

More than "some" by the way she'd felt in his arms. She'd felt thinner, fragile. He'd chalked it up to grief. Now he wasn't so sure.

Kate never went out without looking perfect—hair, makeup, clothing. She called it the "whole package", even though she looked as beautiful to him in ratty, old sweats, a stained T-shirt and ponytail. Today, however, Kate looked as if she'd had to work harder on the package. And he could see the difference.

The energetic, multitasking dynamo, who owned one of the hottest and fastest growing public relation firms in the Pacific Northwest, had all but disappeared. Jared expected to see Kate's normally bright blue eyes red and swollen given the circumstances, but not so wary, stressed, exhausted. Her sunken cheeks and loose fitting designer clothes went beyond grief, and the changes worried him.

"You need to remember to eat," he said.

"I eat."

He raised an eyebrow.

She set her chin. "I just forget sometimes."

Most of the time. Jared used to text message her at lunchtime and dinnertime. Now that he wasn't around to remind her, she probably didn't bother to eat a decent meal. "You should schedule food into your day."

"I do," she said, a little too quickly. "Do you?"

"I don't need to. I enjoy food too much to skip meals."

"I don't skip meals. I forget." Her mouth twitched. "I don't want to argue."

She never did anymore. The only place Jared had seen Kate really lose control was in bed. "We're not arguing."

"Just drop it. Okay?"

He checked the time. The second hand moved slower than his niece's turtle, Corky.

"Sorry to keep you waiting." A middle-aged man, wearing a tailored navy suit and wire-rimmed glasses, burst into the office. "I'm Don Phillips, the Lukas's attorney."

Jared rose and shook the man's hand. "Jared Reed."

Kate remained seated. "Kate Malone."

The lawyer sat behind his desk, and Jared sat, too.

"I'm so sorry for the loss of your friends," Don said. "It's such a tragedy."

Jared nodded. Kate placed her clasped hands on her lap.

"Thank you for coming so quickly." Don reached for a file. "I'd hoped to speak with you personally when I called yesterday, but under the circumstances I felt it was imperative to get you to Boise as soon as possible."

"We understand," Jared said. "Have funeral arrangements been made?"

"Yes." Don pulled out a piece of paper from the file. "Mr. Lukas, Brady's father, took care of that. A vigil will be held at the funeral home on Wednesday and a memorial service on Thursday. The church will put on a reception in the hall afterward. Then the bodies will be flown to Maine for burial."

The lawyer made it sound so easy like a checklist.

"Susan…" Kate's voice trailed off.

"What?" Jared asked.

"It's just—" she tucked her hair behind her ears "—Susan never really liked Maine."

"No, she didn't," Don agreed. "But she and Brady had their burial location put in their wills."

"Oh." Kate wet her lips. "Okay, then."

"A situation like this is never easy, but fortunately Brady and Susan had the foresight to plan for such an occurrence."

Occurrence? A chill inched down Jared's spine. Perhaps that was legalese for death. Either way, all of this was difficult for him to hear.

"No amount of planning will make this any easier to deal with, but logistically, having wills in place will make things proceed a little smoother." Don pulled out a thick document from the file. "I attended the same church as Brady and Susan, and I drew up their wills. Since they had no family in town, I kept the originals here in the office."

"Shouldn't we wait for Brady's parents?" Jared asked.

"Mr. and Mrs. Lukas aren't coming," Don explained. "Although Mr. Lukas handled the funeral arrangements, their doctors felt the trip from the East Coast would be too much for them with their current health conditions. They received copies of both wills after they were written so they know, and agree with, what their son and daughter-in-law decided. May I proceed?"

Jared nodded. He watched for Kate's reaction, but she held herself together tightly. This had to be tearing her up inside, and he ignored the urge to touch her.

"As you know, Brady was an only child and Susan had been in foster homes since she was five. They had no living relatives other than Brady's parents." Don's gaze rested on Kate. "Though Susan considered you more a sister than a friend."

Kate's composed façade cracked for an instant. "I felt the same way."

"The Lukases thought highly of you, Jared," Don said. "Brady and Susan each named you their personal representative to handle their estates. Do you accept their nominations?"

Jared had no idea what sort of responsibilities would be involved as Brady and Susan's executor, but that didn't matter. "I'm honored and happy to accept. May I retain your services? I've never done something like this before so I will need your expertise."

"I'll gladly counsel and offer you assistance. The sooner we get started, the better. I would like to submit the wills and obtain your appointment as personal representative through informal proceedings. That way a hearing won't be required."

Proceedings. Hearing. Jared's muscles tensed. This was too weird. A few weeks ago he'd been making plans to attend a poker tournament with Brady while Kate spent the weekend with Susan. Now he was overseeing their friends' probate.

As Don scribbled notes on a yellow legal pad, Jared glanced at Kate. She acted like this was nothing more than another one of the endless meetings she attended, but he noticed her hands trembling. He wanted to pull her onto his lap and hold her until she felt better, until she smiled again.

"Once you're officially appointed their personal representative, you'll want to call a locksmith and have the locks changed on the Lukas's residence," Don said. "I can provide recommendations."

"I'd appreciate the referrals," Jared said.

"Why do the locks need to be changed?" Kate asked.

"We don't know who might have keys to the house," Don explained. "Baby-sitters, neighbors, housecleaners. The list goes on. You don't want to chance a robbery. Unfortunately such break-ins have occurred."

Jared pictured the two-story house Brady and Susan called home. The couple had been too busy working on the nursery to fix up the rest of the house. Now that task would fall to the new owner. Jared thought of his and Kate's home, the hours they'd spent working on the old house. Kissing on a ladder. Making love on a drop cloth. Kate obsessing over paint chips. That seemed like so long ago.

Soon the house would be hers. He hadn't fought Kate for it, even though he loved the home with all its creaks, foibles and bad plumbing. But his life was no longer in Portland. His life was no longer with Kate. He kept telling himself that, even though the words never seemed to make things easier. And he'd yet to fully believe them.

"Do I have your permission to proceed?" Don asked.

"Please do," Jared said, grateful for the lawyer's help.

Don shuffled papers. "And now Cassidy."

Kate's befuddlement matched Jared's confusion. "What about Cassidy?" he asked.

"You and Kate have been nominated for joint guardianship in both wills," Don said, but his words made no sense. "You realize, of course, you are under no legal obligation to accept the guardian appointment."

Kate's lower lip quivered. "I don't understand."

Neither did Jared. Guardian? Of Cassidy? But...

He shook his head. "There has to be some mistake."

"I suggest clients discuss guardianship with prospective nominees before naming them in their wills," Don added. "Otherwise the nomination can come as a shock."

Shock didn't come close to what Jared was feeling. "You don't understand—"

"They discussed it with us." Kate's voice sounded hoarse, unnatural. "But Cassidy is dead."

The lawyer frowned.

Jared reached for her hand and laced his fingers with hers. "The message I received said the family had been in an accident and the Lukas's were dead."

"I was told the same," Kate said.

"Oh, no. There's been some sort of miscommunication." Don's face went grim. "Cassidy was in the accident, but she survived."

Kate clung to Jared's hand. He understood how she felt, afraid to hope, afraid to believe the news could be true, because the letdown would be even worse.

"She's alive?" Kate whispered.

Jared held his breath.

"Cassidy is very much alive." Don set his pen on the desk. "She's at the hospital recovering from her injuries."

Thank God. An enormous weight lifted from Jared's shoulders. He knew how much Brady loved his baby girl, how much Brady would have wanted her to go on with or without him.

Kate jumped up from her chair, pulling Jared with her.

Tears streamed down her face. She smiled at him. An almost forgotten warmth seeped into his heart. "I can't believe it."

He smiled back. "Believe it."

She hugged him. The scent of her shampoo—grapefruit—filled his nostrils. Her mane of hair brushed against him and he remembered how much he'd miss holding her and touching her and loving her.

"Is it wrong to feel happy?" she whispered, her warm breath caressed his neck.

"It's fine, Kate." Jared held onto her. "I feel the same way."

They both laughed, a sound he never thought he'd hear in the near future let alone today.

"I am so sorry." Don removed his glasses and rubbed his eyes. "It was a difficult day yesterday. I thought I was clear on the phone but perhaps I wasn't."

"Cassidy's alive." Kate sat, but didn't let go of Jared's hand so he sat, too. "That's what matters. Is she okay?"

"Cassidy is in stable condition," Don explained. "The car seat seems to have protected her from more serious injuries."

Kate sucked in a breath. Jared blew his out.

"What?" Don asked.

"Our baby shower gift was the car seat," Jared said.

Don leaned forward. "Excellent gift."

Jared nodded, but he felt strange. Kate had spent hours poring over catalogs and reading car seat reviews in order to pick the right one. He'd thought she was being obsessive again, but her research could have saved the baby's life.

Her lips parted. Was she remembering?

How could she not? Cassidy was alive. Her parents were dead. And the little girl belonged to him and Kate.

Jared remembered when Brady and Susan had flown in for a weekend. Susan and Kate had spent the day shopping for maternity clothes while Brady helped Jared build a trellis for the yard. That night over a bottle of sparkling cider, Brady and Susan asked them to be the baby's guardians. They told them to think about the request. Jared and Kate did and agreed the next morning.

But that was before. Before the separation. Before Kate had filed for divorce.

"How recent is the will?" Jared asked.

"I met with Brady and Susan a week after Cassidy was born." Don got a faraway look in his eyes. "I remember them telling me this was the baby's first outing since coming home from the hospital. Susan said she'd put it into the baby book."

That didn't make sense. Brady and Susan would have known about the marriage problems, about Jared living and working in Seattle and Kate in Portland. Something wasn't adding up.

"What's the problem?" Kate asked. "We told them we would do it."

"This is a life-changing decision," Don said. "Don't rush. You have thirty days after we start guardianship proceedings to accept the appointment."

"We're not declining," she said.

Jared agreed with her. Of course he did. But he needed to be sure this was what his friends wanted for their daughter. Guardians with a disintegrating, soon-to-be-over marriage didn't seem like the number one choice parents would make. "Could you please read the guardianship portion of the will?"

Don paged through the paperwork. "Since Brady and Susan wanted to name both of you as guardians, I suggested additional wording to the wills, which they agreed to."

That made sense to Jared, and he wanted to hear the

wording. Especially since Brady and Susan knew about the marriage problems.

"Here's the passage from Brady's will. Susan's is identical." The lawyer put on his glasses. "'If my spouse does not survive me and if at the time of my death any of my children are minors or under a legal disability, I appoint Jared Reed and Kate Malone to act jointly as the guardian of each child who is a minor or under a legal disability so long as Jared Reed and Kate Reed are both then living and married on the date of such appointment.'"

Kate straightened in her chair.

Jared felt her tension. It wasn't so bad, though. They were living. They were still married. They were fine.

At least as far as the baby was concerned.

Of course Cassidy would become part of the divorce settlement. No doubt Susan would want Kate to have custody.

"Are there any provisions if our marriage ends at a future date?" Kate asked, her voice cool.

"Actually there is. Again both wills contain the same wording." Don flipped the page. "'If Jared Reed and Kate Malone are not married to each other on the date of such appointment or become separated or divorced at a later date, I appoint Jared Reed to solely act as the guardian of each child of mine who is a minor or under a legal disability.'"

"What?" Kate asked.

Jared sat stunned. "Me?"

CHAPTER TWO

KATE'S heart pounded. Every muscle tensed. She didn't believe her ears.

She couldn't.

"There must be some mistake." Her gaze darted between a shell-shocked Jared and a contemplative Don. "Susan would never have agreed to that."

"It's not a mistake," Don said matter-of-factly as if they were discussing the custody of a pampered pet not Kate's precious goddaughter. "Brady and Susan were clear with their wishes and made sure I understood them."

Kate flexed her fingers, fighting to grasp the situation. Fighting for control. "But it makes no sense."

"I agree." Jared's confident voice reassured her. "I may have been nominated as the personal representative, but the sole guardian? Kate and Susan were as close as sisters. There's no reason I should be the one named in the wills."

Relief and gratitude washed over Kate. Thank goodness he understood how ridiculous this was. No doubt Jared would support her in getting this overturned.

His gaze met hers. They were on the same side for once. And that felt…good. Satisfying. In a way it hadn't for a very long time.

"Remember that's only if you and Kate divorce," Don added. "As long as you are together, the provision doesn't apply."

Her relief ebbed.

The split of assets had been agreed upon; the paperwork had been filed. It was only a matter of time, weeks really, until the divorce was official.

Panic threatened. Kate grabbed onto the chair. She couldn't lose control.

Not when she had to think. Kate needed to figure out a way to fix this. First, they had to be named guardians. Together. Then she and Jared could challenge the validity of the will so she could gain sole guardianship of Cassidy. Of course, Jared would have whatever visitation rights he wanted.

She eased her death grip on the chair arms. Now that she had a plan formulated, she could cope.

"If it's any consolation, Kate," Don said, his voice startling her. "You are named sole guardian if Jared dies."

"Don't give her any ideas."

His wry humor reminded Kate of the time he playfully accused her of poisoning him when she made juice using organic kale, rhubarb and strawberries after a trip to the Farmer's Market. A smile pulled at her mouth. She caught herself. This wasn't the time for fun. She pressed her lips together.

"What happens next?" Jared asked the lawyer.

"Well, since you're married you will both receive guardianship if you accept the nomination," Don explained. "But I'm sure this is something you want to discuss in private. No guardian can be named until the personal representative is officially appointed and the wills submitted for probate."

She struggled to make sense of his words, to understand their implications. "What about Cassidy? What happens to her in the meanwhile?

"Cassidy is currently under state custody," Don said.

That was one thing Kate understood all too well. "No. Susan would not have wanted that for her baby."

"But since Cassidy's in the hospital, she won't be put into a foster home, correct?" Jared asked.

"Yes, as long as guardianship has been determined by her release," Don said. "If we run into any snags, we can petition to have a temporary guardian named until final guardianship is determined."

Jared covered Kate's hand with his. "We'll make sure there aren't any snags."

She fought the urge to hug him. With everything they'd been through these past months, she'd forgotten Jared Reed was still a good guy. His reassurance meant so much.

Kate stole a glance at him, and he winked. Her pulse quickened. She mouthed the word thanks and looked away. As fast as she could without seeming rude. Gratefulness. That was all her reaction was, all it ever could be.

"Susan and Brady left letters for you." Don handed Kate a large, thick manila envelope, and Jared received a thin, standard business-size one. "Would you like to read them now or later?"

She clutched the envelope as if it were a winning Powerball lottery ticket. A part of her was afraid to look inside, but the other part wanted to rip the flap off and start reading. "Now."

"Later," Jared said at the same time.

Deadlock. They never could agree on anything. At first their differences had been a joke, and they'd laughed about

it. Over and over again. But their disagreements had been
a sign. Even though she might have loved Jared, even
though she might sometimes long for him, they didn't
work well together.

"You can open yours later," she said. "I'd prefer to
open mine now."

Jared ran his finger under the flap of the envelope.
"Now is fine."

Don rose from the desk. "I'll get the paperwork started."

Kate mumbled a thank you. As she focused on the
envelope in her hand, she heard paper crinkle and unfold
and a chuckle.

With trembling fingers, she opened the manila envelope
and pulled out several typed pages.

Dear Kate,
    If you're reading this, I'm dead and it's a good
thing I decided to write everything down for you.
Brady thinks I'm being morbid, but until I had Cassidy
I didn't give much thought to what would happen if I
weren't here. And now in the middle of all this estate
planning, I've been thinking about it too much.

The corners of Kate's mouthed curved. That was so like
Susan. She thought about things too much. As did Kate.
Obsessive? Perhaps. But she and Susan had called it ana-
lytical thinking.

    By now, Don Phillips has told you that we want
you and Jared to raise Cassidy. This should come
as no surprise. What would come as a shock is if
Don told you that Jared would gain custody of

Cassidy if the two of you divorced. I know you're confused and mad at me.

Kate wasn't mad. How about stunned? Hurt? Bewildered? Betrayed? Her gaze strayed to Jared before returning to the letter.

My hope is you and Jared have resolved things by the time of our untimely and unfortunate demise (gotta love that phrase!) and are living happily ever after. You are truly meant for each other.

Oh, Susan. She was such an optimist. Even under the most horrible situations growing up, she had never stopped believing her life would improve. No matter what the odds. But this dream of Susan's wasn't in the cards for Kate.

And that realization hurt. Badly.

She had wanted a family with Jared, but the timing always seemed off. They spent so little time together with their jobs. He wanted her to have a baby right when her company took off. And then he asked her to give up everything she'd put her heart and soul into and move to Seattle. When she wouldn't do what he wanted, he left without her. Kate squeezed her eyes shut, but that didn't stop the memories or erase the pain.

"Here," Jared said.

She opened her eyes. He held a tissue out to her. She wasn't sure if his offer was out of compassion or pity. She didn't want him to think she was weak. Kate stiffened. "I don't need it."

"Just in case."

His half smile unfurled warmth inside her. And made her feel like an idiot. Jared was only trying to help her, not point out her weaknesses. She had to stop thinking of him as the enemy. Kate took the tissue. "Thank you."

"You're welcome."

His dark eyes seemed to see right through her, to her secret thoughts and feelings.

Heat. Fire. Passion.

Kate forced herself to breathe.

Okay, some sort of volatile chemistry remained between them. She'd go so far as to admit her physical attraction to Jared had increased during their separation.

No big deal.

A marriage couldn't survive on desire alone. She'd learned that lesson. She looked away.

"Are you finished?" Jared asked.

"No."

"I've read mine three times."

Did the letter mention her? Old inadequacies floated to the surface. Had Brady questioned her ability to care for Cassidy? Kate bit the inside of her cheek.

"What did the letter say?" she asked.

Jared smiled. "Typical Brady stuff that helps."

"I'm glad." She only hoped hers helped, too. Up until now, Susan's letter hadn't. "I need to finish mine."

"Go ahead."

Kate read how proud Susan was over Kate's accomplishments, their friendship and their love for one another. As she continued, the paper shook and Kate realized her hands were trembling.

You and I know family doesn't have to mean blood relation, and that's what I'm counting on because I want Cassidy to experience what being part of a loving family is all about. Jared with the crazy, meddlesome Reeds can provide that for her. She can have what we didn't have growing up. I need that for my child.

As tears streamed from Kate's eyes, she struggled to read the rest. She didn't like what Susan had written, but Kate understood and somehow that hurt more. Each word felt like a wound to her already aching heart. She fumbled for the tissue.

Jared handed her another one. She muttered thanks and wiped her eyes.

So much for challenging the will. She couldn't. Not when she knew what Susan wanted for her daughter. Kate would want the same for her own child. Wasn't that one reason she found Jared Reed with his large, supportive family so attractive when they'd first met? He'd had everything she hadn't had growing up.

But knowing the reasons and understanding them didn't make the circumstances any easier on her.

"Katie?" Jared placed his hand on her shoulder. The warmth of his touch nearly did her in, but she couldn't—didn't want to—pull away.

He and Cassidy were all Kate had left.

She dabbed her eyes with a tissue again. "I'm not finished."

Forgive me if I've written something that has hurt you. I'm only doing what I feel is best for my daughter. I love you, Katie. I always have and I always will.

Take care of my baby and love her the way we
wanted to be loved!

Hugs and love,
Susan

She didn't want to let Susan down, but Kate didn't
think that kind of love, the kind you didn't have to earn,
was possible. Not any longer. But for her best friend, she
would give it her all.

She traced Susan's name—the only word handwritten
on the many pages—with her fingertip. Tears dropped
onto the paper, and Kate dried them off. She didn't want
the letter to be ruined. She wanted to keep it. For herself.
For Cassidy.

Kate inhaled and exhaled slowly. Steady. Calm. In control.
She squared her shoulders. With a steady gaze, she met
Jared's inquisitive eyes. "They want you to have Cassidy."

"I know."

"It's…okay." Or would be. Someday. Somehow.

"I'm sorry."

"It's not your fault." No matter how much Kate would
have liked to blame him for this, she couldn't. If only she
knew what to do next. "I want to see Cassidy."

Jared nodded. "Let's sign whatever papers Don has
prepared then go to the hospital."

The children's wing of the hospital was painted with blue-
birds, colorful flowers and rainbows, but the cheery decor
did nothing to ease Jared's growing anxiety. He'd been
trying to come to terms with a divorce he didn't want and
now he was about to become a guardian. A father.

A dad.

He thought about Brady's letter.

You've always wanted kids.

Jared had wanted to be a dad. After he and Kate first got married, she was enthusiastic about wanting kids, but they'd agreed to hold off for a couple of years to concentrate on their careers. Still he'd imagined having a family, the perfect family to go with his fantasy of the perfect marriage—two children, a fancy double stroller and a fully loaded minivan. But when Kate's company exploded onto the PR scene, she resisted starting a family. And then the Seattle opportunity arose. He thought the promotion and transfer was a way to have the family he desired, not destroy his marriage.

Divorce.

Jared hated that word. Divorce meant failure. He hated failing or losing at anything. But there didn't seem to be a damn thing he could do about it.

He was the first to admit they'd both made mistakes that contributed to the collapse of their marriage, but whereas Kate called the problems irreparable damage, Jared believed they could work through them. He missed Kate so much. If only she would get off the divorce kick and give their marriage a go…

Jared waited in the lobby for her. He would have preferred driving together, but she'd wanted a few minutes by herself. He didn't like her being alone when she was tired and stressed, but he understood. Their lives had been changed completely. Whatever the future held, however, they were in this together.

"Sorry." Kate's steps echoed on the tile floor. "I couldn't find a parking place."

Her red eyes suggested she'd been crying again. He wished she would let him help her get through this. "I just got here."

She adjusted the strap of her purse. "I hope Cassidy's okay."

"Don said she would be."

"I know, but there's okay and there's okay."

Her nervousness reminded him of the first time he invited her home to meet his family. She'd brought flowers and a bottle of wine. Kate had been pleasant, personable, perfect. He'd later discovered she'd bought a new outfit and had her hair done that day. Her efforts had touched him and taken their dating to a new level. Jared took her hand in his. "Let's find out how okay Cassidy is."

As they followed the yellow bricks painted on the floor and stepped onto the elevator hand in hand, he felt as if nothing had changed between them and they were still together. Still in love. Those had been the days.

He'd been attracted to Kate since the moment he first saw her, and that attraction had only grown once he realized her brain matched her beauty. They'd been a perfect match. The perfect couple.

He missed their conversations, even their disagreements. He missed everything about her from the sound of her laughter to the birthmark on her left shoulder. He especially missed the lovemaking. Their problems had never reached the bedroom. Yet somehow the marriage had gone wrong. Bad. But that didn't mean it was over. Maybe he could make something new, something good happen between them to show Kate they could still be together.

He stopped at the nurse's station. "I'm Jared Reed and this is Kate Malone. We're here to see Cassidy Lukas."

"I'm Rachel." The nurse smiled. "Don Phillips said you were on the way."

"How is she?" Kate asked.

"Cassidy is recovering well. She's in Room 402." The nurse picked up a file. "I'll make a note to have the doctor speak with you."

"Thank you," Kate said.

The small room had a chair in one corner, a sofa bed under a bank of windows and a strange looking crib against the far wall. The four-month-old baby girl slept oblivious to them or any of the machines connected to her. Cuts—some that had been stitched—and bruises—some purple, others yellow—covered her arms and face. A white bandage was wrapped around her head.

A wave of protectiveness washed over Jared. This baby was his and Kate's responsibility.

"She's so beautiful," Kate whispered with a hint of awe in her voice.

Seeing the compassion in her eyes as she stared at the baby triggered something deep within him. This—Kate, him and a baby—had been his dream.

She sighed. "Cassidy looks so much like Susan."

He saw the resemblance especially around the mouth and eyes. "But she's got Brady's chin. I hope that doesn't mean she's as stubborn as he was."

Kate smiled wanly. "Let's hope not."

He glanced around the room. A stuffed bear and a basket of flowers sat on a cart. He read the cards. The bear was from Don Phillips and his wife. The flowers from Brady's work.

Why wasn't the room full of flowers, balloons and cards? Where were all the visitors? Jared didn't get it. "Why is Cassidy all alone?"

"What do you mean?" Kate asked.

When his sister Heather gave birth to her third child, his family camped out in the waiting room. "There isn't anyone here with Cassidy. How come?"

"We're all she has."

"But friends. Surely Brady and Susan had some friends—"

"Who have their own families and lives," Kate explained. "Not everyone has a family like yours, Jared. A lot of people end up in the hospital alone. Even babies."

His mind accepted the truth of her words, but his heart and his upbringing rejected it. "That's not right."

"She won't have to be alone again. We can take shifts."

Shifts meant they wouldn't be together. He'd been apart from Kate for so long, too long, and wanted to make the most of this time. He needed to show her they could save their marriage.

"Is something wrong?" she asked.

The sight of the baby hooked up to beeping machines gave Jared second thoughts. His needs came a poor second to hers. "You want to take the first shift? I need to meet with Don."

Kate hung her jacket on the back of the chair, tidy as always. "That will be fine."

But it wasn't fine with Jared. He felt funny leaving them alone. His gaze returned to Cassidy.

"The baby will be fine, too." Kate's voice sounded a little strained.

He wasn't worried only about the baby. Kate looked so tired. Jared wondered if she'd eaten lunch. He would be gone for at least a couple of hours. What if she or Cassidy needed something?

"Go." Kate motioned to the door. "The sooner you're named personal representative, the sooner we get guardianship."

"If you need anything—"

"I'll call."

Would she? Kate, ever capable, never had called in the past. But he wouldn't stop hoping. "Please do."

He wondered if she heard him or if it mattered to her because she didn't look up as he walked to the door.

"Jared."

He turned.

"It's been a full day and—" she moistened her lips "—please be careful."

The concern in her voice brought a smile to his lips. Maybe she wasn't so indifferent to him after all. Maybe he stood a chance. "I'll be back, Kate. Just as soon as I can."

CHAPTER THREE

AN HOUR later, Kate struggled to keep her heavy eyelids open. A sleepless night and overloaded emotions had taken their toll on both her body and her brain, but she wasn't about to give into the exhaustion plaguing her. Not here in Cassidy's hospital room. What if the baby woke up, and Kate didn't hear her?

Sure, nurses came in and out with regularity, but she didn't want to let Susan down. Or, Kate realized, Jared.

All she needed was a second wind. Stretching her arms over her head, she wiggled her fingers. Caffeine would help, but she didn't want to leave Cassidy alone in case she woke up.

The minutes ticked by. Kate felt her head fall forward. Dazed and disoriented, she straightened. The smell screamed hospital and Kate knew where she was, but she still took in the cream-colored walls, the overhead lighting, a bed couch and a crib surrounded by noisy machines.

Cassidy.

The baby lay sound asleep. So small. So fragile.

And Kate's responsibility.

She sat with her back straight and the balls of her feet

pressed against the wall. Comfortable, no. But napping while on duty wasn't allowed.

Despite her brave words and determination, she was terrified of doing something wrong, of being unable to care for the baby the correct way. And the last thing Kate wanted was for Jared to find her asleep on the job. He held all the cards, or in this case, the baby. She wouldn't give him any reason to doubt her childrearing abilities.

From across the room, Kate stared at the crib. The machines lit and beeped, but the baby hadn't moved from her earlier position. Not since the nurse had been in here before. Cassidy hadn't made a sound, either. Unease prickled the hair at the back of Kate's neck.

Check her.

She imagined Susan's voice saying the words, and a heaviness weighed down on Kate. She'd lived with fear and uncertainty her entire childhood, and she'd moved beyond the two since becoming an adult. She'd put the past behind her, set goals and achieved them. But now Kate felt as if she'd been tossed into a whirlpool of doubt and confusion. She hated feeling that way again, and the million what-ifs running through her mind paralyzed her.

Kate remembered Susan telling her about checking the baby during the middle of the night to make sure Cassidy was breathing. Kate knew Susan's fears were irrational and told her to take advantage of the free time and sleep herself. Susan had smiled, but said nothing. Now Kate understood the new mother's anxiety. And she didn't like it one bit.

She shifted in her chair, uncomfortable with her new needy, uncertain self.

Where was Jared? Shouldn't he be back by now?

Kate glanced at the clock.

Darn. He'd only been gone an hour and with the paper-work that needed to be submitted to the court he wouldn't return anytime soon. She blew out a puff of air.

Jared.

Even if they disagreed most of the time, his presence here would comfort her, distract her. Especially if he gave her one of his dimpled smiles, the kind that spread all the way to his eyes. She hadn't seen one of those…in months. Not that she'd seen him, either.

A light blinked. Kate scanned the bank of machines. Surely if something was wrong, a monitor would sound an alarm and alert the nurse who would come running. She took a slow, deep breath.

Was this how her life would be from now on? Worried something bad would happen? Worried she would somehow fail Cassidy? Worried she would let Susan down in the worst possible way? If only Jared…

Kate shuddered. She had to stop. Now.

She didn't need Jared. She'd survived all but five years of her life without him. He'd proven he wouldn't stick around forever, that if she didn't do what he wanted he would leave. The realization provided resolve and courage, both of which she needed.

She could handle this. On her own. The way she'd always done.

All Kate needed to do was check the baby. She slipped off her shoes, walked softly to the crib and peered down. The rise and fall of Cassidy's chest brought a rush of relief. The sight of the slumbering child with a peaceful expres-sion on her face blanketed Kate with warmth. How could something so small make her feel so good? She fought the urge to caress the baby's smooth cheek. The last thing she wanted to do was wake the sleeping infant.

Kate stood by the crib. Watching the machines, with all those blinks and blips, would keep her busy until Jared returned. And then it would be his turn.

But she realized with unexpected clarity, her turn wouldn't be over. Not ever again. Her life would never be the same. Cassidy would always be a part of her life and link Kate to Jared. Even after the divorce…

The implications, both past and future, swirled through her mind. There would be no tidy goodbye. No tucking the memories away and forgetting about him. No moving on without Jared a part of her life. They would spend the next eighteen years making decisions about Cassidy, a child who would rely upon them for everything—nourishment, shelter, nurturing, advice and love.

The reality of what their new responsibility entailed hit Kate full force. She stood frozen, assailed by a multitude of doubt. She and Jared couldn't agree on what television show to watch or what they wanted for dinner on the weekends they were home together, how could they agree on what to do with Cassidy? Until she became an adult?

Kate staggered back.

What on earth had Susan been thinking?

Raising a child was nothing like baby-sitting Jared's nieces and nephews. Kate had no idea how to be a…mom. Motherhood had been this ideal, never anything real or attainable, just something she'd tucked away in the back of her mind when she realized her days as a wife were numbered. She didn't have a clue about being a parent. The only thing she knew was what kind of mother she didn't want to be.

And what about Jared? He had no experience being a dad. Sure, he liked kids, but that was different from having one of your own. With his travel schedule and once they were divorced…

Staring at the baby, Kate leaned against a wall. She didn't want to let her best friend down, but…

How in the world were she and Jared going to do this?

"How are you going to do this?" Not even a bad phone connection could mask the concern in Margery Reed's voice.

Jared wanted to reassure his mother, but no words would come. Not when he was as unsure about this situation as the rest of his family—two of whom he could hear voicing their opinions in the background.

"Raising a child isn't easy under the best of circumstances," Margery continued.

She meant his marriage. Or rather, his soon-to-be lack of one. The divorce had not only caught Jared off guard, but the entire Reed clan who had encouraged him to accept the promotion and move to Seattle with the belief Kate would follow him. Jared had assumed the same, that he was more important than her career. He'd assumed wrong.

"Being a single parent is going to be hard on Kate."

"Don't worry, Mom." Especially since he was the one who would end up with Cassidy, but he wasn't about to drop that bombshell on them yet. "We'll figure something out. Reeds always come out on top."

"You sound like your father."

"And Grandpa." A flashing sign caught Jared's attention. The Burger Barn. It was dinnertime. He doubted

Kate had eaten. She needed to put some weight back on. He pulled into the parking lot and lined up behind a red pickup truck in the drive-thru line. "You remember what Grandpa said. Second place is for everyone else."

Margery laughed. "You'll be saying the same thing to Cassidy before you know it."

An invisible weight pressed down on Jared. He had a good job and made recommendations to clients who would invest millions of dollars in companies based on his word, but that kind of responsibility was different than the parental kind. "Yeah. I guess I will."

"Chin up, Jared," Margery ordered. "You'll be a great dad."

Brady had written the same thing in his letter. Jared would do his best.

"I can't wait to meet Cassidy, our newest granddaughter."

He imagined her bragging to her friends about the newest addition to the family. If only it could have been under happier circumstances.

"Would you like us to come to Boise to help you?" his mom asked. "We could be there tomorrow. Tonight if you need us."

Yes. Please. He'd like nothing better than to dump this mess in his mother's experienced lap. But Jared swallowed the words before they were barely formed. He was in this on his own. Or rather, he was in this with Kate.

Once his family swarmed in on them, they would lose any chance of seeing if they could make this parenting thing work. He would lose any chance of showing Kate what she'd given up on. What they were both missing. What they could still have if only she wasn't so damn stubborn.

Okay, maybe that was nothing more than a pipe dream, but he wasn't ready to accept the failure of his marriage completely. Lawyers and divorce settlement aside.

Kate had never been comfortable accepting his parents' well-intentioned advice and assistance. She reminded him of a stray cat they'd found living in their garage when he was a kid. The cat wanted to be petted, but would hiss and arch if it received too much attention.

Jared knew his parents acted out of love, but the Reeds were like the cavalry when they rode into town with a cloud of dust in their wake. It was better to stand back and get out of the way to keep from being trampled. Kate would feel pushed out more than she already did if his family were here. For once Jared was willing to concede that point.

Cassidy was his and Kate's responsibility.

"Thanks, Mom, but let's see how we do on our own first."

"We? As in you and Kate?"

"The two of us were named guardians."

"But the divorce—"

"Isn't final yet," he interrupted. "And Cassidy needs both of us."

"Do you think…?" His mother's words trailed off.

"What?"

"It's none of my business."

That had never stopped her before. "What do you want to know, Mom?"

"Do you think that now with Cassidy in the picture, Kate will change her mind about the divorce?"

"I hope so," Jared admitted. "That would be the best thing for Cassidy."

"Would it be the best thing for you?" Margery pressed.

"Yes." Jared didn't hesitate with his answer. He wanted to avoid divorce at all costs.

"You know we love Kate, but be careful," his mother said. "We don't want to see you hurt again."

The red truck pulled forward. "I've got to go, Mom. I'll call you later."

"We'll be here. Love you."

Jared disconnected the call. He had no doubt his entire family would offer their advice and help. That was what the Reeds did.

You have your family to support you.

He remembered Brady's letter. Jared did have his family's support. And he might need it more than he ever had.

Time to stop wanting to get Kate back and do something about it. Jared would be taking a chance by putting their marriage—himself—on the line. Hell, she could say no and he would be worse off, but she could say yes and that was worth the risks. Because if she agreed…

Jared smiled. He would not only get his wife back. He would have the family he'd always dreamed about.

The smell of grease wafted in the sterile air of Cassidy's hospital room. Kate's stomach growled, and her mouth watered.

This wasn't good. Tired, hungry and hallucinating about food. Maybe she could ask one of the nurses for some crackers.

"How is Cassidy?"

The sound of Jared's softly spoken question brought a smile to Kate's face. She turned, and tingles shot through her at the sight of him. Okay, maybe seeing the bag of takeout and the drink holder with two large cups in his hands caused the tingling.

Whatever his other faults, Jared made sure she ate.

"She's doing well," Kate said. "She was awake for a little bit."

"Shouldn't we whisper so we don't wake her up?" he asked.

"The nurse said noise wouldn't bother her. If we're too quiet the baby will need total silence to sleep. The nurse recommended keeping music on in the house once we get home."

Wherever home might be. Portland, Kate hoped, until the divorce was final.

"That makes sense." Jared placed the bag on a table. "I brought double cheeseburgers, mustard and pickles only on yours, fries and onion rings."

Her empty stomach cheered. "My favorites."

A beat passed. "I remember."

And so did Kate. Grabbing lunch at a local burger joint and heading to the park for an impromptu picnic lunch on the rare occasion when they both happened to be in town on the same day, and it wasn't raining. She remembered eating and lounging on a blanket until the ringing of their cell phones told them it was time to return to work.

"Thanks." She offered him a smile. "I needed this."

But mere words didn't seem enough. Kate might not need Jared to be here, but she was happy he was here. She would have to do something nice for him.

"Thank you for staying with Cassidy," Jared said.

He handed her food and a drink. Kate wanted to gobble her dinner down, but she wasn't about to let hunger replace good manners. She would wait until Jared was ready.

He stood by the crib. "Go ahead and eat."

"I can wait." Kate sipped her soda instead. The jolt from the sugar and caffeine was exactly what she needed.

Jared's watchful gaze, however, made her uncomfortable. "What?" she asked.

He glanced back to the crib. "Let's eat before the baby wakes up."

She wasn't going to disagree.

Jared pulled his dinner from the bag, unwrapped his cheeseburger and took a bite. He wiped his mouth with a napkin. "I don't know about you, but I was starving."

Kate picked up a fry. "This hits the spot. I owe you."

"It's on me."

She hadn't meant owing him financially, but she understood his response. They had kept their own bank accounts after they married. Every month they would each deposit an equal amount into a joint household account to cover the mortgage payment and utility bills. The method worked well and made splitting the assets for the divorce settlement easy. "Thank you."

"You're welcome."

They finished eating in comfortable silence, a difference from the negative undercurrents they usually encountered when they were together.

Kate finished her soda and wiped her hands. "The nurse said the doctor might release Cassidy in two days, three at the most. Did you and Don finish going through the paperwork?"

"Completed and filed." Jared said to her relief. "Don hopes the court will appoint me personal guardian tomorrow so we can start the guardianship proceedings."

"And then the real fun begins."

"I've been thinking about this whole guardianship issue," Jared said.

"Me, too." Kate leaned back in the chair. "It isn't going to be easy. We don't know anything about babies."

"You're right, and this is going to be hard on Cassidy. She doesn't know what's going on or where her parents went so we need to make sure she's the priority."

"I agree," Kate said. "We need to think about Cassidy and the effect on her with every decision we make."

Suddenly the situation didn't seem so overwhelming to Kate. She wasn't alone. She and Jared were discussing matters logically, rationally, without disagreeing. A positive sign. She only hoped their getting along continued in the future.

Jared's easy smile sent Kate's heart beating faster. "Sounds like a good plan."

No doubt he felt the same way about their conversation and getting along. That bolstered her spirits and gave her the courage to ask what had been on her mind all afternoon. "Once Cassidy is released from the hospital, could I please take her back to Portland with me? At least until the divorce is final."

"Another good idea." He glanced at the crib, then back at Kate. "My family can watch Cassidy when you are at work. Unless you had thought of other arrangements?"

Child care. Kate hadn't thought about that, but a nanny or day care didn't make sense when the Reed clan was right there. And Susan wanted Cassidy to be part of a large family.

"I hadn't thought of any child care arrangements," Kate admitted. "Do you think your family will mind?"

He laughed. "They'll be fighting over her."

"That will be good for both Cassidy and me." And Susan. That was what she wanted. She must be smiling up in Heaven.

Except, Kate wondered, would she see the recrimination in Jared's family's eyes? Sure, they still invited her to dinner and gatherings, but she knew they weren't happy about the situation between her and Jared.

"I could come down and help out on weekends," he added.

"That would be great."

"Yeah, great."

His gaze locked with hers. The temperature in the room increased. She needed another soda or a glass of water or a...kiss. Kate looked down.

No, this couldn't be happening. Her reaction was simply due to the situation. The grief following the death of Susan and Brady. The emotion of inheriting Cassidy.

Kate wouldn't let herself think otherwise. "What about after the divorce?"

"I've been thinking about that," he said. "The best thing for Cassidy would be if she had a mother and a father who were married."

"I know that's what Susan and Brady would have preferred." Kate would give Jared that. "But in our case a traditional family is not possible."

A beat passed. "It is if we didn't get a divorce."

His words hung on the air.

Not divorce. That was the craziest idea she'd ever heard. Kate almost laughed except he wasn't smiling. The seriousness in his eyes told her he wasn't kidding. Okay, she could appreciate him making a noble suggestion for the baby's sake, but one of them had to be realistic.

"What difference would not divorcing make?" Kate asked. "We hardly saw each other when we lived in the same house. Now we live in different states. Staying married would never work."

"Don't you want Cassidy?" he asked.

That wasn't fair.

"You know I do." Kate wanted the baby with a fierceness that surprised her. "But staying married under our current circumstances—"

"Let's change the circumstances."

Hope squeezed her chest. Would he move back to Portland?

"What do you suggest?" she challenged, eager to hear his answer.

"I just…" He seemed at a loss for words. "Maybe things could be different between us."

Not good enough.

Kate wasn't about to allow Jared back into her life, into her bed, into her heart only to watch him leave and hurt her again. Unless…

She thought about her wedding rings locked away in a safe-deposit box at her bank. Losing weight had given her an excuse to take them off. She never thought she would put the gold band and diamond solitaire back on her finger. Her heart pounded.

"Things would have to be very different," she said, formulating the plan in her head.

It could work or cause even more problems. She gulped.

Jared eyed her warily. "What do you have in mind?"

Kate couldn't believe she was considering this, but she had no other choice if she wanted to keep Cassidy. And that was what she wanted. More than anything. She rubbed her thumb over her bare ring finger. "A marriage of convenience."

His brows furrowed. "A what?"

"A marriage in name only for Cassidy's sake."

A nerve throbbed on Jared's neck. "You'd go for that kind of marriage?"

She inhaled sharply. Logically she knew that kind of marriage would work. Emotionally… No, she wasn't going there.

"I would." This was the best solution for everyone involved. "How about you? Would you agree to a marriage of convenience?"

CHAPTER FOUR

"JARED?" Kate asked.

All he had to do was say yes, but a marriage of convenience wasn't what he had in mind.

She bit her lip, a nervous habit she'd had since they first met. "So what do you think?"

That she was out of her mind.

At least insanity would explain her "in name only" proposition. He would rather think her crazy than accept she was rejecting him all over again. When Kate said she wasn't moving to Seattle with him, he'd been upset. When she said she wanted a divorce, he'd been devastated. And now this...

His jaw clenched. He just didn't get her.

This morning, drawn together in grief, he'd felt closer to Kate than he had in months. But now he saw that she didn't want the same thing he did. That she didn't want to save their marriage the way he did.

The realization made his decision all the more critical. With differing expectations, this solution of hers could turn into a disaster and drive them further apart. That was the last thing he wanted. Especially with a baby involved.

"How would this work?" he asked.

"One of us would keep Cassidy during the week. Most likely me since your family could take care of her during the day," she explained, expounding on her plan with enthusiasm. Kate was always a great one for planning. "We could spend weekends together so people won't think we are separated."

Being separated, like divorced, would give him custody per the conditions of the will. Jared weighed the options. Okay, he could work with weekends. As long as she wasn't serious about this "in name only" stuff.

"We could alternate between Portland and Seattle," she continued. As she stared at Cassidy, the tenderness of Kate's gaze reminded Jared of how she used to look at him, and something twisted inside him. "Drive up on Fridays, come back on Sundays."

Weekdays apart, weekends together. That was more than she had been willing to do before. Some of his unease disappeared.

Sure, a long distance marriage wasn't what he wanted. Jared wanted Kate in Seattle full-time, but this was a step in the right direction. With the attraction buzzing like static between them, physical chemistry would soon take over. Kate would realize they belonged together and make the move north.

Now that would be a very convenient marriage. And worth whatever challenges and commute the next few weeks and months held. *If* things worked out the way he hoped they would.

"So…you, me and Cassidy will be together on the weekends," he stipulated.

"Well—" she wet her lips "—mostly together. We

would share the same house. You and I would still be legally married. We just wouldn't do some things other married couples do."

Uh-oh, but he'd heard the words "legally married," not divorced. Key point.

"So you'd continue to keep your name," he said, making sure he understood the intricacies. "We'd keep our finances separate. We'd live apart except on weekends."

That was how they lived now. And had before the separation. It had worked well for them then.

She scuffed the toe of her shoe against the floor. "It also means we won't be, um…"

"What?" he asked.

"Romantic."

She was serious. He smiled, hoping to tease her out of that position. "With a baby around, that's a given."

For now.

If they stayed in Portland over the weekend, his family could watch Cassidy so he and Kate could spend time alone and perhaps rekindle the romance.

"It's not just romance," she clarified. "It's also, you know…"

He was afraid he did know, but Jared wanted her to spell out the rules in case he was wrong. "I don't know."

"Sex."

"What about sex?" he asked.

"There won't be any."

There hadn't been any sex for a while. He didn't like that, but assumed once they were back together…maybe not right away, but eventually. "No sex for how long?"

She bit her lip again.

"Kate?"

"Never," she mumbled.

Not good. "Ever?"

She blushed. "Correct."

"But we're married."

"We'll stay married for Cassidy, not each other," Kate explained, as if she were ordering a cup of coffee not talking about their future together. "That's why it's called a marriage of convenience."

"That's totally inconvenient."

Stupid really.

No sane person would agree to something like that.

She shrugged.

"Let me get this straight." Jared imagined living in the same house with Kate and not touching her. Impossible. "There's no fooling around?"

"No."

"What about kissing?"

"I—I'm pretty sure kissing goes against the rules of an 'in name only marriage.'"

Screw the rules.

That wasn't a marriage. That was hell. Sure, he was managing the celibacy imposed by their separation, but he didn't want to live like that forever. With his own wife. "You really think we can live by those rules?"

"We can if we have to." She leaned forward and touched his arm. "For Cassidy's sake."

No way. Kate was too passionate to spend her life in a sexless marriage. Sure, she might think she could for Cassidy's sake and Kate might hold out a short while, but she wanted him as much as he wanted her. He'd bet money on it. She still had her hand on him.

And that, Jared realized, would work completely in his

favor. Plus it gave him an idea. A way to rattle Kate's neat little world and bring her back where she belonged.

"I've got to be honest with you, Kate," he said. "I don't think I can live like that."

She lowered her hand and her gaze. "I know it's a lot to ask to put aside all your own, um, needs and focus on the baby's. But don't all parents have to do that to some extent?"

I hope you and Kate have worked things out.

Brady's letter rushed back. He wanted his daughter raised by a married couple. And Jared wanted his wife back. He hated the idea of a divorce more than a sexless marriage, but if his idea worked, neither of those things would be a future concern. "What about other people?"

Her eyes widened. "What?"

Aha. That definitely got her attention. "What if we saw other people, discreetly of course, so long as our actions don't affect Cassidy?"

"I—I hadn't thought about that."

From her arched eyebrows, she didn't seem to like the idea, either. Good.

"I don't mean right away," he added smoothly, as if he'd given this a lot of thought, not coming up with the game plan as he spoke. "Maybe we could discuss this in say, six months. Once Cassidy is settled and we're more comfortable with the arrangement. I mean, marriage."

"So you're actually considering this?" Kate asked.

He was. He must be out of his mind, too. "Seeing other people?"

"No, the marriage of convenience."

Mentally he counted backward from ten.

"Yes." He forced himself not to smile at the surprise in

her eyes. Keeping the opponent guessing was the way to go if he wanted to win. And he wasn't about to lose. "But this no-sex thing is pretty much a deal breaker for me."

"Have you been seeing other people?"

Jackpot. He had her right where he wanted her. Curious about his social life without her. "No. I didn't think that was a good idea until the divorce was final."

"Oh."

He thought he glimpsed relief in her eyes. "What about you?"

"Me? No." Her cheeks reddened. "I mean, with work and everything, I never thought much about dating."

But she would now.

And that, too, would work entirely in his favor. Kate would never assume she was the only woman he wanted in his bed. "So what do you say?"

A beat passed. "O-kay."

He released the breath he'd been holding. "Okay?"

"The marriage is a legal one, not an emotional one." Her words didn't give him a warm and fuzzy feeling, but hey, it was better than a divorce. "I'm willing to consider this, um, seeing other people once we have the situation under control."

"Good." Because the discussion was never going to have to come up. Soon Jared would have Kate right where he wanted her. He would have what he wanted—his wife in Seattle with him, back in his life and back in his bed. Someday they would share a good laugh over all of this. "This is what's best for Cassidy."

And, Jared realized, it was the only way for him and Kate to save their marriage.

* * *

Later that night, Kate stood on the balcony of her hotel room. The crescent moon look painted on the star-filled black sky. A cool breeze ruffled her nightshirt, and she ignored the goose bumps on her arms and legs. She should be in bed, sleeping while she had the chance. But every time she closed her eyes a million thoughts took over her mind.

What had she done?

The sound of the rushing water from the river below matched the turmoil inside Kate. She clutched the wrought-iron railing.

She had never expected Jared to suggest they not divorce. Yes, he'd claimed he wanted to work things out, but his actions showed Kate he only wanted her in Seattle with him. That wasn't working things out. That was Jared winning his argument. Getting his way again.

But now…

They wouldn't be divorcing. They really wouldn't be married, either.

No sex.

She tucked her hair behind her ears. That would be…interesting. Impossible.

No, Kate amended, not impossible. If they kept their distance and locked their bedroom doors at night.

Correction, if she did that.

Jared seemed to have no problem agreeing to the rules so long as he could see other people discreetly. His request made sense. Sex had always been important to him. Obviously his feelings for her had changed. Her feelings had changed, too.

Still it wouldn't be easy. Boundaries would need to be set and adhered to. The love may have died between them, but the physical chemistry hadn't. Every time they touched, the pull of attraction drew them closer. And that meant she would have to keep her distance.

Or find someone else.

The idea left her feeling unsettled, sad even. Kate took a deep breath.

This whole situation was so unbelievable. What she needed was someone to talk to. Kate glanced into the room and saw her cell phone sitting on the bed, but the one person she could call, the one person she could count on to help her was no longer here to answer the telephone.

Susan.

The thought of her dead friend brought a wave of grief. The jumble of emotions—sorrow, confusion, frustration— brought tears to Kate's eyes, but she wasn't about to cry again. Not even in the solitude of her hotel room, in the inky darkness of the late night sky. This was a time for strength. No matter how weak she might feel.

Cassidy. Kate had to think about Cassidy and what Susan had wanted for her:

She can have what we didn't have growing up. I need that for my child. Grandparents, aunts, uncles, a ton of cousins. Do you understand? I want you to understand this, Kate, and support it. I need you to be a part of Cassidy's life no matter what has happened with you and Jared.

And Kate would.

Knowing she was making Susan's dream for her daughter come true, Kate could do anything. Even spend the next eighteen years being married to Jared Reed.

Cassidy would have both a mother and a father who

loved her. The pattern of Susan's and Kate's childhood would not be repeated. She prided herself on her control and the ability to do what needed to be done. Those skills would never be more important, when Cassidy's well-being and future depended on Kate's action. She would push aside her emotions. She would live knowing Jared would be her husband, but he would never really be hers again. She would make practical, meaningful decisions for herself and Cassidy.

Kate would become the perfect mother.

Because, she realized, that's all she could do.

The next morning at the hospital, Kate juggled a drink holder and a bag from Starbucks. The aroma of freshly brewed house blend coffee made her crave a sip. After another restless night, caffeine would definitely help, but first she wanted to see Jared. No, Cassidy. Kate was here for the baby.

She pushed open the door to the room with her shoulder, took a step inside and froze.

Both Jared and Cassidy were still sound asleep. Part of Kate—the sleepy part—was envious, and the other part—mainly her overwhelmed emotions—found the scene in front of her totally heartwarming. Jared slept on the sofa bed with an arm outstretched toward Cassidy. Kate wondered if he'd fallen sleep touching the baby. Her heart constricted at the sweet image.

In that moment, she could almost believe Cassidy would solve all their problems and make them the perfect couple they'd once been. But a few seconds of daydreaming was all Kate could allow herself because she knew better.

Not even the adorable Cassidy could bridge the gap of

problems that had pushed Kate and Jared apart. Children, and when to have them, had been only one of their problems. Jared hadn't wanted to wait any longer to start a family. He hadn't cared about Kate's company or her employees or her dreams. He'd wanted her pregnant and in Seattle. With him.

No compromise. No discussion.

Sure he suggested marriage counseling, but only to a therapist who was a friend of the Reeds and would take his side. The way his family had.

Misgivings over this marriage of convenience exploded in Kate. Her heart beat triple time. Their differences—what they wanted from their lives, their career, pretty much everything—wouldn't just go away. Divorce or not.

Panic threatened to overwhelm her. Kate placed the bag and drinks on the bed table. She wanted to tell Jared she wanted out. Removing the plates, she looked at him and the baby.

Her best friend's beautiful baby girl.

Kate's heart rate slowed. She couldn't forget she was doing this for Cassidy. Susan and Brady, too. In control, Kate pulled out the fresh fruit bowls, pastries, forks and napkins.

Jared stirred in the sofa bed. As he stretched his arms over his head, his gaze zeroed in on Cassidy. He turned Kate's way. "You brought coffee and a continental breakfast buffet."

Ignoring his charming smile, Kate picked up a scone. "I thought you might be hungry."

"Thanks." Jared stood, his shirt wrinkled and his pants creased. He looked sleep rumpled and adorable, reminding her of the times he'd come straight home after a long flight and tumbled into bed with her. Sleep the last thing on either of their minds. Heat emanated deep within her.

"Is something wrong?" he asked, grabbing a pastry.

No sex. No fooling around. No kissing. Seeing other people discreetly.

"Why do you think anything's wrong?" she asked.

"Well, you lost your best friend, gained a child and you have that tongue between your teeth look you get when something's on your mind."

She didn't know what to make of his observation. "There is a lot on my mind." But she wasn't about to admit thinking about making love to him was one of them. "That's how it's going to be for a while."

"A long while I'd imagine." He sipped his coffee. "This hits the spot. You went above and beyond as usual."

As usual. She ate her scone. It felt weird to be having breakfast with him like this. To remember how life had been between them and how different life would be from now on. Kate wasn't sure how to act or what to do, but she guessed pushing the hair that had fallen across his forehead back into place wouldn't be a good idea.

"Did you sleep?" Jared asked.

"Some." Kate would guess four, maybe five hours. After exhaustion had extinguished the thoughts in her head. "How about you?"

"I slept pretty well." He rubbed his neck. "Though the sofa bed was about as comfortable as a seat in coach on a trans-Pacific flight."

Kate glanced at Cassidy. "How did the baby do?"

"She fussed a bit." He walked over to the crib. "It took a while to get her to take a bottle."

"You fed her?" Kate asked.

"I did." His mouth quirked in a lopsided smile. "I got to hold her, too."

No fair. Her skin prickled. "The nurse wouldn't let me do that."

Laughter glimmered in his eyes. "You must not have the right touch."

He was only kidding, but his words stabbed Kate's heart like a dozen daggers. She'd wanted to hold Cassidy and feed her, too, but the nurse had said no. Kate hadn't taken it personally. Until now.

Stricken, she looked at him.

"They finally disconnected the machines," he explained. "That's the reason I got to hold her."

Kate felt foolish. She had to stop with all the insecurities plaguing her. She had more important things to worry about. "That means Cassidy is improving. And if she's released early…"

"I'm meeting with Don this morning to talk about the guardianship." Jared's tone brought reassurance. "Don't worry, Kate. This is all going to work out. I promise you."

He'd promised to love her, in good times and in bad. That had only lasted three years. Cassidy needed them for the long haul. A shadow of doubt crossed Kate's heart.

"We have to make this work," she said.

"We will."

She wanted to believe him, but leaving their problems—and the emotions associated with them—in the past wasn't so easy. Kate wasn't sure she wanted to try. All they needed to do was be civil to each other on weekends. Anything more was asking for trouble.

She removed her jacket. "I guess you'll be off now."

He took a sip of coffee. "I don't mind staying a while."

But she minded.

Yes, they would have to work together for Cassidy's sake, but Kate wanted—no, needed—some space. The way he looked, the words he said, the response her body had to him. She was too upset to think clearly. She would be better off alone with Cassidy and get used to how life would be once they got home.

"Don't you have to meet Don?" Kate asked.

"Yes, but I have time." Jared's gaze returned to the baby. "Cassidy needs her family with her."

Family.

The word made Kate's head swim. She sat in the chair. Her entire life she'd dreamed of being part of a family. Sometimes she had been until fate or the state of Oregon interfered. She was a member of the Reed clan by marriage. But now with Cassidy and Jared, the three of them would be their own family, too.

The baby screeched. The sound, more pterodactyl than human, pierced the silence of the room. Kate jerked to her feet, and Jared hurried to the crib. He picked the baby up as if he'd been doing this all his life, not random nights when they baby-sat. The crying continued. He rocked Cassidy in his arms and then...silence.

Kate stared in amazement.

"Good morning, princess," Jared said. He cuddled Cassidy close, and Kate's heart lurched. "Did you have sweet dreams?"

Her mouth went dry. Unlike other women she knew, she'd never felt the ticking clock. She'd never experienced the overwhelming desire to have a baby. But seeing Jared with Cassidy in his arms sent Kate's world spinning off its axis. He'd always said he wanted children, and for the first time she could see he was meant to be a dad. An incredibly sexy, desirable dad. She couldn't tear her gaze away.

"Want a turn?" he asked.

She wanted…him.

No, Kate corrected, she wanted to hold the baby. "Please."

She cradled the warm, wiggly girl against her. She made sure to support the baby's head and neck the way she'd read online last night. Cassidy made a sucking motion with her mouth.

"She likes you," he said.

"She's hungry." But that was enough for the time being.

Kate touched her finger to the baby's tiny hand. Little fingers wrapped around hers. An instinctive reaction? Kate didn't care. All she knew was she could get used to this.

And that scared her.

She'd lost everyone she'd come to love. How would this be any different? "You can take her."

Jared placed his hands on her shoulders. "It's going to all work out, Katie."

She wanted to believe him. Desperately.

Staying married to Jared was the best thing for the baby, Kate knew that in her heart, but with his touch burning through the fabric of her blouse and his warm breath heating the blood in her veins, Kate wished she knew if this marriage was the best thing for her, too.

Because she wasn't sure.

She wasn't sure of anything.

CHAPTER FIVE

As JARED sat behind the wheel of the idling rental car two days later, the reality of what he'd inherited slammed into him. He gripped the gearshift. Forget speeding around town in his fully restored 1966, cherry-condition Corvette. He needed a new car, a family car, maybe that minivan he'd imagined. But that wasn't all he needed.

He glanced at Kate in the passenger seat. Her whole package sure had come together nicely today with her black pants, blue shirt, crystal jewelry and shoes. The only thing missing—her wedding rings.

"Are you ready?" he asked.

Cassidy squealed before Kate could answer.

Using the rearview mirror, he saw the back of the car seat. At least the most important passenger was ready to leave the hospital. The little cutie.

"Do you think the baby is strapped in tight enough?" Kate asked.

"Yes. She's not going anywhere." Jared thought about the accident, about Cassidy in that same model of car seat and surviving the horrific crash that claimed the lives of her parents. There'd been no doubt in Jared's mind which car seat to buy when he'd gone to the store yesterday. He would make sure nothing happened to Cassidy. "I stopped by the fire station and they double-checked the car seat installation and the nurse made sure Cassidy was securely strapped in."

Kate glanced back. "I wish we could see her face."

"The car seat has to face backward until she's one year old," he explained. "We can buy a mirror to see her face tomorrow."

"Maybe I should ride back there with her until then."

"Is that what Susan did?" he asked.

"No, but maybe if she had…"

Jared's heart hurt for Kate, but what-ifs would only make the grief process harder. With all the work getting the estates in order, there hadn't been much time to think about Susan and Brady. Maybe Jared and Kate needed to concentrate less on the To Do list and more on themselves, and each other. "Do whatever makes you comfortable, Katie."

The baby made popping noises with her mouth. At least Cassidy didn't seem to mind being in the car.

"Just drive," Kate said finally. "The baby seems happy."

That was good enough for him. He shifted the car into gear and released the brake. Kate sucked in a breath.

"Nervous?" he asked.

"No," she said. "Why would you think so?"

The tightness around her mouth was a dead giveaway, but he wasn't about to admit that to her. "We're on our own. No button to call the nurses' station if we need help. No one a few feet away to answer our questions. No one to pop into the room to give us a break."

"You sound like the nervous one."

Jared shrugged. "Life as we knew it has changed, but people deal with a new baby every day. We'll be fine."

"Yes, we will."

"Though I expected a little more than the nurse handing us the discharge papers, wishing us good luck and sending us on our way," he admitted. "Most people have nine months to prepare for parenthood. You think the hospital would have given us a manual or something."

"I know," she said. "Not much you can do with 'good luck.'"

That was more like the Kate he knew and loved.

Come back to me, baby.

"At least we have Susan's baby books," Kate continued. "I've been going through them."

"Good." He turned out of the hospital entrance and onto the road. "At least one of us will know what we're doing."

"You seem to have a pretty good handle on parenting." She glanced his way. "Cassidy likes you."

"She has excellent taste." If only Kate felt the same way about him. Patience. He had to give them time to work things out. "But all I did was hold her."

"And walk her and rock her and sing to her," Kate said. "The nurses gave me a full report."

Taking credit for doing what he needed to do in this case felt…wrong. He might be using the baby to get Kate back, but Cassidy's needs were the top priority. "It was the least I could do. The same as you."

Kate nodded. "We have a steep learning curve head of us. Vaccines, checkups, illnesses, diaper rash. I don't even want to think about trying to feed her solids. What if she's as picky as Brady?"

"Then we buy a side of beef and learn how to disguise vegetables as candy."

We. Not I. This was going to work. Jared tapped his thumb against the steering wheel. Soon Cassidy would soon have a mommy and daddy who lived together and loved each other, too.

"What?" Kate asked.

"You sound like a mom."

"Really?"

The hope contained in the one word surprised Jared. Kate always seemed so in control, so self-assured with everything, but her eager tone made her seem vulnerable and more…real. He liked that. "Yes, you sound like a mom."

A satisfied look settled on her face. "That's the nicest thing you've ever said to me."

"Interesting. Saying you sound like a mom works better than saying you look hot." He laughed. "I'll have to remember that."

"Trying to put a game plan into place if you need a night out with the boys?"

He smiled. "More like how to get out of the doghouse."

She smiled back. "Don't forget flowers and chocolate are good for that, too."

Yes. A point in his favor. Jared pumped his fist.

"Both hands on the wheel," Kate said.

"Sorry." He grabbed the steering wheel. "I won't forget."

He glanced at his rearview mirror. Flashing lights rapidly approached. A siren grew louder. Slowing down, he changed lanes. An ambulance roared past, its siren blaring.

The baby cried.

"She must not like sirens," Jared said.

"She doesn't like being woke up so suddenly or with so much noise." Kate reached back. "It's okay, Cassidy, we're here."

The baby wailed.

Kate sighed. "I should have sat in the back seat with her."

"Maybe she'll settle down."

"I can climb back there."

The image of Brady's mangled car flashed through Jared's mind. He didn't want Kate to unbuckle her seat belt. "We only have a few miles to go."

The crying worsened. No matter what either of them said, Cassidy wouldn't be consoled. Jared couldn't concentrate on the road. "Did you read anything in the baby books that would help calm her down?"

"No. She could be tired, hungry, wet… I don't know." Kate twisted in her seat. "We're going to be home soon, Cassidy. Do you miss your room? All your toys?"

The baby's cries squeezed Jared's heart. "I'm getting off the freeway at the next exit."

"We have to do something now."

"The radio," he offered.

"Noise is only going to upset her more." Frustration laced each of Kate's words. He knew exactly how she felt. The wailing reverberated around him.

"What do you suggest I do?" he asked.

When she didn't answer, Jared turned on the radio. A classical song played. Mozart, if he wasn't mistaken. The baby screeched. So much for those classical CDs he'd packed for her.

Jared hit one of the radio's preset buttons. A country music singer sang of lost loves and dented fenders. More crying. He pressed another button. A rock and roll tune filled the car with an electric guitar solo. Cassidy shrieked.

Tension in the car ratcheted. Kate grimaced. "This isn't working."

The baby hiccupped between her sobs.

Jared wasn't about to give up. He hit the AM dial and searched the stations, stopping when he heard stock quotes. Brady used to listen to this.

"Why are you putting on this station?" Kate reached for the radio. "It's only going to—"

Cassidy stopped crying as if someone had flicked an off switch.

"No way." Kate's arm hovered in front of the radio for a moment before she placed her hand on her seat. "How did you know financial news would work?"

"Brady listened to this station."

As a reporter spoke about an upcoming meeting to discuss interest rates, the baby squealed, a happy noise this time.

"We're going to have to add the money station in Portland to our presets," Kate said.

"It's already one of mine."

"Then maybe it's one of mine. I rarely listen to the radio."

"Too many phone calls."

"Yes, but I can maximize my productivity. That will be even more important now with Cassidy."

"I have no doubt you can do whatever you set your mind to." He wanted to reassure Kate. Hell, he wanted to take her in his arms and kiss some sense into her gorgeous head. "We both will do whatever it takes."

"You sound so sure."

"I am."

"Aren't you worried about the future?" she asked.

"All we can do is our best."

"What if that's not enough?" She leaned her head back against the seat. "I keep thinking about all these things."

"Like what?" Jared asked.

"I wonder what Cassidy will remember as she grows up. Will she remember Susan and Brady?"

"We will keep her memories alive," Jared said. "Even if she never remembers being born or living in Boise, we can tell her about that. We can tell her stories about Brady and Susan so Cassidy will always love them. And we can take her to Maine to meet her grandparents."

"It sounds like you've been thinking about this."

"Yes," he admitted. "Going through Brady and Susan's things has made it hard not to. I realized that's one reason they chose us. Who better to keep their memory alive in their daughter's life than their best friends?"

Kate nodded.

He caught a glimpse of affection in her eyes. Unexpected emotion rushed through him, and Jared struggled to maintain his composure.

"I've been setting aside the items I think we should keep for Cassidy, but there's probably stuff I haven't thought of," he said. "Guys aren't programmed to think that way."

"You're not like most guys, Jared Reed." Kate covered his hand with hers and squeezed. "Most guys wouldn't have done half of what you've done this week. And fewer would have thought about what things to save for a four-month-old baby."

As she pulled her hand away, Jared wished she could keep it there. Still her words gave him hope that one day soon they would put the past behind them and be a real family. The way Susan and Brady had wanted. The way Jared wanted. He only had to persuade Kate to want them to be a real family, too.

Sitting on the floor of Cassidy's nursery, Kate taped the lid of the box full of toys and board books. She glanced at Cassidy. The baby sat in her stroller, patting the activity bar with chubby fingers. The sight brought much needed comfort to Kate. After two days of sorting through items at Susan's house, a heavy sorrow had taken permanent residence in Kate's heart. She made a conscious effort to breathe.

"All done," she announced to Jared.

"Good timing," he said, looking as good in his sweats and T-shirt as he did in a suit and tie. "We have to leave for the airport in a few minutes. Though with this weather, the flight could be delayed."

Thunder and lightning had set an ominous mood this morning, and sheets of rain fell from the dark, gray skies. The constant pelting against the roof had worsened with each passing hour. The dreary weather fit Kate's mode better than the warm, sunny days they'd had all week. Finally the Heavens were mourning the loss of Susan and Brady, too.

But you would never know anything was wrong by Cassidy's cheery disposition. The baby looked so happy, so content, playing with the spinning toy in front of her. And why not? She was home, playing in the bedroom her parents had spent months decorating, lovingly painting pink and yellow stripes and stenciling flowers and butterflies. Cassidy might not notice the details, but the baby had to sense she was where she belonged.

Unfortunately she wouldn't be here much longer.

On Monday, the house would be put up for sale.

Poor Cassidy. She had no idea what was in store for her. A part of Kate didn't want to leave Boise, didn't want to take Cassidy away from the house Brady and Susan had called home.

"Hey." Jared tapped Kate's shoulder. "You okay?"

Not trusting her voice, she nodded.

"Leaving is going to be hard," he said, matching her own thoughts. "But we have to do it."

Kate nodded again. Selling the house made sense, but left her feeling guilty for taking the baby with her to Portland.

He carried the last box from the bedroom to the pile of stuff in the living room. Movers would transport everything to her home in Portland. The rest of the items would be sold or donated to charity.

Getting rid of a houseful of possessions seemed sad and wrong. She wished Susan and Brady were still alive and none of this had ever happened. If only… Kate hugged her knees.

The cloudy skies seemed to lighten. The rain stopped. Sunlight streamed into the room through the nursery's pair of double-hung windows. The rays, defined by the particles in the air, surrounded the stroller. Giggling, Cassidy reached toward the sunshine.

The baby, who had never seemed so animated before, mesmerized Kate.

"What do you think she sees?" Jared asked from the doorway.

"I don't know," Kate admitted. "Maybe she can feel the sun's warmth. Susan used to call it a sun kiss."

Kate wished she could reach out and grab hold of one of the rays, one of the sun kisses. Her house needed a dose of sunshine badly. So did she. Maybe Cassidy would bring some with her to Portland.

"Whatever the baby sees, she likes it," Jared said.

Cassidy's little arms wiggled in the air as if she wanted to be picked up but she wasn't looking at either Kate or Jared. And she wasn't crying.

"She's happy," Kate agreed. "That's what matters."

"You're right about that."

She took comfort in their ability to agree about the baby. The willingness to get along for Cassidy's sake would make things—okay, their future—easier.

"You've got a smudge of newsprint ink on your cheek." Jared wiped her face with his thumb. "There. All gone."

His nearness disturbed her. He smelled good, a mix of fresh soap and raw earth from his work in the yard. "Th-thanks."

His gaze captured hers. "You're welcome."

Kate expected him to remove his hand from hers. He didn't.

She waited. And waited.

Common sense told her to look away, but she didn't want to listen. Cassidy's coos and giggles told Kate the baby was fine so there was no need to look at her.

"I feel weird not going with you," Jared said.

"You have important business to finish up here."

"I know, but…"

The tone of his voice worried her. "What?"

He didn't answer.

She searched his face for a sign as to what he was thinking, feeling, but found nothing. "Jared?"

"It's going to be strange not having you—" he looked at the baby "—and Cassidy with me."

Cassidy. This was about the baby. Kate ignored the twinge of disappointment inching down her spine. She should be pleased he cared so much about the baby already. Maybe he wouldn't walk away again. What was she thinking? Jared might have left her, but he would never leave Cassidy. "You'll see her next weekend."

"And you."

What he said shouldn't affect Kate, but an unexpected lump formed in her throat. Jared had been a rock, supporting her during the moving funeral service and boxing up Susan and Brady's house. He'd kept things moving and her going. Suddenly a week apart seemed like forever.

"Kate…"

The way he said her name made her pulse quicken.

"I'm happy we had time together this week," he said.

Her temperature shot up.

His lips curved in a half smile. "I'm going to miss you."

Her mouth went dry.

Jared lowered his face toward hers, toward her lips.

He was going to kiss her.

Her heart slammed against her ribs.

Grief, loss, exhaustion. Those emotions explained the physical reactions she was having to him. That was all her body's responses were, all they could be.

She should step back, put distance between them. But Kate couldn't. She didn't want to move away.

"It's time we headed to the airport," he whispered and kissed her forehead.

Relief mingled with regret at the brush of his lips. A silly reaction, really. Good thing she and Cassidy were leaving.

Kate appreciated all Jared had done this week. She'd leaned on him, more than she ever had in the past, but she had to get used to being on her own again. A peck on the forehead, a tender glance and a sincere word changed nothing. She was the one who had to juggle her routine with the baby's. Kate had misgivings, but she could do it. She'd always done everything herself.

But the thought didn't cheer her up. After this week with Jared, it only made her feel a whole lot worse.

Back in Portland, the telephone rang. Grimacing, Kate ran from the pile of pink and pastel-colored laundry sitting on the couch to the receiver on the kitchen counter. She didn't want the ringing to wake Cassidy.

"Hello." Kate sounded rushed and frustrated. She didn't care. Chances were the caller had the wrong number or was a telemarketer. She'd had one of each tonight. Why would this be any different? People she knew called her cell phone. She should just turn off the ringer.

"Hello, Kate."

The sound of Jared's voice brought a rush of anxiety. He never called on the home number. "Is something wrong?"

"No, I wanted to see how you and Cassidy were doing."

"We're doing, um, okay." Kate tried to sound enthusiastic, but she felt like an absolute failure at motherhood. Talk about on-the-job training at its worst, and she only had Cassidy in the morning and after work. She felt a tremendous rush of relief and guilt each time she dropped Cassidy off at Jared's parents' house or picked her up at one of Jared's sisters' houses. Kate couldn't imagine being the full-time caretaker. Of course, the weekend was coming up. "We're adjusting."

Sort of.

"That's great," he said, sounding pleased.

"Yes, great." So long as she continually held Cassidy, only slept a few hours a night and totally let the house go. Kate adjusted the cordless receiver and folded a pink onesie. The amount of laundry one baby generated amazed her.

"My mom says Cassidy's grown."

Kate attributed the baby's weight gain on her own exhaustion. How much could a baby grow in less than a week? "She's still the same diaper size."

"My sister said she uses cloth diapers," Jared said. "Do you think we should use cloth diapers?"

"No." The word tumbled from Kate's mouth. She could barely keep up with the laundry now. "Brady and Susan used disposables. Let's not change anything more in Cassidy's life."

Or mine.

"That's a good point."

Thank goodness he agreed. Kate folded a burp cloth and made a mental note to buy more of them to protect her clothes.

"Do you need anything?"

You. Strike that.

She needed an extra six hours a day to catch up with work here at home and at the office. Despite all the books and magazine articles she'd read, combining work with motherhood required a tricky balance. One she wasn't close to mastering.

"No, thanks. I'm figuring things out." Or would. Getting used to having another person completely reliant upon her wasn't easy. She didn't know how other moms managed especially those without a husband to help. "Though I see the benefit of maternity leave now."

Kate had dreamed of a smooth transition, of how wonderful being a mother and working a fulfilling job would be. Reality crushed her expectations. Her life at home was a far cry from the perfect baby who slept at night and smiled all the time. At work, she finally understood the undercurrent of tension between the women in the office who had children and those who didn't.

Exhausted and completely unorganized for the first time in her life, she didn't know how to make things work when she barely had time to think. Kate folded a lavender sleeper.

"Do you think that would help?" Jared asked.

Oh, no. What was she going to say? "It, um, might."

"Is a leave of absence a possibility?"

"No. Not right now." A part of her felt guilty for not taking this week off to be with Cassidy, but she wasn't about to admit that to Jared. Since she owned the company, she wouldn't have to qualify for family leave. She could simply stay home, but that wouldn't be good for her clients or employees. "I shouldn't have brought it up."

"You sound tired."

Of course she did. Sleeping in three to four hour bursts drove a person to exhaustion. Ever since arriving in Portland Cassidy wouldn't sleep during the middle of the night. She wanted to be held and rocked or held and walked. So that was what Kate did, and she was feeling the effects. She'd fallen asleep at lunch today. "It's been a busy week."

"I know how that goes."

He might think so, but he didn't. Jared couldn't.

Once upon a time, before pink clothing, bottles of formula and wet diapers had become a way of life, Kate believed she'd known the definition of a busy week just like Jared.

She hadn't even been close.

Not until Cassidy. But Kate couldn't tell him that or he would think she couldn't cope.

"Where are you?" she asked.

"Raleigh, North Carolina."

"I thought you were going to Chicago."

"Change of plans," he said. "I'm flying to Portland on Friday, and I'll take the train to Seattle on Sunday night."

Kate glanced around the house. She'd yet to unpack the boxes from Boise. The clutter and mess embarrassed her. She wanted the house to look perfect when Jared arrived. "Do you need a ride from the airport?"

"I'll have my parents pick me up or I'll take a shuttle."

"I don't mind," she said.

"Don't worry about me."

"But I do worry." The words escaped before she could stop them. "I mean, not all the time. But sometimes."

She should shut up before she made a bigger fool of herself. Maybe she needed another nap. Or a good night's sleep.

"I worry about you sometimes, too," he said. "So that makes us even."

Somehow Kate couldn't ever see the scales between them being equal, but she appreciated the thought.

"I'd better get going," he said. "I have work to finish. I'll call you later."

"Only if you have time." She had stuff to do, too. Her list of things to check off by Friday kept growing by the minute.

"I'll make the time."

"For Cassidy," Kate said.

"And you," Jared said. "I miss both of my girls."

"Your girls miss you." Kate had missed him, more than she thought she would.

His rich laughter filled the phone. "Give Cassidy a kiss for me. And here's one for you."

Smack. With that, he hung up.

A burst of heat pulsed through Kate's veins. Too bad she couldn't get a real-honest-to-goodness-husband-to-wife-kiss—from him because that was what she really wanted.

Stop. She shouldn't be having those kinds of feelings about Jared.

She'd told him not to kiss her. She'd told him they would discuss seeing other people in six months. She'd told him their marriage would not be emotional. But, she realized, those were all the things she wanted from him.

Oh, no. Kate sunk to the ground. Now what was she going to do?

CHAPTER SIX

THE porch light wasn't on. The door was locked. And since Kate had filed for divorce, Jared no longer had a key. He grimaced and rang the doorbell.

A minute ticked by. And another.

Not good. He wasn't sure what to expect when he arrived home, but Jared's hope that Kate would be happy to see him plummeted. Standing out here in the dark, he feared she might have changed her mind about their arrangement. And if that happened… He jammed his finger on the doorbell again.

After another minute passed, he pulled out his cell phone, but before he could call her, the door opened.

She stood holding a flushed, crying Cassidy. "Sorry I took so long."

The sound of Kate's frustrated voice made him want to wrap his arms around her, but no matter how much he might want to embrace her, he couldn't. Not yet. They were still tiptoeing across a tightrope with no net below. One wrong move and they would go splat. "Looks like you have your hands full."

He wasn't kidding.

The stark-white bandage around Cassidy's little head, the tears streaming down her round cheeks and the "save me" look in Kate's eyes, reminded Jared he wasn't the only one adjusting to a new set of circumstances. He wanted to help make things better for all of them.

She shrugged. "I was upstairs rocking her, but that only irritated her more."

"Having a tough time, baby." Jared ran his finger along Cassidy's smooth cheek. She screamed. He jerked his hand away. "Is she okay?"

"Yes." Kate rocked back and forth, and Cassidy stuffed her fist in her mouth and sulked. "She doesn't like going to bed."

Jared didn't understand. She was a baby. His sister said babies slept a lot. "Maybe she's hungry."

"She just had a bottle."

"Could be gas," he offered.

"I burped her."

"Wet?" he asked.

"I just changed her."

"Does her head hurt?" His did, from the noise and hunger. If he were a baby, he'd probably cry, too.

Kate glared at him. "Are you suggesting I don't know enough to take care of her?"

"No." Hell, no. "You're taking great care of her."

"I'm trying." Kate's shoulders slumped. "But she wants to be held. All the time."

That explained the dark circles under Kate's eyes and why she looked a bit messy with stains on her purple silk blouse and spots on her brown pants. And he'd never seen her with her hair haphazardly piled on top of her head and clipped that way. Jared couldn't believe how much she'd let her "whole package" slip. Even with a crying baby in her arms.

Seeing Kate look so...untidy took a little getting used to, but the tousled style was cute on her.

He liked that she hadn't forgotten the most important piece of jewelry in her wardrobe. She wore her wedding set—a plain gold band and an engagement ring. The diamond sparkled as if newly cleaned. He wondered if she'd had it resized or started eating better.

Jared placed his luggage inside. Ready to be the go-to-guy, he closed and locked the door. But facing his two girls, he wasn't sure where to begin. Kate looked as if she needed a shoulder to cry on. Cassidy, all teary-eyed and slobbery, clung to Kate. Maybe he should remove his jacket with all this crying action going on. "I, uh, don't mind holding her."

Cassidy wailed. Jared gritted his teeth.

Kate turned her away from him. "I've got her."

Barely.

He wasn't sure he could do any better, but he owed it to both of them to try. "You do, but I'm here. Get some sleep."

"I'm fine."

But she wasn't. He could see the tiredness in her eyes and the strain on her face. The screaming baby was a pretty big clue, too. Kate, however, was being Kate and doing everything herself. He didn't want her handling child rearing the same way she handled everything else in her life.

"We're in this together," he said.

Not that he knew what he was going to do once he had Cassidy. Truthfully the idea of holding a fussy—okay, crying—baby appealed to him as much as a visit with the IRS about his tax return. Still he had to do something.

Kate gave no response. She simply swayed with the baby in her arms.

Tension simmered in the air. Cassidy fussed and flailed.

Usually when Kate acted like this, needing to do things her way, they'd go head to head then have hot makeup sex. Jared wouldn't mind the latter, but he wasn't sure that was the way to go this time. She didn't seem up for a disagreement, let alone a fight. The only thing she seemed up for was bedtime. He kind of liked it.

This new disheveled Kate was growing on him. She seemed less in control, more vulnerable and to be honest, sexier than her normally put-together, perfect, whole package self. Not that he would ever admit that to her.

The baby punched the air like a fighter warming up for the second round.

"Please." Jared extended his arms. "I want to hold her. I kinda missed her."

And you.

But he wasn't about to go there. Not yet.

Patience. He needed to tattoo the word on his brain so he wouldn't push her too hard and too fast.

"Are you sure?" she asked.

"Positive."

With only the slightest hesitation, Kate handed him the baby. As her hand brushed his during the transfer, he felt a shock. Electric static? Or physical attraction? Maybe a little of both. Jared didn't care. Having her soft skin against his skin, even if it had been for less than a nanosecond, felt good.

"Hello, sweet pea," he said to Cassidy.

A sob greeted him.

"Now is that any way to say hello to me?"

Another cry.

As Jared held the warm bundle close, the baby's scent surrounded him. Not all sugar and spice. And he missed the smell of Kate's grapefruit shampoo. Cassidy smelled different…funny. Formula? Or maybe that diaper needed changing again.

She wiggled. Sighed. And then her entire body seemed to go boneless. Magic. Relaxed didn't begin to describe how content she looked. Something inside of him melted. Jared smiled. "Have you been giving Kate a hard time?"

Kate pushed an errant strand of hair back into her clip. "Except for not sleeping, she's been great."

Cassidy reached her chubby little hands to touch his chin, but missed. "Ah-goo."

"Ah-goo?" Flattered, disarmed, he touched her nose. "Really?"

The baby grinned, all toothless gums and drool, and Jared knew he was a goner. Okay, maybe Kate had another reason for wanting to keep hold of Cassidy instead of control issues—baby love. "You are so cute."

Kate tsked. "You better be careful or she'll have you wrapped around her little finger."

Too late.

"Nothing wrong with that." As he rocked back and forth, Jared glanced into the living room. The house, as usual, reminded him of a model home with nothing out of place. Even the magazines on the coffee table were aligned perfectly. Not that he expected any less. Kate was a neat freak plus she had a housecleaner come every other week. Except something—boxes to be exact—were missing.

"Did the movers come?" he asked.

She nodded.

"Where is everything?"

"Some is in Cassidy's new room," Kate said. "The rest is in the attic or garage."

"That must have been a lot of work."

"I hired someone to unpack and move the boxes."

As she always did whenever something needed to be done. Kate ran an efficient household for someone who worked sixty plus hours a week.

Cassidy clicked her tongue. Her eyes widened and she made the same clicking sound again. And again. And again.

His gaze returned to the living room. Same couch and coffee table, but the walls… "You painted."

"Last month, I did some updating to the interior."

Tension from the past week crept into his shoulders. Update her life, update her house. Jared tried not to take the change personally. They were talking a new paint color, not a new man. "The blue is nice."

Kate raised her chin. "I thought so."

The challenge in her tone made Jared take a closer look at the living room. The paint wasn't the only difference. Their wedding portrait had been removed, and new pictures, framed and matted botanical prints in black frames, hung on the wall. The multicolored patterned rug they'd picked out one rainy afternoon at Pottery Barn had been replaced with a straw looking mat. And the book-shelves seemed less full. Were his books missing?

"What do you think?" she asked.

"A lot of changes." Jared felt strange as if she'd taken their home and made it all hers. He didn't like that. Or the differences. Yes, they had been planning to get divorced, but couldn't she have waited until the dissolution was final? Unless she'd already divorced him in her heart and the paperwork was just a formality. He shrugged off the idea. He couldn't believe that was true, not when he remembered what they'd had. He would woo Kate back. He would win her heart. "Where's our wedding picture?"

"I'm having the frame changed to match the blue better."

Okay, good. She was fitting the idea of their married life into her new room, not throwing the old away altogether.

The baby yawned.

He shifted her in his arms. "Are you tired, Cassidy?"

"Baaaah," she replied and stuck her fingers in her mouth.

"Don't be fooled," Kate said. "She's only lulling you into complacency."

"She's a baby."

"She's a smart baby who won't sleep.

Jared laughed. "Tonight will be the night."

He wished.

Kate rolled her eyes. "In your dreams."

His dreams revolved around his wife, not Cassidy. He'd missed making Kate smile. "Wait and see."

"I will."

The baby's eyelids fluttered shut then sprung open.

Kate crossed her arms. "Told you so."

"Patience." He rocked Cassidy and kissed her head above the bandage. "Isn't that right, sleepyhead?"

"You're not giving up?" Kate asked.

"Never. It's called perseverance."

"Or stubbornness."

"As long as I win—" he stared at the sleeping baby in his arms "—and I just did. It worked."

"No."

"See for yourself," he whispered.

"You've got the touch that's for sure," Kate said, and he hoped he'd get to use that touch on her. "Now can you make the transfer to her crib without waking her up?"

He wasn't at all sure he could. But with Kate smiling at him, teasing him, reminding him of what they'd once shared, he was willing to try.

Jared winked. "Watch the master."

"Where do I buy a ticket?"

The amused gleam in her eyes lit a spark in Jared. Maybe once he put Cassidy to bed, Kate would let him tuck her in, too.

Kate stood in the doorway of Cassidy's room and watched Jared in action. Wearing a navy suit, light blue dress shirt and blue striped tie, he looked more like a Hugo Boss model than a new father. Yet his daddy instincts were spot-on. She found that incredibly attractive as well as a tad bothersome. A tiny part—one Kate hated to admit—resented him for succeeding where she had failed.

As Jared gently placed Cassidy in the crib, Kate held her breath. This was where the baby always woke up with her. Yet Cassidy remained asleep. Again, Kate didn't get it. Sure, he'd baby-sat before, but he'd never had to do anything like this. Still Jared acted as if he'd done this a million times as if he'd been a dad for a really long time.

He quietly backed out of the room. "Mission accomplished."

The guy must have an angel on his shoulder or made a

pact with the devil. He never lost when he set his mind to something. Even, Kate realized, their divorce. He was getting his way. As usual.

Darn him.

For a second she felt like kicking the door or making some other loud noise, but common sense took over. Or maybe self-preservation. A block of uninterrupted sleep would make all the difference for her fatigued body and brain. With some rest, she could finally be the mother she wanted to be.

"If I didn't know better," Kate whispered, "I'd think the two of you were in cahoots."

"It's been that bad?" Jared asked.

She didn't want to admit the problems she'd had this week. "Bad might be a bit extreme."

"Let's go downstairs and talk so we don't wake Cassidy," he said. "It's been a while since I've been home."

Kate remembered the last time he'd returned from a business trip on a Friday night. She'd helped him undress, relishing in the scent of him and not caring whether the buttons on his shirt remained attached or not. They'd tumbled into the bed and knocked over the nightstand. And then they'd... She took a deep breath. Looking as handsome as Jared did tonight, she'd better put those memories behind her once and for all.

Pretending to be in love when they hardly saw each other had been easy. She didn't want to fall into the same trap again.

In the kitchen, Kate pulled a brown paper bag from the refrigerator. "If you're hungry, I bought you a sandwich from the deli."

He took the bag with a chuckle. "Thanks."

"What's so funny?" she asked.

"I didn't expect dinner tonight."

"What were you hoping for?"

"A cup of coffee and, maybe, a smile."

Thank goodness he hadn't wanted sex. Relieved, she grinned. "You hit the jackpot. You got the smile and I already brewed a pot of decaf. Though I have beer if you want one of those."

"After all that crying, a shot of whiskey might not be so bad." He took off his jacket, sat on one of the bar stools at the breakfast bar and unwrapped his turkey and provolone sandwich. "But a cup of decaf will be great. Thanks."

"You're welcome."

See. They could be pleasant and platonic. No problem. This might actual work. Of course once they started seeing other people... No, she didn't want to think about that.

He loosened his tie. "Would asking for dessert be pushing it?"

Kate removed two mugs from the cupboard. The cups, white with mini blue coffee mugs painted all over them, had been a wedding gift from one of his co-workers. She'd boxed them up, trying to put all reminders of their marriage away, but this week Kate decided to unpack them. Removing all the reminders of Jared from the house might upset him. "It depends on what you want and whether I have any to give you."

He rolled up his sleeves. "I want..."

Uh-oh. The desire in his eyes made her feel like she was the only dessert he wanted. He smiled, complete with dimples. Her heart hammered against her chest. Oh, boy. His smile was better than she remembered. Kate looked away, but she could still feel his gaze on her and see those dimples. She was in so much trouble.

"Cookies," he said finally.

"Cookies," she repeated, trying to regain control of her raging hormones. "I have a bag of Oreos in the pantry."

"Another one of my favorites."

She didn't want him to think she had gone to any special trouble. Sure, she'd purchased a few of his favorite foods, but that was common courtesy. Nothing more. She poured coffee into the two cups. "Well, I knew you were coming."

"You're the perfect hostess."

That was her intention.

"Here you go." As Kate handed him one of the steaming mugs, her arm brushed his hand. Accidental, but she felt a burst of heat at the spot of contact. Distance. She needed to get away from him. She went to the pantry and pulled out a bottle of vanilla flavored syrup and the bag of cookies.

"Thank you," he said.

She wouldn't meet his eyes.

"Something wrong, Kate?"

You. That wasn't correct. Her own feelings were the problem. "Nothing's wrong."

He took a sip. "Perfect."

He liked his coffee strong and black. He wasn't the type for sugar or cream or flavored syrups. She added a shot of vanilla into her cup. "Someday you'll join the rest of us and drink lattes and mochas."

"Never."

And he was probably right. Jared and his entire family stuck to traditions. Big ones, like naming children after older relatives, and small ones, like how they took their coffee. She, on the other hand, had zero family traditions unless you counted eating Thai food while watching the Academy Awards every year.

Kate wouldn't mind acting out a love scene with Jared. The thought melted her insides like butter. Not good. Shivering, she wrapped her hands around her mug.

"Are you cold?" he asked.

Actually she was quite warm. Okay, hot. "I'm fine."

"So have you talked to the pediatrician about this not-sleeping-hold-me-all-the-time problem?" he asked.

Good, maybe if they talked about the baby she could stop thinking of him as a, well, a man. One who she wanted to touch her again. "I'm not sure I'd call it a problem, but no, I haven't."

"What about my parents?" He picked up his sandwich. "Does she act the same way at their house?"

"Cassidy has no problem napping there during the day, but when she's here at night, sleep becomes a foreign word."

"Her internal clock might be screwed up."

"I don't think so. Susan would have mentioned something like that. I remember when she told me the baby had started sleeping at least four hours at a stretch during the night. She said she felt like a new woman."

"Maybe Cassidy's gotten spoiled," he suggested. "At the hospital she had round-the-clock care and attention."

"The books say you can't spoil a baby." Besides Kate couldn't spoil her if she wanted. Not working all day. "Why all the questions?"

His interest confused her. Jared, like all the male Reeds, might hold the babies during family get-togethers, but they never joined in the baby talk.

"I need to know what's going on," he said.

So he took the new responsibility seriously. Kate wondered whether his caring dad act was well, an act. She was surprised, but happy to discover he did care.

"I don't think that's the problem with Cassidy," Kate said. "She's lost her parents, spends her days at one house and her nights at another. That's a lot to take in for a baby."

Too much? Guilt slithered up her spine.

Jared wiped his mouth with a napkin. "Maybe she'll be better now that we're all here together."

Kate's muscles knotted. They were only together for a couple of days. And then the situation would change. Again. "One can hope."

"Yes, one can." Mischief glinted in his gaze. "So where am I sleeping tonight?"

His suggestive tone made her set her cup on the counter before her unsteady hand dropped it. "You're sleeping in the guest bedroom."

Jared didn't say anything, but his eyes darkened. He couldn't be surprised. Upset, maybe. But this was what they'd agreed upon. The rules they'd set.

And ones they would stick to. No matter what.

She expected him to say something. He didn't. And the silence magnified the stress between them. Kate could fix that.

"I had the room cleaned out, including the armoire." She refilled his mug, hoping her words didn't sound as lame as she thought they did. "I had pictures hung on the wall, too."

As if Jared would care.

He took another bite of his sandwich.

"All you're missing is a dresser." She wanted to keep the silence from returning. "We can buy one this weekend."

His gaze focused on her, and her pulse skittered. "You've thought of everything."

The tone of his voice told her he hadn't meant the words as a compliment. "I, um, tried."

Because that's what Kate did. Considered all the possibilities. Made plans for all the contingencies. Or at least she had until...tonight.

Jared had thrown her—not to mention her hormones—for a loop. And that left her worried about what the rest of the weekend would hold.

Maybe she was the one who needed that shot of whiskey.

Or better yet, an entire bottle.

So much for there being no place like home. Right now, being home pretty much sucked. His new room was small—eight by nine if he were being generous—without a closet. Without his wife.

Lying on a full-size mattress with his feet hanging over the edge, Jared glanced at the clock. Midnight. Sleeping wasn't easy when his wife, the woman he hadn't slept with in two months and twenty-three days, was sleeping down the hall. Alone. In a king-size bed. Probably wearing some short little nightshirt that had ridden up the curve of her hips. He missed touching her soft skin, feeling her warm body pressed against his in a perfect fit.

As he calculated ways to make Kate fall for him all over again, his eyelids grew heavy. He'd been on East Coast time all week, and the time difference was catching up to him. He rolled over. Sleep came fast and hard.

A cry shattered the silence of the house like a rooster's call at dawn. He looked at the clock. Two. Another cry.

Cassidy.

He scrambled out of bed, hit his calf on his luggage and hurried to her room. But Kate had beat him there.

A small lamp provided a dim light, enough for him to see her, wearing a nightshirt that showed off her long, slender legs, holding the baby.

"Let's get you a bottle, hungry girl," Kate said.

Hungry girl. If only Kate were saying she was hungry for him. He felt a twinge in his groin. The baby sobbed.

He concentrated on the task at hand. "Want some help?"

Kate sucked in a sharp breath. "I didn't hear you come in."

"Sorry." He yawned. "You want me to get the bottle?"

"I can do it." But instead of heading to the kitchen, she lowered the fussing baby to the changing table and pulled a diaper from the lower shelf.

"Let me change her," he offered, not wanting to replay the scene earlier tonight. "While you warm the bottle."

Kate unzipped Cassidy's pajamas.

"If we work together," he said. "We can get back to bed that much sooner."

Alone, together, he'd take what he could get at this hour.

"Cassidy needs to be changed." Kate strapped the baby to the table and handed him the diaper. For a moment they both held onto it, and then she looked away. "Everything is here, including a new sleeper if the one she's wearing is wet. I'll be back with the bottle."

Victory. She was actually letting him help.

He undid the diaper, and his satisfaction evaporated. Gross. He should have opted for the bottle.

After the diaper change, Jared rocked, swayed and walked Cassidy, but nothing made the baby happier or sleepy.

Kate returned with bottle in hand. "I can take her."

"You've been doing this all week." Jared reached for the bottle, purposely brushing his fingers against Kate's and watching her pull away her hand. So she felt the heat, the connection, too. Good. He placed the bottle in an eager Cassidy's mouth. "Go back to bed."

"Are you sure?" Kate said. "She doesn't go to sleep right away."

"All the more reason for you to grab some shuteye now."

She bit her lip. "Yell if you need me."

He needed her. Badly. But not in the way she was offering. But hey, at least she hadn't argued with him about this. A positive step. "I will."

With that, she left the room. He pictured her crawling into bed, sliding under the covers and her nightshirt riding up again. One peek was all he wanted.

Jared glanced at Cassidy, who sucked down her bottle as if it were a chocolate milkshake, not formula. "Let's see if you need to burp."

Once she'd burped, finished the bottle and burped again, Jared walked Cassidy to her crib. She fussed, tears falling from her eyes. "Do you want to rock?"

She answered him with a sigh.

Jared sat on the rocker he'd helped Brady refinish. Cassidy settled down for about five minutes until she cried again.

He walked around her room, and that seemed to do the trick. Until he stopped. The crying started again.

Now he understood what Kate had been talking about and why she looked exhausted. How had she done this every night without losing it? This was only his first night, and he was already tired of the routine and ready for sleep himself.

"It's late, baby." He walked more like a robot on automatic mode but the movement calmed Cassidy. "You had your bottle. Your diaper's clean. Time for nighty-night."

But Cassidy didn't seem to understand. Or maybe she didn't care. He respected Kate dealing with this and still managing to go to work each morning.

"I'll take over," a quiet voice said from behind him.

"Kate," he said surprised. "I thought you were asleep."

"I was, but woke up."

He wasn't about to accept defeat. And those rings under her eyes seemed darker. Jared wondered if she'd actually slept. And that upset him. She never wanted to give up control. "I can do this."

"I know, but tomorrow will be a long day if we're both tired." She reached for the baby, but he didn't let go. For a moment the three of them were locked together. Not quite a group hug, or passionate in any sense of the word, but he'd take it. "Really, Jared, get some sleep."

He heard the familiar determination in her voice. Stalemate. He couldn't count the number of times it had happened before. Arguing with her would only lead to a fight.

Jared let go. "I'm not going to be able to sleep knowing you're still awake."

"Then stay up," she said. "It's your choice."

As he walked to the opposite side of the room and leaned against the wall, Kate sang a quiet lullaby. Funny, but he'd never heard her sing except one time at karaoke. This was different. Love filled the sweet sound. Patience, too. Her song captivated him as did Kate herself.

She was a mom. Cassidy's mom.

They'd made the right choice for the baby. Jared knew

that without a doubt. He also knew something else. He needed Kate and Cassidy in his life, and they needed him, too. Kate just didn't realize it yet, but she would. He would show her just how much she needed him, stupid no sex rule or not.

CHAPTER SEVEN

CASSIDY usually woke up at six o'clock in the morning. This time, with Jared in the house, Kate wanted to be prepared.

At five-thirty, she showered and dressed, putting on gray pants, a pale pink blouse, pearl necklace and matching earrings. Perfect mom clothes, she thought. Kate brushed mineral powder foundation over her face, added a touch of blush and lip gloss. A bit early for a Saturday, but walking around in her nightshirt didn't seem like a smart idea. Especially after she'd noticed Jared checking out her legs last night. Thank goodness she'd shaved.

Not that she wanted him to find her attractive.

Kate didn't.

But she felt better knowing her legs looked good. At least, she hoped they had.

At precisely six o'clock, she sneaked a peek into Cassidy's room. The sight of an empty crib sent panic rolling through Kate. She struggled to breathe. "Cassidy."

"Downstairs," Jared called up.

Kate hurried down the stairs and into the kitchen. She skidded to a stop. Cassidy sat in her high chair, and Jared fed her from a bowl.

Kate's blood pressure spiraled. "What are you doing?"

"I'm feeding Cassidy her breakfast."

"She's not eating solids yet."

"There was a box of rice cereal in the pantry."

Kate placed her hands on her hips. "Your sister gave the box to your mother to give to me."

"I know," he said. "My mom told me."

"You called your mother?" Kate asked, though as soon as the question was out, she realized how stupid her words must sound. Jared talked to his family all the time. His parents, his sisters and brothers. Aunts, uncles and cousins, too.

"Yes, I called her. The bottle didn't seem to fill Cassidy up." Jared spooned more cereal into the baby's mouth. "Don't worry. After I talked with my mom, I double-checked the baby book on the counter. Solids are okay for four months olds."

"But they don't recommend starting solids until six months to alleviate allergies."

"Well, my mom fed us solids at four months and we turned out okay." Jared stuck another spoonful of rice cereal into the baby's open mouth. "Besides Cassidy likes it. Maybe she'll sleep longer with something more substantial in her stomach."

If they wanted to be perfect parents, they needed to stick to a plan. Not make changes as it suited them. "You should have asked me first. I was awake."

"You were in the shower," he said. "I could have come in, but I didn't think you'd appreciate that."

Okay, he was right about that. The thought of Jared walking into the steam-filled bathroom raised her temperature a few degrees. "You could have waited."

"Why?" he asked. "We are both her guardians, Kate.

Her parents, now. I realize you like things a certain way and you've spent more time with the baby than I have, but I need to be a part of this, too."

"You are a part of this."

"Am I?" he asked. "You could have slept last night and left Cassidy with me, but you didn't."

Okay, she'd give him that one. "You were tired, but stayed up, too."

"I'm only home a couple of nights a week." He wiped Cassidy's messy white face with her bib.

"A wet washcloth would work better," Kate offered.

He glared at her. "This is what I'm talking about."

"What?" Kate felt as if she had to defend herself. "I'm only trying to help. And I wanted to wait until Cassidy was six months to try solid foods because Susan had a peanut allergy. Cassidy could be more susceptible to food allergies."

"I didn't know," he said. Not much of an apology, but knowing Jared that's all she would get. "But if you're worried about allergies, we don't have to feed her anything else except rice cereal until she turns six months."

Kate didn't want to fight. They'd done too much arguing before they broke up. "I guess."

"If it's any consolation, Cassidy seems to like it. She's scarfing down the cereal like it's ice cream." He made a face. "Don't know why. The stuff tastes pretty bland."

"You tried it?"

Jared nodded. "Isn't that what you're supposed to do when you're a parent?"

"I have no idea, but I've never seen that in any of the baby books."

"Maybe you need to stop relying on the baby books."

His suggestion brought a flash of hurt. Jared could always call on his family for help, but with their strange marriage arrangement, she hadn't felt comfortable doing the same. His family did enough caring for Cassidy during the week. Besides, Kate didn't want to appear incompetent. "And do what instead?"

He raised a brow. "Try winging it."

The concept went against every one of Kate's instincts. "I'm not sure that's a good idea."

Cassidy knocked the spoon with her hand. Rice cereal flew through the air and landed on Jared's face.

The baby squealed.

"Very funny, sweet pea." Laughing, he wiped his eyes with a napkin. "At least Cassidy seems to understand the definition of winging it."

Kate wanted to remain indifferent to him, and not care what he did, said or looked like. But at this moment indifference was the last thing she felt for Jared. Especially when he looked so adorable with splotches of cereal and a dimpled smile on his face. "You look—"

"Like a clown?"

"No."

"A papier mâché model?"

"Close, but no, you look like a dad." She grabbed a paper towel, wet it and wiped his face clean. "The kind who all the kids in the neighborhood will want to play with."

"What about you?"

She swallowed. "Me?

"Would you want to play, too?" he asked.

Oh, yes. Kate met his warm, intent gaze, her heart thudding.

Oh, no.

* * *

Winging it worked great, Jared thought smugly a few hours later. As they walked around the neighborhood full of cozy bungalows and English-style cottages on the partially cloudy May morning, Cassidy fell asleep in her stroller without so much as a peep. Maybe they'd finally learned the secret to naptime—keep the baby away from the crib.

"So…Chinese takeout, barbecue or pizza for dinner?" Kate asked.

"Whatever would be easiest," he said.

Walking with Kate, talking with Kate reminded him of when they'd first got married and would stroll through the tree-lined sidewalks hand in hand and catch up on their week. Except this afternoon they pushed a stroller, kept their distance from each other and avoided any source of controversy with their conversation topic. No work talk, only food talk.

"Pizza would be the easiest," Kate said after they'd gone around and around, about various restaurants and the block. "Pepperoni and mushroom."

His favorite.

"Don't you like olives and sausage?" he asked. "On a thick crust?"

She nodded. "But you like thin."

They were trying so hard to get along. Maybe too hard.

But he understood the reasoning. If they were polite and nice, they could pretend no underlying passion and heat brewed between them. Of course maybe he should just admit he was too tired to do anything but be a good boy and follow the rules. "Let's order a regular crust."

"Sounds good," she said.

But good wasn't enough for him. He wanted things

back to the way they were. Even though they were outside, the atmosphere, like the conversation, felt forced and strained. He didn't like that. But focusing on the negatives wouldn't help, Jared realized. Bottom line— they were together. They were a family. Perhaps not a totally functional one, but even this much had to be enough for now.

He noticed an empty lot on the corner. "What happened to the Pahls's house?"

"Someone bought the house and tore it down," Kate said. "The land was worth way more than the structure."

On that one intersection alone, a house was for sale, one had been demolished, another was being remodeled and a fourth had been primed for a paint job. "Things are changing," Jared said. "I've noticed more traffic from non-locals."

"True, there are more cars on the streets, but our property value has gone up." She sounded pleased. "It's that old saying—location, location, location."

"I always thought the location was great."

"Now others agree with you." Kate's mood seemed to improve. "It makes financial sense to do the remodel."

And give them more space, another bathroom and an updated kitchen.

"I think we should still hold off." Jared didn't want them to live in Portland, but he couldn't tell that to Kate. "Too many changes at one time—"

"Would be too much for all of us," she finished for him.

There it was again. That feeling of oneness. Strain, stress, whatever else that kept them apart couldn't hide the bond between them. She *had* to feel the connection, too, and Jared suppressed his guilt over keeping quiet about his real reason for not wanting to pour money into the house.

Back home while Kate fixed lunch, Jared read board books to the baby. After lunch, they played with Cassidy under her floor gym. Sure, tension remained between him and Kate, but nothing had gone wrong as far as the baby was concerned. No need to refer to any baby books or Google information on the Internet. He and Kate were getting parenting down and that felt great.

"It's afternoon naptime," he said, holding Cassidy on his lap. "My mom says the baby takes two naps at her house."

"Why don't we take her on another walk?" Kate suggested. "She can fall asleep and we'll get some exercise."

"You said she was dealing with a bunch of changes. Maybe we should try to keep to her routine at my parents' house."

"You're right."

Her dubious tone made him smile. He rose, ready for the challenge. "Then let's do it."

"I can put her down."

"So can I."

Impasse. Again.

Only this time, Jared held the prize. That meant he won. "Since I've got her, I'll put her down."

"I've got your back covered."

He laughed. "You sound like we're going to war."

"Don't you remember last night?" she asked.

"It wasn't that bad." He carried Cassidy up the stairs. "It's time for your nap, baby. Show us how well you can go to sleep on your own."

The baby gooed.

"That's right," he said. "Show us how tired you are, sleepyhead."

Kate followed him up the stairs. "I wouldn't talk too much or get her excited in any way."

"So I shouldn't tickle her toesies?"

"I wouldn't recommend it."

"What about yours?" he asked.

"Well—" her mouth curved "—this probably isn't the best time."

But she hadn't said no. Progress.

"Right now we should just put the baby to bed," Kate said.

Jared changed Cassidy's diaper and carried her to the crib. He kissed the top of her head, just above the white bandage. "Sleep well, princess."

Mommy and Daddy need some more alone time.

He lay the baby in the crib. Wide-eyed and innocent, she gazed up at him with her big blue eyes, and she wailed. The blood-curdling scream made every single one of his nerve endings stand at attention like Buckingham Palace guards.

"Pick her up," Kate said, rushing to the crib.

"No." He patted Cassidy's back. "We're here, baby, but you need to go to sleep."

The baby's face turned red, and tears shot from her eyes.

Clutching the crib rail, Kate's knuckles went white. "This isn't working for me."

Him, either. "Give it—"

"Shhh." She picked the baby up. "Don't cry, sweetie. We're here."

A minute.

Cassidy rested her head on Kate's shoulder, held onto Kate's hair with one hand and cried.

The minutes passed slower than the concession lines on opening day. With every tear the baby shed, Jared felt his composure unraveling. After thirty minutes of the baby's tantrum, he wanted to scream himself.

"I can't take this much longer," he said finally.

"I know, but I'm not sure what else to try."

Swaying hadn't worked. Rocking, either.

He had to give Kate credit. Her voice remained calm. She kept in constant motion even though she looked ready to fall asleep herself at any minute.

"We've got to figure this out and make her stop," he said. Before Cassidy's naptime behavior pushed he and Kate over the edge. They had enough problems on their own to work out. They didn't need this, too. "I'm going downstairs."

"For what?" she asked.

"To check the baby books."

Kate sat on the rocking chair for the third time. She arched her eyebrows, but her smile was sympathetic. "What happened to winging it?"

He shrugged. "So I'm an idiot."

"No, you're a new parent, that's all," she said with the understanding of a mom. "It's not as easy as you think it will be."

"You're right," he admitted. "I don't know how you managed on your own."

"You do what you have to do."

Exactly. And Jared wasn't going to let a tiny baby defeat them. A man on a mission, he stormed downstairs. Thumbing through the stack of baby books on the table, he ran through all the checklists with flowcharts and what-if scenarios. Nothing explained why Cassidy hated going to sleep so much. Nothing told him what to do.

So he did what any other man would do in this situation. He picked up the telephone and called his mother.

"I don't know what the problem is, dear," Margery, mother of five and grandmother of seven, said. "Cassidy has no problem going down for a nap in the morning and in the afternoon here. Have you checked her temperature?"

Jared hung up the phone, feeling worse than before, and returned to Cassidy's room. "Where's the thermometer?"

Kate walked the perimeter of the room with the baby in her arms. "She doesn't feel warm."

"Just tell me where it is?"

She patted a sobbing Cassidy. "In the hall bathroom. Second drawer."

A minute later, he ran the thermometer over the unbandaged portion of her forehead, but the reading was way too low. What little remained of his tired spirits disappeared completely.

"Hold the button down as you scan," Kate explained kindly. "You'll hear double-beeps when it's finished."

"Thank you." Jared hoped he sounded sincere, not irritated like he really felt. This wasn't Kate's fault. She was trying to help him. The way he wanted to help her.

He scanned the baby's forehead again, and this time the device worked. The action, however, aggravated Cassidy more, but he kept going. If she had a fever, they could fix that. At the double-beep, he checked the readout. His entire body seemed to sag. "No fever."

A good thing, really, but no temperature meant he had to keep looking for the reason she acted this way.

"What do you want to try next?" Kate asked.

"I'm out of ideas." Jared patted her shoulder. "I just can't believe you did this all yourself."

"I only had to deal with nighttime, not naptime."

That was enough. And earned his undying respect and admiration. "I'm still impressed."

"Thanks."

"So do you have any other ideas?" he asked.

She gave a half smile. "Are you up for another walk?"

As Kate hoped would happen, the afternoon stroll around the neighborhood worked. Cassidy fell asleep in her stroller as soon as they reached the end of the street, but by nine o'clock that night, she threw another tantrum. Cassidy did not want to go to bed. Again. It was too dark and late for another walk. Not that Kate had the inclination or the energy to take the baby out once more. Thank goodness Jared was here because she could not take any more. Physically exhausted and emotionally drained, she collapsed on her bed.

She had no idea how Susan had done this. Her friend may have spoken about being tired or wanting to lose weight, but she had never complained about the baby. And that was all Kate had wanted to do today.

"We should wave the white flag and surrender," she yelled to Jared, who walked Cassidy in the hallway. "Maybe then she'll stop crying."

Though Kate doubted it. She crawled under the covers as if the cotton blanket could shield her from the baby's latest fit. Anything for a reprieve.

Cassidy sobbed.

Jared walked into the room and sat on the bed. "I think we're reaching the saturation stage."

The baby hiccupped.

Kate felt light-headed from the fatigue of trying to get the baby to sleep. "I'll take over, but I'm going to need some help getting up."

"Mind if we join you instead?" Jared asked.

Anything to stay in bed. Staring at the ceiling, she patted the space next to her. "Please do."

He placed the baby in the center of the king-size bed so Cassidy lay between them. "Why don't we rest for a little bit?"

Rest. The word was ambrosia to Kate's ears. And then she realized she had invited Jared into her bed. Her body tensed. What had she been thinking? She hadn't. That was the problem. Biting her lip, she tried to control her erratic pulse.

"That means you, too, baby," he said.

Cassidy's tears stopped, as if she realized she'd won another round, and she cooed.

The baby. Kate's worry was premature. Cassidy would keep anything from happening between her and Jared. Of course, if Kate stuck to the rules, nothing would happen anyway.

"She likes this bed," Jared said. "Just not her own."

"I don't understand." Kate rolled on her side so she faced the now content baby and a relieved Jared. "How could this cute little girl also be the crying crib monster?"

Cassidy reached into the air with her arms and kicked her yellow footie clad feet.

He laughed. "I don't know, but she's happy."

"Yes," Kate said. She wished she felt happy, too, but she only felt…stressed. Especially the way Jared's shirt tightened across his chest and the muscles on his arms as he lay on his side. She swallowed.

Peals of laughter escaped from the baby's mouth.

"This sure beats tears," Kate said, trying to sound cheerful. And not stare at him.

"Too bad it's not always like this," Jared said.

He meant Cassidy. He had to mean Cassidy. Kate wet her lips. "Maybe we've reached a crossroad."

His gaze locked on hers. "I hope so."

Jared reached his hand across the pillows and touched her head. Kate stiffened, unsure what to say, but knowing she couldn't allow him to touch her. Not like this. In bed. Together.

He combed his fingers through her hair, and her body went limp. She couldn't help herself. Having him touch her felt so good and so right. And that was so wrong. But Kate didn't want to think about all the reasons she should stop him. She wanted to enjoy this a few minutes longer.

All these months sleeping alone, she'd forgotten how good having him in bed with her again felt. Kate almost sighed. "If you keep that up, I'm going to fall asleep."

"That will make two of you," he said softly.

The sight of Cassidy's closed eyes and curved lips brought relief. Finally. Quiet.

"What if she wakes up?" Kate whispered, watching the baby's steady breaths.

He placed one of the shams between their feet. "With you blocking that side and me on this side and the pillow down there, Cassidy isn't going anywhere."

That meant neither was Jared. So many buts and what-ifs ran through Kate's mind. She was too tired to deal with them. Maybe in the morning they'd have to set new rules to deal with situations like this, but for now she'd just go with it.

Leaning over, Jared brushed his lips across hers. "Sleep well."

The kiss had been platonic—a gesture out of camaraderie. Saying good-night, that's all he'd been doing. She shouldn't read anything into the action. Too bad her throbbing lips hadn't gotten that memo. She forced herself not to touch them.

"Close your eyes, Kate."

She did, but that didn't stop the thoughts running through her head.

"Night Katie."

Kate waited for him to take his hand away. He didn't. O-kay. She cleared her dry throat. "Good night, Jared."

Except for sleeping in his own bed last night—albeit with Cassidy between him and Kate—the rest of the weekend didn't improve. Cassidy, a teeny, tiny, helpless baby, turned into a raging, demanding demon any time the crib was involved. Naptime and bedtime became battles. And Cassidy, by sheer willpower alone, had been victorious.

Kate didn't want to get Cassidy in the habit of sleeping with her, and he was onboard with that. He wanted to be the only person in bed with Kate.

But there were only so many walks a person could take and by Sunday night, Jared felt like a war zone refugee—sleepless, homeless, shell-shocked. He couldn't wait to get back to Seattle though he would miss Kate. His job, even during the most critical of times, had never been as hard as taking care of a baby. And he was ready for some R & R.

The only good to come out of this was he and Kate had become a team trying to get the baby to go to sleep without a World War III reaction.

Jared hated leaving her to deal with Cassidy. Kate was exhausted when he arrived. His visit had barely given her a respite. How would she survive another week of the Crib Demon routine on her own?

"I'm sorry I have to go," he said, watching Cassidy play under her floor gym.

"You have your job," Kate said evenly. "I understand."

Her understanding increased his guilt. "But we have to do something about Cassidy."

"I know." Frustration clouded Kate's pretty face. "She never does this at your parents' house."

"That's what my mom told me."

"Maybe Cassidy needs more consistency."

"Consistency?" he repeated.

"If Cassidy spent more time here during the day so this isn't only the place she comes to for a bottle, bath and bedtime, she might not have such a terrible reaction."

"That sounds like a good theory," he said. "But I don't think my parents would want to spend their days here."

"No, you're probably right."

He hated to see her so discouraged. "You mentioned maternity leave or a leave of absence."

"Yes, but I can't do that. I'm still trying to catch up from the time I spent in Boise." She bit her lip. "Things would fall apart."

Things were already falling apart. If she didn't get some sleep, if Cassidy didn't settle into her new home, Kate was going to make herself sick. "At the office, you mean."

She stuck out her chin. "Yes."

He should have known. Her career and her firm came first. Before her health, before their marriage, before Cassidy.

But that was unfair, he realized. Lots of new moms worked by choice or necessity. Kate was doing her best to juggle a demanding job during the day with a demanding baby during the night. In fact, she was doing a lot more than he was.

Jared took a deep breath. "Kate, you can't go on like this."

A long silence ensued.

"I'll be fine," she said. "I just need to quit running every time Cassidy makes a sound."

Kate sounded confident, and her plan made sense. But he didn't believe her. Ordinarily Jared would take Kate at her word and take off, but this time…he didn't want to leave.

He stared at his two girls. Something had to change or the happy future, the perfect family, he was striving for was never going to happen. He needed to step up to the plate and hit the grand slam. "I'll take time off from work and stay home with Cassidy."

Kate's mouth gaped. "What?"

"I'll use some of my vacation time and stay here." Jared couldn't believe he had thought of the idea let alone suggested it, but what choice did have if he wanted to do what was best for his family? "That should help Cassidy adjust quicker."

Kate stuck her tongue between her teeth. "You'd do that for the baby?"

"Not just for the baby. For you, too. For me," he added hastily when her mouth tightened. Kate never could accept his help. "I'd worry about you here alone."

"That is so thoughtful of you, but I've managed so far."

"You've done great, but remember what I said. We're in this together. I mean that, Kate."

Gratitude filled her eyes. And he knew he was making the right decision.

"I have to talk to my boss, but they managed without me while I was in Boise. I'm sure they can survive another week or two," he said. "I've accrued so many weeks of vacation. I don't think I've used any since our honeymoon and last week."

Which, thinking about it, was a pretty sad statement about his life. And their marriage.

She looked wistful. "There wasn't enough—"

"Time," he finished for her. "Remember Maui?"

She nodded. "How could I forget? We were at the airport ready to go."

And as quickly as that, the tentative rapport between them faded as old hurts, old conflicts surfaced. "I told you to turn off your cell phone."

"How was I to know my biggest client had been slapped with a class action lawsuit?"

"You wouldn't have known if you'd listened to me."

"I would have had to fly back anyway."

"You could have had someone else handle the situation."

"Situation? It was a crisis. My firm's reputation was on the line. I couldn't hand the client off to someone else and go on vacation." She brushed her hair behind her shoulder. "At least I got our money back unlike the trip to Cancún."

"Hey, I had no choice but to fly to New York. Boss's orders," he explained. "We were supposed to reschedule the trip, but then…"

"We never did."

And probably never would. Jared swallowed.

"There's not going to be a lot of time in the future for

big vacations so I might as well use the time now," he said. "As long as you don't mind me being here during the week, too."

"I won't mind you here," she said softly, making him wonder if she was having a change of heart about the two of them.

He hoped so. "I'll try not to get in your way."

They used to joke about being two planes passing in the night. Except for the week of Thanksgiving and the time between Christmas and New Year's, they rarely spent weeknights together due to travel schedules. At least they would only be working around one of their work schedules now.

A stay-at-home dad.

Temporarily, he assured himself. Just until they tamed the Crib Demon and he made sure Kate ate and slept. He could relieve her of the bedtime battles and make the next move in his game plan to win her back. He would quadruple the progress he'd made this morning. No doubt.

"I'll talk to my boss in the morning," Jared said.

"Having you here will be good for Cassidy."

His being here would be great for all three of them. Kate would realize that soon enough. Putting on his game face, he clapped his hands together. "Just call me Mr. Mom."

She smiled. "Somehow I never pictured us as Mr. Mom and Mrs. Dad."

"What about Mr. and Mrs. Jared Reed?" he challenged.

Her smile faded. "I don't think so."

"So what do you suggest?"

"Hmmm." She pressed her lips together and winked. "What about Mr. and Mrs. Kate Malone?"

CHAPTER EIGHT

WEDNESDAY evening, Kate turned the car from the alley onto her driveway in the back and noticed the lights on in the house.

Jared was here.

A strange mix of apprehension and relief flowed through her. Kate parked the new four-door Ford Freestyle in front of the garage housing her beloved silvery blue BMW Boxster. She turned off the engine, but remained in the car.

She was relieved to have Jared back. Bedtime with Cassidy had only gotten worse since he'd left on Sunday. But knowing he would be here day and night, for at least a week, maybe more, made Kate nervous and uncertain. Jared had been nothing but cooperative, trying to make this arrangement work, but she hated unpredictability. She hated not having control. And that's what she feared would happen with him here.

Cassidy squealed.

Kate glanced in the mirror and saw the baby's smiling face through another mirror attached to the back seat. Affection for the little one overflowed in her heart. Surely Cassidy and doing what Susan desired for her daughter would make Kate's struggles worthwhile. "Give me a minute, okay?"

The baby cooed.

She'd take that as a yes.

Staring across the backyard, she saw Jared in the kitchen. Fluttery sensations overtook her stomach. She clutched the steering wheel. The butterfly aviary fluttering in her tummy had nothing to do with apprehension, and everything to do with attraction.

Uh-oh. Maybe that was the real problem. The temptation having Jared around 24/7 would bring.

A bed-size lump of worry lodged in her throat.

She couldn't afford to be tempted. She couldn't do anything to upset the precarious relationship—make that situation—between them. Too much was at stake. She glanced in the mirror at Cassidy.

And Kate knew what she had to do.

She needed to encase her heart in armor to immune itself from him. From his good looks and witty charm, from his willingness to use his vacation time to care for a baby he hardly knew and to help his almost-but-not-quite-ex-wife make the transition from working woman to working mother.

She exhaled slowly.

Cassidy giggled, another happy sound, but Kate wasn't about to push the baby's good mood. She didn't want Jared's second homecoming to be filled with tears. That would happen soon enough when bedtime rolled around.

She exited the car, swung her laptop case strap over her shoulder and opened the baby's door. "Are you ready to get out?"

"Ah-goo," Cassidy said.

Kate repeated the sound. "That's your favorite word, isn't it?"

"Ah-goo."

She reached into the center of the back seat, removed Cassidy from the car seat and carried her to the back door that opened as if on cue.

The scents of basil and garlic drifted out. Her stomach growled. She hadn't eaten a real meal with all the food groups or drank a liquid without a heavy dose of caffeine since...Sunday. When Jared had been here last.

"Perfect timing," he announced as she stepped inside. "Dinner's almost ready."

"You cooked?" Silly question once she got a glimpse of the kitchen. Something red simmered on the stove. An empty pasta sauce jar, a bag of spaghetti noodles and a bottle of Chianti sat on the tile counter. Water boiled in a huge pot. Something—garlic bread, she hoped—baked in the oven.

Kate recalled the dinner she'd given him when he'd arrived last Friday evening—a cold sandwich—and felt bad she hadn't cooked a meal for him. Of course Jared hadn't been taking care of a baby while trying to fix dinner tonight, and she had done the best she could at the time. But Kate realized she should have had a meal prepared for him by a professional chef. That was what a perfect wife would have done. Next time...

"It smells delicious." Her nervousness in the car seemed silly. He'd cooked her dinner, not tried to seduce her. She glanced at the bottle of wine. No, she had nothing to worry about as long as he didn't offer to rub her back. Kate cleared her throat. "When did you get here?"

"Around three." He dumped the bag of pasta into the

boiling water and set the timer on the stove. "My boss wanted me in on a conference call this morning."

"Is he okay with you taking vacation time?"

Jared nodded. "He asked me to check in with him at the end of the week. I told him I'd probably be gone two weeks."

Two weeks. She could handle that if Jared could.

She noticed a bottle in the warmer. "For Cassidy?"

"It should be ready."

Kate set her briefcase on the floor and tested the temperature of the formula in the bottle. Perfect. She shouldn't be surprised. Not with the competence he'd already demonstrated tonight. "Thanks. You've thought of everything."

He smiled. "I gave it my best shot."

She sat at the kitchen table—set with plates, silverware, napkins and wineglasses—and fed the bottle to a hungry Cassidy. Kate had no idea what she'd expected when she walked in the door, but this—a scene out of an alternate reality 1950's television show—wasn't it.

Jared stirred the sauce with a wooden spoon. Amazing. She didn't know they had a wooden one. A satisfied grin formed on her lips. Sure he'd only cooked a dinner, but the care he'd gone to make her feel special. Cherished. A way she hadn't felt in a long time. And she liked it.

"Do you need any help?" she asked.

"Thanks, but I'm almost done."

As the baby slurped down her formula, Kate watched Jared. He checked the boiling noodles, lowered the heat on the bubbling sauce and removed the bread baking from the oven. He'd always been comfortable cooking, more so than her, but she'd never seen him look so…domestic. He seemed perfectly at home in the kitchen. Her kitchen. Their kitchen, now.

Unfamiliar heat burned deep within Kate. She pressed her toes against the hardwood floor. "I could get used to this."

He glanced her way. "You think?"

Uh-oh. She hadn't meant to say the words out loud. She nodded, when her answer was really "most definitely."

And that, Kate acknowledged, was a problem. She wanted to establish a stable home and a routine for Cassidy, but Kate knew better than to depend on the same for herself. She would only end up disappointed and heart-broken again. They'd agreed on a marriage of conveni-ence, not a happily-ever-after.

She patted Cassidy on her back and a loud burp exploded from the baby.

"That's my girl." Jared stirred the sauce again. "You'll show up all the boys when you are older."

His words sounded like something a dad would say, es-pecially his dad. Kate fed the rest of the bottle to the baby. "Your parents didn't mention you were back when I picked up Cassidy."

He sliced the garlic bread. "My parents don't know."

Kate fumbled with the baby's bottle. Jared told his family everything. Good news, bad news, silly news. Nothing was off-limits with the Reeds. "You haven't talked to them about this?"

"I wanted to speak to them in person," he said. "I'm telling them over breakfast tomorrow while you're at work."

Sparing her the inevitable recriminations. Kate appre-ciated that. Dropping the baby off in the morning and picking her up in the evening had gotten easier. Her dis-cussions with his parents and siblings revolved around

Cassidy, but Kate still wasn't sure how to act around them. She burped Cassidy again. "Are you concerned about their reactions?"

"My mom won't have a problem with my being here, but my dad…" Jared placed the bread on a plate and covered it with foil. "He may have some issues."

In other words, Vesuvius—the family nickname for his father's temper—was going to blow.

Frank Reed was a throwback to the days of a man who expected a cocktail in his hand when he walked in the door and dinner at six o'clock on the dot no matter whether his wife, Margery, was nine months pregnant, fighting the flu or chasing after her brood of five children. Frank still couldn't understand why Kate hadn't moved to Seattle and had filed for divorce instead, so Jared taking over primary child care duties might not go over so well.

"What time are they expecting you?" Kate asked.

"Oh, I'm not going there." He dumped the pasta in a large bowl, poured the sauce on top and stirred the mixture with the spoon. "I invited them to come here."

Here. Tomorrow. Kate gulped, making a mental note to clean the house later. His parents hadn't been here in months, and she wanted everything perfect for them. "Why here?"

"Home field advantage."

Forget home being any advantage. His father wasn't swayed in the slightest.

Flipping pancakes on the stove, Jared realized cooking a meal for his father while telling him he was staying home with the baby hadn't been one of his smartest moves.

"People are going to call you Mr. Malone," Frank Reed said. "I can't believe you, with an MBA from Stanford, are going to spend your day changing dirty diapers, doing housework and cooking."

"That's what I did, Frank," Margery said before Jared could speak up. She fed Cassidy another spoonful of rice cereal. "You didn't have any complaints about me doing the same thing for the last forty-five years."

"You're a woman." Frank's nostrils flared. "That's your responsibility."

She shook her head. "Times have changed, Frank."

"Gah," Cassidy said.

"See." Margery smiled. "Cassidy agrees with me."

Frank harrumphed.

At least his mom was on his side. Jared knew she would talk some sense into his father, but he wasn't ready to give up himself. He transferred the pancakes to a plate. "Besides, Dad, we have a housecleaner. There's no need for me to scrub toilets or the floor. And I won't be cooking every night."

Frank grumbled under his breath. "It's abnormal for a man to stay home while his wife goes to work."

Jared carried the plate to the table.

His father frowned. "The next thing you know, he'll be wearing an apron."

"*He* is standing right here," Jared said. "Pancakes anyone?"

"I'll take a couple more," Frank said.

As he dished up two pancakes, Jared grimaced. His father might complain, but he wasn't above eating the food he'd cooked. Seconds, even.

"Don't forget, Dad." Jared sat at the table. "I didn't quit my job."

Though he'd lost a big opportunity with a longtime

client by taking time off, but he wasn't about to tell his parents or Kate about that. Whatever sacrifices he made would be worth it when he and Kate were together, living as husband and wife.

Frank added a pat of butter and poured maple syrup over his pancakes. "Are you being paid?"

"Full salary and benefits." The only thing missing were marital benefits, but he was going to work on those. Starting tonight if he got the chance.

"And when will you return to your job?" Frank asked.

"I don't know yet." Jared cut into his pancakes. "Probably two weeks."

The lines on his father's face deepened.

"Frank, this is a good thing," Margery said. "We'll not only get to see Cassidy, we'll get to see Jared, too."

"Does that mean you'll still bring her over?" Frank asked.

Jared nodded. "We want Cassidy to be comfortable at both places, but we need to establish a routine and get her used to sleeping in her own crib first."

His dad leaned back in his chair. "Why don't you let the baby stay with us all the time?"

Margery laughed. "So you can stay home all day with Cassidy, but not Jared?"

Frank puffed out his chest. "I'm retired. I've earned my keep."

"Your father has fallen in love with this little girl." His mother's tender gaze focused on Cassidy. "And so have I."

Jared could tell with the attention his parents paid to Cassidy while she ate. He wondered if they ever left her alone for a minute. They hadn't since they had arrived this morning. "We appreciate all you've done so far and will be doing for us after I go back to Seattle."

"You could always do this full-time," Margery suggested.

"Yeah, right," Jared and Frank said at the same time.

Margery shook her head. "What does Kate think about all this?"

"I've only been here a day." Jared thought about Kate's reaction to his offer, to her pleasure over the dinner last night and her concerns about his father's reaction. Forward steps, definitely. "But the weekend was…encouraging."

And if she allowed him back in the master bedroom again, things would be even better.

Margery leaned forward visibly curious about her children's lives, as usual. "So the weekend went well?"

"'Well' might be a tad optimistic." He picked up his coffee cup. "It's hard to work on being a couple when all our energy is spent on a baby who won't sleep and fusses and cries all the time."

His parents laughed.

"What?" Jared asked.

"Welcome to our world, dear." His mother's eyes twinkled. "Just multiply what you're going through by five."

"So is this what parenting is always going to be like?" Jared asked, unsure he wanted to hear the answer.

"They sleep eventually," Frank said.

"And cry less." Margery wiped a speck of cereal from Cassidy's chin. "But once you have kids, your world does tend to revolve around them. Finding time for romance, and each other, gets more difficult."

They'd had enough trouble with romance before Cassidy arrived. Jared ate his pancake. Somehow he and Kate needed to find time for each other.

"It helps maintain your perspective, not to mention your sanity, when you have a spouse who's there to share in all the ups and downs," Margery added.

He set his fork down. "I have Kate."

His parents both sipped from their coffee cups.

Their action put him on the defensive. Jared understood why they might feel like that—Kate had decided not to move to Seattle and she had been the one to file for divorce. But those things had to be forgotten. The sooner his family realized that, the better. "Kate and I are committed to raising Cassidy together."

"That's what you've said."

"We're going to make our marriage work," he added.

"We only want you to be happy." Margery placed her cup on the table. "And we'll do whatever we can to help you."

But they didn't believe the marriage would work. He could see the truth in their eyes and feel their skepticism in his heart. And that hurt. More than he wanted to admit.

He was not going to fail.

Jared set his chin. "You'll see."

And they would. Once Cassidy settled into a routine, once Kate came to accept his ongoing presence in their house, her bed and life, they would have the kind of partnership, the kind of marriage his parents were talking about.

He just hoped it happened soon.

Kate walked into the living room. Jared sat on the couch with the laundry basket at his feet and Cassidy in the bouncer on the floor. On the bottom of the television screen, stock symbols rolled by on the electronic ticker tape. If only Kate found the stock market more interesting, she could concentrate on something other than how relaxed and handsome Jared looked in his green polo shirt, khaki shorts and bare feet.

Forget her knees being like wet noodles. They were already at the Jell-O stage.

Oh, boy. She sucked in a breath. Not the reaction she'd hoped to have when she saw him next. Kate steadied herself by kicking off her sling backs and holding onto a nearby chair. "Hi there."

Jared looked up from the pink gingham crib sheet he was folding. Concern filled his eyes. "What are you doing home so early?"

Good question. She wished she had an equally good answer. "I, um, let everyone have the afternoon off."

He tossed the sheet into the basket. "Are you feeling okay?"

Funny, but a number of her employees had asked her the same question. "I'm feeling fine, a bit rested, too, since you took the middle of the night shift for me."

She'd wondered whether his plan to stay home with Cassidy would work, but today had been a near normal day for Kate. The familiarity reassured her after the panic and disarray of the last week and a half. She felt more like her old self and Sean Owens, her dedicated assistant, had commented on her "return." And Kate couldn't deny the results—a wonderful and productive day, make that two-third's day, at the office.

"So why did you let everyone go home early?" Jared asked.

"Because I wanted to go home." And see him and Cassidy. Kate couldn't remember the last time she'd left work early unless she was catching a flight for a business trip. "I didn't feel right leaving unless everyone could go home, too."

"You're one helluva boss, Kate."

She wasn't sure if that was a compliment or not. She walked over to Cassidy and sat on the floor next to her. "Hello, baby, did you have a good day?"

As drool rolled from Cassidy's mouth, the baby smiled. Kate knew she'd made the right decision to come home early.

"Tell us about your day," Jared said. "I need adult conversation desperately."

She looked at Jared and felt her heart go bumpity-bump.

"Kate?" he asked.

She checked out the toy bar hooked to the baby's bouncer. She spun the mirror around much to Cassidy's delight. "We signed a new client, beBuzz Sportswear."

"Congrats."

"Thanks." A feeling of exhilaration washed over Kate. She'd forgotten how nice sharing her accomplishment with someone other than her staff could be. Kate didn't have that many friends. Susan. A couple of girlfriends from college. The rest she'd met through Jared who had all taken his side when they broke up. "Today capped off a long and unsteady courtship."

"Sometimes those are the most fruitful."

"I hope you're right."

"Me, too," he said, his intense gaze on her.

She wondered if he was talking about her new client or the two of them.

"We should open a bottle of champagne and celebrate."

Sharing a bottle of bubbly might not be the smartest move when she couldn't keep her eyes off of him. She remembered the last time they'd shared a bottle of champagne. Strawberries and whipped cream had been involved. They'd had to buy new sheets. "I was thinking I could take you and Cassidy out to dinner instead."

Jared's surprised look brought a rush of uncertainty. His lack of response only intensified those feelings.

"Would you like to eat out tonight?" She kept her voice steady when her insides shook worse than those of a nervous schoolgirl asking a boy to a Sadie Hawkins dance. "Your choice of restaurant, but it's not like a date."

"A date would be against the rules."

He still hadn't answered her question. She tilted her chin. "Yes, but we could, um, consider it practice. For, um, later, if we…when we see other—"

"I'd like to go out to eat," he interrupted to her relief. "But I'm not sure Cassidy would want to go. Why don't we have my parents watch her? We'd probably enjoy ourselves more."

"True. But aren't we supposed to be establishing a routine for the baby?"

"You're right," he said, sounding disappointed.

"We could go out after she went to sleep," Kate suggested.

"I'll give them a call." He picked up the phone before she could say wait or better yet no. A minute later he hung up. "They'll be here at seven."

"I just hope we don't have to spend hours getting her to fall asleep."

"Cassidy took two naps in her crib today." Pride filled his voice.

"How did that happen?" Kate asked.

"My mom taught me the importance of a bedtime routine, not just a schedule, and something called a binky."

"A what?

"A pacifier." Jared smiled. "She figured we were using one since Cassidy took one so easily at her house."

Kate racked her brain. "I don't remember Susan using one."

"Would you have paid that close attention?"

"No, but I can't believe a pacifier made the difference."

"Not just the pacifier," he explained, refolding the crib sheet. "But having a set routine we follow every time we put her down. I was skeptical myself and she cried a little, but nothing like her never ending crib demon crying fits."

"Good job."

A shy smile curved his lips. "My mom gets the credit. I only offered an assist."

"I'll thank her when she gets here," Kate said. "Speaking of your mom, how did this morning go with your parents?"

"They enjoyed the pancakes."

"What did they think about you taking time off to be with Cassidy?" And me, a little voice in Kate's head whispered.

"My mother supports my decision." He folded a pink, trimmed dress. "She said I had evolved and become a man for the twenty-first century by putting the needs of my family ahead of my career goals."

"That's great."

Jared shrugged. "My father wasn't as pleased."

He tried to sound lighthearted, but Kate knew how much his father's opinion meant to Jared. "I'm sorry."

"He'll get over it."

Of course, his father would. Jared was the golden child, the son who never did wrong, never disappointed. Frank would never stay mad at him for long.

"If it's any consolation," Kate offered. "I agree with your mom. What you're doing for Cassidy is pretty incredible."

Jared's gaze held hers, and she had to force herself to breathe. "Thanks."

Kate hadn't done anything to deserve his thankfulness. Not really. And that made her feel bad. Useless.

Cassidy reached up. "Gah."

"Are you ready to get out?" Kate looked at the baby dressed in a pink and yellow jumper and did a double-take. "Oh, no."

She unhooked the strap holding the baby in the bouncer and lifted her out. "Did you and Cassidy go out today?"

"We walked to the store."

"Was she wearing this?" Kate asked, her frustration rising.

Jared studied the baby. "Is something wrong with what she's wearing?"

Kate stifled a groan. "Her outfit is on backward."

"The snaps go in the front," he said.

"In the back," she said.

"No, they don't."

"Yes, they do." She unsnapped the jumpsuit and showed him the tag. "They go in the back where this belongs, too."

Kate took off the baby's outfit and put in on the right way. "See."

A beat passed.

"No wonder all those women kept staring at us in the produce department. And I thought they were looking at me. Not Cassidy's clothes." Jared released a heavy sigh. "No doubt they were whispering about my inability to dress my baby, not my remarkable pecs."

The humor in his voice evaporated her frustration. She laughed. "Okay, so maybe Cassidy wearing her clothes backward isn't such a big deal."

"You think?" he asked.

Kate nodded, feeling stupid for almost ruining a pleasant afternoon. "Overreacting is probably my way of compensating for my lack of parenting skills and knowledge."

He feigned disbelief. "No."

"Yes." Kate stared at Cassidy's orange and blue socks. Not the ones she would have chosen to go with the baby's pink shoes and clothing, but the baby didn't have to coordinate from head to toe. At least not under Jared's watch. "I'll try harder."

"You already have." He stared at her. "You're doing a fantastic job, Kate."

"Thanks." His compliment meant the world to her. She needed to hear she was doing well, even if it wasn't a hundred percent true. "I've been feeling a bit like a lone wolf mom."

"You don't have to feel that way anymore, Katie," Jared said with a smile. "Daddy wolf is here to help."

"You taking the 2:00 a.m. wake-up last night was huge."

"Those are a daddy wolf's specialty. I just have to keep my howling at the moon to a minimum."

She laughed. Cassidy did the same.

"I doubt the baby would mind the howling," Kate said. "She loves mimicking sounds and would howl alongside you."

"You're probably right."

He howled.

Cassidy released a high pitch squeal.

"You don't have to worry about the baby when she's with me," Jared said seriously.

"I know." No matter how much Kate might want to run everything, doing so wouldn't be fair to Jared or good for their arrangement. They would both have to compromise to make the marriage work. "I will make a point not to interfere with what you do with Cassidy."

"And I'll do my best to dress her properly with the tag in the back." With a hopeful smile, he extended his arm. "Deal?"

Kate shook his hand. "Deal."

CHAPTER NINE

DEAL?

The only deal Jared wanted to make with Kate was about her being his wife...for real. Sure, he was supposed to be patient. He'd only been in town one day. But each time he saw her, the pull grew stronger, as did the ache inside.

Now that she was sitting across from him with the candlelight flickering, he couldn't deny his need any longer.

He wanted her. Bad.

A waiter removed the plates from the linen covered table.

"I'm glad we went out tonight," Kate said, looking more beautiful than ever. Her shimmery blue dress matched the color of her eyes.

Good thing they were in a public place or Jared might be in trouble. Who was he kidding? He was already in trouble.

She looked at him expectantly, waiting for his response.

"Me, too," he said.

The way she casually tucked her hair behind her ears made her look younger, almost innocent. But the smoldering heat in her eyes was like a kick in the groin.

Couldn't she see sex wasn't the problem? Sex was the solution to their problems.

The air around them seemed electrified. He reached for his water glass. "We'll have to do this again."

Anything to bring that warmth to her smile and the radiant glow to her face.

Unless he found other ways of doing that. He grinned.

A spark of laughter danced in her eyes. "Especially if we can find another place as quiet as this one."

It wasn't quiet like a church, but the soft conversation from the other diners seemed like whispers compared to Cassidy's chattering and crying. "You noticed that, too?"

She nodded.

"It's amazing how much noise one baby can make."

"Cassidy talks back to her bottle when she's drinking her formula," Kate said. "But I'm getting used to the racket."

"I'm going to need a few more days before I can say the same."

"It won't be easy, and there will be a transition period, but give it time. You'll get there and things will be fine."

Interesting. That sounded like his game plan for winning Kate back.

"I hope you know how much I appreciate you taking time off from work." She smiled shyly. "It's pretty incredible what you're doing."

Her words made him feel ten feet tall, but he wanted to give credit to her, too. "You're the one who's incredible, Kate. I'm amazed at how much you've done with Cassidy. You can handle anything."

"I still have a lot to learn, but thanks." Kate's eyes softened. "It's kind of strange, but sometimes I think I hear Cassidy crying when I'm at work."

"That's not strange, you've changed."

"Changed how?"

"Look at what you did today. You gave your employees the afternoon off, and you came home early yourself. When was the last time that happened?"

"Never."

"I bet it won't be the last time." He saw his future. Kate, Cassidy, more babies. "You're a mom, now. You've learned to be more flexible, not so set in your ways."

"Everything just feels so different."

The anxiety in her voice coupled with her sudden interest in the salt and pepper shakers suggested she wasn't only talking about the baby. "What do you mean?"

"Tonight. Being here with you." She toyed with her napkin. "I can't remember the last time you and I had a meal together in the middle of the week."

"Burgers in Boise."

"I meant here at home. Before."

Before the separation. Jared thought back and came up blank. But that wasn't surprising given their work schedules. "Dinner out on a Wednesday night is a lot more satisfying than a call from a hotel room."

"I agree," she said. "We'll have to make the most of the time while we can. Once you go back to work…"

It would be back to phone calls. He tried to reassure her. And himself. "We'll figure something out. Video calling. You'll think I'm right here with you."

"Except I'll be the one taking out the garbage."

"Builds muscles," Jared teased. "But I just got here yesterday. Let's not think about me going away already."

The sommelier approached with two flutes containing champagne. "I hear you are celebrating a special occasion."

Jared nodded. "My wife is."

Kate gave him the arched eyebrow what-are-you-doing look.

He leaned forward. "You never said no to champagne."

"But the baby—"

"Is asleep," he said. "My parents would have called if something was wrong. I only ordered us each a glass, not an entire bottle."

The sommelier waited patiently.

Kate smiled at the wine steward. "Thank you so much. I do enjoy a glass of celebratory bubbly."

"My pleasure." The sommelier placed the glasses on the table and bowed. "Enjoy."

Once the man walked away, Jared raised his champagne. "To a successful partnership."

"And a lasting one."

He hoped she wasn't only talking about her new client.

She tapped her flute against his. The chime of the crystal hung in the air like the song of a bird on a sunny day.

As she sipped her champagne, she seemed uncertain, a little nervous.

"Is something wrong?" he asked.

Her cheeks flushed. She set her glass down. "No."

He didn't believe her. Definitely a new Kate, and one he liked.

The waiter arrived with an order of profiteroles with two forks, a cappuccino for Kate and a cup of decaf for him.

"Profiteroles are my absolute favorite." She stared at the ice-cream filled pastry puffs sprinkled with powder sugar and drizzled with chocolate syrup. Jared wished she'd look at him with the same desire. "You're spoiling me."

That was the point. "I'm only getting started."

"Promises. Promises."

She would see soon enough.

He scooped a bite onto his fork and brought the taste toward her mouth. "For you."

Temptation flashed across her face, but caution tempered it. "I don't think this is such a good idea."

"The rules."

She nodded.

Screw the rules. He wanted to feed his wife.

"Come on, baby." He brought the fork closer. "Show me the tunnel so the choo-choo can come inside."

A relaxed smile formed. "It's a hangar and the plane needs to go inside."

"Open up."

She did. He placed his fork inside her mouth and her lips closed around it. "Mmm."

Talk about sexy.

Slowly he pulled the fork from her mouth. "Was it good for you?"

She laughed, the melodic sound wrapping around his heart. "Delicious."

He agreed.

A drop of chocolate sauce hung on her lower lip. As the pink tip of her tongue darted out to wipe it away, Jared's temperature skyrocketed. Sweet torture. He wanted a taste himself.

As Kate ate more of the dessert, the waiter brought the check. Jared reached for the bill, but Kate was faster.

"It's my turn," he said.

When they used to go out, each would take turns paying.

"You can pay for the champagne and dessert," she said. "But I invited you. I want dinner to be my treat."

He didn't want to spoil the night by insisting on picking up the tab. With a shrug, he handed her cash to cover his portion. "Thank you for dinner, but I hope you know I'm not an easy date."

The corners of her eyes crinkled. "I'll try not to be too disappointed."

He cocked a brow and did his best Latin lover impersonation. "But for you, baby, I could make an exception."

Laughing, she placed her credit card inside the leather-covered folder. The waiter promptly took the bill away.

Kate ate another bite of the dessert and wiped her mouth. "Thank you for the dessert, Jared. And the champagne. I really appreciate your support."

"You deserve it."

"Lots of people worked on winning the beBuzz account."

"I'm not just talking about your firm signing a new client, Katie."

She glanced up. "What then?"

"Cassidy."

"I'm only doing what anyone else would do if their best friend died." Eyes glistening, she looked up and blinked. "Besides, Cassidy is so easy to love. Even if she won't sleep at night."

Her humility touched him. He reached across the table and took hold of her hand, thin yet strong like the woman herself. "You've opened your heart and your life to the baby. You've become a mom. You've surprised me, my family, no doubt everyone else you know."

She bit her lip. "I never said I didn't want children."

"No, you didn't," Jared admitted. "But saying you wanted a family and then putting off getting pregnant made me wonder."

"I'm sorry. I didn't mean to send mixed signals."

"Me, either." He squeezed her hand. "You're a wonderful mother and a beautiful woman. I'm so proud you are my wife."

The gratitude shining in her eyes took his breath away.

The waiter returned with the bill. Kate pulled her hand from Jared's so she could fill out the charge slip. She placed the pen inside the folder and her napkin on the table.

"Finished?" he asked.

Kate nodded. "I'm ready to go home."

Home. Their home.

Maybe tonight would be the turning point. The start of their having a real marriage…

Anticipation rippled through him. If she desired him that meant she still loved him.

He stood and pulled her chair out. As they walked out of the restaurant, he placed his hand on the small of her back. She didn't stiffen; her muscles didn't tense. A good sign.

"Thank you, Jared. Tonight was really…special. I wish I could do something in return."

"You can," he said.

"What?"

Jared unlocked the car, opened her door and helped her into the seat. "You were never an easy date, either, but…"

Her eyes narrowed. "But what?"

Grinning, he walked to his side and slid into the seat beside her. "I wouldn't turn down a good-night kiss."

"A kiss?" She didn't sound horrified. More…intrigued. "This isn't a real date."

Could've fooled him. He locked his seat belt into place. "Not a date kiss. A slow, hot, take your breath away date kiss wouldn't be appropriate."

"Not appropriate at all." Kate shifted in her seat. "What kind of kiss are you talking about then?"

"A kiss between friends," he said. "That's all."

"To get us back in the game so to speak."

"Exactly."

"O-kay." She leaned over and kissed him lightly on the lips. The fresh scent of her surrounded him, making him heady. Her mouth lingering an instant longer than any other kiss from a friend he'd experienced ignited a fire inside him. His boiling blood pushed him toward the edge.

He was ready to jump. She only had to say the word.

"Friendly enough for you?" she asked with a slow, seductive smile. The woman didn't have an innocent bone in her body. Kate knew exactly where she wanted him. And had him.

Jared cleared his throat. "Yes. Very friendly."

He was definitely back in the game and so was she. Now all he had to do was to convince Kate to be his friend. His friend with benefits. Marital benefits, that was.

The days passed quickly for Kate, the nights not so much. Kissing Jared had been a mistake because all she could think about was…kissing him again.

She lay in her bed. Three o'clock in the morning. She should be fast asleep, not wide-awake, but thinking about Jared sleeping down the hall in his underwear or maybe nothing else wasn't helping. She kept waiting for Cassidy—

The baby.

Kate bolted upright. Cassidy hadn't woken up tonight. That wasn't normal.

Her heart pounding, Kate hurried to the baby's room. The door was ajar. She peeked inside.

Cassidy lay with her hands behind her head sound asleep. Her tiny chest rose with her even breaths. So small, so perfect.

Even when Cassidy fussed or cried.

Kate's heart rate returned to normal, but love for the child welled up inside of her. She'd finally found what had eluded her all these years—unconditional love. Kate thought it wasn't possible for anyone to love her no matter what she said or did.

But Cassidy did.

Thank you, Susan. Thank you so very much.

As Kate watched the baby sleep, she sensed a presence behind, Jared. Could he ever love her the way the baby did? Without reserve. Without conditions. Totally. Completely. Forever.

She backed out of the room and closed the door so only a small crack remained.

"I heard you get up," he said.

Dark razor stubble covered his face. His tousled hair and sleep rumpled T-shirt and boxer briefs made him look sexy. A tad dangerous. Her pulse quickened.

Forget cardio exercise. Between Cassidy and Jared, Kate's heart got enough of a workout.

"Sorry," she said. "I was worried about Cassidy."

He took a step toward the baby's room. "Is something wrong?"

His concern made him even more attractive. He adored Cassidy, and had jumped into his new role as stay-at-home dad without looking back. Kate respected that, respected him.

"She didn't wake up tonight," Kate said. "I wanted to make sure she was okay."

He straightened. "And?"

"She's fine. Sound asleep. The way she should be."

"Good."

He looked good. She thought about her big, empty bed. But that was only loneliness talking. And attraction. Two things she couldn't allow to get in the way and complicate matters.

"We may have turned a corner," he said.

A knot formed in her throat. "Corner?"

"Cassidy sleeping through the night."

"That would be great."

Except he would be free to go home. The baby had adjusted to her nap schedule at home and no longer threw tantrums at bedtime. A part of Kate hoped tonight was an anomaly. She wasn't ready to say goodbye to Jared.

"You'd better get some sleep," he said. "Don't you have a big meeting tomorrow?"

She always had a big meeting, but she appreciated Jared remembering. If only he'd sweep her off her feet and carry her to bed the way he used to. "I do have a meeting."

"I'll take care of Cassidy if she wakes up."

"Thanks."

Kate trudged her way back to her bedroom, making sure she didn't look back because if she had and still saw Jared standing there and watching her, she wouldn't be able to close the door.

She stepped into her room, shut the door and clicked the lock in place.

What was she going to do? Jared made life so much better. His handling the house and the baby helped, but his being here to lend a hand or an ear made such a difference. They ate dinner together, shared their days and helped each other with the chores around the house. They'd become partners, teammates, parents. Kate didn't know how she would get along without him.

And that was a problem.

The problem.

They were playing house. She got that part.

But being "mom" when she was used to having great sex with "dad" who walked around the house in a T-shirt and underwear looking better than your typical Abercrombie & Fitch model wasn't that much fun. Or easy to do. Especially when the lines between playing and real life kept blurring.

Having Jared here, having him help with Cassidy was wonderful. But, Kate realized, it wasn't enough.

It would never be enough.

Jared pushed Cassidy in her stroller along the waterfront path in downtown Portland. His sisters, Heather and Hannah, pushed strollers alongside him.

"How are things going?" Heather asked.

"Good," he said. "It's going well with Cassidy."

"So any change in your arrangement with Kate?" Hannah asked, with a suggestive lift of her eyebrows.

Not the kind of change she meant. "Not as much as I was hoping for."

"And what were you hoping for?" Heather asked. "That she'd show up in your bed naked and attack you?"

"Pretty much."

His sisters laughed.

But it wasn't only about sex or the lack of it. Somewhere between caring for Cassidy and living together as a family, he and Kate had become a team, a parental unit, a couple. The bond between them grew stronger every day. Jared didn't want to lose that when he went back to Seattle.

"She's my wife," he said. "It shouldn't be this difficult."

Hannah sighed. "You've never had a conventional marriage, little brother."

"And Kate did file for divorce," Heather said. "It's not going to be an easy road ahead."

"I'm not giving up," he said.

"Have you thought about what will happen if everything you're doing, all the sacrifices you're making don't change things?" Heather asked.

"No." He glanced at a ship sailing on the Willamette River. "Losing isn't an option. I'm going to make my marriage work no matter what."

He would do whatever it took. He would not fail.

Kate was going to fall in love with him again.

It was just a matter of time.

Unfortunately his boss had called and wanted him back. On Monday. That only gave him three more days to make it happen.

Friday morning, the alarm clock blared. Eyes closed, Kate pounded the top of her nightstand until she hit the snooze button. Good. She wanted to sleep. And then she remembered. Her morning staff meeting. Kate glanced at the clock.

Oh, no. Late.

She must have hit the Snooze a couple of times before this. She threw off the covers, scrambled off the bed and ran to the bathroom. Turning on the shower, she noticed all the towels were gone. Oh. She was supposed to fold the clothes in the dryer last night.

Kate hurried to the laundry room, dug a towel from the dryer and was halfway up the stairs when she bumped into Jared coming down them. She sucked in a breath.

No man should look this good so early. He wore a pair of shorts. And nothing else. She swallowed. Hard.

"Good morning," he said with a smile. "In a hurry?"

Was she? Kate couldn't see past his sweat-drenched chest and his tight abs. Her dry throat could teach the Sahara desert a thing or two. "Uh-huh."

"What are you doing down here?" he asked.

The sweat on his skin gleamed. Her temperature inched up.

"Kate?"

She showed him the towel, trying to concentrate on the damp tendrils framing his face so her gaze wouldn't drift downward.

"I need one, too," he said.

She needed to see whether he'd chosen to wear boxer briefs under his shorts this morning or old-fashioned boxers. Not that knowing mattered. Much. "Dryer. The towels are in the dryer. I forgot to fold the laundry."

"I'll fold it this morning."

His good looks, his rich voice and his glistening skin wreaked havoc with her senses. She didn't like that. "It's my turn."

"I don't mind."

But she did. "I want to do…fold the laundry."

No, what Kate really wanted to do was him. Forget the rules. Forget any more friendly kisses. She gulped.

His gaze raked over her, reminding her she was wearing only a T-shirt. And a pretty short one at that. Her cheeks warmed. She tugged on the hemline.

"Don't do that." His voice sent a ripple of awareness through her. "Your curves are coming back. I like it."

And she liked him. A singsong rhyme from her school-days played in her head. Kate and Jared sitting in a tree K-I-S-S-I-N-G. Forget the tree. The stairs would work fine.

Oh, boy, she had to get a grip. Or take a spin on the dryer's cool down cycle.

Remember the rules. Set boundaries. Keep her distance.

So what if he had an amazing body? And looked hot after finishing a rep of crunches or push-ups or whatever he did to keep himself looking so great. He was still just a guy. Man. Dad.

Who was leaving for Seattle on Sunday.

She clutched the towel.

Unless she wanted to hand him her heart with a Fragile Do Not Break sticker attached, she had to stop ogling him like a new pair of shoes from Nordstrom. "I need a shower."

"Me, too." The invitation in his eyes sent her heart slamming against her chest, and she struggled to breathe. "Want to join me?"

Yes. No. What if the baby woke up? "No, thanks. I'm running late."

"You can go first, Katie."

"Thanks." But she wasn't so sure he was doing her any favors.

He walked past her, brushing his shoulder against her bare arm. Accidental or on purpose, she didn't know, but heat exploded at the point of contact. The attraction between them had grown. Bad. Very bad.

"And Kate," he called.

She glanced back.

"Make sure you leave me some hot water."

That wasn't going to be a problem. The coldest setting was probably going to be too warm for her. "Don't worry," she said. "You'll have plenty."

She wanted him. Thanks to their early morning encounter on the stairs, Jared knew it. He'd won.

Won.

He was going to talk to Kate about making this marriage of convenience more convenient and real. Tonight. He wanted his wife—body, heart and soul.

His cell phone rang. He recognized his lawyer's number on the display. "Hello."

But as his attorney updated him, Jared's hope and conviction died. His day had been great up to this point, but now...

He snapped his phone shut in a state of shock that failed to block his rising anger. Or his hurt.

Kate didn't want him. She never had.

He scooped a crying Cassidy from her crib and prepared her bottle with jerky efficiency.

When he heard Kate's car in the driveway a few minutes later, he stalked to the door to meet her.

"Hello," Kate said with a smile. She kissed the baby's cheek, then his. "How was your day?"

The collar of his shirt tightened around his neck. "My day was going fine until I got a phone call from my lawyer telling me the judge signed the judgment of dissolution of our marriage."

"Oh, no." The color drained from Kate's face. She covered her gaping mouth with her hands. "I'm so sorry. I never told my attorney to stop the divorce proceedings."

Her obvious shock reassured him. A little. "Did you forget—?"

"Of course I forgot." She glared at him. "Do you think I would do this on purpose?"

And chance losing Cassidy? Hell, no. But the betrayal, intentional or not, cut deeply. Letting it go wasn't so easy. "Probably not."

"Definitely not." Kate might have changed and softened some of her edges, but she still had a spine. She looked him squarely in the eyes. "Between Cassidy, work and you showing up, I've been a little busy. I agreed to the arrangement and I'm sticking to that. No matter what."

The sincerity in her voice removed what doubt remained. His anger dissipated. "I believe you."

Her gaze held his for a moment. The connection between them was still there, though dimmed by a fog of distrust and hurt.

"So what happens now?" she asked.

"There is a thirty-day waiting period until the dissolution is final," he explained, having memorized his lawyer's words. "If we want to stay together and give notice to the court, our marriage will continue as if we never filed for divorce."

Kate picked up the telephone. "Let's call now."

Her eagerness pleased Jared, but not even Kate's determination would be able to turn back the clock. "It's after five. The courts are closed until Monday."

She put the phone back in place and looked up at him, her eyes anxious. "You'll be in Seattle on Monday."

Kate sounded so sad, looked so lost.

"It'll be okay." But Jared's words did nothing to remove the heaviness centered in his chest. "We're in this together, remember?"

But suddenly that didn't seem nearly enough.

CHAPTER TEN

"I CAN'T believe it's time for me to go," Jared said as he opened his suitcase. Especially when he'd wanted to go home with his family in tow.

Sitting crisscross on the guest room floor, Kate folded his clothes. "The time's gone so fast."

He was glad she thought so, too.

Jared glanced around the small room. "I wish I could pack the entire house and bring it with me to Seattle."

"I thought you had a two-bedroom apartment."

"I'd make it fit," he said. "I'd do anything to have us be together."

"We'll be together on weekends."

"And that's enough for you?"

She stuck out her chin. "It has to be."

"Does it?" he pressed, knowing tomorrow he didn't want to say goodbye to her for one day let alone five.

"Yes, it does." She looked away. "Please don't make this any harder than it has to be."

The emotion in her voice gave him hope. "I don't want this to be hard on us. I just want us to be together."

"Me, too." Kate folded a T-shirt with the same competence she did everything else and handed the neat, white square to him. "Make sure you leave some clothes here so you won't have to pack an extra bag when you come down on weekends."

"You're so practical, Kate." He'd always respected that about her, but her practicality was getting in the way of what he wanted, what was best for her, him and Cassidy. Jared placed the T-shirt on top of his shorts.

"I have to be, to take care of Cassidy."

"It won't be easy for you." And that bothered him. Eating regular meals had helped her put on weight. Sleeping through the night had gotten rid of the dark circles under her eyes. She looked healthier and rested. He didn't want her to fall back into the old routine of neglecting herself when things got hectic. "I hate leaving you."

"I hate to see you go." She smiled ruefully. "It's been great having you here. I'll be the first to admit I have no idea how I'll get along without you."

"So come with me."

"To Seattle?"

"Yes."

For a second, he saw the idea take hold in her eyes and then her familiar caution, her damn practicality, returned. "You mean next weekend?"

"I mean for good." He tossed a pair of pants in his suitcase, not caring if they were folded or not. "I don't want us to be apart."

"I'd love if we could be together, but this isn't only about us."

"Being together would be good for Cassidy."

"I meant my firm," Kate corrected, her voice strong and determined. "Don't forget, twenty people rely on me for their livelihood. The potential for growth is phenomenal. It makes financial sense for me to stay here and guide the company through this period and ensure our family's future."

Financial sense, sure. But with his suitcase half-packed and facing a week of late night telephone calls from a hotel room, Jared wasn't feeling sensible. He'd even keep the no-sex rule in place if it meant having her with him.

"Emily Butler could run the firm for a while," he said. "She seems sharp with a lot of savvy."

"She is and a dedicated worker. But she's also pregnant and will be taking maternity leave this summer," Kate explained.

"There has to be someone else."

"It's my company. My name on the placard."

"You're my wife and Cassidy's mother."

"That's not fair." Kate frowned. "I shouldn't have to choose."

He thought about Brady and Susan. "Sometimes life isn't fair, Kate."

"I want to be your wife and Cassidy's mom, but you're asking me to give up—" Kate took a breath and exhaled slowly "—my home, my career, my life. Everything I've worked for and dreamed of since I was young."

He sympathized with her, but too much was riding on this to let it go. Weren't his dreams as important as hers? Wasn't their family?

He needed to play to win. Even if it was dirty. The means justified the ends, as his father always said.

"Isn't having a family part of your dream?" he asked.

"You know it is."

"So how can you walk away from our family? From us?"

"I'm not walking away from anything." She crossed her arms over her chest. "I don't want to fight."

"We need to discuss this."

"The last time we discussed this we ended up in divorce court." Her eyes pleaded with him. "It's too soon for me to make the kind of decision you want."

"It's been two weeks."

"Two wonderful weeks," she admitted. "And that's part of the problem. We shouldn't make a decision when our judgment is clouded."

"My mind is made up. I want you, Kate. I want you and Cassidy in my life."

"We are in your life."

"But not where I want you." He took her hands in his. "We could have a real marriage if you moved to Seattle with me."

"We could still have a real marriage if I didn't."

"Is that what you want?" he asked, tension charging the air. "A real marriage?"

He'd offered her a real marriage. A real family. Kate had wanted both, more than anything, but she didn't want to accept his terms.

She spent a restless night in her big, empty bed thinking and dreaming about Jared. Kate missed him so much. And he wasn't even gone yet.

"Happy Mother's Day."

Pathetic. He was leaving, and all she could do was dream about him complete with realistic audio. She needed to gain control over her emotions.

The mattress depressed.

She opened her eyes and saw Jared sitting next to her

with Cassidy in his arms. He'd ditched his everyday T-shirt and shorts for a black polo shirt and khaki slacks. The smart casual look suited him well, as did the way his damp hair curled at the ends. She fought the urge to reach out and touch his smooth, recently shaved face.

He looked good, so mouthwatering good.

Kate wondered if she was still dreaming. She propped herself up on her elbows. Nope. She was awake. "About last night."

He smiled, those dimples of his appearing with a vengeance, and she felt sucker punched. "Not now."

But they hadn't come to any conclusion, decision. And he was leaving. Tonight.

He watched her with an odd expression in his eyes and motioned toward the other side of the bed. A pink smoothie, a chocolate doughnut, a white envelope, a blue box and a single red rose sat on a tray.

Wow. Kate sat up. "What's going on?"

"It's for you."

Presents. After they'd fought. That didn't make any sense. Confused, she looked at him.

"Happy Mother's Day," he said.

Cassidy giggled and waved her hands.

Mother's Day. Kate was a mother.

A swell of emotion swept through her. Tears stung her eyes. She hadn't expected this. She'd never thought of today being anything other than the day Jared went back to Seattle.

"Did you think I would forget?" he asked.

Not trusting her voice, she shook her head. "I forgot."

"You've been busy."

"It's not that," she admitted, feeling overwhelmed by and unworthy of the attention. "I spent so many years celebrating this day with different mothers, but never my mother. I know today is a big deal for your family, but the holiday never seemed important to me."

"Today is the start of a new tradition then," he said.

Their first family tradition. She stared at a grinning Cassidy. Kate wiped the drool from the baby's chin with the sleeve of her nightshirt.

"Koo," the baby said.

She felt a sudden squeezing pain. "This should be Susan's day."

"Susan would be proud of you. She would appreciate everything you do for Cassidy." Jared traced Kate's jawline with his fingertip. "The way I do."

"Thank you so much for everything." Kate sniffled. "You don't know what this means to me."

She kissed Cassidy's cheek. She went to kiss Jared's cheek, but he turned so she kissed him on the lips instead. Warm and nice, his kiss tasted like a mix of coffee and chocolate doughnuts.

Jared grinned. "Gotcha."

He did. He had her. All of her.

The realization left her speechless and more than a little scared. She didn't want him to leave tonight, but she couldn't go with him, either.

He reached over her and picked up a rectangular navy-blue box patterned like the strips on a grosgrain ribbon. "This is for you."

She untied the navy and white ribbon imprinted with the name Aaron Basha and removed the lid. Inside laid a silver—no, white gold—charm bracelet and the prettiest pink enamel baby shoe charm with a diamond strap and diamond hearts on the toe. "I love it."

"Let me put the bracelet on you." He clasped the chain around her wrist.

"This was so thoughtful of you." She stared at the dangling charm. "Thank you."

He handed her the white envelope. "Now this."

Kate pulled out a lovely card with a little girl walking through a field of purple irises and green grass. The printed sentiment brought a lump to her throat, but the handwritten words at the bottom made her heart skip a beat. Okay, three.

She reread them again.

You are my wife and my life. Whether I'm here or in Seattle that won't change. Forget the rules. I want a real marriage with you. I want us to be a real family. All you have to do is say the word.

Love,
Jared (& Cassidy, too!)

Kate stared into his eyes. She knew the risks, but she was willing to take the chance. She wanted a real marriage. She wanted them to be a real family.

Long distance didn't matter. The marriage would work.

She cleared her throat. "Yes."

A nerve twitched at his neck. "Yes?"

"Isn't that the word I'm supposed to say?"

A smile erupted on his face, not only with dimples but lines crinkling the corner of his eyes. He gathered her up in his arm.

Jared looked down at her with such tender affection she thought her heart might burst with happiness. He lowered his mouth to hers.

The moment his lips touched her, emotion burst through Kate with the force of a rocket launcher. She could no longer pretend she didn't feel anything, no longer hold back all her feelings for Jared, all her longings.

He pressed his lips against hers. The warm taste filled her up, but she didn't think she could ever get enough of him. This was what she'd been missing, what she needed. And Kate never wanted the kiss to end.

Heat emanated deep within her, sparking a need she knew could not be filled. At least not with the baby here. Kate could tell by the way Jared held back, not touching her, that he was conscious of the baby's presence, too.

They were a family, and sometimes that meant having to wait even if you didn't want to.

"Ah-gah, gah."

Jared slowly drew the kiss to an end. "I think Cassidy is getting bored."

That was the least boring kiss ever. Kate's mouth felt bruised and utterly loved. She inhaled to calm her rapid pulse and fill her lungs with much needed air. "Um, Jared, that wasn't a friendly kiss."

Mischief gleamed in his eyes. "Now that we're husband and wife for real and not in name only, the marital kiss takes precedence over the friend kiss."

"I can live with that."

"I thought so."

Cassidy squealed with delight.

"Group hug," Jared said. "Or should I say, family hug."

"We're a family, Cassidy," Kate said. "A real family."

He smiled. "I like the sound of that."

"You know what I'd really like right now?" she asked.

"Me, too." He glanced at the clock. "But it's too early to put Cassidy down for her nap."

"I hate to burst your bubble but this—" Kate patted the mattress "—isn't what I was talking about?"

Lines creased his forehead. "What do you want?"

"Breakfast." She grinned mischievously. "That doughnut sure smells yummy."

"I'm supposed to be the yummy one." Looking at Cassidy, he sighed. "Your mommy has the wrong thing on her mind this morning."

"No, she's just more practical about our other commitments like meeting your family at church in an hour," Kate said.

"You're no fun," Jared complained.

"Wait until we get home," she promised. "I'll show you how fun I can be."

He raised a brow. "What do you have in mind?"

"I thought maybe you could give me one final present for Mother's Day."

"What's that?"

She met his gaze directly. "You."

He sucked in a breath. "Should I wear a bow?"

"Please do," she said in her huskiest voice. "And nothing else."

"That baby gets cuter every time I see her." Staring at Cassidy sitting on Kate's lap, Frank flipped the steaks and hamburgers cooking on the grill in the backyard. Every Mother's Day under the shady canopy of the towering Douglas firs and the blossoming cherry trees, he threw a barbecue for his wife, daughters and daughters-in-law.

One of the many Reed family traditions. "Kate looks good. Not so skinny and pale."

Jared nodded. She looked radiant, her face glowing.

"So you're heading back to Seattle tonight?" Frank asked.

"Yes." But Jared wasn't thinking that far ahead. He only wanted to get home. Speaking of which, he needed to swipe a bow from the pile of presents on the picnic table. "I'll be back on Friday."

Sooner if he got the opportunity.

"So you think this long distance arrangement will work out?" Frank asked.

"Yes," Jared said, tired of rehashing the details with every single member of his family, as if they knew more about the situation than he did. "Kate and I are going to make this marriage work."

"Your mother mentioned the official dissolution being signed by the judge."

"Seems like Mom told everybody." Jared took a sip of his iced tea. "We're going to take care of that tomorrow."

Frank peppered the meat. "What if you used the threat of divorce to force Kate to move to Seattle instead?"

Bitterness coated Jared's mouth. "Funny, but you're not the first person to tell me that today."

His siblings had suggested a similar idea. His father must have been the ringleader.

Frank adjusted the heat on the gas grill. "So…"

"I can't do that to Kate, Dad."

"Can't or won't?" his father asked. "Sometimes a man has to do things he'd rather not, but the means justify the end, son. Kate will thank you for this later."

Jared looked across the grass at Kate tossing a ball in the air. "She'd hate me. And she'd have every right."

"You've been watching too many of those daytime talk shows while you've been home." Frank laughed. "You're going soft."

Not soft, Jared thought. Just a bit more evolved. He shook his empty glass. "I need a refill."

His father nodded. "Think about what I said."

"I don't have to think about it, Dad. I won't do that to her. To us."

"Somebody has to do something," Frank muttered.

Jared hoped his father cooled down. But after lunch, as his mother and sisters cleared away the litter of wrapping paper and dirty dishes, Frank approached Kate.

"You ought to be going with him," his father said.

Kate held the baby a little tighter. "I'm sorry, Frank. We feel this arrangement is better for us right now."

"It's not good for Jared."

"Dad, that's enough," Jared said sharply.

Frank ignored him. "The judge signed the paperwork. Jared would have every right to go through with the divorce if you won't go with him to Seattle."

Kate drew in a breath, her stricken eyes seeking Jared's. "Would you do that?"

"No." He'd never understood her concerns about his family's intrusiveness, but he did now. And it was time to put an end to it. "You guys know I love you, and put up with the nosiness and all your advice, but today a few of you Reeds went a little too far suggesting I do what Dad just told Kate I should do and that's…wrong."

"You all should be ashamed of yourselves," Margery announced, rushing to Kate's side like a bear protecting her cub. "I apologize for all my misguided children. Especially the old one who should know better."

A red-faced Frank mumbled an apology.

"We wanted to help," Sam said.

Hannah nodded. So did Tucker. And Heather.

Jared listened to his family one by one justify their reasons. He'd always considered family, family. Extended, immediate, distant. It hadn't mattered. Until today. He still loved each one of them, but he had his own family now and they needed to come first.

"I'm not the one you should be apologizing to." Jared stared at his father and four siblings. "I know you want to help. That's what we do for each other. Help. But think about what you asked me to do. The end does not always justify the means. Especially if it hurts the one person who means the most to me. My wife."

Jared hated making a scene, but his family had left him no choice. He put his arm around Kate and the baby. "It's time to go home."

On the drive home, Kate dabbed tears from the corner of her eyes. She thought she'd respected and loved Jared before, but those feelings couldn't compare to how she felt about him now.

She was used to handling everything and making a place for herself. She needed to do that on her own in order to avoid being disappointed. It was easier that way. Safer. But today Jared had taken on his father, his family, for her. Without any prompting. Without being asked.

Her astonished heart overflowed with joy. "I can't believe you said those things."

He glanced sideways at her. "I'm sorry it had to come to that."

She heard the regret in his voice, but the sincerity filled her with warmth. She was no longer alone. "I'm not."

"You're not?"

"Nope." Kate smiled. She would not take his championing her for granted. She would prove herself worthy of his support. "No one has ever stood up for me like you did. You made feel good. Special. Thank you."

"I only did what needed to be done." Jared covered her hand with his. "I should have spoken up earlier, but I didn't realize…"

Staring at their linked fingers, at the pink baby shoe charm on the new bracelet around her wrist, she felt everything she needed dangling at her fingertips. If only she could reach out and grasp it. If only she could prove herself worthy of his love the way he had just proved himself deserving of hers.

Kate knew she could make their marriage work. She loved him. No doubt. She wanted to with him. No question.

Jared's actions today showed her he hadn't abandoned her by moving to Seattle without her. Instead of dealing with the troubles in their marriage, he'd listened to his family. He could have done the same thing today, but he hadn't. He'd defended her. He'd changed.

She felt renewed, alive, loved. She didn't want that to end. "So what you said about moving to Seattle…"

He squeezed her hand. "I'm not going to force you to move."

Kate drew strength from his touch. She could feel the love flowing from him, and she knew it was her turn to give that feeling back to him. "But that's what you want."

"I want us to be together," he said.

"I want that, too."

Before she'd tried to control Jared because she'd had so little control of her own life. But now they were a couple, a family, and she couldn't continue to operate the same way. Family made sacrifices for each other. If she wanted to keep their family together, to make their marriage work, Kate would have to prove herself worthy of his love.

She took a deep breath. "What if Cassidy and I moved to Seattle, and I tried telecommuting? I'd still have to travel some, but I could set up a satellite office."

Jared pulled into the driveway and turned off the car. "You would do that?"

"I'm willing to try to see if it works," she said. "If it does, we can talk about what the next step would be."

Like the house. Her firm. So many things. "But I'll need to find child care. I know I can't work while taking care of Cassidy at the same time."

"No problem. We can hire a nanny or use a day care." He sounded pleased, happy. "Are you sure about this, Katie?"

She had the family she'd dreamed about. A husband who'd stood up to his family in her defense. A daughter who loved her no matter what. Kate wasn't about to risk that. She would do whatever having a real marriage and keeping her family together took. She would be the perfect wife and mother. And businesswoman, too. She could do it. She would do it. "Yes, I'm sure."

Jared opened his car door. "Stay here."

"Why?"

He removed a sleeping Cassidy from her car seat and

grabbed the diaper bag. "Give me five minutes. That's all I ask."

"Okay." Kate would use the time to formulate a plan on how her move to Seattle would work and telecommuting and child care...

Four minutes later, a text message appeared on her BlackBerry: Go upstairs.

Kate did. All the doors were closed except the one to her bedroom. She stepped inside. "Jared?"

"Are you ready?" he called from the bathroom.

"For what?"

He walked out wearing nothing but a red bow. "To unwrap your present."

CHAPTER ELEVEN

JARED had won. He'd gotten exactly what he wanted. Kate and Cassidy had been living in his apartment for the past two weeks. So how come victory felt so hollow?

He stared out the window of his hotel room on San Francisco's Union Square. His meeting with the CEO had gone well. Tomorrow he would tour the manufacturing facilities; the next day he had more meetings and the day after that…

He hoped to finish in the morning so he could catch an earlier flight home.

Home.

Jared had only been home for five days since Kate and Cassidy arrived in Seattle. Unfortunately the move hadn't solved the problem of their spending more time together. Granted, he would see them less if he had to add a weekly commute to Portland, but was the limited time together worth disrupting their lives?

He'd tried to think of a solution, but his consulting job required constant travel, often weeks away at a time, visiting companies his clients wanted to invest in. What could he do? He loved his job, except…

He had so much more in his life to go home to now.

Jared stepped away from the window and sat on the bed. Numbers needed to be crunched and research completed, but he didn't open his laptop. Instead he grabbed his cell phone and hit the number three on his keypad.

On the fourth ring, he heard a "hello" that sounded better than the song of a heavenly choir. Okay, he was exaggerating, but only slightly.

"Hey, gorgeous," he said.

"Jared? Hang on a minute."

Silence filled the receiver while he felt a twinge of disappointment. He wanted to hear Kate's voice, not wait and wonder what she was doing without him.

"I'm back," she said less than thirty seconds later.

"You sound surprised to hear from me," he said. "Who else would be calling you at this hour?"

"I don't know," she teased. "Maybe a tall, dark and handsome stranger."

"Well, I'm not a stranger."

Though he worried with all the time he spent on the road, Cassidy would forget who he was.

"You're not very modest, either." She sounded like she was smiling.

"So how are my two girls?" he asked.

"Cassidy's been a little fussy," Kate admitted. "Her first tooth came in."

"Yeah?" He sunk back into a king-size down pillow. "Sorry I missed that."

"There will be other teeth," Kate said, trying to reassure him.

It didn't work.

"Other teeth aren't the same as the first one." Jared wondered what milestones he might miss. Cassidy's first step, her first word, her first boyfriend.

"I can e-mail you a picture."

His dissatisfaction grew. "I don't want to watch Cassidy grow up on a computer screen."

Silence. "Well, I could always send the pictures to your cell phone."

Her lightness sounded forced.

"Are you getting any sleep?" he asked, instantly concerned and wishing he could see her face.

"Cassidy's still sticking to her schedule," Kate said, not exactly answering his question.

He'd try a different tactic. "How's work?"

"Heating up a bit."

"Trouble?"

"beBuzz has turned into a bigger project than we'd anticipated."

Her strained voice bothered him. "Are you okay?"

"A little tired, but I'm okay." As she spoke, he heard a muffled sound in the background. "How about you? Are you okay?"

"I'll be better when I'm back home with you and the baby." He had memorized his itinerary. "Only three more days."

Silence greeted him.

"Kate?"

"Sorry," she said absently. "I thought I heard the baby."

She sounded distracted. She must be worried about Cassidy. He should let her go.

"I'm going to do a little work before bed."

"Me, too," she said. "Good—"

"Wait." Jared wasn't ready to say goodbye. "I miss you, Kate. I really miss you and Cassidy."

"I miss you, too," Kate said. "A lot."

"I'll call tomorrow." He hated to hang up, but the longer he stayed on the phone the later she would have to stay up to finish her work. She sounded tired despite her denial that Cassidy had gotten off her schedule. "Bye."

He disconnected the line. The phone call hadn't helped fill the void inside him. He sat in lonely silence, thinking about her voice and her words.

I miss you, too. A lot.

She wanted him home; he wanted to be home.

Three more days. Less than seventy-two hours until he saw her again. Jared could make it. He had no other choice.

Kate stared at the receiver in her hand. Her heart ached. She missed Jared so much more than she ever thought possible. If only he were here now…

But he wasn't and wouldn't be. Kate had moved to Seattle, but he was still gone all the time. She'd known that would be the case. Still… She sighed.

At least she got to see Cassidy's new tooth.

Kate returned to the small apartment kitchen that had been turned into a satellite office for her public relations firm. Two of her employees worked at the table covered with laptops and paper and speakerphone. Next to them on the floor, Cassidy sat in her lilac Bumbo baby seat.

Kate smiled at the baby. "That was your daddy. He misses us."

Us.

The word warmed her heart. That counted for something.

Sean Owens, her twenty-something assistant and the crush of all the unmarried females in the office, adjusted his black-rimmed glasses. "Is Jared coming home?"

"He'll be back as soon as he can." Kate didn't like her employees knowing about her personal life, but in this case she'd had no choice. "Friday at the latest."

Maisie McFall, a thirty-something writer with short, spiky black hair and four years nanny experience, looked up from her laptop. "If you were in Portland, this situation would be a lot easier to manage."

Her words echoed Kate's own doubts. If she were back in Portland, her life would be easier and back to normal, too. She stared at the charm bracelet around her wrist.

"I told Jared I'd give Seattle a go," she said. He'd proven his love. It was her turn. "I have to do that."

And she would. She had to.

Kate understood what was at stake. She needed to make sure they remained together because she was the only one who knew what the lack of a family could do, not just to her and Jared, but Cassidy. Kate had spent her entire childhood trying and failing to fit in, to be a part of other people's families. She wasn't going to fail with her own family.

Sean refilled her coffee cup. "If this situation with beBuzz gets any worse…"

Her newest client was facing an onslaught of bad press. Accusations their latest financial report had been misrepresented had resulted in the "resignation" of the CEO and CFO, and a downward spiral of the once highly touted stock. If the negative publicity and hints of criminal activity continued, the once successful company could face bankruptcy. Or worse.

"I know what's at stake." Not only for her client, but for her own firm. "I appreciate you coming up here today. Between you and the team in office we'll get this done."

Another all-nighter, do doubt. The second in a row for Kate, but she hadn't told Jared. Why worry him when there was nothing he could do from so far away?

Cassidy yawned.

"I'm going to put the baby to bed and I'll be right back." As Kate picked up the baby from the Bumbo, Cassidy puckered. "Don't get that look on your face. It's bedtime. Be a good girl and go to sleep."

Cassidy pouted, her lower lip quivering.

Kate kissed the baby's cheek. Hot. "Oh, no."

"What is it?" Maisie asked, already on her feet.

"Cassidy's burning up." Kate touched the baby's forehead. "I'm sure she has a fever."

"Have you run over the schedule for the new CEO's interview on CNBC?" Kate asked two days later, holding Cassidy. Antibiotics had helped the baby's ear infection, but she was completely off-schedule and so was Kate. If not for caffeine, she'd be flat on her back comatose.

You're the one who's incredible, Kate. I'm amazed at how much you've done with Cassidy. You can handle anything.

Kate hadn't told Jared about the ear infection, about the problems with beBuzz or pulling all-nighters. He believed she could handle anything. And she didn't want to disappoint him.

She heard murmuring on the other end of the speakerphone and massaged one of her aching temples.

Sean hit Mute. "This isn't looking good."

"Have faith." At this point that was all they had left. Cassidy whimpered. Frustrated, Kate sighed. She needed to take her own advice and have faith herself. "Are you hungry, baby?"

"I'll take her." Maisie stood. "Cassidy and I have an understanding when it comes to eating. The messier, the better. Isn't that right, baby?"

"Thanks." Guilt mixed with gratitude. Kate owed both employees for going above and beyond with beBuzz and Cassidy. Jared would be back tomorrow and by then, she hoped things would have settled down both on the home and work fronts.

"Look at this, Kate," Sean said.

As Maisie strapped the baby into the high chair, Kate sat at the table and stared at the chart on Sean's laptop. beBuzz's stock had risen eight percent since the market opened two hours ago. A good sign after a fifty-seven percent drop since Monday. "The damage control is working."

Sean nodded. "You're the spin master."

Kate wouldn't disagree. The room *was* sort of spinning.

She rubbed her forehead and glanced at the baby eating her rice cereal. White mush seemed to be everywhere but inside Cassidy's mouth. "We're not out of the woods yet."

Maisie wiped the baby's face with a…dish towel. Were they out of washcloths and napkins?

"Okay," Emily Butler, second in command, said finally. "We have the schedule and I will be accompanying Mr. Leclerc to the studio for his interview and the press conference."

Kate hit the speaker button. "Sounds good. The stock

is up slightly, but we have a long way to go. We need an all-out blitz today."

As she stood, the chart on the screen blurred. Kate blinked and refocused. Lack of sleep was catching up with her. She headed to the overused, but well-appreciated coffeepot.

Reaching for a cup in the upper cabinet, she felt woozy. Shaky. Something crashed on the counter.

"Kate?" a voice asked from behind her.

Her legs wobbled. She reached for the counter.

I'm sorry, Jared. I failed you.

And saw…

Black.

Jared entered the hospital with only Kate on his mind. He hadn't been able to stop thinking and worrying about her since he received the call five excruciating hours ago. An older woman with blue-gray hair and a pink smock directed him to a waiting area where he found Sean, a woman named Maisie and Cassidy, in her stroller fast asleep.

The content look on the baby's face brought a momentary relief. At least Cassidy was fine.

"Where's Kate?" Jared asked. "How is she doing?"

"She's with the doctor," Sean explained. "Kate has a concussion. She hit her head when she collapsed."

"How did Kate collapse?" Jared asked, noticing the exchange of glances between his wife's employees.

"Talk to Kate about that," Sean said.

Jared wanted to do just that as soon as he could. "Would you mind watching Cassidy again?"

"I don't mind at all, Mr. Malone," Maisie said, and Jared didn't feel the need to correct her. "She's a great baby and takes her medicine from us without much of a fuss."

"Medicine?" Kate had never mentioned anything about Cassidy needing medication. "For what? Her new tooth?"

"An ear infection," Sean explained.

What was going on? Jared's unease grew. Kate's employees knew more about his daughter than he did. "I'll be in Kate's room if you need me."

Walking down the hospital corridor brought back memories of Boise. Running into Kate at Don's office. Seeing Cassidy for the first time. Saying goodbye to their best friends. But he couldn't concentrate on the past, not when Kate needed him.

Jared went into her room. She lay in the bed, an IV in her left arm, a white bandage on her forehead. Her pale face brought a rush of guilt. Would this have happened if he hadn't been away? A wave of nausea overtook his stomach.

The doctor, a young Indian woman with thick black hair, cleared her throat.

Forcing a smile, Jared put on his game face. "Hey."

"Hi," Kate mumbled, looking dazed. "Cassidy?"

"She's fine. Napping." Jared touched Kate's right hand. She seemed so fragile. "Sean and Maisie are with her in the waiting area. My parents are on the way."

"Okay. Good," Kate said, her voice fading.

The doctor greeted him. "I'm Dr. Pradhan."

"Jared Reed."

"Your wife has suffered a level 3 concussion," the doctor said. "The CT scan showed no skull fracture or bleeding, but we are going to keep her overnight for observation."

"Is it serious?"

"Head injuries, especially with loss of consciousness are always taken seriously, but a concussion is a type of closed head trauma and generally not considered a life-threatening injury. However, there can be short-term and long-term effects."

Not life-threatening. Key point.

"I am concerned about the level of fatigue that caused Kate's collapse in the first place," the doctor said.

"She fell because she was tired?"

Dr. Pradhan checked the chart. "Fainted would be a more accurate term based on the description of what happened."

Jared had wondered whether Kate would take care of herself when he wasn't around, but he never thought she would wind up hospitalized. He didn't understand. She had told him she'd been a little tired, but so was every working mom. She never hinted something was wrong or the baby ill. He scratched his head.

"Cassidy?" Kate asked.

She'd asked the same question before. That couldn't be good. Worried, Jared looked at the doctor.

"Repeating the same thing over and over again is called perseverating and a symptom of a concussion," the doctor explained. "Just answer Kate's question."

"Cassidy's fine." He patted her hand and stared at the charm bracelet around Kate's wrist. "She's in the waiting room with Sean and Maisie."

"Okay," Kate said.

Not okay. Jared hated this. He hated seeing Kate this way. He hated feeling as if he were somewhat to blame. He wanted to know what had happened. He needed to know.

"So what do we do, Doctor?" he asked.

"We wait."

* * *

Oh, boy. She hurt. Her brain felt like leftover oatmeal. Either that or someone had stuffed soggy cotton balls into her head. Kate opened her eyes. The light made her squint.

Hospital. She was in the hospital. And Cassidy…was okay.

Her pounding head and blurry vision made her squeeze her eyes shut. She opened them and blinked. Jared came into focus, his intense gaze resting squarely on her.

He'd come back.

Her heart thumped.

"You're here."

His soft smile practically caressed. "Where else would I be?"

"I—I missed you," she croaked. "Water, please."

As he pushed a button, her bed raised so she was sitting up. Kate felt wobbly. As she adjusted to being upright, Jared poured her a glass of water.

She smelled flowers. Looking past Jared, Kate saw bouquets of all shapes and sizes. She also noticed a box of her favorite chocolates.

He handed her the glass. She drank. The water quenched her thirst and cleared a few of the dust bunnies from her mind. Enough so she remembered.

Reality crashed down on her. Everything she'd done, the perfect image she'd projected for so many years, had collapsed with her.

Over. It was all over. Kate nearly dropped her glass.

Jared took the glass. He sat on the edge of the bed, his thigh pressing against her. "Do you need anything?"

You.

The compassion on his face twisted her insides. Fear and uncertainty rooted themselves in her.

"Where is Cassidy?" Kate asked.

"With my parents," he said. "My entire family is here. Cassidy is getting used to all of them."

The throbbing pain in Kate's head was nothing compared to the ache of her heart. She swallowed a sob. "I'm sorry. If I'd been holding Cassidy when I fainted…"

"But you weren't holding her." His warm, calm voice kept Kate afloat. "She's fine and you're going to be fine."

She wanted to believe him.

Since Cassidy had come into their lives, Jared had given her no reason to doubt him. Kate clung to that. She wanted him to hold her and tell her it was okay. That no matter what, he would love her; that no matter what he would never leave her.

"I don't understand how this happened," Jared said. His hand covered hers. Warm and strong and protective. "We talked every day. You mentioned being tired, but you never told me about Cassidy's ear infection or a big crisis at work. Why didn't you tell me what was going on, Katie?"

Guilt coated her throat. He'd been nothing but a good husband and a wonderful dad. He deserved an answer. She just didn't know what to say. Past hurts gripped hold of her. If she told him the truth, he would know that she couldn't do it all. That she wasn't perfect. That she had failed.

Kate wanted to believe the truth wouldn't matter. He'd proven he cared about her. He'd wanted to save their marriage. But what if Jared was like the other people in her life? People who didn't want her, who didn't love her, who would abandon her?

Did she trust him enough not to leave her?

Because if Jared left, he would take Cassidy with him.

An iron vise clamped around Kate's heart and squeezed hard, but the pain of the thought of losing the two people she loved most in world would be nothing like the real thing.

Fear scraped her bare. Trust him or not, that was the question. She pressed her lips together.

As she pulled her hand from his, he tightened his grasp. "Please, Kate."

His anguished tone cut into her like a knife. A wound would heal, but this… She looked around the room, at everything except him. If she avoided his eyes, maybe she could avoid talking to him.

"Talk to me," Jared said.

Kate wanted to believe in him, but she couldn't stop thinking about the consequences. If she talked to him, she could destroy the family they'd built together.

She stole a glance at him, expecting to see accusation and anger, but the only thing she saw was concern. For her. Emotion clogged her throat.

A muscle flicked at his jaw. As he closed his hand around hers, his forehead creased with worry. "If you can't trust me enough to talk to me, we're…we're never going to make it."

CHAPTER TWELVE

THE truth of Jared's words brought tears to Kate's eyes. She teetered between self-protection and full disclosure. Both had their risks, consequences that could change her life forever. But if she refused to tell him the truth, if she couldn't trust him with that same truth, what did that say about their marriage? Their future? She entwined her fingers with his.

Logically she knew what to do, but her heart wasn't convinced. Not after years of having to prove herself worthy of a home, a family, love. Kate gnawed on her bottom lip.

He scooted closer. "I want to make this work, but you have to meet me halfway."

"I let you down." As soon as the words tumbled out of her mouth, she wanted to stop, to walk out on him before he walked out on her, but her heart…her heart wouldn't let her. "The day you left for San Francisco we found ourselves in the middle of a media circus due to financial discrepancies in beBuzz's latest financial report."

"You never said a word about this before."

"I thought…I thought I could handle it. Sean and Maisie came up to help. But Cassidy got sick and there wasn't as much time during the day so I worked at night. All night."

Jared's brows knotted. "You just had to call me."

"And say what?" Frustration and fear burned in Kate's throat. "Fly home, I really need to be in Portland because my company is falling apart without me?"

"Yes." His voice was strong. Positive. "I would drop everything if you needed me. If I knew what was going on…"

"You have a responsibility to your boss and your clients."

"I have a responsibility to you. You're my wife. I didn't even know something was wrong until I got the call you were in the hospital. I couldn't think straight. I only wanted to get back to you. As soon as I could."

"I didn't plan on this happening. I never wanted you to…"

"To what?"

She swallowed. "To know."

"Why?"

"Because I agreed to move to Seattle." Kate struggled to keep her voice steady. "How could I make our marriage work and keep our family together if I kept running back to Portland whenever something came up at the office?"

"But you said this was a crisis." Jared's jaw tensed. The moment of silence increased the tension between them. Even though he sat next to her, she'd never felt further from him. "If you would have told me how important—"

"I was afraid to tell you."

"Afraid of what?"

You can handle anything.

Kate forced herself to look at Jared. She was either going to destroy her marriage with the truth. Or save it. "I was afraid of disappointing you. I didn't want to lose you again."

"You would never lose me."

"Yes, I would. If you saw I was weak. Vulnerable. Not perfect. You would leave me."

There. The truth was out. But instead of feeling better, Kate felt as if her world was about to crash down on her. Her shoulders sagged.

She stared at his hand linked with hers. "And since I'm none of those things…"

"Those aren't reasons for a person to leave," Jared said. His words made her want to cry.

"But that's what always happened before." Her voice broke. "If I did something they didn't like, they'd send me away."

His lips parted. "Your foster parents? They would send you away?"

She nodded, ashamed. "Not every foster home was like that. There were some good families. Really decent caring people. The one family Susan and I lived with during high school was great. Well, until they had to move out of state our senior year and couldn't take us with them, but we'd been accepted to college and were turning eighteen so it wasn't so bad."

Jared squeezed her hand. "I never knew."

His tenderness gave her courage, enabling her to continue. "Another family talked about adopting me when I was ten. They were really nice, but the father lost his job and the mother got pregnant and… I figured out if I was perfect, everything would be okay. So I tried to be the perfect daughter, the perfect student, the perfect wife."

His eyes softened. "Oh, Katie."

She didn't want his pity. She wanted his love.

"I thought I'd gotten over my past, but then you wanted

to move to Seattle and I didn't and you went anyway and well, history was repeating itself. Unfortunately I wasn't perfect then, and I'm not perfect now." She looked down at the blanket covering her, feeling lost and alone. "I'm sorry I failed you."

Jared stared at his wife, stunned. He wanted to wipe away her fear and sadness. He wanted to make her smile and feel loved. Not for what she did or didn't do, but for who she was.

"You are Ms. Practical. Ms. Take Charge. Ms. Planner Extraordinaire. I admire those traits, but I love Kate, the whole package. I'm sorry now I didn't dig deeper and get to know that whole package better. But we have our whole lives ahead of us to discover each other."

Her wide eyes filled with wonder. "Our whole lives?"

"You're not getting rid of me that easy." His smiled waned. "But I need to tell you something, too."

"You can tell me anything."

Jared hoped so. Years of living with strangers, many who didn't want her or wouldn't love her, had made Kate vulnerable. She might appear tough, opinionated, stubborn, but she wasn't. Those were ways to keep her heart from being broken again. He'd broken her heart anyway. He'd hurt her. They same as the strangers she'd grown up with, but it wouldn't happen again.

Still for them to move forward, they needed to face the past.

"My entire life," Jared said. "I've only been interested in winning. A video game, an argument or our marriage. I didn't care as long as I came out on top.

"I wanted our marriage to work, not for you or me or us, but so we wouldn't be considered a failure." She stared up at him with her emotions so exposed Jared struggled to continue. "That's why I agreed to the marriage of convenience. That's why I took the time off and went to Portland."

"And now?" she asked.

"Now, I owe you an apology," he admitted. "I thought I loved you when I proposed four years ago and we got married. But that is nothing like the love I feel for you now."

The love she needed. The love they both needed.

And Jared finally understood.

"The only thing I want, Katie. The only thing I need is you."

He pulled her on to his lap, mindful of her head injury and IV cord, and brushed his lips across her nape.

"Before I could leave you for a week or more without any problem. I didn't like it, but I figured when our schedules meshed we were meant to be together. Now—" he pushed a strand of hair off her face "—now I want to go to sleep with you by my side and wake up next to you each and every morning."

"In Seattle," she said, sounding resigned.

That was what he wanted, but that wasn't what Kate needed.

Jared had grown up knowing he could fight or argue or tell his family off, and things would be okay. His family gave him security, support and love no matter what. That was something she didn't have, but he could give that to her now.

And Jared would.

Kate shouldn't have made all the sacrifices, uprooting her life and disrupting her career so that they could live together. He should have been the one to do that.

Not because she owned a company that would make her more money or because he was a consultant and had more flexibility to work part-time or a million other things. But because he was more secure than she was. Jared could give Kate what she needed because he loved her. That love was more important than his job or winning or anything else.

"I did," he admitted. "But being in Seattle is not the best thing for us."

"Us?"

"I want us to move back to Portland."

She inhaled sharply. "Your job?"

"My job is taking care of you and Cassidy. That's what I need to do right now," he explained. "Maybe once we're settled I'll look into doing work at home, consulting or something new."

"But your family—"

"You are my family. You and Cassidy."

Her eyes darkened. "I don't want to alienate your parents."

"My parents will be thrilled to have Cassidy closer. And my dad can use his contacts to help me set up a business."

"Really?"

The hope in her voice brought a smile to his face. "Really. But you need to promise me we'll talk to each other. We'll communicate what's going on in our lives and our hearts no matter what. Our needs, our fears, our dreams nothing will be off-limits."

Her smile lit up her face. "I promise."

"And if we get into an argument or disagreement, nothing is going to change anything. I love you, Kate Malone." He embraced her, wishing they could be this close forever. "I will always love you."

"I love you, too."

"I have something for you." Jared pulled a familiar looking navy-blue box from his jacket pocket. "I've been waiting for the perfect time—"

"There is no such thing as perfect."

He laughed. "Then now is as good a time as any."

She untied the blue and white ribbon and opened the top. Inside the box lay a pink heart charm with diamonds and white flowers on it. "The charm is beautiful."

"Like you."

"Thank you." She removed the heart from the box. "I love it. And you."

"My heart will always be with you." He clipped the charm onto her bracelet. "So be careful with it, okay?"

"I'll cherish your heart always." She held her arm with the bracelet to her chest. "And never break it. Deal?"

"Deal."

Jared sealed their bargain with a kiss. He had only meant to brush his lips against hers, but the way Kate raised up to meet him sent his blood roaring through his veins. He couldn't get enough of her. Of her sweetness and her warmth. Need pulsated through him. He wanted her, but not here. Not now. There would be a lifetime of kisses ahead of them so he drew the kiss to an end.

Oh, boy, Kate thought, trying to control her breathing. What a kiss. What a man. Her man.

"I never thought love could ever be like this." The smile on her lips matched the one in her heart. She'd never experienced such happiness. "I'm so glad I was wrong. I thought you were the one for me, but we got married and nothing really changed. We still acted single, living our separate lives during the week and being married on weekends.

"But since Cassidy came into our lives I saw a new side to you." Joy bubbled inside Kate. "And I fell in love with you all over again. Only this time the love was so much deeper, so much stronger than the first time. And I know this is only the beginning."

He lowered his mouth to hers, his lips soft and gentle. His kiss made her feel special, beautiful, alive. She soaked up the essence that made him the man he was. The man who showed her how amazing love could be. His heartbeat thundered against her chest. Kate smiled. Nothing had ever felt so right.

"You've taught me to trust, Jared." His love for her shone in his eyes and sent a warm glow pulsing through her. "Not only you, but my heart. And my heart keeps screaming over and over again, how much I love you."

"I love you, too."

She relished in the pleasure his words brought. "I want to be with you. I want to be married to you. And I think Cassidy needs a brother or sister. Or both."

His dimpled smile reached his eyes. "No argument here. I agree on all counts.

"It's not going to be easy being parents or have a successful marriage. But we will make it work."

"We."

Not I. "Yes, we."

She and Jared were meant to be together as Susan had written in her letter. Their love was strong enough to overcome whatever came their way. Good or bad. They would succeed. For Cassidy, and for each other.

Kate pressed her lips against his. Forget caffeine. This was the only jolt she needed. He pulled her closer. She went eagerly, her mouth moving over his, taking all he had to give. In his arms, she'd found security and strength, peace and happiness, love and a family. She wanted it all; she wanted him. Today. Tomorrow. Forever.

Jared pulled back. "You're wrong about one thing, though."

"What's that?"

"I know something that's perfect."

Her eyes widened. "What?"

"You." He kissed the top of her hand with all the chivalry of a knight from so long ago. "You are perfect for me."

MILLS & BOON®

The Chatsfield Collection!

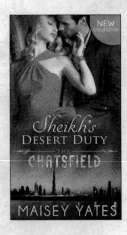

Style, spectacle, scandal…!

With the eight Chatsfield siblings happily married and settling down, it's time for a new generation of Chatsfields to shine, in this brand-new 8-book collection! The prospect of a merger with the Harrington family's boutique hotels will shape the future forever. But who will come out on top?

**Find out at
www.millsandboon.co.uk/TheChatsfield2**

MILLS & BOON®

Seven Sexy Sins!

CATHY WILLIAMS
To Sin with the Tycoon

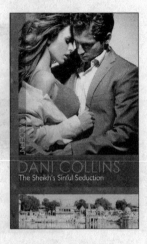

DANI COLLINS
The Sheikh's Sinful Seduction

The true taste of temptation!

From greed to gluttony, lust to envy, these fabulous
stories explore what seven sexy sins mean in
the twenty-first century!

Whether pride goes before a fall, or wrath leads to a
passion that consumes entirely, one thing is certain:
the road to true love has never been more enticing.

Collect all seven at
www.millsandboon.co.uk/SexySins